THE STA

CW00434924

**The first book in the *Hunted* se
steamy thriller of crin**

**Blackmail. The price of reputation.
Raw passion. Crime. Love. Betrayal.**

Lillian Morgan would do anything to regain the status she lost by marrying beneath her. This includes blackmail and the hand of marriage of her own daughter…
Tori's father would have stopped his daughter's misery. He'd have stopped it in a heartbeat, but he couldn't because he was dead. He'd been dead for years. Murdered, in fact…

When Tori's fiancé attempts to further his high-profile career, she finds herself mixed up with Ash Hunter and his crew - the sort of people she blames for her father's death. She *hates* Ash Hunter and the feeling is mutual, but life moves in mysterious ways and things unexpectedly change.

Someone is not being honest and secrets have the power to rip everyone to shreds.
Especially when life is built on lies.

Arch nemesis or salvation?

What readers are saying about *The Status Debt*:

- *"…Wow! Edie delivers again…"*
- *"Gritty, steamy and real – a true five star read…"*
- *"I'm a massive fan of Martina Cole, Kimberley Chambers and Jessie Keane…I can now add Edie Baylis to the list…"*
- *"Another epic series in the making…"*
- *"I need book 2… Now!'*
- *"A gripping, emotional gut-wrenching thriller…"*

THE STATUS DEBT

HUNTED SERIES #1

EDIE BAYLIS

ATHAME
press
· LONDON ·

First published in Great Britain in 2019 by Athame Press.
This paperback edition published in 2022 by Athame Press.

Front cover design Copyright © Athame Press/Edie Baylis 2022
Front cover photography: heckmannoleg/envato.com, daemaine/envato.com
Back cover photography: Fotographierende/Unsplash

Paperback ISBN 978-1-9998110-8-2
e-ISBN 978-1-9998110-7-5
Hardback ISBN 978-1-7398114-4-0
Large print ISBN 978-1-7393009-8-2

Athame Press
Unit 13230 - PO Box 6945 – London – W1A 6US

1981

TWELVE-YEAR-OLD Victoria Jacobs and a group of friends decided to ride their bikes three miles away to a little village on the outskirts of town. As long as she was back for tea at 6 o'clock her parents didn't mind her exploring during the school holidays.

Bounding with energy they set off, each armed with packets of sandwiches, a drink and a few coins. Travelling down narrow country lanes, with trees knitting overhead forming a cool bower from the sun, they rode past the reservoir and found their usual spot.

Ditching their bikes on a long-grassed verge speckled with wildflowers and edged with a thick hedge covered with brambles, they ran off. They came here regularly, especially in the Autumn when the hedges dripped with blackberries waiting to be picked and taken home to be made into jam and pies, but the *best* bit was the train track.

Each time they got the chance they placed two pence pieces on the lines, then sat back to wait for a train to thunder through. On hearing the tell-tale whine from the rails signalling the approach of a coming train, they'd rush from the track just in time, allowing the coins to be flattened by the heavy metal wheels. The wind from the passing train would blow their hair all over their faces and the second the last carriage had passed they'd be back on the humming shaking rails, searching for their prize.

Tori had a collection of these mangled, strangely shaped coins in a jar at home and she loved to compare which had the most interesting patterns or fluted edges.

This day was no different until the police car arrived.

Tori's first thought was that they were in trouble for trespassing, but it was just *her* the burly policeman needed to speak to. At this point she sensed something was very wrong.

Despite his size, the man was kindly and tried to put her at ease during the short journey home, but it felt like a thousand hours before she arrived back home.

Walking into the living room Tori saw her mother sitting on the floral-patterned sofa clutching a cup of tea in her shaking hands, whilst being comforted by a policewoman. Her mother raised her tear-stained face and sobbed loudly as the police informed Tori that her father was dead.

Tori made a guttural howling noise as she crumpled to the floor in shock, finding it impossible to take on board that she'd never see her beloved father again.

. . . .

WHEN THE DOOR slammed signifying the police had departed, Tori sat on the floor hugging her knees to her chest wanting her mother to do or say something to make her feel better.

As she rocked backwards and forwards rhythmically in an attempt to stop the pounding devastation from suffocating her, her mother coldly wiped away the smudges of makeup away and stood up, her display of grief replaced by impatience.

'It appears your father wasn't what you thought he was Victoria,' Lillian said, smoothing her hair.

'W-What do you mean?' Tori sobbed. Her father was *everything*. He was the best and she loved him more than anything.

It was her dad who played with her, made her laugh and told her fabulous stories whilst her mother stared at them in open contempt.

'Has he killed himself?' Tori forced herself to ask. If he had then it would have been her *mother* who had driven him to do it. She was always moaning at him to get a better job, a better house, better holidays. Better *everything*.

Lillian laughed, seemingly oblivious her daughter was wracked with heart-wrenching anguish. 'Don't be ridiculous!' she spat. 'Of course he hasn't. Apparently, he was involved in something he shouldn't have been and it's caught up with him.'

Tori had no idea what her mother was talking about. What did she mean *involved in something*? Her Dad was the kind one. The good one. The one who *cared*.

'Oh, for God's sake, Victoria,' Lillian snapped, eyeing Tori's puzzled expression. 'Do I have to spell it out?'

Seeing the blank look in her daughter's eyes, Lillian sighed petulantly. *The girl was just like her father.* 'Your father was shot in the street as he left work like a common criminal. It wasn't an accident - it was deliberate.' Her eyes shone with ill-disguised contempt. 'It certainly wasn't for his fucking money, so it can only mean he was involved in something.'

Tori's eyes became as wide as saucers. *Her mother NEVER swore. And her father had been shot? People didn't get shot, did they?* 'B-But why?'

Lillian huffed as she reapplied her mascara. 'I really don't want to know and I suspect I never will. That man must have been lying to me for *years*. I always said he was never good enough for me, as did my parents.' She pulled her lipstick from her handbag. 'I'm sure there must have been a very good reason for what's happened. In fact, it's totally bloody typical of him to do this and leave me to face the embarrassment and pick up the pieces! He probably did it on purpose to spite me!'

Tori stared at her mother in disbelief and tears began to flow once again. *Didn't she care that he'd died?*

Lillian crouched down on the floor level with Tori's tear-stained swollen face. 'Now listen! You need to pull yourself together. Do not breathe a *word* of this to anyone. Go to your room and sort yourself out. I need to get on the phone to the insurance company before they close and I don't want you putting me off and then I'm going out.'

ONE

1989

'SIT UP DEAR, you're slouching,' Lillian said sharply, eyeing her daughter sitting on the plush three-seater sofa. 'Are you not seeing Matthew today?'

Tori forced herself to raise her eyes to meet those of her mother's. 'Yes, he'll be here soon,' she muttered.

Lillian nodded impassively. 'Do you realise you're lucky to have someone like that, Victoria? Make sure you don't ruin it.'

Tori concealed a sigh. 'We're *engaged,* Mum. I wouldn't call that ruined!'

'Don't be sarcastic. It's not ladylike,' Lillian scoffed. 'I'm well aware you're engaged, but you're twenty years old and I won't have you jeopardising things by stalling getting married. Matthew will tire of waiting before long and you don't want to risk being left on the shelf.'

Tori stood up. She had to get out of here before she said something bad. Not that it would achieve anything. *Nothing ever did.*

She wouldn't want to jeopardise anything by not going through with her marriage to Matt. How could she? Her mother had made it *very* clear no one decent would want her if the suspicions surrounding *that* incident – the embarrassing one where her father had been dispatched like an animal, became common knowledge. Apparently, even worse than that - her mother would be ostracised and it was the *least* Tori could do, considering *she'd* been the one to cause additional problems to an already difficult situation. For almost ten years it had been drilled into her over and over that she *owed* it to both of them to do the 'right thing'.

She glanced at her mother eyeing her suspiciously from the chair. According to her, things would have been and still would be impossible if Matt's family hadn't promised never to breathe a word over what they knew. Of course, it had been *her* fault they knew anything about it in the first place because *she'd* been the one who'd opened her mouth. For this reason, she owed it to her mother not to trash the meticulously maintained life that she'd engineered for herself since her husband's death which had enabled her acceptance back into the affluent society circles that she'd been previously ripped from.

After all, her mother had said, *they'd been lucky things had been able to be salvaged and had worked out so fantastically well.*

Tori's brow furrowed. *Worked out well for who?* Things might have worked out well for her mother, but certainly hadn't worked out for her and as time passed it became more and more difficult to put up with everything. *All of it.*

Lillian studied the expression on her daughter's face and smiled condescendingly. 'Victoria, you seem to have learned absolutely nothing in your life. Ladies do not dally over setting a wedding date. What was the point of putting you through that extortionately expensive school if you don't put the knowledge you gained to good use?'

Tori bit her lip to stop the retort itching to escape. She hadn't asked to go to that bloody school. She'd have preferred to go to a standard school with her friends from her first school like a normal person. A school where social etiquette and place settings weren't deemed important subjects. Neither had she wanted her surname changed from Jacobs to her mother's maiden name of Morgan so they could 'start again'. This had been done before her father's body had even got cold, but it wasn't like she'd had a say in it.

Getting up from the armchair, Lillian rearranged a china ornament on the polished bay window. 'Furthermore, what is all this rubbish with that ridiculous job you do? I mean, it's not like you've achieved anything by being a typist!' she sneered. 'It's completely futile and a waste of time because you won't need to work once you're married.'

'What's wrong with being a typist?' Tori snapped. 'It's a good job and I like working!'

'Women shouldn't work, Victoria. It's not fitting. That's *men's* business. Have you learnt *nothing*? This fascination you have with feminism just isn't nice! There's certain things I don't expect my daughter to be lowering herself to.'

Tori closed her eyes waiting for what would undoubtedly be coming next. *It always did.*

Lillian sniffed and shakily sat back down in the chair, gently dabbing at invisible tears with a lace-edged handkerchief whilst Tori looked away from her mother's sympathy act, yet again swallowing the things she wanted to say.

Changing her attitude at the speed of light, Lillian glared at her daughter. 'It's embarrassing. *Everyone's* talking about your reticence to set a date. The Stevens will change their mind about wanting us in their family the rate you're going. Your father would be so disappointed.'

Tori stood up, hating it when her mother brought her father into her diatribe. The woman was deluded. She'd always had a misplaced sense of grandeur. She'd been manufacturing her own bullshit for so long she believed her own lies. She'd never cared about her husband. *All she'd cared about when he was killed was HOW he was killed may raise questions. That and how much money she'd get from his insurance, of course.*

'Did you not hear me, Victoria?' Lillian bleated. 'I said the

Stevens will think twice about accepting us if you carry on like this.'

Tori walked calmly towards the door. *Accepting us?* It was *her* who was marrying Matt, not her mother. Personally, she didn't much care if Matt or his bloody family shunned either of them. She knew the arrangement over her marriage had been agreed years ago, but the Stevens made no bones they didn't think her good enough for their son, which raised the question she'd asked herself many a time as to why any of it had been agreed in the first place. The whole state of affairs was getting more and more difficult to bear.

'Where are you going?' Lillian cried, watching Tori reach for the door handle.

'I'm going to meet Matt.'

Lillian got up. 'Oh, is Matthew here? You didn't say.' She rushed to the bay window and pulled the net curtains to one side. 'What a handsome young man he is too. Don't forget how luc…'

'Yes, I know. I'm lucky. See you later.' With escalating irritation, Tori left the house and walked down the pathway towards Matt leaning smugly against his brand-new red Porsche Carrera.

• • • •

MATT PEERED OVER his sunglasses as they sped along the road. 'Are you going to be like this all evening, or will you lighten up at some point?'

Tori continued staring out of the window watching the trees rush past. 'Where are we going?'

'Just popping to my folks to have a quick shower and then we'll go and meet the others,' Matt said, blasting his horn indiscriminately at a cyclist.

Flinching as the car cut worryingly close to the bicycle, Tori tried not to look disappointed with the prospect of the evening ahead. She didn't fancy another interrogation from his parents and fancied another night with Matt's friends even *less*.

Sensing her unease, Matt sighed irritably. 'Tori, I've just finished work. You live on the way back, so it makes sense picking you up on route rather than going all the way back again for nothing.'

Tori nodded. *Yeah. She was nothing. She knew that.*

Matt took one hand off the small steering wheel and gripped Tori's thigh painfully. Her slapped-face expression was grating on his teeth. 'At least *try* to make a fucking effort, will you?'

Tori winced. 'Matt! You're hurting me!'

'Oh sorry...' Matt sneered. 'Forgot you were so fragile.'

Refusing to rise to his barbed comment, Tori instead wondered why Matt rarely used his own apartment. His parents had bought him the property in an exclusive gated development for his eighteenth birthday and it was, as far as she was concerned, a complete waste of money. He'd only been there a handful of times over the last four years. It was criminal not to use the bloody thing, but to Matt everything was a commodity for his convenience as and when he liked. *Including her.*

'So how was work?' Tori muttered, shifting the conversation to something Matt would like - which was one of two things: his job or himself.

'Hectic!' Matt grinned. 'I had a meeting with a property investor who doesn't know what to do with his money, so I thought I'd help relieve him of it.'

Tori smiled thinly. Matt had received yet another promotion and now held the esteemed position of Business Banking Account Manager for the area. It was an unheard-of post for someone at the age of twenty-one, but courtesy of his father, who conveniently held the post of bank manager, he'd risen up the ladder at lightning speed.

She studied Matt's chiselled jawline and his neat short blond highlighted hair. It was no secret he'd be the overall branch manager before he was thirty with a salary to match the coveted role. His father had already earnt triple of what was required to maintain his luxurious lifestyle until the sea froze over, so he'd planned to retire by the age of fifty-five – which wasn't too far off.

Tori shook her head. All these attributes Matt and his family offered were further reasons why her mother was more than desperate she marry him as soon as possible.

'If I can pull this customer in I'll get a nice bonus,' Matt boasted. 'Jeremy can do the initial grunt work and then I'll take over and clinch the deal myself.'

Another bonus? Tori thought sarcastically, forcing herself to smile. 'That's great. Well done!'

'*That* put a smile on your face didn't it! I thought it might.' Matt smirked, squeezing her leg once more, his fingers creeping rapidly up her skirt. 'The prospect of extra money *always* makes women happy!'

Tori squirmed away from Matt's probing fingers and ignored his insult. She didn't want his money. She didn't want *anything* from him. He didn't make her happy and his money wouldn't either. She'd been so busy making everyone else happy for so long she genuinely couldn't remember what, if anything, made her happy. *But she knew what didn't.*

'Matt, stop that. We're almost at your parents' place,' she admonished, hoping he'd take the hint. His touch made her skin crawl.

Matt scowled. 'For fuck's sake. You need to chill out! If you're so uptight now, what will you be like once we've been married ten years?'

Tori stared blankly out of the window again as Matt screeched around the corner and pulled on to the long gravelled driveway of his parent's large detached house on the outskirts of town. *She had no idea how she'd be in ten years from now. Dead with any luck.*

Two

TORI SIPPED AT her wine in the beer garden of the quaint black and white timbered riverside pub. The early evening sun was still strong and it was pleasant overlooking the riverbank.

Well, it would have been if she hadn't been with Ginny, Jeremy's horrible girlfriend.

Tori spied Matt deep in conversation with Jeremy as they stepped out from the large open glass doors leading on to the patio and eyed the bottle of wine in an ice cooler he was holding. She knew most of the women sitting around tables on the paved area had their eyes on her boyfriend. She could understand why. Regardless of anything else he was an attractive man. His tall, athletically toned frame and sparkling blue eyes, coupled with his clean-shaven well-defined face and confident personality ensured he was never short of admiring glances.

Tori scowled acidly. What a pity these traits didn't detract from the fact that he was a controlling snob who treated her like she was somebody who should be grateful for his attention.

She brushed a tendril of her dark brown wavy hair away from her eyes and frowned, convinced Matt was filling in his dreadful friend with the latest grilling she'd received from his parents. Not that he'd witnessed most of it, but it been clear by her face when they'd left that she'd failed *once again* to get on with her future in-laws.

Tori's face heated uncomfortably. Whilst Matt had his shower she'd sat in his parents' immense open-plan lounge in uncomfortable silence and Richard and Susan had made no secret of scrutinising her. It had been only a matter of time before *it* started again and she'd been right.

'Victoria, my dear,' Susan had said in her patronising nasally voice. 'You do realise it's a personal insult to our son in front of all our family, friends and clients if you don't finalise the wedding date soon, don't you?'

Tori had stared at Susan's fuchsia-coloured lips set in a hard line and tried not fixate on the large backcombed blonde monstrosity which resembled a gigantic candyfloss perched on her head. Instead she'd wondered what would happen if she swapped the woman's hairspray for a can of neon pink spray paint, or even a flame thrower.

'I'm not trying to insult anyone, Susan,' Tori had explained with more conviction than she'd felt. 'We just can't decide on the venue.'

Susan's fluorescent mouth had pursed in irritation. 'From what Matthew tells me, it's *you* who doesn't like any of the venues we've suggested rather than it being a case of indecisiveness.'

Tori had fidgeted on the sumptuous leather armchair. 'Well, it's just that…'

'A big wedding is expected for people like *us*,' Richard had interrupted as he stood stiffly behind his wife, his hands clasped behind his back.

People like US? Tori wasn't one of them and they knew it, which was why they felt the need to constantly comment. She'd tried to think of something which wouldn't get misconstrued or appear insulting but couldn't think of one thing.

Everything that was important to *them* wasn't important to her and it was becoming increasingly difficult to pretend otherwise. She didn't want any of those wedding venues. *Capacity for a thousand people? It was ridiculous. She wasn't Princess Diana and neither did she want to be.* She had very little confidence and was even *worse* in front of people.

She'd only found out the details about her own wedding after they had been decided. It had already been agreed *exactly* how everything would be - from her dress, the poxy table decorations, down to what shape baskets the host of unknown flower girls would be carrying as they followed her down the aisle. She hadn't been consulted over any of it. She hadn't even chosen her own bridesmaids – not that she really had anyone she could ask.

She'd had no say either in who was invited to what was *supposedly* the most important day of her life. In fact, she hadn't even been asked who *she'd* like to invite and the thought of all those strangers staring at her was enough to make her pass out.

Even more horrifying was that the press would be there. Susan and Richard hadn't been able to wait to announce that *Country Life* magazine would be doing a story about their wedding.

She didn't want this fuss. She didn't want any of it. She didn't even want to get married.

Susan had twiddled an oversized pearl stud earring between her manicured fingertips, further stretching the already sagging earlobe. 'Anyone would think you don't *want* to marry into this family.' She'd raised a plucked eyebrow and emitted a high-pitched tittering noise which sounded like an out of tune ancient harpsichord. 'How ridiculous would that be?'

Richard had nodded in agreement and stared at Tori down his slightly over-long nose. 'I don't know how many times we've pointed out we've managed to see past something which would have caused you irreparable damage had we not been good enough to keep it to ourselves – for you and your mother's sake.'

Tori had felt anger simmering and she'd bit down on her bottom lip to retain her self-control. *She knew how many times they'd pointed it out. MILLIONS of times, that's how many.* She believed the only reason Richard and Susan Stevens had agreed to keep anything to themselves was because it made them feel important for helping out someone Richard had known from the old days.

Susan had smiled overbearingly. 'We all know questions would have been asked as to *exactly* what your father had been involved with to warrant what happened and we didn't want that to happen to you and Lillian, but there's no smoke without fire remember…'

Tori had stiffened, sick of Susan's obvious pleasure in her use of metaphors. 'Susan, my father wasn't invol…'

'Agreeing with Lillian that Matthew would marry you when you came of age was again to secure you a place in our world out the goodness of our hearts,' Susan had cut in loudly. 'But your slowness in securing a date may exacerbate the need for people to question our association. Most suspect your status didn't come from breeding and we don't want to be forced into the position where we have no choice but to break our arrangement.'

'Ready to go Tori?' Matt had said cheerfully as he'd burst into the lounge.

Tori couldn't remember the last time she'd felt so glad to see her horrible fiancé. She was aware she'd been about to lose her temper or burst out crying with frustration and she hadn't wanted either of those options.

Quickly getting to her feet, her face tinged unmistakeably with humiliation, she'd left the room.

• • • •

TORI GLANCED BACK to Matt still talking to Jeremy by the patio doors and sighed. Admittedly she'd been very attracted to him initially. He'd been one of the most popular boys at the private school and she'd noticed him the very first day she'd started, but that was *years* ago and before she'd found out what he was really like.

She, however, had been an object of curiosity from the off being as she'd mysteriously appeared out of the blue. Her family were unknown in any of the other kids' parent's prestigious groups, so everyone had been extremely inquisitive as to her background.

She had previously been briefed with military precision by her mother to in *no way* let on as to the truth surrounding her father's death. Instead she'd been instructed to state he'd been killed in a car accident on his way to work as a stockbroker in the city.

Emphasis had been made that it had been *vital* not to mention his real job had been a shop floor manager of a manufacturing company and to say after his death they'd moved to escape the painful memories. Tori had never felt comfortable with lying. She wasn't embarrassed by her father, but as usual she hadn't been able to let her mother down.

To her surprise she'd had Matt on side from day one. He'd appeared from nowhere to fight her corner during the gauntlet of questioning. She hadn't thought at the time to ask how he'd known what she'd been supposed to say because she'd been flattered by the attention from the popular handsome boy and had stupidly thought his involvement to quell the nosy rumour machines had meant that he'd liked her. She'd quickly realised it hadn't as he'd never bothered acknowledging her unless she was being questioned.

It was only by the age of seventeen at one of the countless summer garden parties she'd been dragged to, courtesy of her mother's successful infiltration of the upper-class cliques, had Matt finally showed real interest. She hadn't realised at the time that everything was, and always had been, pre-determined.

When Matt had unexpectedly begun paying her attention she'd been seduced by his charismatic confident personality and bona-fide assured future as well as his attentive behaviour, but this had not lasted. Three years down the track and as many years of being controlled and constantly reminded how grateful she should be – both by him and everyone else, it was all becoming more than tiring.

Tori blinked away the forming tears, grateful it was still light enough to justify wearing sunglasses.

'Are you capable of having a conversation, Tori?' Ginny asked sourly whilst scrutinising herself in her gold-plated compact mirror. 'Or have you just got absolutely *nothing* of any use to say as usual?'

Tori met Ginny's eyes and willed herself to smile pleasantly. She'd almost managed to forget the woman was there. She *hated* the supercilious vapid cow almost as much as she hated Jeremy and Matt.

'Enjoying yourself ladies?' Jeremy drawled as he and Matt finally made their way over.

'We were wondering how long you boys were going to take with that wine!' Ginny purred, running her talon-like fingernails suggestively along Jeremy's thigh as he sat down next to her.

Tori swallowed her scowl and smiled sweetly, but realised it probably held more resemblance to a grimace than anything else.

Matt draped his arm heavily around her shoulders and placed his mouth next to her ear, looking outwardly like he was whispering sweet nothings. 'Cheer up, you miserable bitch,' he hissed, digging his fingers painfully into her shoulder. 'You're embarrassing me.'

Plastering on a wide bright smile like she was accustomed to having to do, Tori topped up her wine from the new bottle. 'Are we staying here for the evening?'

'What's say we go for a cruise in my car? Let's have a drive through the cheap streets for a laugh and play 'Spot The Scrubber',' Jeremy sniggered.

Ginny giggled, her tinkling laugh irritatingly loud. 'Oh, I *love* that. We haven't played it for *ages*!'

'We did it last week if I remember rightly,' Tori muttered. Why they felt the need to cruise around in a brand-new car to places where the average house had less than eight bedrooms and a gated driveway, blasting the horn and cat calling through the windows was anyone's guess, but they seemed to enjoy it. However, it wasn't her idea of a good time.

'Scared of seeing someone you know, Tori?' Jeremy sniped, winking at Ginny, causing her to emit another peal of high-pitched laughter.

Tori thought about replying and then decided better of it. It would only anger Matt.

'She can't stay out too late,' Ginny said smugly. 'Not when she's got to go to work in the morning for her oh-so-important job.'

Colour rose up Tori's cheeks. Her job *was* important - to her anyway. It was the only place where she felt normal.

Matt increased his grip on Tori's shoulder and pulled her close. 'She won't be working there or *anywhere* much longer, will you babe?' He smirked. 'I'll be damned if she's doing something like that once we're married.' He rolled his eyes. 'With what *I* earn she doesn't need to work. Christ! Imagine it at a dinner party. *'Meet my wife.... She's a TYPIST...'*, Jesus, no!'

As everyone broke into laughter, Tori felt like smashing the wine bottle in each and every one of their faces. She knew what her life was and she'd just have to put up with it. *What else could she do?*

Matt pushed his hand into the pocket of his tan-coloured chinos and pulled out a small bag of white powder. 'In the meantime, let's get some of this up our noses, shall we?'

Three

THE WHITE HART, a coaching inn dating back to the mid-1800's which looked not to have been decorated since then, was noisy and dimly lit. The blackout shutters left over from the second world war sat either side of old sash windows, framed by moth-eaten shabby curtains.

Stained walls, once cream, were now nicotine-brown and surrounded the large room where men and women sat around rickety wrought iron tables, the chipped, scored and sticky tops covered with a thin layer of greasy, green faux leather. Bench seats running the perimeter of the room boasted torn maroon PVC and sported tears leaking smelly upholstery foam.

Colin Mathers busily served drink after drink through the haze of cigarette smoke and dogs on chains lay languidly on the sticky carpet liberally covered with cigarette ash and ground out butts.

He smiled. It may not be The Ritz, but he was extremely proud of his pub. Well, it wasn't *his*, he only leased it from the brewery, but considering what state it had been in when he and Sarah had taken it over a couple of years ago, they hadn't done too badly in turning it around.

When he said 'state', he was of course referring to the

clientele rather than the décor. He'd been determined to rid the White Hart of its reputation of being a hang-out and dosshouse for drug-addled junkies, glue-sniffers and general losers who just wanted a fight. Between them, that lot had caused no end of grief and explained the quick turnover of previous landlords.

Like himself, Sarah hadn't flinched at the prospect of taking the place on. He'd known Sarah would rise to the challenge as much as he'd wanted to. That was why she was his wife and another reason why he loved her so much.

The area might be run down, but the majority of its inhabitants were proud, hard-working folk who deserved somewhere decent to drink without having to put up with the percentage that had caused the White Hart to have so many problems.

Looking up, Colin watched Ash Hunter saunter into the pub, his presence evoking a series of acknowledgments, nods of greeting and offers of drinks. Politely returning the greetings, he brushed away the offers of drinks and made his way to the bar where he leant his leather jacketed arm against the dark wood.

'The usual, Hunter?'

Hunter smiled. 'Please, Colin.'

Colin cheerfully set about pouring the pint for the big man in front of him. It hadn't been just his and Sarah's determination that had managed to turn this pub's reputation around. It had been Sarah's friendship with Hunter that had clinched it. With Hunter's backing, they'd successfully driven out the majority of the troublemakers. People behaved themselves when they saw the Gypsy Reaper patch on a leather jacket.

For a small fee – substantially less than what other establishments were charged – Hunter and various members of his crew were in residence on a regular basis in the raised alcove area housing a pool table and dart board, which ensured the White Hart remained trouble-free.

Initially, Colin had not wanted the Reapers in his pub – he'd heard all about them more than he cared to remember, but

Sarah, having lived around these parts all her life, knew Hunter of old and she was adamant that now he'd taken the reins of the group it would be run in an entirely different way to the previous president. From what he'd been able to tell – Sarah had been right and whatever changes Hunter had made to his club, it still commanded an unspoken amount of respect and control in the city.

Now, apart from the occasional good-natured scrap privy to all pubs, there were no longer any untoward happenings in this gaff and that's how everyone liked it.

Colin smiled. Yes, it had been *well* worth having the Reapers use The White Hart as their regular drinking establishment for the lack of trouble it had brought and worth every penny they paid for their presence.

He placed the pint on the beer towel in front of Hunter and watched some of the other Reapers beckon him over to their usual area. 'Looks like you're wanted,' he said amicably.

Hunter took a slug from his pint and raised an eyebrow in acceptance before walking over to the alcove.

Colin had to admit from what he'd seen Hunter did seem like a decent man. Not that he could say the same for most of the other members of his crew. Especially *Noel*.

His nose wrinkled up in distaste. That man he *certainly* did not like. There was something about him that made every hair on his body point the wrong way and if he had the choice, Noel wouldn't be welcome here at all. But he was part of Hunter's crew, so he had to take the rough with the smooth.

Noticing another three people clamouring to be served, Colin pulled his eyes away from the alcove area and began to serve, wishing Sarah would get a move on collecting the glasses.

. . . .

HUNTER MOVED ACROSS the room. He knew all eyes were on him – they always were, so he was used to it, but tonight he wasn't in the mood for pleasantries.

Something he'd learnt today had both annoyed and intrigued him and he needed to work out what he was going to do about it. He wouldn't, however, mention his concerns to the boys right now. Not until he'd found more out about whether there was any need to.

Hunter sat down heavily on a wooden chair and stretched his long legs out in front of him. He said nothing until he'd taken his fill of his drink and shrugged his leather jacket off his wide shoulders, slinging it sloppily onto an empty chair.

He shook some strands of his thick dark blond hair which had escaped from his ponytail off his face and looked between Noel and Grin in turn. 'We have a new shipment coming in tonight, just thought I'd remind you. Anything else to report that I should be aware of?'

Noel was busy rolling a cigarette between his thick fingers. 'Nope. Everything's fine.'

Hunter moved his grey eyes to Grin. 'You?'

Grin smiled, revealing the crooked teeth which had given him his name. 'All good.'

Hunter nodded. 'I've sent some of the others to give a friendly reminder to a couple of people,' he began, then stopped abruptly sensing someone approach.

'Don't mind me!' Sarah beamed, bustling over and wiping spillage from the table top with a sodden beer towel.

Hunter smiled jovially at the woman in front of him. 'How you doing, Sarah?'

'All the better for seeing you, handsome!' she laughed, reaching out and squeezing his bearded chin like he was a child. 'Now, don't you lot dare make any more mess! Beer goes in your bloody mouth, not on my tables, you hear?'

'Yes Sarah…' Hunter replied mockingly, teasingly slapping her backside. 'Now sod off back behind that bar like a good girl and go give your man a hand rather than chatting up the customers.'

'Chatting up the customers? In your dreams, love!' Sarah said, her ample chest jiggling as she laughed heartily. 'Rather be here all day than in that bleeding office though, that's for sure!'

'Stop moaning, woman!' Noel winked. 'Two jobs? What the fuck are you complaining about?'

'You'd understand if you were there!' Sarah retorted.

'Yeah, that's why we're not!' Grin smiled.

'Ah, go on with you! Put your teeth away!' Sarah glanced back to the bar, aware she'd left Colin to cope on his own whilst she'd been gasbagging. 'Right, best get back and help the old man before he starts bleating.'

'Yes please, Sarah,' Hunter said, nodding towards the empty glasses. 'Three more over here when you're ready.'

'You cheeky bastard!' Sarah laughed, collecting the empties from the middle of the table. 'Your legs not working or something, no? Being as you're so good looking, I'll let you off. Give me a minute and I'll bring them over.'

'You're a star,' Hunter smiled. Regardless of what people did or didn't think of him and his crew in this town, Sarah and Colin were one of the few people who didn't feel the need to stand on ceremony or tread on eggshells around him. He'd known Sarah since they were young and she was genuine. He couldn't have picked a nicer boozer for his base – helped of course in his choice by Sarah's request.

Yes, the White Hart had definitely been the right choice and he was damned if that would change. It was a good arrangement which suited them both and he would have *nothing* spoil that. It was also nice to see a couple like Sarah and Colin so genuinely happy and at ease with each other. That in itself was rare and if he could feel as at ease – even with himself, he'd be grateful but that was unlikely to happen.

'I'm sure you've got a soft spot for that girl,' Noel commented, eyeing Hunter watch Sarah make her way back over to the bar.

Hunter's resolve to stay in a good-natured mood evaporated and his eyes swung around, holding the steely gaze that everyone was used to. 'I've a good deal of respect for that woman and her husband. It's a shame you don't,' he snapped.

He knew Noel resented him being the Reapers' President. He'd never said so, but he hadn't needed to. Oh, he knew the man pretended he was happy about it, but if Noel could, he'd step into his shoes before he'd have had chance to fully remove them.

Sure, Noel played the game, but he wasn't good enough to completely hide his resentment. It was a shame because Hunter had tried to do right by the man and it had cost him more than he wanted to admit. Not in money, but peace of mind and conscience, but that was something which had to remain in his knowledge only.

Needing to put some space between them, Hunter rose from his chair. 'I'll be back shortly. I need to make a call.'

. . . .

TORI TRIED NOT to let her uncomfortableness show as Matt, Jeremy and Ginny giggled inanely each time one of them made a loud derogatory comment.

As usual, it had been Matt's idea to 'rough it', as he put it, insisting they go for a drink at a pub in one of the city's backstreets for a laugh.

After first drawing attention to themselves by making an overly grand entrance screeching up to the pub and parking Jeremy's shiny new motor half up the kerb, Tori had felt immediately threatened the minute they'd walked through the doors of the Pitcher's Arms.

Greeted by a sea of unfriendly stares she couldn't work out why on earth they'd insisted on coming somewhere like this purely to take the piss. *But what did her opinion matter? Answer was, it didn't.*

'For God's sake,' Matt sneered. 'The beer's flat and look at the state of that moose over there. Fancy that one, do you Jeremy?'

Jeremy followed Matt's gaze and his eyes locked on a middle-aged scrawny woman leaning unsteadily against the bar. Her thin pale legs covered in thick varicose veins stuck out like sticks from under her stained white lycra mini skirt.

'You pissed yourself, love?' he shouted, gaining several more bristling stares from the other people slouched around the room. 'Fucking disgusting that is. Putting me right off!'

Tori cringed. What did they get out of ridiculing other people? If they felt everyone to be so beneath them then why come somewhere like this?

She looked around, quickly turning away after catching the eye of a man opposite who was staring at her, his grubby hand kneading the crotch of his ripped jeans and a trail of dribble cascading from his mouth.

With difficulty she freed her arm which had stuck to the top of the table and grabbed Matt's sleeve. 'Can we go soon?' she whispered.

'*Go?*' Matt cried. He turned to the others. 'She only wants to go! We've only just got here.'

'Come on Tori, you can't be *that* stuck up, surely?' Jeremy slurred. 'Worried you'll catch crabs from the chair?'

Flushing pink, Tori hastily got up.

'Where are you going now?' Matt hissed, digging his fingers into her arm.

'Toilet,' Tori muttered.

'Don't forget to put paper on the seat before you sit on it. You can't be too careful in dumps like this,' Ginny shouted before dissolving into peals of shrill laughter.

Tori continued towards the door which had 'TOILETS' written on it in black marker pen, horribly aware that every pair of eyes in the room were fixed on her.

She pushed through the sticky door into a hallway and stood for a moment, taking a deep breath. Inhaling the strong smell of urine mixed with something nameless, she felt her stomach heave.

Quickly moving towards an open window, her feet unexpectedly caught as she rounded the corner and she fell forward. Instinctively putting her hands out, Tori crumpled to the floor landing on something soft and the overpowering smell of glue assaulted her nostrils.

Blindly trying to pull her surroundings into focus she realised she'd landed heavily on a man slouched against the wall.

'Fucking hell!' a voice slurred. 'All my angels have landed.'

To Tori's horror, as well as having fallen on a random man who looked like a tramp, her hand and the sleeve of her jacket were covered in glue.

Looking at the man's red glazed eyes as he smiled crookedly, she tried to get to her feet. The smell of glue wafting from the man's body was already beginning to give her a headache.

'You want some of this, girly?' The man held out a clear bag and grinned, exposing his toothless smile.

Scrambling to her feet, Tori attempted to brush her hair away from her face without getting glue in it. 'N-No thanks.'

'Suit yourself, you stuck up bitch!' the man snapped.

Tori stared at the bag of glue in the man's hand as he raised it to his face, then lowered his nose and mouth over it and inhaled deeply. Swallowing down nausea, she watched in horrified fascination as the fumes hit the man's brain and his body visibly relaxed. A dreamy smile passed across his face and he slumped back against the wall.

Her lungs tight, Tori stumbled into the toilets, glancing around like a nervous animal, hoping no one was lurking in one of the cubicles behind the smashed doors. *She needed to get out of here.*

Finally wrenching on the rusted tap in the small wash basin, Tori sluiced water over her hand, frantically scrubbing at the glue and trying her best to remove the sticky residue from her burning skin.

She glanced around fruitlessly for some soap and paper towels, rapidly realising there was none, so wiped her hands down her jacket. Moving towards the door she hesitated, unwilling to walk past the glue-sniffer again. *What if he lurched forward and grabbed her?*

Taking a deep breath, Tori yanked the heavy door open and rushed into the hallway seeing the man was still there, but now looked comatose. She scurried past, trying not to look too hard in case he was dead.

Pulling open the bar door, Tori gratefully hurried towards the table, only to find it empty. Panic overwhelmed her. *Where were Matt and the others? Where the hell had they gone?*

Aware that all the people in the bar were finding her panic amusing, Tori stumbled blindly through and onto the pavement outside only to be greeted by hysterical laughter from within the waiting car.

'Come on! We were just about to leave you in there being as you seemed to like it so much!' Matt cried, whilst Jeremy revved the engine impatiently.

Without wanting to give anyone the satisfaction of seeing the tears forming in her eyes, Tori determinedly blinked them away and silently got in the car.

• • • •

HUNTER WATCHED GEORGIE hoover up a further line of his coke off the table and frowned. Calling her hadn't been the brightest idea he'd had all day, but he'd needed something to release his burgeoning frustration.

From his position on the floor he lay back against the sofa and stared up at the large skylight spanning half the ceiling of his open plan room. He'd bought the old dilapidated Victorian factory building for a song over ten years ago. It had never been his intention to squander his hard-earned cash tarting it up, but admittedly he should have at least done *something* to improve the desperate need of repair.

Saying that, it hadn't been his intention for it to be used as the base for the Gypsy Reapers either, but since he'd taken over as President he'd made the decision to move from the old chapter house and use his own building. *New place, new president, new start and new ways of working.*

What the building *had* done was serve well in not drawing attention to them or their dealings. He'd done up the roof space – in as much as it no longer leaked and he'd put in some fine windows, but that was primarily to give him a good vantage point in overlooking the surrounding area rather than for aesthetic qualities.

He'd planned on doing something at some point with the rest of the building, but it had become nowhere near the top of the list. There were always more pressing things to deal with but to hear that a property developer had been sniffing around this morning had genuinely shocked him. He'd thought no one in their right mind would want to take it on. The man had been making enquiries as to who owned the building and whether it was up for sale. Apparently, this district was earmarked to become the next big thing in desirable areas.

Hunter scowled. No doubt the plans would be to convert it into extortionately priced flats for the yuppies, turning his territory into a playground for the 'bright young things'. All the surrounding shops, cafés and pubs would morph into designer boutiques, delicatessens and bloody wine bars.

But would he be selling his building? *Over his dead body would he.*

'Hunter?' Georgie wheedled, pushing herself up from where she knelt in front of the coffee table and straddling his lap. 'You going to give me a freebie wrap of your lovely Columbian?'

Hunter raised his eyebrow at the girl who was now grinding herself against his steadily hardening cock. She jiggled her large breasts and smiled in anticipation.

'Think you've snorted at least two wraps worth since you got here, don't you?' Hunter said, absentmindedly tweaking Georgie's nipples into hard points. 'Besides, you're getting my attention for the evening, aren't you? Isn't that enough?'

Georgie flicked her long blonde hair over her shoulder and sniffed hard to dislodge the remains of coke clinging stubbornly to the inside of her nostrils. 'I'll *never* get enough of you,' she purred, moving backwards so she could undo his button fly. 'But you only want me when it suits you…'

Hunter grinned. *That much was true.* 'Just as well really, otherwise I'd run out of coke and that wouldn't be good for business, would it?'

Pushing Georgie to one side, Hunter leant across and expertly hoovered up a couple of lines himself. He kept a handle on his own personal intake these days, but he tonight he'd bypass that.

Standing to his full height he stared down at Georgie's small figure sitting on the floor naked. He completed the undoing of his jeans and his rock-solid cock sprang out, hard and resplendent.

He smiled smugly seeing Georgie's eyes run slowly over his thick hard length, the tip of her tongue skimming her bottom lip in anticipation. 'You getting up, or do I have to come and get you?' he growled huskily.

Georgie smiled mischievously and remained seated, her eyes daring.

'Fine…' Hunter smirked. Bending down, he pulled Georgie's tiny frame up from the floor. His mouth crashed down onto hers as he slammed her against the wall and wrapped her legs around his hips.

As he entered her, she gasped, her fingers digging into his broad shoulders, and with hips pounding, he relentlessly slammed into the girl, who for quite some time had been the one to call when he needed a diversion from his crashing mind or to release some pent-up frustration.

He'd make her come. Make her come hard. He always did. Despite her expensive drug dependency that he funded half the time, the girl was ok and he wished he could give her what she wanted. He knew she loved him, but he didn't love her. *He didn't love anyone. He couldn't.*

Hunter's teeth ground together in concentration keeping up the frantic pace he knew Georgie needed and her legs jerked spasmodically underneath his steady grip.

Hunter's teeth nipped at Georgie's throat then crashed back onto her mouth, his tongue invading. He needed to shut her up before she told him she loved him like she usually did. *He didn't want to hear it because he didn't deserve it.*

FOUR

'WHAT'S UP, SUGAR TITS?' Sarah poked Tori in the ribs as they sipped their cups of tea during morning break.

Tori looked up, realising she'd been staring into space. 'Sorry. I was off on one.'

'You could say that. You've been gazing at the wall the past five minutes like you've had a bloody lobotomy!'

Despite her miserable mood, Tori couldn't help but smile. Although ten years older than her, Sarah's energy and personality were so refreshing it made her feel almost normal. It was only being at work which kept her sane.

'Here, that man of yours isn't playing you up, is he?' Sarah asked. She knew things were going on behind the scenes with this girl that she was reticent to share, but sometimes she got clear glimpses into the personality of this woman who spent so much of her time as a closed book and it both intrigued and worried her.

She liked Tori Morgan – liked her a lot and was uneasy that someone so pretty and kind should be so subdued and bogged down with a general sense of malaise.

'No, nothing like that. Matt's fine,' Tori replied a little too hastily.

'Go anywhere interesting last night?' Sarah pressed.

Tori sighed. *Surely she could let off a bit of steam if she didn't say too much?* 'It was a nightmare to be honest. Matt and his friends, which I have to admit I don't like very much…' she smiled shyly. 'Actually, I don't like them *at all*… Anyway, they insisted on going to a pub and then moaning about it. It was embarrassing.'

She blushed slightly, unwilling to admit just how rude Matt and Jeremy had been. 'Then they all disappeared, leaving me stuck in a corridor with a glue-sniffer!'

Sarah raised her eyebrows. 'Bloody hell! My Colin would have gone batshit about that. He hates glue-sniffers. Thankfully we don't have that sort in our pub anymore. You should come over for a drink one night.'

She grabbed Tori's hand. 'In fact, I'd love it if you and Matt would swing by. I'm *dying* to meet him and I know Colin would love to meet you!'

Tori smiled. She very much admired that Sarah worked full time in the office *and* helped run a pub. 'I'd love to meet Colin too. He sounds lovely.' She'd very much like nothing more than to spend a night in Sarah and her husband's pub, but she'd never put either of them through that.

From what Sarah had said, Tori knew the pub they ran would be classed as a 'dive' by Matt and his cronies. The sort of place he'd relish taking the mick out of and she was damned if she would have them insulting her friend. *Her only friend.*

Sarah watched the emotions passing across Tori's face. 'Seriously, please come over. We have people playing music occasionally and there's never any trouble. Well, *hardly* ever because we have our very own set of heavies,' she added, smiling mischievously.

Tori's face hardened. 'I don't think I'd like them too much,' she said sharply. She had no idea what Sarah classed as 'heavies', but in *her* mind they were the sort of people who went around ruining people's lives or worse. *The sort that had killed her father.*

For years even though she'd failed to get any further information from her mother, she was adamant her father would never have been involved in any dodgy dealings. He just wasn't the type.

She didn't believe the force-fed stories that her father had been leading a double life. Neither did she believe he'd been involved in dealing drugs and had upset a rival firm who had ordered a hit on him by a group of bikers. She had no idea why her father had really been killed but was determined one day to find out.

All her mother's stories had achieved was to cause her to have an attitude against anyone she believed the 'type' and until she knew for definite what had occurred, why and by whom, *everyone* fitting that mould was a suspect.

Each time she saw someone who could be a possible contender, her stomach would lurch and her blood would run cold. Hearing the roar of one of those awful motorbikes from that biker club made her feel sick and she wished they'd take up residency somewhere else – preferably a thousand miles away.

Sarah realised she'd inadvertently hit a nerve. 'I still think you'd enjoy it, sweet cheeks.'

Tori smiled, knowing that apart from not wishing to expose Sarah to Matt's rudeness she'd never willingly put herself in a position where she would be surrounded by people who terrified her, however it was easier if she said the right thing to close this conversation. 'Maybe we will, but we'd best get back to work otherwise the boss will be on the warpath!'

• • • •

'THAT MORON WAS back again today,' Noel said, helping Hunter stack crates in the cellar.

Hunter wiped sweat off his brow with the back of his arm. 'Which moron?' There were too many people fitting that description infiltrating this area so it could have been anybody.

'That one sniffing around about this gaff,' Noel nodded

around the large expanse they stood in.

Hunter shoved another crate into place and plonking himself down on it to take a breather, pulled out his cigarettes. 'What did he want?'

'Still digging around. He didn't say much. The fucking ponce had brought another one with him – some skinny twat in a pin-striped suit. Looked about fifteen, the prick,' Noel spat. 'Rocked up in a flash motor with a clip board and stood staring up at the Factory. Fucking yuppy bastards!' he raged. 'Looked at me like a piece of shit, he did.'

Hunter sighed. He knew Noel hated people who paraded their wealth around like a trump card and he went out of his way to fuck them up at every opportunity. It wasn't like Noel was jealous of their money – he had more than enough of his own, but he did have a very justifiable reason for despising them, as he also did himself.

He stared at his friend and trusted fellow member. He hated the pompous filthy rich too. He'd hated them with a vengeance and had done since the moment a posh city twat had slammed into his parent's car whilst they'd travelled back from hospital with his new-born brother, killing them all.

The man driving the Bentley had been pissed from lunchtime drinks at the golf club by all accounts. Pissed up so bad that the cunt had no memory of wiping out an entire family.

Hunter had memories though. Like the years he'd spent in care where he'd had a long time to work out how to kill the bastard who had managed to escape jail on a technicality. But by the time the club president, Rafe and his missus had managed to legally get him out of the system and formally adopt him, he was robbed of his revenge when the old fucker who had smashed his family had died of a heart attack before he'd grown big enough to get his hands on him.

He hadn't been the only one to have fallen prey to the way the upper class worked. Another posh bastard had dragged the daughter of one of the Reapers off and forced himself on her. The result of this rape had been born nine months later – *Noel*.

Sadly, unable to cope, Noel's mother had topped herself shortly after he was born.

Rafe had tried to keep the sordid details from Noel as he'd grown up alongside Hunter under the club's wing, but invariably he'd eventually discovered the truth of his conception.

Unsurprisingly Noel wasn't well balanced. In fact, that was an understatement. It was almost a full-time job getting him to keep a lid on his viciousness against half the population, but it had its upsides... Noel was a great enforcer because he had no morals but was admittedly difficult to control.

The only reason Noel listened to him was because *he'd* been the one to take revenge, which had also given him payback for his *own* family – of sorts at least. That was he'd *thought* that to be the case at first.

Due to Noel's mother's death it had taken a lot longer than usual to avenge her. The club had sat on it for many years, having no real clues to go on, but with Hunter's initiation looming he'd been given the job of sourcing an ID for the pervert.

It had taken him months and months of digging, but after a lot of work, confusion and dead ends, he'd finally found the information pointing to the culprit. Hunter had proudly shown Rafe his work and it had been agreed he could carry out the hit personally for his initiation.

Hunter had enjoyed it. Enjoyed it a lot. It had been quite an accomplishment for a prospect to have singlehandedly ID'd a man the club had been after for years and remove him. His first killing had been ruthless and that man had been despatched in a way even vermin wouldn't have been subjected to.

Yes, he'd shot him as requested, but before pulling out his gun, he'd taken it upon himself to inflict a whole host of other unsavoury things just to make sure the man *really* had paid for his heinous crime.

Rafe and the club had been more than impressed with his hardcore ability. It hadn't been difficult. The pent-up rage he'd held for being unable to avenge his parents' death had proved a useful conductor to aim against that man instead.

Afterwards he'd felt he'd relinquished of a lot of his rage, anger and grief– like a salve to his wounds. That was until he'd discovered he'd fucked up.

Rafe had taken him for a drive, breaking the news that he'd ID'd the wrong person and Hunter's life had crashed down for the second time. Sure, he'd done what had been asked and done it well, but he'd got that one *major* detail wrong and nothing could detract from that and never would. It had played on his mind ever since.

He was well aware he should have been thrown out of the club for a mistake of that magnitude. Reapers didn't get things wrong – not like *that* anyway. It was a banishment offence with no argument. But Rafe insisted the screw-up should be concealed.

As well as not wanting the truth to destroy Noel, Rafe wanted Hunter to be the one to take over the club when the time came. Hunter was his 'son', had an 'extremely good business head on his young shoulders' and was 'the natural choice'. And so the truth had been buried, along with the wrong man.

Hunter had been forced to live with his mistake ever since and several years later, feeling like a phony and a fake, he'd accepted the President's patch after Rafe's death.

He knew Noel had been disappointed that he had been passed over to become President, but there was nothing he could have done, apart from run the Reapers in the way he believed was right.

Pulling a silver zippo from his jeans pocket, Hunter sparked his cigarette up and inhaled deeply. He felt like shit thanks to far too much coke last night and his cock was still sore from overuse. Georgie would still be clambering back onto him if he hadn't eventually told her to make herself scarce because he had things to do.

'Do you know what this dickhead said?' Noel said, snapping Hunter from his thoughts. 'He actually had the fucking cheek to pull me to one side and ask if I knew where he could score some gear!'

'Which dickhead are you referring to now?' Hunter laughed.

Noel rolled his eyes. 'The finance guy. The skinny prick in the suit. I mean, do I look like a fucking drug dealer?' he said, raising his arms theatrically.

'I guess it depends who's judging!' Hunter grinned. 'I take it you told him to sling his hook?'

'Of course not!' Noel smirked. 'He wants a shed load.' He wasn't sure why he was even telling Hunter this. He could have just said nothing and pocketed the cash himself. As far as he was concerned, Hunter didn't have a clue what he needed to do to run the club properly. It seemed the man was far too busy trying to turn it into a legit business, rather than concentrating on what they did best, but as always, he had to swallow what had been decided.

His time would come though. Of that he had no doubt. *It had to.*

Noel plastered a bigger grin across his face. 'Oh and by the way, I've quoted the dickhead *triple* the usual price and thought we'd offload that shite stuff we've been struggling to shift.'

Hunter laughed. It would be good to offload that coke which had been overcut. It was no use to anyone who knew their salt but being as it had been an unexpected freebie they'd lifted on a collection, it was an extra bonus to pull something in for it. He'd been all set to just dump the useless stuff, but if some jumped-up wanker was stupid enough to part with his readies for it, then all the better.

Besides, his overall aim was to gradually reduce the club's involvement in drugs – eventually bypassing that side of things altogether. Another facet he'd inherited that he planned to change.

'I've told him where to find me so I'm sure it won't be long,' Noel winked.

Grinding his cigarette out on the cellar floor, Hunter smiled,

unable to think of a better suited customer for the heap of shit.
'Come on. Let's get this wrapped up.'

MATT HELD TORI'S head down firmly by her hair and thrust himself deeper into her mouth. 'Come on baby, put some effort into it,' he groaned.

Tori's eyes watered as she overcame the gag reflex and tried to summon up the effort to work Matt with her mouth. He'd been in an extremely good mood since the date for their wedding had been officially decided last night. *Six months, three days and twelve hours from now.*

Unsurprisingly she'd had no choice about it. Richard and Susan had hosted a dinner party and Matt hadn't appeared at all surprised when his parents had proudly announced the wedding date whilst they'd been eating their main course. Tori, however had almost choked.

They'd passed around the official invitations and she'd stared in horror at the thick cream folded card, embossed with large raised gold lettering – *'Matthew and Victoria'*. The gold ribbon with a sumptuous tassel hanging at the folded corner was the final embellishment sealing her fate.

Dying a little more inside, Tori had glanced at her mother who sported her usual saccharine smile and accepted air kisses from everyone, whilst surreptitiously shooting her looks which screamed she should not even *think* about challenging anything.

Matt acted like the proud groom-to-be, but had he, her mother, or *anyone* bothered to look, they'd have clearly seen the unmistakeable look in her eyes akin to an animal in a slaughterhouse.

The thing Tori never understood was why Matt was so insistent they marry. Considering it was and always had been an arrangement and he'd never been particularly interested in her, she couldn't work out what he was getting out of the alliance. She still couldn't. He didn't even *like* her the majority of the time and he most certainly didn't love her. *So why?*

'Oh Victoria!' her mother had exclaimed on the way home, patting her over-coiffed hair in the car window's reflection. 'It was obvious the decision had to be taken out of your hands. You were becoming a liability and making a mockery out of everything as usual.'

Tori had felt utterly drained and hadn't the energy to do anything but numbly stare out of the window.

'Matthew had been just as exasperated as we all were with your silly games, so when we all got together the other day and de…'

Tori had turned sharply towards her mother. 'When you all got together? When was this?'

Lillian had flapped her hand dismissively and smiled sweetly. 'You were at work. We'd already decided if you hadn't set a date by last week, we'd do it for you, so we did!'

Tori had returned to staring out of the window. *They'd taken it out of her hands… AGAIN.*

Feeling a sudden suffocating sensation, she'd scrabbled for the window handle in the hope that opening it would ease the intense feeling of rising claustrophobia, but it hadn't.

Lurching back into the here and now, Tori wanted to choke once more when the tip of Matt's cock touched the back of her throat and was relieved when he pushed her away. Pulling her up from her knees, he sat her on the edge of his bed.

She felt self-conscious as Matt's eyes scrutinised her naked body. He was the only person she'd ever slept with and although after three years she should feel completely at ease with him, she was far from that. The way he looked at her made her feel substandard. *It always had.*

The truth was, she felt something must be very wrong with her because she didn't enjoy sex. It did absolutely nothing for her and was just yet another thing which was expected.

'How am I supposed to get it in there, Tori?' Matt moaned, jabbing his fingers into her painfully. 'As usual you're as dry as a bone.'

Scowling, he spat on his fingers contemptuously before pushing them back in. 'That's a bit better,' he muttered.

Tori looked up at the man she was due to marry standing over her like he owned her. *Which he pretty much did and definitely would do soon.*

Feeling nausea rising, she forced herself to smile when Matt lowered himself down to her, his fingers still desperately attempting to elicit a reaction.

'For fuck's sake!' he spat, angrily withdrawing his hand. 'I know you're a frigid bitch and all that, but the expression on your face and the way you just lie there makes me feel like I'm a dirty bastard screwing a corpse.' He glared at her, his blue eyes cold and snatched his trousers from the chair. 'Go and get dressed. We're meeting the others shortly.'

Tori rose from the bed and rushed into the en-suite bathroom, her eyes brimming with tears. It was *her* who felt dirty. *He* made her feel dirty.

• • • •

'WHY ARE WE stopping here?' Tori asked nervously as the car pulled up outside a pub.

Matt scowled. *Firstly, she'd fucked up his chance of getting off and now she was asking stupid questions.* 'Why do you think? Do you think perhaps we could be going for a drink?' he snapped sarcastically.

Tori's heart sank quicker than a broken lift as she looked at the pub sign. *The White Hart. Wasn't that Sarah's place? Oh God – please don't let it be Sarah's place...*

She eyed the paint peeling from the old sash windows and the rusty sign squeaking noisily from its old iron hook. A man slouched against the battered wooden front door holding a lead with a thin-looking dog attached. If this was Sarah and Colin's place, then if the outside was anything to judge by, Matt and the others would rip it to shreds and she'd never be able to face Sarah again.

'We're going in *here*?' Ginny squealed, clapping her hands together excitedly like a child. 'We're roughing it again I take it?'

'Not as such,' Jeremy said, running his tongue along Ginny's heavily powdered cheek whilst she giggled. 'I know a bloke in here.'

'*You* know a bloke in here?' Tori cried sarcastically. She couldn't help it. It was too tempting after all the digs he'd dished out to her over the years.

'Actually, Jeremy doesn't *know* him, but let's just say he's arranged to pick something up from the man,' Matt interrupted.

'Drugs, is it?' Tori questioned, turning to Jeremy. She hated drugs and the people who sold them. It was probably those people who Sarah said kept order in here. *Scum like those who had killed her father.* 'I'm not going in there so you can score drugs!' She crossed her arms over her chest.

'Oooh! Listen to Lady Muck!' Ginny teased. 'You're always the one telling us off for being disrespectful and now you won't go in somewhere because of the people. How hypocritical!'

'It's not that. I just don't want anything to do with drugs,' Tori snapped.

'It's not drugs, *drugs* though, is it? We're not druggies! It's different,' Jeremy said.

Matt leant forward and grabbed Tori's face between his hands, squeezing her jaw painfully. 'She's just winding us up, aren't you baby?'

Placing his ear next to hers, he spoke quietly. 'Behave, unless you want me to mention your father's dealing and ruin your bloody mother for good, yeah?'

Tori paled. *Her father was no dealer. Never. It was lies!*

This was her fault. If she hadn't opened her mouth all those years ago and told Matt those extra details about her father's supposed underhand involvement, thinking he was on her side, then she wouldn't be in this position.

'I would say we'd best curb the comments though. I want to get this deal done. I've got a lot of people riding on it at work and we'll make a nice profit. If it goes to plan then it'll be a regular thing, won't it Matt?' Jeremy grinned proudly.

'You're part of this too?' Tori stared at Matt. *This was getting worse by the minute. Money, money, money. Was that all anyone thought about?*

Matt sighed loudly as he got out of the car. Walking around to the other side he made a show of chivalrously opening the passenger door. 'Now get out and stop embarrassing us. I won't tell you again, Tori.'

Tori got out of the car obediently knowing there was no point in arguing. *There never was. There was no point in anything.*

Her heart was in her mouth as she stepped into The White Hart. A heavy hush descended over the room the moment they crossed the threshold and her eyes rapidly scanned the room searching for Sarah, but there was no sign of her. Tori relaxed slightly. If Sarah wasn't here to be insulted by these arrogant people she was lumbered with then that was one less thing to worry about.

'Jesus Christ!' Ginny exclaimed, taking in the surroundings as they stood in the doorway like sore thumbs.

'Drinks?' Matt sauntered confidently through the room, oblivious all eyes were on them.

Tori looked for anyone resembling the people Sarah had mentioned. She didn't want to see them. She didn't want to be in the same room or breathe the same air as that scum, but to her relief she could see no one fitting their description.

• • • •

'JESUS, THIS PLACE is a shit-tip!' Matt muttered as they sat a table with their drinks. He slowly scanned the room. 'And who the fuck's that?' He nodded towards a man sitting cross-legged on a bench seat strumming on a guitar.

'Looks like a busker,' Ginny tittered, eyeing the man's shoulder length curly hair falling loosely around his shoulders and his linen shirt open to the waist, proudly displaying a long string of beads.

'Looks like a fucking hippy if you ask me,' Jeremy remarked. 'I think we've time warped back to Woodstock festival!'

Tori's eyes moved away from the stocky man, who she presumed was Sarah's husband, serving drinks behind the bar and studied the man with the guitar. She smiled as he looked up, his kind brown eyes meeting hers as he continued strumming.

She decided she liked it here. It had – how would it be described – a good vibe? *Yes, she liked it. Liked it a lot.* She bent down to fuss a Staffordshire Bull Terrier who had got up from his place on the sticky carpet and made his way over.

'Ew! Don't touch *that*! It must have fleas!' Ginny screeched.

Tori fidgeted uncomfortably, aware people nearby must have heard her remark.

'So,' Matt said, facing Jeremy. 'Where's your man and who is he?'

'I can't see him and I don't have a clue who he is. He was lurking around the industrial area when that investor took me to see some potential sites for regeneration. I thought he looked the type who would know where to score gear, so I asked him and I was right. He said he was in this pub most nights, but at least we can get in some good 'scum watching' whilst we're waiting,' Jeremy laughed. 'Fancy a game of darts?'

Matt grinned. 'Yeah ok. Why not!'

'TORI!' a voice suddenly called loudly.

Tori's heart lurched as Sarah bounded though the door towards her wearing a wide smile. She didn't dare look at Matt, nor any of the others. She knew they were staring at her open-mouthed in shock and disbelief as Sarah pulled her into a tight hug.

'It's *great* to see you in here. Can't believe you came!' Sarah shrieked. 'Colin! COLIN! Come over here and meet Tori!'

As the stocky man lumbered over smiling widely, Tori felt Matt kick her sharply in the ankle and glare at her with unasked questions.

'Great to meet you, Tori,' Colin boomed, leaning in to kiss her cheek.

'You too,' Tori muttered, sensing Matt's bristling rage.

'So, which one of you is Matt?' Sarah chirped, putting her hands on her hips and looking between the two men sitting at the table.

'Oh, erm... this is Matt. Matt, meet Sarah. We work together,' Tori said, speaking like she'd swallowed razor blades.

'Pleased to meet you, *Sarah*...' Matt said sourly, shaking Sarah's hand stiffly and then brazenly wiping it against his trousers.

Silently cringing, Tori turned to the others. 'And this is Matt's friend Jeremy and his girlfriend Ginny.'

'Hello Sarah,' Ginny said loudly. 'How very nice it is to finally meet one of Tori's friends. All this time we presumed she had none!' She laughed bitchily. 'What a *lovely* place you have here. So very *classy*...'

Sarah frowned for a spilt second and then smiled. *Tori had been spot on when she'd said this lot were twats.* 'Make yourselves at home. Rog here is going to play a few tunes for us tonight.' She nodded towards the man with the guitar. 'I'm sure you'll enjoy them.'

'I doubt that,' Matt muttered. 'We won't be staying long.'

Tori looked at Sarah, hoping her eyes conveyed the apology she was desperate to get across but didn't dare utter.

'Right then!' Sarah forced her voice to remain cheerful for Tori's sake. 'Best get back behind the bar.' She grabbed Tori's arm. 'Come and have a chat before you go, love.'

Tori smiled weakly, waiting for the comments she knew were inevitable.

Matt's eyes were alight with amusement. '*Seriously,* Tori?' he laughed. 'You think I'll let you continue associating or working with *that* sort after we're married?'

Tori bowed her head and wished they'd all go away.

SIX

MATT WAS PLAYING Jeremy with bent darts taken from a collection in a glass tankard on the bar. He glanced over from the alcove and scowled seeing Tori still sitting at the table in the bar with Ginny.

She was fixated with the man playing guitar who had degenerated into strumming some kind of hippy tune. He had no idea what the bloody song was, but most of the people in this dump must know it because they were all joining in. Even Tori was tapping her foot and smiling. She almost looked like she was *enjoying* herself.

Irritation flooded him. He snatched his darts from the board and turned to Jeremy. 'When's this man turning up? I don't want to stay in this shit-hole any longer than I have to.'

Jeremy shrugged. 'I don't know. Does it matter?'

'Yes, if it means he might not come at all,' Matt spat, his eyes still firmly fixed on Tori. 'If he doesn't show up in the next few minutes th…'

A hand on Matt's shoulder promptly cut him off mid-flow.

'What are you doing?' the voice growled.

Spinning around, Matt glared in contempt at the large man with slicked back dark hair pulled into a ponytail. He shrugged the hand from his shoulder. 'What does it look like? We're playing darts!'

Grin smiled coldly, revealing an expanse of crooked teeth. 'This is *our* area, mate. It's not for general use.'

Matt laughed. *Was this greasy twat for real?* He squared his shoulders up. 'Are you seriously telling me we're not *allowed* to play darts? It's a fucking dart board, isn't it? And I'm not your *mate!*'

Jeremy eyed the man's wide shoulders underneath his leather jacket and the rather intimidating tattoo on his neck with unease. He didn't look too friendly and Matt clearly had his nose out of joint. Why was he being difficult? He was trying to get a deal done, not antagonise things.

With dread Jeremy spotted the Gypsy Reapers patch on the man's leather jacket. *Shit. This was one of those psycho bikers. He didn't want to argue with them.* He nudged Matt. 'Listen, I th…'

'No, Jeremy,' Matt cut in. 'Why are we being told we can't play darts? I want to know.'

Amusement flashed in Grin's eyes as he watched the two posh boys. 'Because *no one* steps into this area without our say so,' he growled.

Jeremy knew he needed to intervene. Matt might be on his high horse, but this guy might know something about the gear – he looked the type. Noticing the rest of the pub had fallen worryingly silent he stepped forward. 'We didn't mean to offend anyone, we…'

'What are you doing?' Matt hissed at Jeremy in amazement. *Was he going to let this guttersnipe lord it over them?*

Jeremy ignored Matt and instead leaned towards the big man. He lowered his voice. 'We're waiting for someone.'

Grin folded his arms across his chest. 'Oh yeah and who may that be?'

'I don't know his name. I met him today and he looked a bit like…' *Shit. He couldn't say he looked like the drug dealer type.* 'I'm buying some, erm, something from him.'

Immediately realising this pair must be the dweebs Hunter mentioned Noel was offloading the shite gear to, Grin's face broke into a wide, but gruesome smile.

He hooked each of his arms around Matt and Jeremy's necks playfully. *He might as well have a bit of a game with the pair of pricks.* 'Why didn't you say so!' Grin boomed. 'Yeah, I know all about that.'

Dropping his grip, he jerked his head towards a table, beckoning Matt and Jeremy to follow. He watched with ill-concealed amusement as they exchanged glances with each other and rubbed their necks.

'Noel was due tonight, but a party's kicked off,' Grin muttered. 'I'm on my way there so come along and he'll sort you out. I know he's got your goods with him.'

'He won't sell it to someone else, will he?' Jeremy panicked, still unable to believe he'd unwittingly brokered a deal with a member of the Gypsy Reapers. Well, how was he supposed to know? The guy he'd seen earlier hadn't been wearing a leather jacket, nor was he on a bike. Still it was done now and he'd got too many people waiting on this and would be a laughing stock if he didn't deliver.

Grin shook his head. 'Nah, not if he's said it's yours.' He looked across to the main part of the room. 'Feel free to bring your girls.'

'Great!' Jeremy cried happily. 'Thanks. We'll do that. When?'

Grin held back a chortle. 'Give me ten minutes and I'll meet you out front. You can follow me.'

'Cheers,' Jeremy said, smiling as Grin disappeared in the direction of the toilets.

Matt stared at Jeremy in amazement. 'You're not seriously suggesting we go somewhere with *him,* are you?'

'We want the gear, don't we? We've got plenty of customers for it and you didn't help matters by trying to act hard.'

'I'm not scared of that! All gob and leather jackets who ride on an old-fashioned reputation,' Matt snorted. 'The man should take some of the money and go and get his bloody teeth fixed!'

'Shut up, for Christ's sake! Let's go and tell the girls to finish their drinks. It could be a laugh. A real-life skanky party!' Jeremy smiled.

• • • •

TORI PERCHED UNCOMFORTABLY on the arm of a moth-eaten armchair in the front room of a small terraced house in one of the less salubrious areas of town. She had been less than happy to hear they were going to a party because she'd been happy listening to the songs, knowing Sarah was close by. She hadn't even had chance to tell her friend they were leaving when she'd been rapidly ushered out of the door.

On leaving the pub she'd been horrified to find a large scary looking biker revving his machine outside. Matt knew how she felt about them and she'd been sure she'd been about to pass out from a combination of fear and hatred, but despite her uncontrollable shaking, she'd been pushed into the car.

She glanced around the room packed with a mixture of scantily clad women and mean-looking men and felt her fear spike once more. *This was a nightmare.*

Tori refused to meet anyone's eyes, aware they were being scrutinised by everyone. She forced herself to sip from the can of lager which had been shoved unceremoniously in her hand by a man who'd busily undressed her with his squinty eyes.

She didn't know where Matt and Jeremy had gone either. They'd followed the biker with the teeth somewhere and the thought that she might never see them alive again brought both terror and relief. At least this place wasn't *full* of bikers. She'd have had to run away or pass out if that were the case.

Ginny however was in her element perching on the knee of a stocky man in a black sleeveless Metallica vest, his long beard trailing creepily onto her arm.

Tori watched her happily accept drags from a joint that was being passed around, whereas she remained frozen to the spot, trying to be polite and steadfastly refusing when it was offered to her. *How she wished they were back in the pub.*

'Hey, you ok?' A girl with blonde hair approached, her tiny frame looking like it had been poured into the shiny lycra catsuit.

'Erm, yes, I…'

'I'm Georgie, by the way. This is my place. How do you know our boys then? I haven't seen you before. What's your name?'

Tori swallowed, panic rising like a phoenix at the barrage of questions. 'I'm Tori and I don't know any of them. My erm, friend came to pick up something.'

'Oh, like that is it?' Georgie winked. 'I see. Say no more. Tori? Is that short for Victoria?'

Tori nodded. *Another example of her mother thinking she was highbrow by naming her after monarchy.* 'Yes, but I hate being called Victoria, so I always shorten it.'

'I get that. My full name's Georgina, but no one *ever* calls me that,' Georgie smiled. 'Are you alright for a drink?' She pulled a small packet from her pocket. 'Or you do fancy a line?'

Tori eyed the wrap in the girl's hand. 'Erm, no thanks. I don't do an…'

'My, you're posh, aren't you?' Georgie laughed. 'If I could speak like you, I'd probably be able to get a good job.'

Tori forced a smile, inquisitive to know what the girl did for a living but didn't want to get into a conversation. She just wanted her to go away. *She wanted everyone to go away so she could go home.*

'Which one's your fella?' Georgie continued, opening the wrap.

Tori watched the girl take a pinch of the white powder between her thumb and finger and sniff it up one nostril. 'I'm not sure. He's gone off somewhere.'

'You'll have to watch him, honey. Plenty of girls here to choose from,' Georgie giggled, her laugh fluid like water. '*My* man will be here soon so no one would dare touch me.'

Refraining from asking as to why that would be the case, Tori forced herself to smile once more. The girl was clearly being friendly, which was nice being as no one else was, but she just didn't want to be here. Didn't want to be here at all. These sorts of people freaked her out.

• • • •

NOEL GRINNED AT the guys Grin had shepherded into the small back room at Georgie's house. *They were even more eager than he'd thought they'd be, the mugs.*

It was taking all of his power not to laugh out loud at the utter ridiculous way the pair of them were putting on a cool bravado to make out they knew what they were doing, even though it was plain to see by anyone who had functioning eyes that they didn't have a clue. Or he might just punch them in the face for being the epitome of what he despised.

Their girls were ok, mind. He'd seen those birds when they'd arrived and wouldn't say no to either to be fair, but especially not to the little dark-haired one who was so stuck up her own arse that she deemed it below her to even look at him. He'd give her an excuse to be silent alright once he'd shoved his cock down her throat. Women always happily put out for him, giving him no need to act like those bastards who thought money gave them the God's given right to take what they wanted regardless.

Noel's brow furrowed as the buried details over the circumstances surrounding his conception forced themselves into his mind. He wondered how people like that sour-faced little rich girl over there would like it if the boot were on the other foot?

He moved his attention to the blond man with the sneering face, seeing the evident contempt for all around him despite the flowery bullshit coming out of his mouth. *Him and his equally poncey sidekick thought they could call the shots, did they?*

'Heard you caused a bit of trouble at the White Hart?' Noel said, determined to try and stir up this pair of arse-bandits.

Jeremy lounged back in the chair, the spliff he'd smoked giving him confidence to be more relaxed in front of the rather intimidating biker. 'Trouble? No, it was a misunderstanding.'

'Yeah,' Matt sniped. 'We didn't realise you lot had the exclusive rights to the dartboard area at that establishment.'

Establishment? La-de-dah! Noel surveyed the blond man again. *This one really believed his shit didn't stink!* If he wasn't so amused with offloading this crap gear on the ponce, he'd have no hesitation in showing him a close-up of his fist.

Jeremy eyed Noel's expression and knew Matt was intent on pushing his luck as far as possible, whereas he didn't want that. It was kind of cool being at this party. He'd put away several more beers since they'd arrived, not to mention there was no shortage of drugs. Furthermore, a lot of the scenery was exquisite.

He smiled at the girl with a fuchsia pink bandeau top barely covering her nipples and the belt-like mini skirt grazing the top of her thighs, provocatively leaning against the wall opposite him, winking and running the tip of her tongue over her bottom lip.

Jeremy decided he could get used to being invited to parties such as *these*. 'So, Noel. It *is* Noel isn't it?' he said, hoping he was coming across in a way which didn't seem stiff. 'I've got the money.'

Noel nodded. 'All of it?'

'Yes of course. What we agreed. That's ok, isn't it?' Jeremy hoped the man wasn't going to up the price. Not that the money was an issue, it was more to do with his legs were becoming progressively unsteady and he could do without having to try and find a cashpoint.

'How do we know if it's any good?' Matt piped up.

Noel raised his eyebrows with interest. *He really thought he was the dog's bollocks this one.* 'Are you saying I'm trying to turn you over?'

Jeremy stiffened. *Why was Matt causing problems?* 'I doubt th…'

'It's decent, but as you don't believe me, feel free to have a taster,' Noel said, irritably pulling a wrap from the pocket of his dirty jeans. *The stuff in this taster was good, but he didn't say the gear they'd be paying for would be, did he?*

Smirking, Matt took the wrap from between Noel's fingers and rubbed a fingerful onto his gum. Feeling his mouth immediately deaden he nodded, placated. *It was good stuff. He had to give this guy that.*

'Help yourself to a line,' Noel smiled amicably, silently planning how he could hack this ponce up without anyone noticing, or – what the hell – he'd do it in front of everyone!

Nodding acknowledgment, Matt cut a line of cocaine on the coffee table and effortlessly hoovered it up. The powder rapidly hit his brain and he drew in a large intake of breath. 'Whoa!' he gasped. 'That's *really* good stuff!'

Jeremy also took the opportunity to take a free line and was equally impressed. *This was the best coke he'd had in a long time, if not ever! He knew he'd been right to approach this guy, despite popular opinion.*

As the door of the small room suddenly pushed open, Noel sat up sharply, his senses on alert. 'Get the fuck out. I'm busy!'

The door slammed shut before it was even clear as to who was on the other side and Jeremy raised his eyebrows. By the looks of it this guy had some clout around here and would be good to have on side. He'd speak to Matt later and make sure he wound his neck in. He wouldn't have Matt's personal hatred muck up his money-making schemes and he'd just have to swallow it on this one.

Pulling a fat envelope from the inside of his blazer pocket, Jeremy held it out. 'It's all there. Count it if you like.'

Noel smiled widely, hastily took the envelope and placed it in a zip-up pocket of his leather jacket. 'No need. I doubt you'd be stupid enough to rip us off.'

The sideways glance Noel gave him didn't go unnoticed by Matt. It was a blatant dig that the meathead thought *he* was untrustworthy, but he didn't give a shit. Jeremy was right. It was good stuff and there would be a substantial mark up with the people at work for this. All they needed to do was ensure a steady supply and if that meant having to be civil, or even *friendly* to this dirty biker tramp, then he would.

Noel rose to his feet and walked over to a built-in cupboard. Reaching in between a stack of cassette tapes he pulled out the bag he'd stashed there earlier. Georgie was cool about stuff like this – providing of course that she got her cut. He handed the bag to Jeremy. 'There you go. As promised.'

Jeremy greedily eyed the contents. The main bag contained lots of small bags with wraps and a small clear bag containing visible cocaine.

'I threw in a taster bag,' Noel said watching the pair of ponces scanning the contents. 'For occasions when your customers insist on sampling the gear. You know... like *you* did...'

Jeremy reddened. 'Thanks. Much appreciated.'

Noel nodded. *Smarmy twat.*

'Is this something you could provide on a regular basis?' Matt asked haughtily, wondering whether the question was worded clearly enough for this bonehead to understand.

Jeremy bristled. Noel was *his* contact. *He* should be the one broaching and arranging deals, not Matt.

Noel sealed the joint he'd been putting together. 'The same amount or what?'

'Yes, I think so,' Matt said. Although he was unsure how quickly this lot would shift, he suspected it would be gone relatively quickly and he fully intended on taking a percentage for his own personal use. Jeremy was bound to get his arse into a twist that he was stepping on his contacts, but the man didn't have the brains to broker deals at the best of times.

'That won't be a problem,' Noel grinned. 'There's a proviso though if you want to do regular business.'

'Oh, and what's that?' Matt asked. *Wait for it. 'Can I drive your car?'* Everyone wanted a Porsche, didn't they?

'One is that you *never* mention my name or anything about

anyone here and that goes for your girls too.' Noel bared his teeth resembling a grimace rather than a smile.

'That goes without saying and the girls will do whatever we tell them,' Matt replied.

Noel grinned. 'Then I'd say you've got yourself a deal.' He spat loudly onto his palm and held his hand out.

With gritted teeth, Matt gingerly shook Noel's hand, ignoring that his fingers were being crushed and also that he was possibly at this very second contracting something horrid like Hepatitis or AIDS.

SEVEN

TORI HAD FOUND herself drinking more than she realised, because despite what she had envisaged, Georgie had continued chatting and she'd fallen into conversation with the woman.

After she'd finished the can of lager, Georgie had passed her a glass of vodka which had been topped up several times and the result was that she was now feeling very drunk.

The room was spinning and Tori's panic returned in abundance. She still hadn't seen either Matt or Jeremy and it must have been well over an hour since they'd got here. Ginny however seemed happy and not bothered over Jeremy's lack of presence. Her obnoxiously loud laughter could even be heard over the music blasting from the stereo.

Tori followed the sound of the laughter and saw her perched on the arm of a different chair across the far side of the room, leaning over a man with waist-length dreadlocks and no shirt. Her fingers were playing with the chains hanging around his chest as she pulled on a fat joint, her glazed eyes fixated happily on the smoke she exhaled.

Feeling suddenly nauseous, Tori realised she would have to use the bathroom and *fast*. She grabbed Georgie's skinny arm. 'Where's the toilet?'

'The bog? It's up the stairs, first on the right.' Georgie eyed Tori as she got unsteadily to her feet. 'Here, are you ok?'

'Yeah, I think so…' Tori stumbled across the room bumping into several people in her haste to get away from the thumping music and the closing-in walls. Her breathing became rapid as blurred faces of strangers flew past.

Reaching the hallway, she squinted into the darkness, blindly fumbling for a light switch, but found nothing. Stumbling onwards as her eyes adjusted to the gloom, she located the staircase and clumsily stepped over people engaged in activities she'd be too embarrassed to describe.

Taking a deep breath, she made her way upstairs as quickly as possible and was relieved to shut herself in the bathroom, glad to get away from everyone, if only for a moment. Leaning against the wall she swallowed down the urge to vomit and tried to pull herself together. Splashing cold water onto her face, she took some deep breaths and studied herself in the mirror, focusing on her glazed eyes in the reflection. *What a mess!*

Grateful that leaning on the washbasin served as a prop to stop herself from falling over, she knew she would have to find Matt and ask him to take her home, but when the door suddenly flew open Tori nearly fell to the floor in shock.

'Ah, hello! I didn't realise anyone was in here,' Noel lied. *He knew full well she was in there because he'd followed her.*

Tori looked at the man filling the doorway with his wide frame and felt a rush of fear steam through her. She took in the contemptuous expression across his hardened face and even though she was drunk, she didn't like the look glinting in his eyes. 'I was just leaving.'

She made to walk out of the bathroom, but the man made no effort to move. Instead he placed his arms either side of the doorframe and smiled savagely. 'You're the girl of one of those posh blokes, aren't you?' he drawled, his tongue running over his bottom lip. *This one was tasty alright. Very tasty indeed.*

'If you see it that way, then yes I suppose so,' Tori snapped, finding the resolve to sound and act more courageous than she felt. *She just wanted to go.* 'Can I get past please?'

'Get off your high horse, Miss Aristocrat!' Noel shut the door behind him and moved towards Tori. 'I think we'll be seeing a bit more of each other from now on.'

Tori stared at the big man blocking her way. She wouldn't panic. *Not just yet.* She had to tell herself that otherwise she would pass out immediately from pure fright.

'Yeah, your other half just cut a deal.' He reached out and brushed his fingers over her left breast.

The man was so close Tori could distinctly smell spirits and cannabis on his breath and the overpowering scent made her stomach lurch. She put her hand over her mouth as the room began to spin again. 'Oh!' she gasped, turning away.

Noel grabbed Tori around the waist and pulled her closer. 'Don't turn away when I'm talking to you, love. It's rude.'

Without warning, Tori threw up violently and vomit splashed onto Noel as well as the bathroom floor.

'For fuck's sake, you stupid bitch!' Noel roared.

Stumbling towards the toilet, Tori grabbed some toilet roll and wiped her mouth, then splashed more water on her face. She felt slightly better now she'd been sick, but not better in the respect that she was still penned into the small bathroom with one of her worst nightmares.

Noel grabbed Tori's arm and swung her around to face him. 'You'd best be clearing this up. *And* me whilst you're at it.'

Panic washed over Tori in waves. *She had to get out of here.* 'I-I'm sorry,' she stuttered. *Quick, quick – think of something!* 'I'll go and get a cloth.'

'Wipe it up with your fucking tongue,' Noel roared, not impressed that this posh cow who couldn't hold her drink had yakked up all over him.

Tori stared at the rabid look in his expression and knew she was not in a great situation. She reached for the door handle.

'You won't be going no fucking where until you cl…'

'NOEL?' A voice roared from the other side of the door.

Seeing the man freeze in his tracks, Tori took this as her

chance to escape. She grasped the handle and yanked the door open. Lurching forward, she slammed straight into the hard chest of another man. *Two of them? Oh no. Oh no, no, NO!*

Almost hyperventilating and without even bothering to look at who she'd run into, the fear overtook her like an express train and she flailed around in a desperate attempt to free herself from the man's steady hold of both her arms.

'What the fuck have you done, Noel?' the voice boomed.

'Nothing,' Noel sneered, moving out of the bathroom. 'The silly posh tart puked all over the gaff.'

'I'm no tart!' Tori raged, finding her voice. 'Let me *go!*'

Finally looking up to see who the arms holding her belonged to, Tori's heart almost stopped beating. Her mouth went dry and she felt slightly limp as she took in the man in front of her. He was tall – well over six foot with scruffy dark blonde hair tied in a loose ponytail. The loose ends fell in an unkempt mess around his square-jawed bearded face. His eyebrows knitted together as he studied her intently with his steely grey eyes.

Tori's heart went from almost a standstill to racing point. Unable to help herself, her gaze travelled from the man's full lips and down to the tight white T-shirt he wore. His large biceps bulged from the material and a tattoo of a snake wound its way up through the neck.

'Fuck off downstairs, Noel,' Hunter growled, the vibrations of his voice passing straight into Tori's body. 'I'll sort this out.'

Tori watched Noel stomp down the stairs muttering under his breath something which was undoubtedly derogatory about her. Acutely aware the man in front of her had not said a word and nor she to him, she found her eyes drag back to his, his steel-coloured gaze locked on hers.

'I, erm, I'm sorry about the mess,' she muttered, embarrassedly referring to the bathroom not knowing what else to say and more than aware unwanted desire was burning unexpectedly between her legs. 'I was going to get a cloth but…'

'Did he touch you?' Hunter hissed, his voice holding raw anger.

Tori shook her head. 'N-No, not really.' She watched Hunter raise one eyebrow whilst a vein in his temple throbbed.

She realised she was still being held captive in very close proximity to this disturbingly beautiful specimen of a man and that she was crushed closely against his chest. She could smell the heady aroma of his spicy aftershave and could feel his erection hard against her stomach. *Shit. He was hard?*

A never before experienced urge to run her hand between them over his hard length passed over her and her breath hitched. *What was wrong with her? Stop this Tori – are you insane?*

From instinct she pulled against his grip and to her surprise he immediately released his hold. He was staring at her breasts, which to her horror, the nipples had hardened and were visibly straining through both her bra and her thin white top.

Flustered and aware her breathing was short and laboured, Tori crossed her arms over her chest, mortified to see the trace of a smile pass over the man's full mouth.

Through her drunkenness the mere movement caused her to stagger slightly. Breathing quickly both from embarrassment, arousal and confusion she regained her balance.

'I think you'd better go and sort yourself out, don't you?' Hunter murmured. *Before I press you up against that wall and take you.*

Watching the woman hurriedly turn and make her way down the stairs as quickly as she possibly could, Hunter leant back against the wall and ran his hand through the top of his hair agitatedly. *What the fuck? What the hell was he thinking?*

He pressed himself further back against the wall in the blind hope that the pressure on the back of his head would quell the racing of his heart.

That woman. When she'd rushed out of the bathroom into him, the mere sight of her had done something. Done something so *intense* he'd barely been able to breathe. Having mastered the art of not giving away any feelings for as long as he cared to remember it hadn't been a problem holding himself together outwardly, but on the inside... *Fuck, he'd been melting.*

Hunter's mind had imploded into a mass of hot lava as he'd taken her in. The dark hair cascading in waves to her waist and her elfin-like, perfect porcelain face with those baby blue eyes framed with thick lashes and oh, so kissable lips.

His breathing quickened once again as the vision of Tori's face flooded his mind tauntingly. He'd wanted to press his hungry mouth to hers, pulling her bottom lip down with his teeth and explore her mouth with his tongue. For fuck's sake, he hadn't even cared that she'd just thrown her guts up. He'd have gladly licked it off the floor himself for the chance to possess her.

Hunter emitted a low strangulated groan when the picture of ripping clothes from her lithe body settled in his mind. He pushed his palm down hard onto his crotch in an attempt to ease the relentless aching from his still rock-solid cock.

Pull yourself together, he admonished himself. He was used to Noel's heavy-handed bully-boy tactics, however for the first time he suspected that if he'd had time, Noel may have crossed the line with a woman and it had lit a fiery fury within him.

Just from that woman's voice alone, Hunter had been able to tell she wasn't one of them. She was one of those rich bitches and belonged to the people he despised. However, it didn't matter *who* she was, or where she came from, he didn't appreciate *any* woman being treated with disrespect and Noel knew that.

His mind raced back to the rush of uncomfortable emotions he'd experienced. *It's just lust*, he told himself. *Just lust.* But it wasn't. He was no stranger to lust and never had trouble satiating his needs with women he took a fancy to, but this was *more*. This was strange. *This was...*

Frustrated, he inhaled deeply. He'd go and find Georgie. She'd get his mind off this unnerving experience.

EIGHT

LILLIAN STUDIED HER daughter mindlessly pushing fruit around in her breakfast bowl. She hadn't seen her at all last night but knew something had happened because the phone had rung several times around 1am. Her eyes narrowed. *Screwing things up again was she? That girl was a liability – just like her father.* 'What's going on, Victoria?'

Tori focused on her mother's face as it screwed up into a vindictive scowl. 'Nothing…'

'There's no point in lying, Miss! I know you. Who was ringing?' Lillian spat. 'You've obviously upset everyone again for some pathetic selfish reason I expect.'

Tori stared at the mixture of melon and kiwi fruit in her bowl and felt sick. She didn't like fruit for breakfast at the best of times, but with a hangover, her dislike of this slimy stuff was worse than usual.

It had been Matt who'd phoned. She'd had absolutely no wish to speak to him, but after he'd called for the *third* time she'd had no choice but to pick up otherwise he'd have turned up and then her mother would have had a field day.

'What the hell gives you the right to disappear, Tori?' Matt had screamed, the drugs and drink thick in his voice. 'It was embarrassing. It looked like you'd walked out on me.'

Yeah, wouldn't that have been catastrophic? How dare anyone give him the cold shoulder in public. It hadn't crossed Matt's mind that he hadn't spoken to her or even bothered to see if she was ok. For the entire time they'd been at that party she hadn't seen him *once*, so she'd been amazed he'd even noticed she'd gone, but as she'd mumbled the expected apologies it had become clear why he'd noticed her missing.

'I came to find you because Noel said you were having a tantrum and had chucked up all over him,' Matt had raged, his voice getting higher with each word he'd spat. 'I mean, Christ, how degrading is that? You're pathetic! You can't hold your bloody drink and yunder over the man I'm setting up deals with! Nice one, you stupid cow!'

Tori had remained silent. *So, that awful man was called Noel?*

'God, Tori. I'm getting so sick of you. Ginny's cool, so why can't *you* be?' Matt had raged. 'I'd have thought you would have appreciated seeing how the other half lives? See how your father would have spent his time? It should have made you grateful to witness where *you* should have ended up if it wasn't for *my* family!'

Swallowing her rage at Matt's need to have another dig at her father and how much she was 'benefiting' from her association with him and his parents, Tori had continued mumbling apologies until eventually, marginally placated when she promised not to let him down again, Matt had put the phone down. *He hadn't even asked how she'd got home, which spoke volumes.*

Feeling blood pounding in her veins, Tori gritted her teeth. How she'd love to kill him. She'd love to kill him for treating her like shit and also so she didn't have to marry him.

She was fast beginning to hate herself. What did it say about her as a person for letting herself to be treated like this? She was *allowing* it and doing nothing to change that. She gritted her teeth. Matt was correct on one thing. She was pathetic.

Completely and utterly pathetic.

'Are you even on this planet, Victoria?' Lillian screeched, slamming the kettle down on the work surface and jolting Tori from her thoughts.

Lillian stormed over to the table and yanked Tori's head up. 'Look at the state of your face!' she hissed. 'It's all puffy and your eyes are red. You've been getting drunk, haven't you? Getting drunk like a fishwife and embarrassing yourself no doubt. You stupid, *stupid* girl.'

Tori continued pushing her now mangled fruit around her bowl whilst quietly wondering whether she could suffocate her mother without anyone noticing.

'If you ruin everything for me, I'll *never* forgive you!' Lillian raged, her overly made up face red with rage.

'What about *me*?' Tori yelled loudly, finally unable to contain her frustration.

'What about you?' Lillian sneered.

'I don't want to marry Matt,' Tori screamed. *There. She'd said it. She'd actually said it.*

Realising her daughter was being serious, Lillian's eyes narrowed into slits. Raising her hand she delivered a hard stinging slap to the side of Tori's face. 'I don't care what you want! You're *worthless* and you'll do what I say!'

Raising her hand against the red mark in shock, Tori stared at her mother. Her previous anger and frustration dripped from her like a leaking bath. *There was no point. No point in any of this. She didn't have the energy or the courage to fight.*

• • • •

'YOU HAD ANY complaints from those posh pricks who bought the dodgy gear?' Grin asked, slurping at his mug of tea. He'd seen them parading around at Georgie's house, completely oblivious that they were the source of everyone's amusement.

Noel laughed. 'You're joking, aren't you? They wouldn't be able to tell the difference between baking soda and coke!

They'll be back for more, you watch.' He ground out his roll up in the foil ashtray. 'I bet they put another order in by the end of the week. I'm telling you, we'll get a nice regular income from those dicks, won't we Hunter?'

Hunter stared through the large glass window of the café facing the seafront ignoring the suspicious and contemptuous glares they were getting from the other customers. He'd made the decision to pop down to the coast for the afternoon with the plan of letting the sea breeze clear his mind, but as he'd grabbed his helmet to leave, Grin and Noel had got wind he was jetting off and had tagged along.

He hadn't wanted company. He'd wanted some time out but that hadn't happened.

'Hunter? Are you receiving me?' Noel jibed in a pretend electronic voice, realising Hunter wasn't listening to a word he'd said.

Hunter had very much heard what Noel had said. He heard everything. He never missed a trick, but he couldn't be bothered to join in their pointless conversation. His mind was still on that woman from last night and he didn't want it to be. He didn't want to be distracted because he *never* got distracted. On top of that, he was resentful. Resentful because he never got any time to himself without *this* lot in his face.

'How much of that crap gear have we got left? Enough for another few orders for the dweebs?' Noel continued.

Hunter frowned. He didn't want to start setting up new drug deals, his plan was to run that side of the club down, not take on new customers, for God's sake. Especially yuppies!

His aim was to steer the club away from its association with drugs, but it was becoming very clear that it was going to be a lot harder than he'd thought to change everybody's mindset on that one. Ok, so he knew the club had to make money, but he wanted to do it *differently* and plough more effort into the legitimate side of things.

He'd done enough shit to last a lifetime and needed to break the mould of what was expected. He didn't see why he and the club couldn't put their minds to a *proper* successful business? There was good money in security and hopefully, if things went to plan, property. Why couldn't they buy a few pubs or bars? Unfortunately, from what he'd picked up on so far, his ideas may not be as popular with the others as he'd hoped.

Hunter's forehead furrowed into thick creases. Although he hadn't yet spelt out his long-term plans to the rest of the club, he knew that several members, most noticeably Noel, felt he was steering the club away from what they were. *They were bikers, not businessmen*, had been Noel's exact words.

Noel would resent *anything* he did, Hunter knew that, but he'd thought some of the others would have been more open-minded. Most of them were far from stupid men, but he was beginning to think he'd been well off the mark.

Noel broke Hunter from his thoughts. 'I said, how much of the shite gear have we still got?'

'When do they want the next batch?' Hunter muttered without averting his gaze from the sea.

'Dunno,' Noel shrugged. 'No doubt they'll ask. I told them to come to that rave we're doing the security for at the weekend if they want more.'

Hunter glanced up. *Would that woman be with them?* 'And are they?'

'I reckon so. Posh twats love being associated with 'our type' behind the scenes. Gives them something to brag about to their mates.' Grin laughed.

'Hoping to get your dick wet on that dark-haired chick are you Hunter?' Noel grinned. 'Well, don't bother! I saw her first, so you'll have to wait your turn.'

A flash of anger passed through Hunter's eyes. 'Don't overstep the mark, Noel. I call the shots around here,' he seethed.

Grin sat back in the plastic chair and exchanged glances with Noel. It was unlike Hunter to pull rank. *What had rattled his cage?* No one doubted his ability to turn on the violence when necessary, but he was also extremely good at keeping it in check too. He wasn't hot-headed like Noel and very rarely lost it over something and nothing – especially with one of their own.

Grin frowned. Maybe this interest in the Factory had rattled him more than he was letting on, but it seemed something else was bothering him too. Unfortunately, he had no idea what.

Sensing Noel was preparing to come out with another jibe, Grin nudged him in the ribs. Judging by the look on Hunter's face he was liable to lose his rag and that would *not* be pretty.

Hunter took a long pull of his cigarette and resumed staring out of the window. He knew he'd just overreacted, but his nerves were jangling. He gazed into the distance and watched the sea, its waves lapping at the shore whilst kids ran about happily in the shallows clutching buckets and spades. He envied them. *He'd never been to the seaside as a kid.*

Noel sneered. He knew Grin was attempting to deter him from opening his mouth again. He watched Hunter gazing out over the sea. *Where had his sense of humour gone?* Now that he thought about it, the man had never had much of one. He took everything seriously and had been the same when they were younger. The only reason Hunter had got anywhere in the club was because he'd been lucky enough to get taken in by Rafe and of course, what he'd allegedly done for the club and for him. And why Hunter was so bothered about that stuck-up chick from last night was a mystery.

'Come on, man. Why are you taking things so personally about that snobby bird? You're not thinking about changing sides, are you?' Noel laughed.

Hunter shook his head in frustration. Noel knew full well what had happened to his parents and baby brother at the hands of people with more money than sense, yet here he was, *purposefully* trying to get a rise out of him. He could feel the adrenalin pounding heavily in his veins.

Noel grinned, unable to resist pushing it further. 'Ooh, something's hit a nerve. I think perhaps I was right… Are you finally selling out over a bit of skirt? I think th…'

Without warning, Hunter jumped up from the table and pulled Noel from his seat by his leather jacket. 'Where the fuck do you think you get off saying shit like that?' he spat, his eyes forming cold, narrow slits.

'Whoa!' Grin cried, getting to his feet. Would he have to step in between Hunter and Noel? He hoped not but could sense the eyes of the other customers in the café were on their group and they were liable to call the cops, which they could do without.

He grabbed Hunter's arm. 'Leave it, mate,' Grin said, clocking the rabid look in his friend's eyes. 'Don't let him wind you up. He's only having a laugh.' Grin glared at Noel, who looked happy to have gleaned a reaction.

Releasing Noel's jacket, Hunter threw him roughly back into his seat and snatched his crash helmet from the table.

Storming out the café without a backwards glance, he put his helmet on and sitting astride his bike parked outside, fired the engine.

He sped down the road, shooting over a roundabout and ground his teeth in anger. He'd been about to lose his temper back there and he didn't like it. He was always in control of what he did, regardless of what it was, but the first time in *ages*, he'd been very close to flipping. And at one of his own too. *This was not good.*

Hunter glanced in his mirror, glad to see no one was following. At least they had that much sense. This time he would be riding on his own and he'd ride until he'd got this anger out of his system, along with his irritation over the feelings that woman engendered in him.

NINE

'I'M SORRY GRIN had a go at your man about the dart board at the weekend,' Sarah said. She'd been studying Tori's melancholy expression since she'd walked into work this morning. 'I'd have warned them the alcove was out of bounds if I'd noticed them go up there. I'll be having words with the Reapers next time I see them. You won't get any more trouble.'

Receiving no reply, Sarah frowned. 'I'm presuming that's why you left?'

'What? Oh no, it wasn't that. They sorted it out between themselves.'

Sarah smiled. 'Glad to hear it. The Reapers can be heavy-handed sometimes, but they're ok once you get to know them. Providing you don't rub them up the wrong way, that is!'

Tori pursed her lips. *She had no intention of rubbing them up in ANY way – least of all that awful Noel.*

'So,' Sarah pressed. 'How come you all left so quickly. I didn't even see you go.'

Tori felt awkward and rude for disappearing without saying anything. 'I'm really sorry. I didn't realise we were going. It was all very rushed.' She didn't want to go into detail about *why* they had left and especially didn't want Sarah to discover her fiancé was part of a ridiculous drug deal. She hadn't liked any of it and still didn't.

Sarah watched Tori closely. Something was not quite the ticket. She'd sensed it at the time, mainly from the body language between her and her boyfriend, fiancé, or whatever he was. She hadn't been impressed by the way he'd spoken to Tori either. It was plain he called the shots and treated her like an idiot and personally she had no time for people like that.

The man had as much charm as a brick and couldn't have made it much more obvious that he didn't think very much of the White Hart. As for the rest of them… Frankly they were rude and jumped up, but it was hardly her place to voice that to Tori.

'What did *you* think of our pub?' Sarah asked, trying to change tack. 'I could tell it wasn't the sort of place you'd normally visit. Listen, I know it's a bit rough and ready around the edges, but…'

Tori put her hand up. 'Don't you *dare* feel you need to justify your pub. The comments Matt and Ginny made were cringeworthy and I'm *so* sorry. Now perhaps you see why I dread going out with them?' She smiled shyly. 'I, on the other hand, *loved* your pub! I'd have quite happily stayed there all evening. That guy – Rog was it? He was *really* good on the guitar and I loved the atmosphere.'

Sarah beamed. 'Well I like it and I'm glad you do too. By the way, Colin thinks you're very pretty.'

Tori forced a weak smile. 'I don't think so! I've *never* been that.'

Sarah raised her eyebrows. *Was she blind?* The woman was drop-dead gorgeous, but sadly unable to see what everyone else could. She smiled mischievously. 'He also thinks you're far too good for your fella!'

Tori giggled – a fresh-sounding, genuine laugh. 'Oh Sarah, that's funny! I love Colin already!'

Sarah grinned. *It was nice to hear Tori laugh. She'd begun to think she didn't have the ability.* 'I'm not trying to pry love, but is everything ok with you and your bloke? Fiancé, isn't he?'

Tori's face fell hearing the word 'fiancé' in conjunction with Matt Stevens. Sarah had seen with her own eyes the way Matt treated her so there was little point trying to pretend otherwise. 'Not really, but that's just how it is. I've just got to get on with it.'

'Why? You could have anyone you wanted! You don't have to marry someone if you don't want to. Ditch him! Find someone you *really* want to be with.'

Tori flushed deeply as the image of Hunter flashed into her mind. She hadn't been able to think of much apart from him since. Once she'd finally got to bed, she'd laid there imagining his hands and mouth on her. The feel of him pushing deep into her…

Sarah watched Tori's face colouring and grinned. 'And what or *who* are you thinking about?'

Tori shook her head frantically. 'What? No one! I'm with Matt, remember.'

Sarah laughed loudly. '*Please* tell me it's not that retard from Accounts!'

'No way!' Tori wailed, picturing the spindly man with bad breath and an ill-fitting toupee who followed her around the work canteen.

'Oh, come on Tori! Spill the beans!' Sarah nagged.

'There's nothing to say!' Tori snapped. 'But if you must know I was thinking about someone who helped me out at a party I got dragged to last night, that's all.'

'What party?' Sarah asked, her smile fading.

Damn! She hadn't meant to mention that. 'Oh erm, Jeremy had to pick something up from someone…' Tori babbled.

Sarah's eyes narrowed. *Noel was heading to a party…* 'Not Noel? Your friend was getting drugs from Noel?' *She'd told those fuckers not to use her pub as a dealing point.*

Tori bowed her head. 'Trust me, Sarah, it had nothing to do with me. I didn't even know about it until the last minute, I promise you. I don't *ever* do drugs. I hate them.'

Sarah patted her hand. She believed her. 'I didn't think your lot would get involved with Noel.'

'Neither did I,' Tori spat, clearly recalling the way that man had treated her. If it hadn't been for that other man then she dreaded what might have happened.

'Did he try it on with you?' Sarah asked angrily, momentarily forgetting about the drugs for the time being. 'He'd better not have! He's a bastard, that one!' If Noel had been disrespectful to Tori she'd have his guts for garters. Tori wasn't like the people around here and wouldn't be able to cope with his heavy-handed tactics. She was far too fragile to be frequenting *their* parties.

'It was getting that way, but like I said, thankfully someone deferred him.' Tori didn't want to go into detail about how horribly close the situation had been to turning extremely uncomfortable, neither did she want to cause trouble between Sarah and her customers.

'Who stepped in?'

'I don't know,' Tori muttered, blushing again despite herself, embarrassed she was even having this conversation.

Sarah suspected she knew who it might be. There weren't many people around here who would pull Noel up over anything. 'Your knight in shining armour wasn't tall with long shaggy blonde hair and a beard by any chance, was he?'

Watching Tori falter, Sarah knew. *Knew beyond any doubt.* She raised her eyebrows. 'And a face to die for?'

Tori blushed a brighter shade of pink. 'I-I didn't notice.' *Of course she'd noticed. How could she not have? The man was a Greek God!*

'Oh my! *Hunter*! You're talking about Ash Hunter!' Sarah cried.

Tori shivered. *Ash Hunter. So that was his name?*

Sarah grabbed Tori's hand. 'Oh fuck, honey. 'Scuse my French! Listen – Hunter… Face of an angel but the heart of the devil. Don't go there, babe. He's a good man, but cold and will rip you to fucking shreds!'

Tori stood up, her face returning to its usual passive state. 'I won't be going *anywhere* with anyone! I'm with Matt remember? Besides, it wasn't like that. The man just told Noel to give me some space, that's all.' She looked down, embarrassed. 'We didn't even have a conversation, so stop being ridiculous.'

TEN

RICHARD GLANCED AT the diary on his desk irritably. This morning he'd got two meetings and he wasn't in the mood for either of them. In fact, he wasn't in the mood for *anything*. He scowled at the cup of tea which had gone cold whilst his mind had been working overtime.

Susan had been doing nothing but constantly flapping over this bloody wedding which was making him annoyed about this whole business with Matthew and Victoria. *More* than annoyed if truth be known. It was all Susan *ever* talked about and to top it all off, he'd got the suit fitting with Matthew later, which meant aside from rearranging his day, they had to meet up with the women afterwards and there were lots of things that he'd rather be doing.

Personally, he'd have rather not have had anything to do with Jack Jacobs' goddamn family. As far as he was concerned, all links to that man had been removed *years* ago. Virtually no one would ever have known their connection had it not been for Jack dying and then Lillian appearing again out of the blue.

The minute she'd unexpectedly turned up at his workplace eight years ago, Richard had known it meant trouble and he hadn't been wrong. Ushering Lillian into his office away from prying eyes and ears, he'd listened to what she'd had to say.

He'd been surprised to hear that Jack had been killed. He hadn't heard anything about it, but then why would he have done? He hadn't seen the man, nor Lillian since they'd wed and it wasn't like they shared any social circles. The thought alone was laughable.

Richard hadn't the faintest clue why Lillian had felt the need to come and see him after all that time just to tell him about Jack's demise, but it had soon become apparent when she'd laid her cards on the table.

Lillian hadn't been shy in stating she would let everyone know of Richard's previous association with her late husband if he didn't introduce her to his social circles. Far too long had she not been around her 'own kind', she'd barked.

Richard sighed deeply as he remembered how she'd gone on and on and ON...

Someone of *her* breeding should never have been ostracised from her own in the first place, she'd moaned. It wasn't like she had an option to return to the circles from back in the day – they all knew who she'd bloody well ended up having to marry, whereas he'd made a nice life for himself in the city he'd moved to. He'd made lots of influential acquaintances and his social circle was *more* than acceptable.

Lillian's eyes had narrowed as she'd reminded Richard that *he'd* been the one to fix her up with Jack in the first place, therefore *he'd* been the one who was ultimately responsible for ruining her life. For this alone, it was down to *him* to rectify things.

Initially Richard had been angry and almost incredulous when Lillian had then proceeded to make further demands. Granted, he hadn't wanted anyone to know that he'd had any connection, however slight, with a man originating from a council estate, but it hardly warranted what she was asking for. A large sum of money – enough to purchase a property of the correct stature in an area which reflected her true status, as well as the additional funds to live in the style she'd been brought up to expect, plus of course, the assurance that his son would marry her daughter when they came of age.

Surely all of this was rather over the top in exchange for her silence?

He'd been seconds away from standing up and as politely as possible suggesting she leave, when Lillian had dropped something else into the conversation. The minute she'd said she wondered what people would think if Richard's shared interest in Jack's previous girlfriend was made common knowledge, his blood had run cold.

It was this which had made him take her seriously. Until that point he'd never considered it a possibility that Jack might have told Lillian about the gypsy. Neither had he realised he had been so obvious about wanting to bed that tart himself. But how much had Lillian actually known?

Richard sighed. He'd only known Jack through college where they'd all been studying business. He supposed in fairness the man would have been described by others as 'decent', but that trait never figured in *his* judgement. It was what people could *do* and what they were *worth* that mattered. Everyone knew that. *Anyone that was successful anyway.*

Surprisingly, despite his lowly status, Jack always had his pick of the women. And the pretty ones, at that! The man was nice looking, but what the hell could he have seriously offered them? At the very best he'd have only ever amounted to a small semi-detached house and the ability to holiday somewhere dreadfully cheap every couple of years. And his speculation had been right from what Lillian had ranted about.

But even though Jack had had his pick of the girls, he'd been infatuated with just one. The gypsy girl was stunning and so therefore alright for a good seeing to, but marrying the woman? What had Jack been thinking of?

Richard's nose wrinkled up with the memory. It was true Jack had little status or reputation to lose, but that hadn't been the point. Dear God, it wouldn't have surprised him if that girl hadn't known how to use cutlery! The most she'd have ever amounted to would have been a toilet cleaner or something. *Imagine it?*

Things like that had underlined just how different their classes were. *He had loads. Jack had none.*

Richard glanced at the clock on his large desk and sighed in resignation. He needed to keep an eye on the time as he couldn't risk being late for the upcoming meeting particularly as he needed to leave early for the damn suit fitting.

Back in the day he'd known *his* money would guarantee him a much better option – and it had. His lips formed a slight smile as he thought of Susan. His status alone had ensured him the arms of a socially acceptable girl of the same class, but that hadn't meant it wasn't his right to have a go on the pretty gypsy. Why should Jack have been the only one to take that pleasure? Not that he'd ever even done that from what he'd heard because the man had been stupid enough to *respect* the woman. He'd even *listened* to her, for God's sake!

Jack Jacobs had been a joke and Richard and his mates had spent many an enjoyable hour in the college canteen laughing at his stupidity, but none of it had mattered in the end because the gypsy girl had disappeared, which was probably a good job for both Jack *and* himself.

Jack had been broken-hearted, but Richard thought he'd had a lucky escape as he'd have probably ended up with twenty-eight kids otherwise. Despite acting so virtuous, those sorts of girls popped babies out like peas. *Virtuous, my backside. Women like that always wanted it and Jack had been an idiot not to take his turn when he'd had the opportunity.*

Richard frowned. He, however, could have had a lot of problems if she'd ever said anything about certain things, but it was hardly his fault. People purposefully tried to screw up successful people out of spite and if she had, then things could have worked out a lot differently, so he'd been exceptionally glad when she'd chosen to leave.

Still, that had been a long time ago and he'd never heard or seen from her again, so he hadn't worried about anything resurfacing. The most insulting thing was that their paths would never have crossed in the first place had it not been for Jack-bloody-Jacobs.

The only other people who knew of the connection were also now in good jobs and wouldn't want the boat rocked either. Richard was confident the agreement he'd set out at the time with his mates wouldn't be broken.

It was a few months after the disappearance when Richard had set Jack up with Lillian. It was only meant as a bit of a wind-up and to get Jack's mind off his lost love.

Ok, so Richard hadn't been entirely honest with Lillian about Jack's background when she'd agreed to a date. She had good blood and was a nice looker in her day, but personally he'd never had much time for her. He'd thought her acidic and had felt the same ever since he'd first met her when they'd been kids, therefore it would have done her good to be brought down a peg or two by being jibed at for being involved with a bit of rough like Jack. He had, however, felt a little bad when Lillian's parents, on discovering she'd been seeing a man below her status, disowned her. She'd then had little choice but to marry the man.

But that had been her problem, not his.

Richard had zoned out Lillian's voice as she'd sat in his office droning on about how awful and depressing her life had been. How she'd had to live amongst the common paupers, rather than her own sort. And now, even though he was dead, Jack had embarrassed her further by being murdered.

Richard had found it difficult not to tell her to shut up. Jack's death had been nothing to do with *him*. He hadn't killed him, had he?

He'd still only been half-listening but when she'd muttered something about 'retribution from bikers', and a creeping finger of fear wormed its way into his brain.

Lillian had waved her arms around animatedly, wailing about how she hadn't understood any of it. Retribution for what? What was he supposed to have done? And with bikers?

Even the police hadn't any suspects. They'd just hinted he must have been 'involved' in something unsavoury. None of it had made sense, she'd cried.

Richard turned the jar of paperclips around in his hand. He distinctly remembered that day and how the sweat had slowly trickled down between his shoulder blades. *He'd known exactly what that retribution had been for.*

At least by that point he knew for definite that Lillian genuinely didn't have a clue. He'd thought for a split second she'd somehow known *everything,* but he'd been stupid thinking that. He'd known enough about Lillian that if she had, she was far too poisonous not to use it against him in its entirety *immediately.* But most importantly of all, Jack had, years later, unknowingly done him one final favour and he didn't want that jeopardised by raking anything up.

Richard had found it easy to quickly think of something to fuel Lillian's urge to blame her husband for his own demise. The lies had tripped unhindered from his tongue as he'd casually mentioned what a shame it was that Jack had gone down the peddling drugs route again…

Jack had been the *last* person who would have ever been involved in that sort of thing. The man refused even a drag from a cigarette, let alone anything else, but Lillian would grasp at anything to justify her resentment. She had been both horrified, but unsurprised at Richard's words, yet had grabbed them with both hands, as predicted.

With that story placed firmly in Lillian's mind it had then been relatively simple to stipulate their agreement would only hold if no one ever learnt of Jack's real history. He'd known that would have pushed her social embarrassment over the edge and she'd have been desperate to hide it.

Between them they'd agreed on a fictional job for Jack which was palatable to Lillian and changed the murder into an unfortunate car accident. Richard smiled. As usual, he'd been a genius in his thinking.

He'd pointed out *that* way, her poor choice of husband

would not be revealed when she was introduced to his circles and there would be no uncomfortable or embarrassing situations to explain. Of course, it had also meant that Jack Jacobs – and Richard's own association with that period of his life, would never need to be mentioned again.

It had been imperative Lillian stuck to the story, otherwise the deal would not happen. The only exclusion to this was that Victoria be told the 'truth'. The girl had needed to know *something* about why her father died and what a loser he was. *That was what she'd needed to believe anyway...*

Lillian, being as mercenary as Richard himself, had been happy with this. She'd more than already paid by marrying beneath her, so was quite content to get back where she belonged. She'd already changed her and Victoria's surname from Jacobs back to Morgan within two months of Jack's death, so there was nothing at all to link her to her unfortunate working-class marriage.

When they'd eventually finalised the money and the promise of Matthew to Victoria, Richard had been silently grateful – not that he'd have ever told Lillian that.

It had been all very well offering her this arrangement, but there had been a couple of other slight issues that he'd also had to deal with... Like, for one, finding the bloody money in the first place and secondly, there was of course his own wife.

Richard had obviously had to tell Susan *something* about it. He'd sat her down that very night and told her the 'awful news'. He was helping the shamed family of an old friend - the least he could do, he'd said. *Imagine finding out your husband was a drug dealer after all that time...*

Susan had predictably agreed helping Lillian was the right thing to do. *The poor woman. Fancy having to go through that shame and coming from such a good family as well...*

Richard smiled. Susan had then mentioned something that haven't even crossed his mind. She'd thought it wouldn't hurt for him to appear a bit nicer and may even help to up his client list at the bank.

He hadn't cared one way or the other whether people liked him. In their world it was all to do with networking and what someone's contacts could offer, rather than bothering about irrelevant things, such as 'liking' someone.

It must be a female thing. After all, it was hardly a secret that most men did what their wives wanted, whether they admitted it or not. Women looked at things differently and could be the most useful influences. Any intelligent man knew that and used it to his advantage.

After a lot of work from his side, Lillian was introduced and accepted into his circles and, in turn, Richard gained plenty of kudos from the wives of the *right* people. *What a nice man he was for taking an old friend's family under his wing after that dreadful accident.*

There was one other part Richard had failed to mention to his wife - he'd been forced to remortgage up to the hilt. She knew he was helping Lillian out financially, but not how he'd funded it and that was the way it had to stay.

There had been a time shortly after he'd forked out for Lilian's silence that he thought his financial troubles, along with everything else, would be exposed. His income had not brought in as much as his bank balance had required to keep up with the hefty remortgage payments, but thanks to the large investments and swathe of elite customers who had recently joined his branch, courtesy of the wives' networking and influential abilities, it had netted him a fortune. Oh yes, Susan had been spot on and her plan had guaranteed his success.

Admittedly, Susan had been a bit unhappy to learn Richard had promised Matthew to Victoria. Matthew was definitely her favourite of their two children, but when he'd reeled off a list of names connected to Lillian's side of the family to appease her, she'd begrudgingly accepted it.

He hadn't been able to see why she'd been that bothered anyway. Matthew had his head screwed on well enough and had done from a very early age, unlike Carmen. Thankfully by that time, thanks to him, their daughter had already been betrothed to a rich French blue-blood and that was good enough for Richard. *It was the girls a parent had to worry about, not the boys.*

But then he'd still had to find a way to broach the subject with Matthew. It had been him who would have to marry the half-breed.

Richard ran his hand over his immaculately shaved chin. Things had been going well until Victoria had opened her mouth.

He had been incensed when Matthew had returned from school and told him what Victoria had said - her father had been murdered by bikers over a drug deal. He'd given Lillian *strict* instructions for the girl not to ever breathe a word about that, but she'd somehow felt the need to confide in Matthew. God only knew why.

Richard hadn't wanted his son to know his father had *ever* been associated with the lower-class in any way. It was imperative to instil standards in children. He also certainly hadn't wanted Matthew to know that the girl they'd agreed would be his wife wasn't one hundred percent well-bred and that her father had originated from a place equivalent to the Black Lagoon. Luckily Matthew had realised it would work to his advantage.

At least he would be marrying someone with fifty percent decent blood. Victoria was a pretty thing but disliked that she voiced an opinion occasionally, which was happening more frequently. She'd always been on the morose and vacant side but was now exhibiting the occasional spark of life and with it, disobedience. However, Matthew shouldn't have too many problems with keeping her in line. He had the proverbial and useful bargaining chip to use if Victoria tried to go against him. His son took after him after all.

He had every faith Matthew would keep her in her place. Victoria was beautiful and articulate enough to be more than acceptable once Matthew had stepped into his shoes at the bank. That was all everything was geared around after all – social standing.

Richard harrumphed in derision. It seemed it was getting more common these days for bloody women to expect a say in things. *Ridiculous. Absolutely ridiculous.*

Take Susan - she knew her place, but she would do because what could she possibly want for? Nothing, that's what. His wife got everything she wanted, when she wanted. She'd produced the correct number of children and he'd rewarded her handsomely in the ways she desired. What else was there in a marriage? They were happy and Matthew would be too if he took the same attitude.

All things aside, Richard would not have Victoria pull rank over his family by stalling on the wedding. Who the hell did she think she was?

Richard glanced at the clock once more and picked up his hardbacked leather-bound notepad. He placed his gold pen in his breast pocket and standing up, left his office to make his way to the board room for the first meeting.

Eleven

'YOU COULD BE more enthusiastic, Victoria,' Lillian sniffed as they entered another up-market bridal boutique.

Tori pretended she hadn't heard what her mother had said, or that Susan was shooting disapproving glares from underneath her candyfloss hair. She glanced around the shop eyeing the rows of exquisite-looking gowns hanging from a myriad of racking along the edges of the large shop and sighed.

There had been some beautiful dresses in the last four places they'd been in and it looked like there were equally gorgeous ones in here too, but no matter how much she thought about it, none of them would make her feel any less nauseous.

It wasn't the dresses which were the problem. Sure, there were some styles that she would *hate* to be seen in, but others were utterly jaw-droppingly stunning and every girl's dream.

She ran her fingers gently over the cream silk of a gown to the left of her. The tailored dress narrowed from the waist down to the floor and sported a small, non-ostentatious train. The bodice was tastefully encrusted with gleaming cream pearls. It was beautiful, there was no doubt about that. It was the *exact* type of dress she'd dreamt about as a young girl when she'd wistfully imagined what her perfect dress would be like on the happiest day of her life.

Well, this dress was the right one, but however beautiful and perfect it was, nothing could detract that her marriage would most certainly *not* be the happiest day of her life.

'Victoria!' her mother hissed, nudging her sharply in the ribs.

Startled, Tori pulled her eyes away from the dress, realising a shop assistant had descended on them.

'I was just saying,' the woman purred in a sickly voice. 'It's a very beautiful design, this one. Would you li...'

'My daughter doesn't like that one,' Lillian interrupted, moving to a rail opposite. 'This one however, is *exactly* what she's been looking for.'

Plastering on an ingratiating smile, the assistant eyed Tori and moved to the rack. 'Of course, Madam. I would say your daughter is a size ten, which...' She lifted one of the gowns from the rail, '...we have here.'

Tori numbly watched the woman heft the hugely flouncy, blindingly white monstrosity with its myriad of ruffles and contained her urge to scream with despair.

The assistant walked toward a curtained-off area. 'I'll prepare a changing room.'

'That other dress was off-white, Victoria. Almost *cream* in fact. Very vulgar. *This* one is a proper gown for someone like you,' Lillian whispered.

'Besides, you'd never get away with such a straight cut style,' Susan added. 'You've got little enough shape as it is. No hips, that's your problem.'

Tori saw little point in commenting or replying to either of them. *What did it matter anyway?*

Lillian glanced at the price tag of an identical dress on the rack. 'Hmm, acceptable. This one's five thousand. I wouldn't consider buying one less than three. Something that cheap signifies inferiority.' She pursed her bright lips together. 'I will also insist they do alterations to make the dress unique. I'm not happy about getting one off the shelf.'

Susan nodded in agreement. 'You should have had one specially made Victoria, like Carmen did. It's embarrassing buying a pre-made dress, but you've left us little choice, thanks to you dallying around with your indecisiveness over the date. We all know it's far too late to get one commissioned. Not by anyone decent, anyway.'

That was one good thing at least, Tori thought. The final insult would have been putting up with months of dress fittings, having pins stuck in her repeatedly and being paraded around like a turkey whilst surrounded by her mother, Susan and a load of flapping assistants. Everything was bad enough as it was.

• • • •

MATT WAS BUSY exchanging flirty smiles with a blonde he'd got his eye on whilst waiting in the wine bar when his mother, Tori and Lillian arrived.

'I was wondering when you'd get here,' he said quickly, hoping that would explain why he hadn't noticed them approach the table until his mother had prodded him. 'It seems I've been watching that clock over there for *hours*.'

Susan eyed Matt disapprovingly. 'Where's your father?'

'He stayed for an hour, then went for a round of golf,' Matt smiled. It was true. His father had made it clear there was no way on earth he was prepared to sit and wait for the women any longer. They could be ages yet and he'd had better things to do. The bank's chairman was expected at the golf range this afternoon and he didn't want to miss the opportunity of networking by discussing lace and tiaras.

Matt couldn't say he blamed his father. He'd rather be anywhere else than here too, but unfortunately he had less choice in the matter. He had to be seen to be playing ball – on the outside at least. He glanced at his fiancée and her mother. 'Hello Tori, Lillian.'

Matt hid his frown well. It was even more galling that he could have been at a rave with the others tonight. Jeremy had arranged to pick up another batch of coke from those skank bikers and could have done with a bit of a mad one. It wasn't like he'd have had an exciting time *wherever* he went if Tori was with him.

He eyed her contemptuously as she stared vacantly at her handbag. She was a boring bitch – nothing *ever* made her anything other than that. At the rave he'd have had the chance to get off his head and perhaps end up with a hot girl for a quickie. Instead he was sitting in a wine bar with the Witches of Eastwick and his dull as ditch-water wife-to-be.

His father had already told him on more than one occasion not to get too stressed over the whole thing. Wives were for a *purpose*, not for enjoyment and there would be many opportunities elsewhere to take his pleasure. Get the wife dutifully popping out well-behaved, nice-looking children, give her adequate money to keep her presentable-looking and the rest was his for the choosing.

It was getting increasingly hard work having Tori hanging around his neck. He knew the score and fully understood the reasons he was getting wed, but he wanted to get it out of the bloody way so he could get on with things. As it stood at this point in time he was spending far more time with her than he'd choose and was unsure how much longer he could keep up the 'nice' act in public.

Remembering himself, Matt grabbed Tori's hand and made a big deal of kissing it.

'Oh, isn't he romantic,' Lillian sighed. Her eyes ran appreciatively over the wide shoulders of Matt's tailored grey suit.

'Would you ladies like a drink?' Matt said, rising from the table.

Susan smiled her saccharine sweet smile. 'Victoria will no doubt, but we won't stay long. We'll give you love birds some time alone.'

'We get lots of time together,' Tori said hastily. 'You're welcome to stay.' Even *their* company would be preferable to sitting here alone with Matt.

Ignoring Tori, Matt turned to Lillian. 'Did you get everything sorted?' It hadn't taken him long to get their suits ordered. His mother had already told him what colour scheme to stick to, so it had been a straightforward exercise of being measured up and that had been it. This had thankfully given him ample time to sit in the wine bar appreciating the talent.

'All ordered and done. A lovely dress isn't it, Susan?' Lillian simpered.

'Well, it's suitable...' Susan sniffed. 'Made by a good designer and in a style that will at least give Victoria the illusion of having a bit of shape!'

Tori kept the smile fixed across her face whilst she silently fumed. Yes, she'd got the meringue dress alright. The grotesque collection of frills and ruffles that made her look like an ice-cream. It had looked even worse on that it had on the rail, which took some doing. The addition of a long veil and an overgrown tiara had completed the horrendous look. It was awful. She'd looked ridiculous and it summed this charade down to a tee.

She'd had to physically bite down on her lip to distract herself from bursting into hot tears with the utter impotence of her situation. She'd stood like a statue whilst alterations had been painfully pinned and the addition of awful gold embroidery placed on to the bodice. *All without her input of course.*

'Yes, Matthew. You'll be extremely pleased with the dress Victoria's chosen,' Lillian gushed.

I didn't choose it, Tori thought, bitterly doubting whether Matt would notice or be impressed with whatever she wore. 'I haven't chosen what colour flowers I should ha...'

'There's no need to worry about that,' Matt interrupted. 'Mother's already ordered your bouquet and the buttonholes.'

Susan flapped her hand dismissively. 'Yes, yes that's all been done. No need to thank me, Victoria. They match the colour scheme of the men's waistcoats and of course the table decorations.'

Tori glanced at her mother. 'Oh, right. So that's all been

decided too, has it?'

Lillian's eyes narrowed. 'Don't be so ungrateful! We couldn't risk waiting for *you* to decide, could we?' she tittered. 'You know what you're like. We'd all still be waiting for a date otherwise, so yes, it's all been arranged. All you needed to do was get the dress fitted, which you've now done, so there's nothing else for you to do. You can just carry on leaving it to the rest of us like you have done so far.'

Tori swallowed a retort and glanced at Matt's sneering face from across the table.

'Right then,' Susan said brightly, rising from her seat and air-kissing Matt's cheek. 'We'll leave you to it. Have a lovely evening.' She glanced impassively in Tori's direction. 'Goodbye, Victoria.'

Tori smiled as much as she could as both Susan and her mother left the wine bar. She stared at the empty space on the table in front of her, noticing Matt still hadn't ordered her a drink.

She'd known the minute their mothers had departed his eyes would be scanning the room again. Sighing, she wished she could leave. Perhaps go and see Sarah at the White Hart, but that was out of the question.

Resolutely, Tori braced herself for an evening of silence, peppered with barbed comments.

· · · ·

HUNTER REMAINED ALERT and scanned the crowd in front of him. He didn't much like doing these security jobs at illegal raves.

His eyes milled over the rows of grinding bodies as he stood, arms folded in front of the stage, his lips forming a straight line and his jaw clenched in annoyance.

Outdoor raves were more difficult to control, compared to events inside a building. He tried to zone his ears out from the relentless throbbing bass blasting from the massive speaker towers piled up either side of the badly constructed metal stage housing the ever-growing pile of DJs. Repetitive music was always difficult to switch off from. It infiltrated the entire system, gradually and subconsciously causing a trance-like state before it had even been noticed and it was taking all his power to make sure his alertness was not compromised.

The strobe lights emitting their bright and tall pulsing beams high into the night sky flashed rhythmically in bursts along with the beat and several scantily clad women stood on high podiums around the perimeter of the dance floor with a spotlight focused on each. They twisted and writhed their bodies, occasionally blowing the piercing whistle hanging around their necks and raising their arms skywards to command the drug-addled crowd's attention.

Hunter surreptitiously eyed Noel standing three feet to his left and his forehead furrowed. He watched carefully as Noel continued an impossible to hear conversation with one of those posh bastards who had arrived at Georgie's place the other night.

He'd grimaced in contempt when he'd spotted the guy and his vacant-headed girlfriend approach. Clearly never having been to a rave before, the snidey bitch had tottered uncomfortably over the uneven grass in her five-inch stilettos. He'd tried not to smile as he'd watched her ankle repeatedly go over and almost laughed out loud when she'd stepped square in the centre of a cow pat which had promptly squidged over her open shoes to coat her beautifully manicured toes.

After a tantrum-like meltdown, whatever the girl had taken had kicked in, because now she was sitting unladylike on the grass, leaning against the edge of a chicken-wire cage looking extremely zonked out.

Hunter glanced Noel's way once more. He was still talking to that skinny twat. He'd told him several times that *no deals* were to be carried out whilst they were working, *regardless* of what he had arranged, but it appeared that he was doing just that. He knew the posh kids had asked for more gear, but like he'd said – *not* whilst they were working.

Hunter shook unwelcome thoughts from his head. When he'd seen those two making their way over, against his better judgement he'd unconsciously searched for the girl that had been with them before. The girl in the bathroom. *The beautiful one and the one that had made his heart react in a way that it shouldn't have.*

Hunter shook his hair away from his face in irritation. *Why was he even having this conversation with himself?* He'd happily show that her a good time, but she didn't strike him as the type who would 'lower' herself to carnal pleasures. Especially with a man who didn't have a flash car, membership of the right circles, or hadn't already put a ring on her finger. She was *far* too uptight for that, he could tell. More fool her and her choice, but the less he was forced to have her condescending expression forced into his face, the better.

Hunter sneered. Let these people think what they wanted to think. If they were happy to live a lifetime of lies, then they could get on with it.

He'd had more than enough lies and deceit to bear over the years and would not masquerade as something he wasn't. Life was hard enough.

Irritated, he moved towards Noel and spoke directly in his ear over the pounding drums. 'I told you, NO deals tonight!'

Noel nodded. 'I know. I'm just sorting it out now.'

'Hi again,' Jeremy shouted, extending his hand towards Hunter.

Hunter narrowed his eyes and forced himself to abruptly nod at the man before moving back to his original place. *He wouldn't be shaking his hand however long he held it out for.*

Against his will, his mind moved back to the girl in the bathroom. He didn't even know her name, but suspected she didn't know, nor wanted to know his.

TWELVE

TORI HADN'T EXPECTED to be going away this weekend and had been surprised when after a very long uncomfortable silence in the wine bar last night, Matt had informed her they were all going to the hunting lodge.

And when he'd said 'all', she'd been correct in assuming that meant Jeremy and Ginny were also invited. She didn't want to spend time with *any* of them, but when she'd suggested they go and she'd stay, Matt had quickly reminded her that she had very little choice in what she did if it was what he wanted.

Tori was not about to break her ankle by trudging through the woods wearing high heels like Ginny would, even though that would be another much-expected source of amusement, so she'd made an effort to search for her walking boots.

She glanced around the attic at the pile of boxes and items gathering dust and frowned. She knew she had some boots knocking around somewhere, but it had been many moons since she'd last seen them. If she couldn't locate them soon she'd have to give up on the idea because she couldn't put up with additional bitchy digs that she'd made them late.

She'd already looked through four boxes and hadn't come across anything, apart from a collection of her mother's last season designer clothes which she deemed too good to throw away, but too good to donate to a good cause. For God's sake, she'd only worn them once or twice and some, not even that.

Tori sighed heavily. Sarah had asked if she'd fancied going to bingo tonight, but of course she'd declined. Even if she wasn't shoehorned into going with Matt, she'd never hear the end of it if he found out she'd gone to a *bingo hall*.

Retrieving another box which looked like it might be a contender for her missing boots, Tori brushed a cobweb off her face. Her mother probably had no idea what was even up here. Most of this stuff had been placed here by the removal men all that time ago and the only other person who had ever put anything up here was her – again at her mother's request.

Pulling out the box, Tori lifted the lid, coughing slightly as a plume of dust shot into the atmosphere. She peered into the box in the dim light, quickly realising this one didn't contain what she was looking for either. All it contained was old shoeboxes.

It was no good. She didn't have time to rummage through anything else. She'd just have to forget about the boots and make do with the flattest shoes she could find in her wardrobe.

Tori was shutting the lid of the box when something made her pause. *There was paperwork in those boxes, not shoes.*

With difficulty she lifted one of the tightly packed boxes from within the larger box and gingerly opened the lid. Immediately seeing a photograph of her father on the top of the pile inside, Tori's mind raced.

Everything to do with her father had been packed and removed within a week of his death and she hadn't seen one thing relating to him since. It had been almost like he'd never existed. She picked up the photograph of her father and carefully ran her finger down the side of his face. *How she missed him.*

She leafed through more of the contents. There were all sorts of bits and pieces in there as well as a lot of paperwork.

Frustratingly aware that she needed to be ready for when

Matt arrived, Tori replaced the lid of the shoe box and closed the larger box. She would have a proper look through this when she got back.

Flicking off the attic light she made her way back to her bedroom to put some things in an overnight bag.

• • • •

'I'M LOOKING FORWARD to tonight, Tori,' Ginny said from the back of the car. 'We'll have a nice girly chat while the boys talk shop.'

Tori turned and smiled. She knew the woman was being sarcastic and had about as much wish to spend the evening with her as she did the other way around but wouldn't rise to the bait. *What was the point?*

Instead she stared at the large dashboard of the Range Rover Matt had decided to take today. As well as having more room, he obviously wanted to get into character of the upper-class country dweller. She sniffed back her irritation. That family had a car for every possible scenario – a bit like some women had clothes. They had more money than sense, the lot of them.

She had no idea how she would bear an entire afternoon, evening and night with this lot, but whichever way she looked at it she'd have to. Besides, this is what her life was and it would be *exactly* the same for the rest of it, which didn't bring much comfort.

'Hope you're in a better mood today,' Matt said, speeding along the road. 'You were as interesting as a brick yesterday.' He raised his eyebrow and glanced in the rear-view mirror ensuring he had an audience. 'You should have seen her! Most women would be full of it after ordering their wedding dress, but not *this* one!'

'That's pure ungratefulness,' Jeremy sneered.

Tori ignored them, hoping Ginny wouldn't ask what her dress was like. She didn't want to picture the monstrosity again, let alone describe it and if Ginny picked up that she hated her own wedding dress it would give her an endless supply of digs to while away the hours.

'Maybe you'll cheer up if you drop a couple of these, Tori,' Jeremy sniggered, pulling a small see-through bag from his pocket.

Ginny's face lit up. 'Ooooh! You've got some extra ones. Are they the same ones from last night because they were brilliant!'

Glancing over her shoulder Tori eyed the small white tablets. 'What are they?'

'Oh God!' Matt snapped. 'They're ecstasy, Tori. *Ecstasy*! Do you not know *anything*?'

Tori didn't dare look at Matt or even answer him. It would only make him angrier. He knew she didn't like drugs. She didn't like what they did to people and how they made them behave. Her life was pointless enough without being chemically induced to act like an idiot.

Her mind drifted to the contents of that shoebox she'd found. She'd much rather be sifting through that today rather than doing *this*. Staring out of the window to avoid Matt's glares, Tori frowned. 'This isn't the way to the lodge.'

Matt laughed nastily. 'God, she's clever, isn't she? Yeah, well done Tori – you're right. What a great observation you've made from noticing that we're in the city rather than heading towards the country.' He ran his hand across his chin in irritation.

Reddening from Matt's humiliating jibe and at the risk of being ridiculed again, Tori continued. 'Ok, but why?'

'We're just picking something up before we head off, that's all.' Jeremy said.

Realising they were now in the back end of the city in a predominately industrial area, Tori felt uneasy. She'd heard plenty of times since Matt and Jeremy had taken that order of coke last week about how popular it was at work and how much of a mark-up they'd got on their 'investment'. Matt had boasted on *countless* occasions that people were *queuing* up for it.

'And what's even better is that I get to see the place Jeremy's been doing the groundwork on for that huge investor,' Matt added smugly. 'I need to see it to make sure it's got as much potential for redesigning as he says before we attach ourselves to a regeneration project for the area.' *Something else he'd been taking charge of.*

'There's no reticence from the buyer. He can see the potential and wants it. It's the bloody moron who owns the place that's causing problems.' Jeremy muttered. 'Why do you think I approached that bloke initially about the drugs. I thought if I could get on side with him it would make things a lot easier.'

Tori went cold. *They were going to that awful Noel's place?* 'So, we're going to see him?' she cried. 'He owns the building you want?'

'No, he doesn't,' Matt interjected. 'Apparently the 'boss' does – whoever that may be. The thick bastard is being far too cagey for my liking. I can't understand why he won't tell Jeremy who owns the bloody place! I mean, by the sounds of it it's hardly Buckingham fucking Palace.'

'Turn left at the end of this road and you'll see for yourself!' Jeremy said excitedly.

Tori stared mutely as they drove over a small bridge crossing a network of canals amongst deserted and dilapidated ancient factories. The huge amount of abandoned or burnt out cars made a suitable backdrop for suspect looking individuals congregating in groups and there was enough general rubbish littered around to rival the dump.

When they pulled up in front of a huge red brick Victorian factory, her heart sank even further.

'Come on!' Matt said impatiently as Tori took her time getting out of the car. Jeremy and Ginny were already making their way towards the large metal door of the building. 'Remember don't say anything to anyone and for once in your life at least *try* to look pleasant. Having a stuck-up expression on your face won't do any of us any favours.'

Tori stumbled over the uneven cobbles as Matt pulled her

along with him, feeling sick at the row of heavily chromed motorbikes. *She didn't want to be here and surrounded by the Noel's of this world.*

Matt could say what he liked, but he hadn't had his father murdered by people like them, had he? He knew the score and why she felt the way she did, yet he continued to put her in positions like this. It showed how little he cared about her feelings. He also knew Noel had acted in a most unsavoury way towards her, but he'd been less than interested.

'Don't take everything so personally, Tori. Why would he be interested in you anyway?' Matt had said scornfully.

Matt had been right. Why would that man have really been interested in her? No one ever was. People like that were only interested in another notch on their bedpost. A bit like Jeremy and Matt, except with less morals. *Disgusting, the lot of them.*

Tori took a deep breath as the door to the building opened. She wanted to get this over and done with so that they could get on their way. Even going to the lodge was preferable to this.

$\bullet \ \bullet \ \bullet \ \bullet$

TORI TRIED HARD not to let her gaze rest on any of the many pairs of eyes belonging to the groups of bikers sitting around scrutinising them.

Even though that dreadful Noel appeared friendlier today – almost *over*-friendly, she knew it was false. His eyes were undressing both her and Ginny and she certainly did not want to give any encouragement in *that* direction.

Tori's eyes wandered around the huge, cold space It was a massive room. Old industrial metal lights hung on chains from the high ceiling and the grey painted walls were shabby and chipped. A pile of unused, broken furniture was stacked up against the back wall and at the other end, nearest to where they were sitting, was a makeshift bar with rows of optics and brass taps. *Was this some sort of weird type of club?*

At least the sofas are comfy, Tori thought, grateful for the old and battered, but soft leather seat.

'Like anything you see?' Noel asked.

Matt nudged Tori sharply when she didn't respond. 'Noel asked you a question,' he said sharply. *He'd told her not to do anything that might cause offence or to embarrass him, but she couldn't help it, could she?*

Flushing, Tori turned to Noel, inwardly cringing at the lust visible in his eyes. 'Sorry, I was just looking around. I-It's very, er, nice,' she stuttered, embarrassed.

Noel grinned maliciously. 'No, it isn't. It's a shithole, but it does us for the time being. It'll be done up soon and then maybe it will be more acceptable to you.'

Tori felt flustered. 'I-I didn't mean that it w…'

'You're doing it up?' Jeremy questioned, panic fluttering. 'I thought selling the building was an option like we spoke about b…'

'The boss isn't interested, I told you that. How many more times?' Noel snapped, glancing at the group of men sitting closest to them, hoping he'd made it sound like he was annoyed with this spindly twat pushing it. He'd told the bastard that he'd try and get the boss to change his mind, but it couldn't be seen like that was what he was doing. Now this dumb fuck had all but made it bloody obvious!

Jeremy followed Noel's stare, his eyes tracking over to the men at the table and realised his mistake. So, Noel was up for working with him and getting this place sold against his boss' wishes. Interesting, but useful – *very* useful. That was cool. Whichever way he wanted to play it was fine by him.

'Sorry, yes you did say that. Just checking there hadn't been a change of heart because the buyer's very eager,' Jeremy added.

'Like Noel said, I'm not interested,' a low voice growled from the other side of the room.

'Hunter!' Noel spluttered. 'I was just saying you don't want to sell.'

Tori's heart lurched into her mouth recognising the low growl. Her eyes quickly tracked over to the other side of the room as Hunter made his way towards them.

With a constricted throat her eyes traced over his bulging heavily tattooed biceps straining against his tight T-shirt and she felt her breath hitch as her gaze lowered over his trim waist and down his muscular legs.

'*You're* the boss?' Jeremy squawked. 'I didn't realise. Maybe we can…'

'There isn't much, if anything which would convince me to sell this place!' Hunter interrupted, his eyes openly conveying dislike. 'Are you here about the order you spoke with Noel about last night?'

Hunter's irritation was escalating. He would be having serious words with Noel over this. Selling these yuppies shite gear was one thing but inviting them *here* was another and he was not happy about it. He didn't want people knowing his business. Especially *them*. And now they were trying to talk to him into selling? What else had Noel been discussing behind his back? His steely glare fell between Matt and Jeremy.

'Noel said to come here rather than do the deal at the rave,' Matt said quickly. *They would need to play this in a different way if they were to make inroads getting this property out of this moron's hands.*

Matt watched Hunter's eyes rest on Tori. 'If we can sort that we'll be out of your way. We didn't mean to intrude.' Oh, he could play the game alright. Having been involved with corporate clients these past few years, having to grovel and arse-lick was no stranger to him. However, he resented acting meek and mild for this joker's benefit. Still, if it bagged him the goods, then it would be worth it.

Matt shot Jeremy a look. The bloody idiot. He hadn't helped the overall situation. He'd told him they'd weigh up a strategy of how best to deal with this, but he'd gone ahead and opened his mouth. This was why Jeremy would never be any good at brokering deals. He had no idea how to play people. Not like *he* did.

'We're on the way up to my hunting lodge to have a night

away in the country,' Matt boasted, slightly miffed to see the condescending look form across the big man's face. 'It has a Jacuzzi and it's in a pl...'

'Yeah, great,' Hunter cut Matt off, his eyes wandering over to the woman sitting next to the irritating prick. *The woman who so far he'd tried to avoid looking at.*

He locked his gaze on her and watched her eyes scrutinise him contemptuously. His breath caught in his throat as he looked at her lips. Pushing his physical attraction to one side, he brought the shutters down in his mind. *The stuck-up bitch.*

Quickly pulling his resolve together, Hunter turned to Noel. 'Get these people what they came for.'

Tori looked away. Unfamiliar heat had spread through her body and she felt indescribably shaky and disorientated. The dislike he felt for them – for *her* was palpable.

Why was she even questioning it? She could hardly be surprised. People like that hated everyone and destroyed everything around them. So why was she feeling so put out?

There was something about Ash Hunter that she couldn't explain or rationalise. She didn't understand it herself. This was confusing. She needed to get out of here.

'Where are you going?' Matt snapped as Tori pushed herself forward in her seat. 'Can't you see we're waiting for our stuff?' It was always *her* that made them look like donuts. He was beginning to think she was doing it on purpose. 'Stay there until I tell you.'

Matt rolled his eyes and grinned at Hunter. 'She's a nightmare! Brain like a sieve and thinks the world revolves around her!'

Hunter stared at Matt, then back at the woman who had turned bright red and sat dejectedly in the chair, clearly used to being publicly humiliated by this jumped-up scrote. 'I can see that...' he muttered.

Matt laughed, glad Hunter appreciated his frustration. 'God only knows what Tori will be like after we get married!'

'A lot worse, I expect,' Hunter's expression remained

impassive, but inwardly he was seething at the way the man had spoken to her. He was also trying to hide that he was drinking in every detail of the woman and hoped the steady hardening of his cock wasn't yet visible.

Tori... So that was her name? 'Now if you'll excuse me, I've got things to deal with.' Hunter turned and walked purposefully out of the door without waiting for a response.

Tori sat blankly in the chair. Her blush was still livid and she felt both naked and humiliated. She didn't have to look in Ginny's direction to know she'd be wearing a huge grin. Oh, she'd have *loved* witnessing that exchange.

Matt gripped Tori's arm. 'You just can't help yourself, can you? You embarrassed me on purpose, you silly cow. Learn how to behave and *fast.*'

THIRTEEN

LAST NIGHT GEORGIE had been surprised to get a call from Hunter but had been even more surprised to get another tonight. She was lucky if he called her once or twice a month. Usually the only way she got to see him was to offer her place up for a party or by inventing a reason to go to the Factory.

She was beginning – or rather should she say, *hoping* her hard work where Hunter was concerned was paying off and that he was seeing her as a bit more than purely a shag. Her heart skipped a beat with the prospect. It was all she'd ever wanted since she'd first clapped eyes on him. He was her *dream* man. Even though he was as hard as nails and no one in their right mind would cross him, he had a good heart. He'd always treated her with the utmost respect, although he'd been clear from the off that what they had was purely physical.

She'd ended up in his bed *countless* times over the last few years and an easy relationship had developed. Well, easy on *him* she suspected because she was available whenever he required. Even if she was busy or involved in something else, he always took priority. She'd drop everything to run to his side and always would.

But having seen quite a bit of him recently – at *his* bequest rather than her manufacturing, maybe – just *maybe* he'd realised they were something more than mere fuck buddies?

They'd always got on well physically, but what she really hankered after was having his heart as well as his body. Unfortunately, Hunter had been closed to that option and it appeared that would never change. She'd initially been happy with this because it had suited them both. After all, he'd been a reliable supplier of her drug of choice, so if she could get free, or on the tick coke, then that had been the primary objective.

Furthermore, it hadn't been a hardship getting into the man's bed. Someone *that* easy on the eye with a body to die for and who more than knew how to use it was hardly a chore, but she'd unexpectedly fallen hard for him very quickly.

Hunter knew she was in love with him. She'd told him countless times when she'd had enough drink or gear to bring her honesty to the forefront, but he'd made it clear he could never give her what she wanted in that department. Was he now seeing things differently and developed deeper feelings?

Tonight, when she'd arrived at his place as requested, Hunter had been in a strange mood. Short of handing her a glass of vodka and throwing a wrap of coke over, he'd hardly said two words. He'd just sat on the low window seat and stared out to the horizon.

Walking up behind him, Georgie wrapped her arms around Hunter's thick neck and planted her lips against the side of his throat. 'Hey honey, what's going on? You don't seem yourself.'

Her fingers gently massaged his shoulders, feeling the muscles knotted and tense beneath her probing fingers. 'You can tell me, you know,' she continued. 'That's what I'm here for, babe. I'll *always* be here for you.'

Without moving his gaze from the horizon, Hunter forced a smile. 'I know, sweetheart.' She was a good girl, Georgie. She'd move heaven and earth for him, but unfortunately it made no difference. *Nothing could change his black heart.*

He continued staring at the spot in the distance which he'd fixated on. He wasn't looking at anything in particular and couldn't have described what, if anything, he was actually even looking at. His thoughts were very much on *Tori*. She'd looked so miserable, dejected and thoroughly downtrodden. *Broken, even*.

He'd wondered whether he'd misread her general expression of what he'd presumed was contempt with a mask to conceal her misery. However, she'd chosen that prick to be her husband, so was it not of her own doing if things weren't good?

A woman who would sell her soul and happiness for money and, in his opinion, plastic status, probably deserved to be miserable. And let's face it – he didn't know her. She could be one of the many creatures playing the submissive subservient wife in public, but behind closed doors, manipulated everything to ensure she got *exactly* what she wanted.

That couple could very well be a match made in heaven. The rich had very few morals when it boiled down to what they'd do for the things they deemed important.

Hunter scowled. But then he was hardly the paragon of virtue or qualified to talk about morals, was he? *Not with what he'd done*.

It still didn't change that against his will he was drawn to the woman. Replaying the image of her which, despite his lack of consent, had stuck in his mind, he felt his cock throb with need with the thought of taking her to bed.

Snapping back to reality, Hunter felt Georgie's hands tantalisingly lower over his hard abdominals and linger over his belt. He knew she was staring at his arousal pressing painfully against his jeans.

Kneeling down, she palmed her hand firmly over his crotch and Hunter inhaled deeply. Reaching up, Georgie pressed her lips onto his, teasing his bottom lip with her tongue. Her hand slipped into his jeans and folded around his length.

'Hunter…' Georgie gasped, willing his tongue to explore her mouth and kiss her with the hunger she knew he had. 'What do you want me to do, baby? What do you want me to do to take away what's bothering you?'

Gently lifting Georgie to her feet, Hunter stood to his full height and bent her over the window seat. He didn't know what she could do to solve his issue of unwelcome confusing thoughts because even *he* didn't know how to deal with those yet. He didn't understand what he was thinking or why, but what he *did* know was that she could deal with the present need to release the build-up of sexual tension he'd had since meeting that woman again today.

'You're doing everything I need right now just perfectly, sweetheart,' Hunter growled, pushing himself deep into her.

• • • •

'JESUS CHRIST! I still can't believe that ape is the boss!' Jeremy remarked, swigging greedily from a bottle of Dom Perignon.

'Yeah, but what does that mean?' Matt sneered. 'Boss of *what*, may I ask? What do that lot actually do – apart from peddle drugs?'

Tori pretended not be interested, but she was. When Sarah had mentioned them previously, she had been vague about it all, so whatever Hunter and his 'staff' did was clearly not legit. *Hardly surprising…*

She still had half an ear on what Ginny was rattling on about and glanced at her lounging in a sumptuous leather armchair, her jodhpur-clad legs draped over the armrest as she stared hypnotised at the fire the men had lit in the grate. It wasn't even over-cold, but they'd insisted on lighting it anyway as it allegedly added to the ambience of their country retreat.

Why Ginny was wearing jodhpurs was another mystery. She didn't have a horse, couldn't ride one and had never even been *near* one as far as she knew. *'Italian designer, darling'*, was all she'd said to explain her choice of clothes.

Tori glanced down at her own jumper and jeans and shrugged. At least the lodge was nice. The wooden walls were decorated tastefully with a collection of expensive antiques and a huge shag-pile rug sat in front of the big open fire. The well-equipped kitchen and dining room led off from the big, but cosy lounge. On top of that, the place sported three big en-suite bedrooms, all containing super-king size beds. It was lovely and set in a private woodland owned by Matt's parents and she'd have quite happily lived here. It was the people in it she couldn't bear.

Tori sipped from her champagne flute. She'd already had three glasses and even though she could feel slight effects from the alcohol it was nowhere near enough to make her want to be talkative, relax or join in with anyone. She wouldn't be taking any of those ecstasy tablets which had been handed around the moment they'd arrived either.

Predictably she'd been slated for her refusal to partake in the drug-taking, but she didn't care. She might have to swallow everything else this lot threw at her, but on that score she was sticking to her guns.

She glanced at Ginny, still entranced by the flickering flames, but hearing Hunter's name crop up again in Matt and Jeremy's conversation, Tori turned her attention back to them.

'The question remains as to how we can change his mind about selling,' Jeremy moaned.

Matt threw a plaid striped cushion at Jeremy's head. 'You didn't help the overall situation either did you, you fucking moron! Did you not see the glare Noel gave you?'

'Oh, Noel's ok when you get to know him,' Jeremy said.

Tori raised her eyebrows. Jeremy spoke like he was best friends with that awful man. He'd only spoken to him twice which hardly constituted as 'knowing' him. *Besides, Noel wasn't alright. None of them were.*

'Have you got something you'd like to add, Tori?' Matt jibed, having seen her expression.

Tori glanced up. She really must curb her facial movements. 'Not really, apart from I don't understand why you're so bothered about purchasing that particular property.'

Jeremy rolled his eyes at Matt. 'Does she understand

anything at all?'

Ginny laughed. 'I think we all know the answer to that! She didn't have a proper education until she was twelve remember, so what do you expect?'

Tori reddened. There was nothing wrong with the school she'd been to before she was unfortunate enough to be forced to go that that private one where she'd met *them*. Matt had promised that he wouldn't say anything about her personal history to either of them, but of course he'd been unable to resist.

Matt leant over and held Tori's hand patronisingly. 'You see darling, you know my job? You remember I work at a bank, yes?' He spoke like he was talking to a little child. 'Well, so does Jeremy and if we can secure this property for the investor then it means we'll make a lot of money. Other investors will flood to the area and they'll all need some level of finance. *Finance*, yes? Like we provide, being as we're at the bank. Do you understand now, sweetheart?'

Tori pulled her hand away in irritation. 'Yeah, very funny.' Getting up she stalked into the kitchen. It was getting harder and harder to hold her tongue.

'Joking aside, mate,' Jeremy lowered his voice, knowing Tori could still hear. 'I don't know how you'll get away with taking *her* to functions with clients once you're married. She'll embarrass the fuck out of you!'

Matt laughed. 'You think I don't know that? She'll learn. You'd be surprised what people can do when they're reminded of being exposed for what they are. She owes me too much. Her and her fucking mother. She'll soon learn not to act retarded in public.'

Jeremy frowned. 'Exposed for what? What's all this?'

Matt sneered. He'd enjoyed telling Jeremy and Ginny that Tori had originally gone to a state school, but the rest he'd kept schtum on – more for his own sake than Tori's, but he'd certainly use it if push came to shove. *He'd tell all and sundry*. 'Never you mind,' he smiled secretively, pulling the test wrap of coke from the order they'd picked up earlier from his pocket. 'Another line?'

'Why not! Set it up!' Jeremy clumsily placed the empty bottle of champagne on the floor where it tipped over and rolled into the corner of the room. 'Tori, grab us another bottle of champers whilst you're out there will you, there's a good girl.'

Sighing, Tori dutifully opened the massive fridge stuffed full of champagne, wine and bottled lager. She retrieved another bottle of Dom Perignon and placed it down on the oak work surface. Leaning against the sturdy wood, she took some deep breaths before returning to the lounge area.

'Going back to the property problem, I think we should continue buttering Noel up. He's the inroad to that meathead, Hunter, so keep him on side.' Matt wiped the residue of coke from under his nostrils. 'If he trusts us I'm sure he'll give us a way of how we can twist the big man's arm. Especially if there's a decent amount in it for him. We need to get the deal closed and I'm going to make that happen.'

'You going to have some this time?' Ginny asked, watching Tori stare at Matt and Jeremy hoovering up more lines of coke. She rose from the chair with an ecstasy-induced grin on her face. 'You might be more of a laugh if you weren't so uptight.'

Tori shook her head and silently sat back down in the armchair. She placed the new bottle of champagne on the large coffee table in front of her.

'I'm buzzing!' Matt exclaimed happily. 'This coke's the business. Let's put some tunes on before the entertainment arrives.'

'This is going to be fun!' Ginny squealed.

'Best make sure we're primed, Jeremy,' Matt grinned, grabbing his own crotch. 'We'll have a lot of work to do!'

Tori frowned. 'What are you talking about?'

Jeremy sneered. 'I can't say I'm surprised you haven't told her, Matt. She'd have freaked out and whined the whole way here otherwise.'

Matt burst into hysterical laughter and Tori looked between each of them in turn. 'What?' *Something was obviously hilarious – at her expense no doubt.*

Ginny leant over the back of Tori's armchair, then ran her fingers through her hair. 'Honey, tonight we'll be giving our men the best night of their lives.'

Tori twisted her head in an attempt to get Ginny's fingers away. She didn't want her touching her.

'You still don't get it do you?' Ginny purred. 'Lighten up, Tori, for Christ's sake! It's almost the nineties. You've got to fall in line with the twentieth century soon before it's all over.'

'Christ, Matt. Is Tori still a virgin?' Jeremy quipped.

'She might as bloody well be. Adventurous she is not!' Matt spat.

'Would someone please just tell me what's going on?' Tori knew they thought she should have worked out what was planned, but she didn't have a clue and it was getting on her nerves. They were frayed enough as it was without all of this ridiculousness.

Matt sighed. 'Ok, we have two beautiful ladies booked to join us tonight,' he said slowly in the voice that he enjoyed using on her. 'You, Ginny and the ladies will enjoy yourselves, whilst me and Jeremy watch.'

'And then we get *our* turn,' Jeremy added excitedly.

Tori's eyebrows knitted together as the penny dropped. *Surely not? They weren't serious?* 'Is this another of your wind ups to make me feel stupid? Ha ha, very funny everyone.'

'It's no joke. We've paid a lot of money for this. High class they are. We've talked about this before Tori, you know that. We're all friends here and we'll never see these women again, so it'll be great fun. Besides, you may learn something and believe me, you could do with that,' Matt smiled.

'I've always wanted a bit of girl-on-girl action,' Ginny drawled, tracing her hand over Tori's left breast. 'It'll be fun, honey.'

Tori stiffened and pulled Ginny's hand away. She stood up

angrily. 'I'm *not* doing anything like that with you or with *anybody*. I'm not a lesbian!'

'Neither is she,' Jeremy interjected. 'It's just *fun*, Tori. It doesn't mean anything. What if the girls just touch you and me and Matt do the rest? How does that sound?'

Tori turned crimson. *They were serious*. She didn't want this. She didn't want to sleep with Jeremy or for him to touch her. She didn't want *any* of them touching her – male or female. *This was not happening*.

With tears threatening, Tori rushed into the kitchen. Using her arms to support herself against the work surface, her mind raced as she regulated her breathing.

Stalking in with a face like thunder, Matt grabbed Tori's arm and swung her around. Pushing her against the work surface he grabbed her face with his other hand. 'What the fuck is the matter with you?' he hissed. 'I'll *not* have you embarrassing me in front of my friends. Get the hell back in there and get yourself in the mood before I get *really* cross.'

Tears escaped as Tori was forced to look into Matt's face. She could see the hate in his cold blue eyes inches from hers. 'I'm with *you*, Matt. I don't want to do anything with other people. I'm not like that. I won't do it.'

Matt applied more pressure to his grip. 'You boring bitch! Yes, you're with me, so if I say it's ok, then it *is*. You need more experience. Now do as I said.'

Tori faltered. Everything he said, everything her mother said, everything *everyone* said was important. What *she* wanted counted for nothing - it never had and it seemed, never would.

'I'm waiting, Tori…' Matt growled, all hint of reasoning now gone. 'I've explained what I want and the women will be here any minute, so don't show me up, ok?' He pushed his fingers either side of her mouth, forcing her lips into a wide grimace. 'And for once in your life, SMILE! Leave your usual miserable face somewhere else. Does *nothing* make you happy? Christ! Most other women would do anything to be in your shoes with what I give you and what you'll get once we're married.'

Happy? By being treated like this? Today had been awful and this was the icing on the cake. Feeling brave for once, Tori decided to stand her ground. 'I'm not doing it. I'm sorry if that upsets you, but if you loved me you wouldn't ask me to do something I don't want to do.'

'What's love got to do with anything, you stupid cow? Nothing, that's what! Besides, you never want to do *anything*, so that doesn't leave much does it?' he raged. He'd got a right bum deal with this stupid bitch. Yeah, he'd marry her – after all, the pay-out he'd get for keeping his end of the deal would suffice his inconvenience, but he was damned if he would put up with insolent bullshit from the cheap pauper.

'Have you any idea where you and your fucking mother would be if it wasn't for me and my family, you ungrateful cow,' he spat. 'You'll do as I damn well say!'

Dropping his hand, Matt agitatedly raked his fingers through his hair. He couldn't wait until he'd got this joke of a marriage out of the way. Then he'd be free to take himself a selection of decent like-minded *proper* women.

'My father warned me you were getting too big for your boots with opinions and all that crap lately and he was right.'

Tori stared at the floor, panic threatening to thoroughly engulf her. Moving away, she stumbled towards the door.

'Where are you going?' Matt screamed.

Tori didn't turn around. If she looked at Matt then there was a high chance that she'd allow him to somehow talk her out of it. He was very persuasive and good with words, as well as threatening and her nerves would not be able to fight him much longer. She knew she was risking everything her mother had desperately manufactured and that she was letting everyone down, but for once she just couldn't do what they wanted. *Not that.*

'I think it's best if I leave. I don't want to spoil your night. We'll talk about it tomorrow.' Tori quietly opened the lodge door. She'd leave her stuff. She didn't need it anyway.

'Bear in mind if you walk out, you'll regret it, Tori.'

'I don't want to argue. I just need some time out,' Tori kept her decision firmly in her mind. 'I'll only embarrass you if I stay, that's why I'm going. Tell them I'm sick. Say what you like,' she reasoned.

'You are sick. Sick in the fucking head, you selfish cow!' Matt spat.

Shutting the door behind her before Matt could say or do anything else, Tori quickly walked down the long path to the country lane. He hadn't followed her, but she'd expected nothing else.

She hadn't got a coat and had no idea how far it was to the small village they'd passed on the way to the lodge, but she had no choice but to keep walking. Tears rolled down her face as she made her way in the direction she thought to be correct.

Tori couldn't quite believe she'd done this. Her heart sank like a stone. Maybe she should have just done what Matt wanted? Cold dread fizzed in her veins but kept up a steady pace in the darkness. *What would she do when she reached the village? Had she even thought of that?*

She'd been ridiculous. The place wouldn't even have a taxi firm. All she'd seen was a pub, a little shop and a few houses, but it was too late now.

Setting her chin determinedly, Tori pushed on. She'd think of something.

FOURTEEN

'GET THAT DOWN your neck, love.' Sarah pushed a large gin and tonic across the table towards Tori. 'Do you want to come upstairs to our private quarters rather than sit in the bar? I'm sure Colin won't mind.'

Tori smiled weakly. 'You and Colin have already done more than enough for me tonight. I'm sorry to have involved you.'

'Don't be daft. I'm glad you called.' Sarah squeezed Tori's hand kindly.

She'd been surprised when Colin had answered the phone to say Tori was on the other end and had known something was wrong the minute she'd heard her friend's voice. She'd barely been able to understand the woman she'd been babbling so much and was clearly in some kind of shock.

Sarah had immediately jumped into her car and driven as fast as her old VW Golf could go. She'd lived around this area all of her life but had never heard of the place Tori said she was. She'd rarely had cause, want or need to venture out into the country.

The village was only eleven miles away, but the drive had seemed endless as she'd negotiated the windy country lanes in the pitch black, grateful she'd only put away one pint before receiving the call.

She'd briefed Colin as to what was going on before leaving and his first instinct had been that *he* should go, but she'd been correct in presuming Tori's twat of a boyfriend had done something to upset her and she'd be more comfortable talking to her rather than her husband.

Sarah had arrived at the tiny village and the only life she could see was from a rickety looking pub. That was until she spied a lone figure standing by the phone box. Screeching to a halt, she'd found Tori shaking with cold and her face streaked with make-up. After hugging her, she'd bundled her into the car and covered her with a blanket to try and warm her up.

Much to Sarah's dismay, Tori seemed unwilling to speak about what had prompted her to ring – apart from that her and Matt had argued, but she was determined to get it out of her.

'You need to tell me what's gone on,' Sarah pushed.

Tori stared at the table. How could she admit to anyone what her life was like? That it was all lies? How she allowed the man she was supposed to be marrying to treat her and what she'd been reduced to. She did, however, owe her friend *some* sort of explanation. She'd dropped everything and raced out to get her after all. 'We argued…'

Sarah pursed her lips. 'I know that, but you'd hardly walk out of somewhere with no coat late at night into the middle of nowhere over just an argument, surely?'

Tori shook her head and gulped at her gin and tonic with shaking fingers. The shock and panic had only set in since she'd got to the safety of Sarah's car. That and the further proof that her life was a hollow shell that was about to get worse.

'Listen, I don't know what that wanker has done, but if he's laid a finger on you, I swear down that he'll pay for it,' Sarah spat.

She couldn't for the life of her work out what on earth Tori was doing putting up with that pretentious dickhead in the first place. She'd only met the man once, but that was all she'd needed to decide the man and his cronies were prize cocks and in no way deserved this beautiful, sweet woman.

'He hasn't hit me if that's what you're thinking,' Tori said quickly. As much as it was tempting to say he had if it meant that someone would wipe Matt off the face of the planet and out of her life for good, she wouldn't lie.

'I know I have no right to call him a wanker, but from where I come from, a spade's a spade. I think the man's a fucking cock-sucker who treats you like shit.' Sarah sighed deeply with frustration. 'I want to know what he's done. I've seen first-hand the way he puts you down and I don't like it.'

Without warning, Tori burst into floods of tears. All the pent up hurt and despair of the last few days poured out in torrents.

Sarah shot a glare at a group of rowdy newcomers who had been playing up all night and were now making jeering sounds, clearly enjoying watching a woman cry. The drunker they got the more obnoxious they became and she guessed it wouldn't be long before they caused real trouble. She glanced around the room and frowned. *Where was Hunter? He should be sorting this out. That's what they paid him for, wasn't it?*

She pulled a crumpled tissue from her pocket and handed it to Tori. 'Right, now speak.'

Tori dried her eyes. She was lucky to have Sarah as her friend. Although she found it almost impossible to believe, it seemed the woman genuinely cared about her, but felt so pathetic and weak. Sarah would think her a joke, but then so did everyone else, so nothing new there...

As Tori hesitantly recounted the evening, Sarah's teeth clenched in anger. *That bastard...*

'Do you think I've been stupid?' Tori asked quietly, dreading to hear the confirmation she expected.

Sarah smiled. 'Yes, I do as it happens.'

Tori's face dropped. *She knew it.*

'I think you're stupid for staying with him and worrying about him. The man doesn't deserve you,' Sarah added. 'No one should be pushed into something they don't want.'

Sarah smiled when Colin deposited two more extra-large gins on the table. He didn't stay or try to speak. He was a good man. He always knew the right thing to do and could see Tori clearly needed to talk.

Tori gulped at the new drink, bolstered by Sarah's words. 'I know I sound like a boring bitch. I'm twenty for God's sake, yet sound like a fourteen-year-old. The thing is, I've only ever slept with Matt. I don't want to, you know, behave like...'

'Sleeping with several people doesn't make you bad, but only if that's what *you* want to do.' Sarah narrowed her eyes. 'I think what you've told me is just the tip of the iceberg. From some of the other things you've said in the past and from the small bit I've seen with my own eyes, I'm guessing Matt is very controlling.'

'Yeah, I guess he is, but I'm used to it, although sometimes it gets me down. My mother's the same. See what I mean, I sound about fourteen.' Tori finished her drink feeling a bit better, both for talking to Sarah and from the large measures of spirits.

'But why put up with it?' Sarah asked. 'You don't have to. Bin him off! Why the hell are you marrying the twat? For God's sake, it won't get any better. Worse, if anything!' It was frustrating. Was Tori one of those women who thought she could be the one to make that sort of man change? *Controlling cowards never did.*

Sarah glanced up again as she heard the third glass in succession smash on the floor, courtesy of the loud group. She watched Colin making his way towards the unruly newcomers. *Still no sign of Hunter and his crew. It was Saturday and they should be here.*

Tori was busy working out how to answer Sarah's question truthfully without it sounding like bullshit. Whichever way she looked at it there was no real rationality as to why anyone would understand why she put up with the way Matt behaved unless they knew the background. They'd then realise that she was stuck between a rock and a hard place trying to do the right thing and what was expected. But would they? In reality most people would struggle to understand. It hardly even made sense to her. She braced herself to formulate an answer when the sound of shouting and more smashing glass put paid to that.

Sarah yelled out in shock as she saw the unruly group upending tables and a man punching Colin in the face.

'Oh my God!' Tori stared in terror at the unfolding scene.

'Tori, move out of the way quickly,' Sarah screeched.

Tori was frozen in shock and horror as she watched a tall greasy man smashing his fist over and over into Colin's face. Blood spurted from Colin's nose and he could do little to defend himself against the onslaught from the much younger, quicker man.

Several of the locals had already come to Colin's aid and were laying into the newcomers, but things were getting out of hand. Tori felt powerless to move. She'd never seen any kind of fight before, apart from in films and even then her mother had quickly switched them off in disgust.

Her eyes searched for Sarah who was trying to help Colin but was at risk of getting punched herself. *Why was she just sitting here? Colin and Sarah were her friends. She should be doing something, not sitting here like an idiot.*

Pushing herself up from the chair, Tori's legs wobbled as the plentiful amount of gin she'd drank since arriving made itself known. Heart beating rapidly, she moved unsteadily towards the thrashing throng of chaos.

'Fuck off, you slag!' One man yelled, launching a full pint at Tori.

The pint glass hit Tori square in the chest and the beer sloshed down her front. Luckily the glass didn't break until it hit the floor. The culprit was not happy that the glass hadn't achieved its intended effect and moved towards her with a wild look in his drunken, glazed eyes.

Tori realised she was in serious trouble when the man raised his fist.

• • • •

HUNTER WAS UNUSUALLY late in arriving at the White Hart. After leaving a reluctant Georgie once she'd managed to successfully relieve his 'tension', he'd headed down to have it out with Noel about bringing those yuppies to the Factory. The discussion had become rather heated and had taken a lot longer to sort out than he'd bargained for.

However, after getting his point across, he and some of the others, including Noel, had hurriedly made their way to the White Hart. It was Saturday night and they were paid to maintain a presence.

Hunter realised there was a problem the minute he pulled up outside and heard the commotion within. 'Fuck!' he yelled, beckoning the others to get a shift on as he made his way hastily through the door.

Barging into the tap room, the first thing he saw was a group he didn't recognise kicking off with Colin and Sarah in the middle. Then he spotted a man with his fist raised to a woman and his blood boiled further. Noel had already steamed into the melee, followed closely by Grin and two of the others and Hunter rushed towards the man he'd got his eye on.

Slamming his huge fist into the side of the man's face, Hunter wasted no time in dragging the man back up from the floor where he'd unceremoniously landed. Pushing the woman out of the way, he slammed the man onto a table and continued punching him repeatedly in the face. 'Don't you *ever* be raising your fucking fist to a woman again! Do you hear me, you slimy cunt? Not on my patch or *ever*!'

Tori stared in terror at Ash Hunter and her legs trembled as she took in the rabid look in his eyes and at the ferocity with which he was beating the man whose face had already been reduced to pulp.

'I said, did you fucking hear me?' Hunter raged at the prone man, spittle flying from his mouth.

Tori stood motionless, nausea rising in her throat and she

felt herself shaking uncontrollably. This was her worst nightmare. People acting like savages was what had killed her father. Her mind was speeding and she started to feel lightheaded as panic and memories of things she didn't want to think about swamped her in a deluge. *She had to get away from this.*

Regardless of the suffocating feelings and the need to leave she remained frozen to the spot, hypnotised by the spectacle of the man in front of her - all muscle, sinews and power.

In slow motion a wooden chair flew through the air seemingly from out of nowhere and Tori braced herself for the inevitable pain when the chair smashed straight into her face. Before she knew it she was pulled backwards with force.

Completely disorientated as she was slammed with her back against a wooden partition, Tori tried to fathom whether the chair had hit her, but realised she was crushed against the hard body of Hunter, who was shielding her from the onslaught.

Her nose was pressed into his hard chest and his heady scent hit her nostrils. Feeling her body thrum, she pushed closer into him, unable to explain her need.

After what seemed like hours, the weight off her was released and Tori stared up into Hunter's face. Her breath caught in her throat once more as she looked at his strong jaw and steely eyes. The urge to press her lips against his was both overwhelming and confusing. *What the hell was the matter with her?*

Hunter gently brushed a lock of Tori's hair, wet with beer, off her face. 'Are you alright?' he growled.

Tori could see the surprise register across Hunter's face when he recognised her. His voice was low and husky, but his eyes remained cold as ice. She tried to pull herself together, amazed by the gentleness of his touch and words in contrast with the brutality that she'd just witnessed him doling out. 'Y-Yes, I'm ok. T-Thank you f…'

'Get yourself out of the way while I make sure these wankers are removed,' he interrupted.

'Wait, I…' Before Tori could finish, Hunter turned away

and she watched in awe as he dragged two more of the unwelcome guests off the floor by the back of their necks and moved quickly towards the door with one under each arm.

. . . .

AFTER UNCEREMONIOUSLY LAUNCHING two of the drunk deadbeats onto the pavement outside, knowing Noel and Grin were busy removing the remainder of the unwanted group from the premises, Hunter leant against the wall of the small inner foyer of the White Hart and took a deep breath.

For fuck's sake, sort your head out, he told himself angrily. He hadn't realised it was *that* woman until, without even seeing her face, he'd felt a jolt run through him as he'd pressed his body up against hers. He'd been trying to shield her from any further flying objects, but the minute he'd felt that rush he'd known. *Known it was her.*

He'd presumed he'd been imagining things. After all, she'd been on his mind constantly for the last week, but he'd been genuinely shocked to find his instinct had been correct.

Why was she here? People like *her* didn't frequent places like the White Hart. They were, in their own minds, far too superior for that and he certainly hadn't noticed her loser boyfriend or tosser mates.

Despite offloading himself several times into Georgie not a few hours past, raging desire flooded his body once more and when Tori had tilted her face up, his immediate reaction had been to crush his mouth down onto hers, but he hadn't. *Of course he hadn't, but by Christ, he'd wanted to with every fibre of his being.*

Pulling down the shutters in his mind, Hunter forced himself to concentrate on what he was doing and what he was here for. He resolutely made his way back towards the tap room to finish his job. *He had no time for distractions – especially pointless ones.*

FIFTEEN

COLIN SAT ON the bench seat wincing as Sarah dabbed at his badly split eyebrow with a ball of cotton wool soaked in TCP. Tori was busying herself sweeping up broken glass from the floor and cleaning up as much of the mess as she could. Although she'd have done anything to help, it was also a welcome distraction rather than sitting down with Ash Hunter.

The man and what he stood for made her skin crawl, but her physical reaction to him had yet again both shocked and angered her.

What was even worse was knowing Noel was staring at her. She could feel his eyes leering over her backside each time she bent down to brush fragments of glass into the dustpan. She'd had to remove her sopping wet jumper, but her equally wet vest top underneath showed her lace bra for all to see. Her hair was soaked and she dreaded to think what her face looked like. Still, it wasn't like she was trying to impress anyone.

'Bend over a bit more would you, Miss Aristocrat!' Noel laughed, a wide sneer across his face. 'First time you've used a dustpan is it? Fucking hell, well done!'

Reddening, Tori ignored Noel's comments and continued clearing up, feeling even more self-conscious. It seemed she was put on this earth purely to serve as the butt of everyone's jibes.

'Watch your mouth, Noel,' Hunter growled. 'You think anyone needs crap like that right now?'

Noel eyed Hunter. *What was his problem?* 'You after dipping your wick in some blue blood are you?'

Hunter's eyes flashed as he leapt from his chair and grasped Noel around the throat.

Sarah swung around angrily. 'For fuck's sake, do you not think we've had enough trouble tonight without you two bitching at each other? Stop it, the *pair* of you!'

Glaring at Noel, Hunter released his grip and sullenly sat back down like an admonished child. If it wasn't for his respect for Sarah he'd have throttled the sarcastic bastard. He'd just about had enough of Noel's attitude. *He* was the one in charge around here, not Noel and if he was going to keep pulling stunts like he had been lately, they he could get the fuck out of the club.

Tori felt like climbing into a hole. She was always the one who inadvertently caused problems. Everywhere she went and everyone she was involved with was infected by her curse.

Attempting to get his mind off the irritation Noel had caused, Hunter raised himself to his feet and effortlessly moved a heavy table to one side that Tori was attempting to push so that she could properly brush underneath it.

'Thanks,' she muttered, risking a tiny glimpse up at Hunter and feeling her betraying heart miss a beat once more.

Hunter sat back down and straightened his long muscular legs out in front of him. He swigged at his pint. 'I'm sorry we weren't here when this kicked off, Colin. We got held up.' He shot a glare in Noel's direction.

'No worries lads,' Colin said through gritted teeth as Sarah ladled more TCP onto his open wound. 'You can't be here all of the time.'

'One or two of you fucking can!' Sarah snapped. 'We pay you to watch the gaff, don't we? It's Saturday night and you don't show up until fucking 10 o'clock? It's not on!'

Colin raised his hand. 'Sarah, it's…'

'No, Col – it's *not* ok. This shouldn't have happened,' Sarah barked.

Hunter nodded. Sarah and Colin were probably the only ones in the entire world who could speak like this without penalty. *Sarah was right in what she said and he knew it.*

'There's not usually any trouble,' Colin said, trying to diffuse the situation. His head felt like a sledgehammer was smashing it up and he could do without extra grief. He knew how argumentative and volatile Sarah got when she felt wronged.

'No there isn't, but they should have been here.'

'You're right, Sarah,' Hunter said loudly. 'There should have been at least two of us here and we've let you down. I'm sorry, I really am. I'll ensure it never happens again.'

Tori listened to Hunter. His voice was clear and smooth. *Like honey.* And someone like *him* actually having the decency to take Sarah's diatribe against them on board? On the same vein it now made sense what they were. *Protection. Bully-boy protection.* Her nose crunched up with contempt. *She might have bloody well known. The epitome of filth.*

Sarah harrumphed. 'It had better not, Hunter.' She stood back to study the clean-up job she'd done on her husband's face. 'It's no use. This cut is too deep. I'll have to take him to A and E to get some stitches put in.'

Noel sat up. 'I've got my kit out back. I can stitch him up, no worries.'

Sarah glared at Noel. 'You've got to be joking, right? You think I'd trust you to make a good job of it?' She snorted derisively. 'If I'd wanted to end up married to Frankenstein's fucking monster, I'd have married one of you lot!'

Hunter grinned. Sarah's sarcasm was back, which meant he was forgiven.

Tori tipped the contents of the dustpan into the bin. 'I'd best get going too.'

Sarah glared at her. 'No, you damn well won't. You're staying *here* tonight, Tori. These two can take me and Colin to the hospital.' She turned to Hunter. 'And I'm expecting *you* to keep an eye on this place until we get back.'

Hunter nodded. *Great. So now he'd be left alone with this woman, who against all his principles, had an unwanted effect on him.* But he wouldn't make things any harder for Sarah – not after what had happened.

Tori felt her nerves jangling incessantly from her toes up to her fingers. The man despised her as much as she despised him. She could see that from his eyes alone. When she'd said she'd better be going she hadn't even been sure where she'd have gone to. The last thing she'd wanted to do was to go home to be questioned by her mother as to why she wasn't at the lodge with Matt. That was if he hadn't already called a thousand times. Besides, Sarah wouldn't be too long at the hospital. A couple of hours, max. It was only a few stitches after all.

Telling herself she was being ridiculous, Tori decided she would busy herself in their absence by continuing to clean the bar area.

• • • •

NOEL SLOUCHED BACK in the plastic chair in the hospital waiting room and sighed. He glared at a man who was clearly worse for wear from drink, drugs or both, shouting obscenities at the tired-looking woman behind the reception desk.

It was packed in here. Saturday night after kick out – he should have known. They'd be here for hours at this rate. It had only been an hour so far and he was already desperate for another fag.

'I've got to ask you this, Sarah. How the fuck do you know that stuck up bitch?' Noel asked. Sarah was down to earth and a good laugh – hardly the sort to be pally with the Lady Mucks of this world.

Sarah narrowed her eyes. She didn't like Noel at the best of times. He had more than one screw loose, hence why she'd left

Hunter to keep an eye on Tori, rather than Noel. Hunter was more than screwed up in his own way, but he'd always been respectful to her and that was she went on.

'Tori's not a stuck-up bitch, Noel. She's a very nice person.'

Noel snorted derisively. 'That I doubt. Looks down her nose at me she does, the silly cow.'

'*Everyone* looks down their nose at you!' Sarah laughed. 'And if you must know, I work with her.'

'*Work* with her?' he sneered. 'That lot don't work! They merely live off their fucking inheritance.'

'She's not like that,' Sarah said defensively. 'And she does work. She works hard.'

'Well, she's still a stuck-up cow. She needs a good damn fucking to make her see sense.'

'Don't even think about it.' Sarah snapped.

'Her boyfriend's a cunt too,' Noel barked.

'That I won't disagree with you on.' Sarah glanced at the clock high on the wall in the large waiting room. *How much longer? Colin would bleed to death at this rate.*

• • • •

HUNTER GROUND HIS cigarette out in the ashtray without taking his eyes off Tori, noting she was still avoiding looking at him. *Did his sort bother so that much she didn't have the decency to even acknowledge his presence?*

Nearly two hours they been on their own in the White Hart and all she'd done was flap about cleaning this, that and everything. Purely, he presumed, to avoid having to interact with him.

Well he'd had enough. Regardless of how entranced he was for some reason with her and her beauty – even if she was wearing scruffy soaked clothes and sporting ruined make up, his strange fascination didn't excuse her rudeness.

He slammed his fifth pint down onto the table. 'I think you've cleaned everything there is to be cleaned by now, don't you?' he snarled, watching Tori stiffen at the unexpected sound of his raised voice.

Tori stared at the beer towel in front of her, unwilling to turn around. What would she say? That she'd purposely been avoiding a situation where she had to sit and talk to him because he stood for everything she resented, but being in his close proximity somehow made her legs turn to jelly. However, she acknowledged she was being rude by avoiding him. She'd cleaned the entire bar four times already.

Hunter became even more irate at Tori's continued silence. 'Who the fuck do you think you are?' Pushing himself up from the chair he strode behind the bar and stood next to her. 'If you're so above everyone, surely you must realise it's rude to ignore people or doesn't someone like me count?' he spat. 'I stopped you from getting chaired earlier, yet you're treating me like something you've just trodden on!'

Tori remained turned away from the man she was so inexplicably drawn to. 'I already thanked you for th...'

'Oh, I should be so grateful that you lowered yourself to speak to the likes of me! I don't want or expect your thanks by the way, but I do expect to be treated with a bit of respect,' Hunter snapped. *She still couldn't look at him, the stuck-up little cow.*

He grabbed Tori's arm and swung her around. 'What makes you so special? Look at me, or does even that offend you?'

Tori flinched. She was fed up with being pulled around and talked down to. Her eyes were angry as they met Hunter's. 'Oh, this says it all doesn't it? We must all give our respect to the people who go around extorting money from all and sundry.'

'Extorting money? You jumped up bitch!' he spat, dropping his grip. 'We don't *extort* anything. People pay for our *security*!'

'And I suppose you'll tell me you don't deal drugs either,' she threw back quickly.

'Like your fucking boyfriend, you mean? Oh, the hypocrisy of the upper class knows no bounds...' Hunter's eyes narrowed as he leaned closer. 'You don't know jack shit, little girl.'

'Yes, everyone keeps telling me that, so thanks for reminding me of my place in life.' The anger deflated from Tori as quickly as it had manifested. *This was the first time in ages – if not ever that she'd stood up to someone who was berating her and she'd only picked the local psycho to take her outburst on. Wonderful!*

Hunter frowned. Something had hit a nerve, but he wasn't sure what. 'Won't your *boyfriend* have a problem? Won't he be worried about you being alone with me? With *my* sort?'

Don't you dare cry, Tori, she thought, angry tears burning the backs of her eyes.

Watching the emotions pass across Tori's face, Hunter sneered. It would be the waterworks next and he hadn't got the time or the inclination to put up with that. He was too tired, confused and irritated both with her and his confusing feelings to deal with any of this.

He shook his head dismissively. 'I'm having a drink,' he muttered, reaching for a glass and helping himself to a large whisky.

Tori pulled a crumpled tissue from her pocket and Hunter turned away, not wanting to chance her seeing his confusion. He didn't understand her one bit. He also didn't understand himself and didn't like it. He poured her a large gin and tonic and held it out. 'You look like you could use a drink, rather than argue.'

Tori smiled weakly, her core throbbing at the way her name had sounded coming from his mouth as he held out the peace offering. 'I didn't mean to take things out on you.' Stepping forward, she gingerly took the glass from Hunter's hand, her body coming alive as her fingers lightly touched his.

Hunter felt the jolt – stronger this time and his heart rate accelerated. Her hand was stuck in exactly the same position as when she'd taken the glass. Unable to pull his gaze away from her face, he knew exactly what he wanted to do. *She was feeling this too. What the fuck was going on?*

Without breaking his eye contact lest it broke the spell, Hunter silently took Tori's glass out of her hand and placed it down on the bar.

Tori felt unable to breathe and powerless to move as Hunter tucked a strand of her hair gently behind her ear and traced his thick finger down the side of her face. She was entranced by his grey eyes locked on hers.

She couldn't stop what was about to happen and she didn't want to. She needed to feel his lips on hers. What would it feel like to kiss another man? *This man?*

Hunter watched Tori unconsciously moisten her bottom lip with the tip of her tongue, his erection throbbing mercilessly within his jeans. Moving his hand from her face to the back of her hair, he pulled her towards him.

'We're back!' Sarah shouted, pushing open the tap room door.

Immediately releasing his grip of Tori and rapidly springing backwards, Hunter swung around, raking his fingers through his hair. *Shit! Fucking shit!*

'Everything alright?' Sarah asked, sensing the odd atmosphere.

'Yep,' Hunter said dismissively. He smiled at Colin. 'All patched up, I see?'

Sarah eyed Tori suspiciously. She looked flustered and uncomfortable. 'You ok?'

Realising she was standing like a statue, Tori forced herself to regain control and not try to make any sense of what might have happened if Sarah and Colin hadn't returned. 'I've been cleaning up,' she said quietly, unable to look in Hunter's direction.

Hunter grabbed his jacket from the back of one of the chairs and shrugged it onto his wide shoulders. 'I'll be off then.'

'Thanks, Hunter,' Sarah smiled.

Hunter glanced in Tori's direction and nodded. 'Tori.'

'Goodnight,' Tori muttered, hoping her voice wasn't as squeaky as it felt.

SIXTEEN

'MATTHEW, THE REASON I've asked for a meeting is because it has come to my attention that you're allowing this potential investment opportunity to slip through your fingers,' Richard said bluntly, tapping his gold Parker pen on the top of his large desk.

Sitting in a leather swivel chair opposite his father in the executive office, Matt casually crossed his ankles and straightened down his suit trousers. He glanced behind his father's head through the window which spanned the entire length of the massive room, giving a bird's eye vista of the city below them from the top of the eighth storey building the bank inhabited.

If he played his cards right this office would soon be his, but he didn't much like how the conversation was going so far.

'I'm not impressed you appear to be allowing whatever personal hiccups you're experiencing with your fiancée to impact on your business acumen,' Richard continued pompously.

Matt tried not to let his irritation show. This man was his father for God's sake, yet for some bizarre reason for as long as he'd worked for him, the man had insisted on speaking to him in the professional corporate manner reserved for staff. *'It's only fitting. I can't talk to you the same way that I'd speak to you at home, Matthew'*, he'd explained when asked previously.

It may have made sense to his father and Matt understood the need for it in a general meeting, but it seemed a pointless exercise when they were the only ones in the room – even if it was in the office.

Matt inwardly scowled. How he wished he hadn't said anything to his mother about Tori's disappearing act at the weekend. She'd been incensed by Tori's behaviour and had immediately summoned both Lillian and Tori to the house to iron out the disobedience.

He hadn't mentioned *why* Tori had left, nor would he. Neither had he been worried that she would inform his parents what he and Jeremy had arranged. He knew as well as she did that she'd apologise and take the blame for her irrational behaviour – she always did and he hadn't been wrong.

For the record, he'd enjoyed himself at the lodge. The two women he'd booked had been on top form and Ginny had put on a cracking show too. Bedding Ginny had been a stark reminder of exactly what a short straw he'd drawn being landed with Tori.

Ginny was a little fire cracker between the sheets and Jeremy was a lucky bastard. It was a shame she didn't come with a hefty purse like Tori, otherwise he'd be insisting they swap, no doubt about that and if he had anything to do with it, he'd be having a repeat performance with the girl too.

After five minutes he'd even forgotten how much Tori had embarrassed him by disappearing. His friends were well aware how dull and boring she was – it wasn't anything new. They'd given her so many chances to have a laugh and to be part of things and all she ever did was throw it back in everyone's faces. It was *her* who always had the sour face, the insolent bitch.

His father suddenly began speaking again in a much lowered voice. 'Like your mother said, if Victoria can't be brought into line then we'll have no choice but to stop the marriage. We *won't* have this family's reputation brought down by the likes of her.'

Richard scowled. He'd had enough of it. He'd kept to his side of the bargain with Lillian, but if her damn daughter wasn't going to play ball and insist on continually embarrassing his family then he'd knock the arrangement on the head. Lillian had got what she wanted out of it and more than enough time had now passed to worry about whether she adhered to her silence.

Furthermore, out of the goodness of his heart when, as time had passed, Matthew had discovered a wife had been chosen for him he'd offered his son a financial incentive to honour the arrangement, but if he couldn't keep the woman on a short leash, then he didn't damn well deserve it.

He glared at his son. 'I should add it will be *you* who will bear the brunt, Matthew. If we're forced to pull this wedding because of your inability to control a woman, then your mother and I will lose all respect for you and react accordingly.'

Matt frowned. *Wait a minute. What was he saying?* 'But it's not m…'

'Matthew,' Richard interrupted. 'Your mother and I have spent a great deal of money, as well as time on this liaison with Lillian and Victoria.'

'Yes, but…'

'But?' Richard raised his hand to quiet his son. 'Don't think for one minute we'll allow the union to go ahead if all it means is that we are to be sullied by public disobedience.' He turned the gold pen slowly around in his fingers. 'I will retract the financial reimbursement for your part in this.'

'You'll do *what*?' Matt said, aghast. He'd always been promised a healthy payout if he married the woman and now that might not happen?

Richard smiled thinly. 'You very well heard what I said, therefore it's down to *you* to ensure it runs accordingly. And I should add it would also look unfavourably upon you assuming the manager position when the time arises.'

Matt stared at his father. *So, was he saying that if Tori didn't behave in the way they wanted in public or at home, then not only would he not get his pay-out, but that he might not take over as bank manager either?*

Richard studied his son's face, pleased to see his words had hit home. 'Nothing is assured if criteria cannot be met, Matthew. We all know how things work.' He smiled smarmily. 'And now it appears you're also losing incentive to bring in the type of investors the bank requires too.' He tutted theatrically. 'It's not looking too bright for you right now, is it?'

Matt retained a neutral expression. His father was making it very clear there was *no* room for error. His success relied on Tori's sorely needed change of attitude. That and him pulling this deal off.

He refused to let his father know how much the conversation was rattling him. *He'd been taught well and could also play at that game.*

Matt smiled widely. 'I think you're worrying about nothing and I'm not sure where you've got this information from. Like you heard when Tori apologised last night, her nerves snowballing over the wedding have been the culprit and getting on top of her. There's nothing more to it than that. Everything is fine between us and I'm confident she won't do anything like that or anything to let the family down again in the future.'

Oh, he had made very sure Tori wouldn't be doing that again and had got the message through loud and clear last night.

'I also need to put you straight over the investment opportunity. There isn't anything to worry about over that either. It's on track,' Matt said confidently. 'It's far from a lack of motivation on my side causing a hold up. It's the owner's reluctance - some sentimental attachment to the property from what I can gather.' *Utter bollocks, but that would do for now.*

'Matthew, you know th…'

'I know what you're going to say and I'm already on it. Steps have been put in place to ensure the owner has a change of heart. I want this to become a massive project regarding investment potential as much as you do and I *promise* I'll achieve that.'

'So, the buyer's changed his mind about selling?' Richard asked. *He'd got a lot resting on this.*

Matt acted nonchalant when really he was inwardly panicking and curling up inside like a dead leaf. 'Not quite, but both Jeremy and I have been working on this around the clock and aim to get a change of heart in place very, *very* soon.'

They didn't have a plan at all. Short of convincing Noel to like them by continuing to buy his drugs so they could get some inside info on Hunter was about as far as they'd got. They'd been far too busy snorting and shagging at the weekend to spend much time discussing shop and yesterday had been taken up dealing with that stupid bitch of a fiancée.

Richard sighed. 'I hope so, Matthew - for your sake.' *And for his, too. There was no way he would pull out of retiring to stay on as Manager, but it wouldn't hurt Matthew to think that. Neither could he face the humiliation of being forced to cancel his son's wedding if he could help it.*

He made a big show of slowly scrutinising his son. 'But maybe you might want to consider doing something which I think may solve at least *half* of the problem.'

Matt frowned as his father opened a drawer in the large desk. 'And what's that?'

'It won't speed up the investors, but it might help Victoria have a change of attitude.' Richard held up a packet of tablets.

Matt stared at the familiar looking box. He'd seen one identical to that many times before. 'What's that for? Tori doesn't need those. She already takes the Pill.'

Richard nodded. 'I thought so and I hope you don't mind, but I took the liberty of getting these from a friend of mine who can source certain 'things'.' He turned the packet around in his fingers. Matthew clearly wasn't grasping the inference he was making, judging by the confusion on his face. He'd have to spell it out. 'You might want to consider getting a child in place as soon as possible…'

'A child?' Matt spluttered. 'You're suggesting I get Tori pregnant? Forgive me if I'm being dumb here, but the Pill stops pregnancy doesn't it? Besides, there's no way she'd agree to trying for a child – not before we're married. She's far t…'

Richard smiled. 'I'm not suggesting you *tell* her and these aren't *usual* contraceptive pills. Listen, women tend to have a complete change of character when they're expecting and sometimes life dictates that certain aspects require controlling. It's guaranteed she'll calm down and won't do the types of things she's been doing of late. She'll lose that need the second her body starts making baby hormones.'

He passed the packet of tablets across the desk. 'These look the part don't they, but all they contain is sugar. Just swap the packets over.'

Matt took the packet and stared at it. *Sheer brilliance.* 'I'm telling you now that she won't be happy and neither will Lillian. God, I can already imagine her face.'

Richard grinned. 'It's only five months before your wedding. Even if Victoria falls straight away it would be doubtful she'd be showing too much by the time you marry. The change in her will be just what we need. She'll be as meek as a mouse!'

Matt was astounded. He hadn't thought for a moment that his father would suggest something such as this. *There was a lot he didn't know about the man.*

Richard could guess Matthew's mind was wondering about a specific question. 'And no, I didn't use these on your mother. I didn't have to. She knew what was good for her and never caused problems – unlike *your* wife-to-be.' He smiled widely. 'I'll get you a few more months supply. You don't want her taking the real ones any time soon. By the way, don't mention anything to your mother about this. She wouldn't understand.'

Matt nodded. As if he'd discuss something like this with his mother! He shoved the packet in his pocket and glanced over when his father's phone began ringing.

Richard picked up the receiver. 'Yes, that's fine. Send them up straight away.'

Matt got to his feet. He knew when he'd been dismissed. *Fuck.* He'd thought the only conditions on him getting his pay-out and guaranteed position was marrying the dumb bitch like his parents wanted. He hadn't bargained on them changing the fucking goal posts.

He'd better have hammered the message home loud and clear to the selfish bitch last night. In the interim he'd get these pills in place and then find Jeremy. They needed to come up with a plan and quick. Still, if his father was right and getting Tori pregnant was the answer to curbing her problematic attitude and make her realise she belonged to him and had to toe *his* line, then that was good as far as he was concerned. He'd been planning on insisting on babies the minute they'd married, so it made no difference to him if it was brought forward. The quicker she was stuck at home whilst he went out and took his fun with *proper* women, the better.

• • • •

MATT KNEW NOEL hadn't been happy that he'd phoned, but how was he to know he'd got grief about bringing them to the Factory at the weekend to pick up that order? He'd given him that bloody phone number, for Christ's sake, so why give it him if he hadn't wanted him to use it?

From now on hc was only to get in contact via the White Hart, which was where they'd agreed to meet.

Matt sat down impatiently at one of the tables, aware everyone's eyes were on him. *Well, they would be wouldn't they, the tramps. His shoes alone probably cost more than their fucking houses!*

'How's Tori?'

Matt looked up to find the barmaid standing over him. *Fuck. He'd forgotten this dozy cow worked with Tori.* 'Oh, erm, she's a bit better.'

Sarah didn't look convinced and eyed him suspiciously.

'When will she be back at work?'

Matt shrugged his shoulders and smiled widely. His winning smile normally went down well with the ladies, but it appeared it had no effect on this sullen tramp. 'I'm not sure. Depends how she feels. Nasty stomach bug.'

That's what he'd instructed Tori to say when she'd phoned in sick, so she'd better have done what he'd said. Make up would hide the bruising in a couple of days, but in the meantime she needed to keep her head down and lie low if she knew what was good for her.

After receiving a most unpleasant glare from Sarah, Matt watched her retrace her steps back to the bar. *Christ. She really shouldn't do anything to make her face any less attractive that it already was, the ugly bitch.*

He tipped the remains of his bottled lager into his mouth, damned if he would drink out the pint glasses in this dump! Now he was glad to have bought two in one go. He'd bought one for Noel but being as the freak had still not shown up, he'd just drink his.

He glanced at his watch hoping the man would get a move on. He needed to get things sorted toute suit and prayed he hadn't weighed up Noel's character and what he thought he'd be up for wrongly. Admittedly he'd have preferred spending a couple of months working on the man, but after what his father had dropped on him earlier he didn't have a lot of choice but to attempt this gamble.

Receiving an extremely heavy slap on the back, Matt almost lost his front teeth on the bottle of lager he'd raised back to his mouth.

'You alright, mate?' Noel said loudly.

Matt forced a smile and glanced around to see if any of the other meatheads were with him. He'd said he'd needed to talk 'privately', but this one wasn't exactly a *Mastermind* contestant so it wouldn't have surprised him if he'd got the whole lot of the Reapers in tow, but thankfully he was on his own.

'Can we go somewhere a bit more private?' Matt hissed,

glancing at a group of long-haired men wearing suspicious expressions on the next table who had a rather unhealthy interest in his presence.

Noel nodded. 'Sit up by the dart board. I'll fetch a drink and then I'll be up.'

. . . .

SARAH NUDGED COLIN and nodded discreetly in Matt and Noel's direction.

Colin's eyes followed Sarah's and he frowned. 'What am I supposed to be looking at?'

Sarah placed a fresh pint on the beer towel in front of her and waited until the punter had taken it and shuffled back to his table before resuming her conversation. 'Why is Tori's fiancé in here with Noel?' she hissed.

'How the hell should I know?' Colin fingered the stitches above his eye which was still sore. 'It's not our business is it?'

Sarah pursed her lips together. 'That bloke's up to no good.'

'Hardly any surprise there!' Colin laughed. 'Everyone knows Noel's a headcase. If it wasn't for his association with the rest of them he'd have been made unwelcome in here a long time ago.'

'I didn't mean *Noel*. I meant the other one. He's a pretentious bastard and something funny is going on with him and Tori.'

'What do you mean?'

'Oh, Col, don't you listen to a word I say? I told you earlier than Tori wasn't at work today. I just asked the boyfriend and he was cagey. Don't forget she stayed here the other night which probably didn't go down too well. What if he's done something to her?'

'Like what?' Colin asked. 'He's far too up his own arse to do anything unsavoury. Imagine what the neighbours would say!'

Sarah couldn't help but smile at her husband's sarcasm. 'He's not too up his own arse to buy gear off Noel though, is he?'

Colin smirked. 'Listen, if he wants to buy crap snort off that psycho and flog it on to the rest of his yuppie friends then let him get on with it.'

Sarah nodded. 'I appreciate that, but I'm just worried about Tori.'

Colin placed his calloused hand on Sarah's arm. 'Try not to get involved. As much as Tori's a sweet girl, it really isn't our business as to what goes on in their relationship.'

Sarah stared after Colin as he busied himself emptying a drip tray. How could she not be worried? She liked Tori. Liked her a lot. The girl didn't have anyone else looking out for her and wasn't made of the same stuff her sort were. Tori was sweet and fragile and there was a lot more going on underneath the surface than what met the eye. Tori had come to *her* when she'd needed help the other night which spoke volumes. Matt was a sneaky bastard and she didn't like or trust him one iota.

Tori needed someone looking out for her, but on the same vein if the woman refused to help herself, what was anyone supposed to do, apart from pick up the pieces or risk getting involved in a scenario which could put the cat amongst the pigeons and make things worse?

Maybe she should have a word with Hunter and see if he knew anything?

Sarah's eyebrows knitted together. If she didn't know better, she'd suspect something had been going on between Hunter and Tori the other night when they'd returned from the hospital because the atmosphere had been odd to say the least. Well, she might have if she hadn't known Hunter of old. His feelings towards the yuppies was legendary.

SEVENTEEN

TORI SAT AT HER desk in her bedroom. She said 'her' desk, but none of it was really hers. She stared at the antique wooden bureau with beautifully carved legs, filigree gold handles and a maroon inlay on the drop-down leaf. She hadn't chosen it – it had been chosen for her like everything else – from her furniture down to her underwear.

How she wished her father was still alive. When he was here she'd had a life – one full of fun and no pretention. All of that had changed overnight the day he'd been killed.

She traced the tip of her finger along the swollen mass of her face festooned with bruises and a cut lip, courtesy of her husband-to-be. Something *else* that had been chosen for her and there was nothing she could do about it.

She'd dreamt for years of walking away from all of this with the justification that her mother would eventually get over it. She herself wouldn't find it too difficult to recover from losing her reputation. What did she care about reputation anyway? She wasn't like the others and it wasn't as if anyone was remotely bothered – short of her mother, Matt and his family, that was.

She could have got a job somewhere else and started again.

It wouldn't have been too hard, but now it was. She was so bereft of confidence and strength these days she'd accepted this was how it was going to be. In just over five months' time she would swap from her mother's warped and delusional control for that of her husband's. Which now, judging by last night, included controlling her with his fists too.

Tori was tempted to glance in the large gilt-framed mirror above her dressing table but thought better of it. She didn't need to see her reflection again to be reminded of what Matt had done and had cried enough last night to suffice for a while.

It seemed that aside from her 'betrayal' of walking out of the lodge, he'd taken umbrage that she hadn't apologised convincingly enough for bringing embarrassment down on him and his family. Apparently, her sullen attitude and ill-fitting public behaviour towards him was causing problems. His father didn't feel she had the poise or correct attitude to accompany him to work functions. She didn't exhibit the correct finesse to be his son's wife and couldn't be, unless she pulled her socks up.

'I won't have you fuck my life up, Tori. I've got too much riding on this.' Matt had screamed when he'd barged into the house yesterday evening.

Tori's mother had been out with her drinks circle again, but she knew that even if she'd been present, all she would have done would have been to raise her eyebrow and make excuses to vacate the room. As far as her mother was concerned, she'd brought all of these 'glitches' upon herself by not toeing the line. She'd not been brought up to be anything other than *grateful* to her husband and needed to remember that.

Matt had dragged Tori upstairs to the privacy of her bedroom and continued to rant about how much she'd let him down. 'What I wouldn't give to swap you for Ginny. At least she knows how to move in the bed and doesn't like there like a corpse!' Matt had raged.

'Y-You slept with Ginny?' Tori had asked, shocked.

'Of course!' he'd spat. 'And the escorts. Even though you

tried your best to spoil the night for everyone, you failed because I had a *fantastic* time.'

'I didn't try to sp…'

'Unfortunately, Ginny doesn't have the same credentials as you do, otherwise you'd be out on your arse like a shot.' Matt had got right into Tori's face as she'd cowered on the bed. 'How long did it take to run home to mummy?'

'I-I didn't come back here. I thought it would raise too many questions, so I…'

'What? Where the hell did you go?'

Tori had been terrified but wasn't going to lie. She always endeavoured to be honest because the one big lie she'd been forced to live with half her life was all she could cope with. 'I went to the White Hart. I stopped there with Sarah.'

Matt had lunged forward, gripping her around the throat. 'You ridiculous little girl,' he'd screamed, his eyes wild. 'Have you any idea what that will look like if word gets back? What happens if people find out you've been slumming it with the local tramps?'

Tori had wanted to jump to Sarah and Colin's defence. They were as far removed from tramps as anyone. It wasn't *them* sleeping with prostitutes and each other's partners was it?

Instead she'd apologised like always, but this time it hadn't worked because Matt had laid into her with his fists. She'd curled up in both shock and pain and didn't attempt to defend herself. *Maybe she'd deserved it? Everyone had always said she caused her own problems, so this had clearly been no different.*

'You will not humiliate me!' Matt had roared. 'Sort yourself out, otherwise I swear to God I'll rip you to pieces. I'll tell the world what *really* happened to your father and expose you and your mother for the fucking liars you are!'

Tori had remained silent. She'd heard the same thing so many times, but this time he was more wound up than usual. He'd never raised his fists before, but now he'd expanded his arsenal of weapons.

After Matt had exhausted his volley of punches he'd sat on the bed. Dragging her upright, he'd stroked her already swelling face. 'I shouldn't have had to do that for you to learn, should I?' he'd said, anger still raw in his voice.

Tori had shaken her head, knowing remaining silent would have only caused more problems.

'You'll make a *proper* effort now, won't you? We won't have a repeat of this. Make me believe I'm not doing the wrong thing by marrying you. I don't want to have to ruin you or your mother's life, Tori. I just want you to deliver your end of the deal, ok?'

'Ok,' she'd muttered, her voice small.

Matt had stood up. 'I'm going now. By the way, you can't go to work for the next couple of days looking like that.' He'd looked her up and down contemptuously. 'Get yourself cleaned up and tell your stupid job you're ill. You won't need to do that rubbish for much longer anyway.'

Matt had walked from Tori's bedroom leaving her a little deader than she'd been half an hour previously.

Tori stared at the desk in front of her once more and wished more than *anything* that she could go to Sarah's. That woman believed she shouldn't put up with the way Matt behaved, but she'd be even less impressed if she knew what he'd done last night. She couldn't say anything. Not now.

Even her mother had been unsurprised. Lillian hadn't batted an eyelid when she'd ventured downstairs this morning, sporting and all but swollen shut black eye, a bruised cheekbone and a cut lip. She'd just eyed her derisively and sighed.

'Will you *now* take on board that you're expected to toe the line?' she'd muttered. 'You've been playing silly devils. If you think this is bad, you don't want to know what will happen to you if you ruin everything I've worked for. I mean it, Victoria. Sort yourself out and play the game.'

Tori stared blankly in front of her, still resolutely avoiding glancing at her reflection. Thoughts of Ash Hunter flooded over her once more and her heart skipped a beat. That was confusing her more than anything else. She'd seen with her own eyes just how brutal and animal-like he was and therefore couldn't explain or justify why being in his presence made her feel the way it did.

Her body began to burn again with unfamiliar longing. How could someone she despised have this unwarranted and unwanted effect? How could a man like *that* make her feel things she hadn't *ever* felt with anyone else? But *he* did. *Ash Hunter made her throb with desire she hadn't realised she possessed.*

She picked up the shoebox she'd retrieved from the attic at the weekend. She'd been hoping it would answer the questions which had always been withheld.

Sighing, she placed it back in the bottom drawer. She couldn't face opening it. What was the point? Nothing it contained could help what her life had become and it might even contain things to make everything *worse*?

What if everything was true and her father had indeed been one of those awful people like Noel and Hunter? *Had she ever thought of that?*

· · · ·

HUNTER SLURPED GREEDILY from his pint. He'd been looking forward to it for hours. It hadn't been the most productive of days. For a start, whilst Noel and Grin had been collecting this weeks' money from the businesses they looked after, he'd been taking delivery of another batch of coke. He'd also been side-tracking Georgie.

He knew he'd been sending out the wrong impression lately, but he hadn't known what else to do to get his bloody mind off Tori. He absentmindedly pulled a cigarette from his packet and sparked it up.

'That one not good enough?' Grin nodded towards the burning cigarette already resting in the ashtray.

Scowling, Hunter picked up the cigarette he'd previously lit. His mind being elsewhere wasn't doing him any favours. He knew damn well he'd been close to kissing that woman the other night and he should have known better. The last thing he wanted to do was start something with a yuppie princess! It was so wrong it was positively *sickening* and went against everything he'd stood for all his life. *That branch of society had ripped his fucking life to shreds.*

Shagging a woman was one thing, but Tori was undoubtedly the proverbial example of the Ice Queen, utterly entrenched in her expensive school of etiquette and upper-class snobbery. Carnal delights were not in her repertoire. Besides, he'd be a laughing stock. He glanced around the table at the men accompanying him.

The trouble was, despite everything, his need for her had become all-consuming. There was something different about her. Something which made her stand apart, but he couldn't put his finger on it. He couldn't explain *any* of it because it made no logical sense. The concept of even acknowledging that he wanted her was a bitter pill to swallow and he felt like the world's worst hypocrite.

Even if Tori was the type who'd be up for a good night of fucking, how would he live with himself for selling out? He couldn't, so that had to be the end of it, but he wished to hell she'd get out of his brain in the interim.

Would he ever see her again? Would she come in here with her boyfriend – that jumped up arrogant bastard, meaning he'd be caught off guard?

Hunter could hardly avoid the White Hart. His lips set resolutely in a firm, straight line. In the event Tori returned for whatever reason, he'd have to ensure he remained as cool as ice – like *she* was.

Noel eyed Hunter warily. The man had things on his mind, that much was obvious. He wondered whether Hunter could read his thoughts and had somehow gleaned what Matt had broached him about, or what he was, at this present moment in time actually *considering*, before realising how absurd and paranoid that was.

No, Hunter had something else on his mind. Something in addition to the investors sniffing around, the protection contracts and the drug sales and Noel suspected he knew what it was. A slight smile formed across his face. He'd seen how Hunter had looked at that stuck up bitch the night she'd puked everywhere and he'd also sensed the atmosphere in the White Hart when they'd returned from the hospital the other night. *He had a thing for the woman.*

Noel studied Hunter's rugged face, his gaze fixed on the room around them. He knew he was looking at nothing but inside his own head. The man had always been a thinker, whereas *he* was a *doer*.

Noel admitted he enjoyed getting stuck in and had no need or want for thinking at the best of times. It was an overrated activity and one he tried to avoid. However, on this occasion he would have to utilise his old grey matter because what Matt had said had made him pause for thought. His initial reaction when listening to the tosspot's words had been outrage, but after forcing himself to hear the twat out, he realised there *was* potential in what the man was saying.

It wouldn't have been the first thing that came to mind to try, but everyone knew the rich were well enamoured with underhand practices, so it would be second nature for someone like Matt to come up with such a work-around.

Besides, surely there was only so long he had to keep up the pretence of being grateful to Hunter? He'd always done everything which had been asked of him without question and allowed Hunter to call the shots – after all it was easier. He'd been happy remaining an enforcer - it was his strong point after all, but things had changed and he was fed up with toeing someone else's line.

As the years had passed his resentment had escalated – especially under the circumstances of which he'd had to hide his knowledge. The sort of money on the table which Matt was offering wouldn't go amiss and it wasn't like he was making something happen that wouldn't happen eventually anyway.

Noel chucked the rest of his pint into his mouth and rose from the chair. *He'd made his mind up.* 'Another round?' he asked.

Receiving nods, he walked to the bar for refills. He'd let Matt sweat another day before letting him know his decision.

EIGHTEEN

'I'M THOROUGHLY ASHAMED of your recent behaviour.' Lillian sat daintily poised in the armchair, her heavily made up eyes scrutinising her daughter. 'I couldn't quite believe it when Susan informed me your attitude has become so untenable that if there isn't an immediate turn around they'll stop the wedding.'

Tori no longer had the energy nor the urge to roll her eyes. Speaking out caused so many issues. It would have probably been more palatable – on the outside at least, to have agreed with Matt's demands at the lodge. All standing her ground had achieved was to chip just that little bit more of her away.

She was inwardly seething that she was now starting to lose the ability of formulating an opinion, let alone *acting* on it. She was turning into an automaton and might as well be dead.

'How humiliating do you think it was for *me* to be told in no uncertain terms that unless you deliver what is expected I'll be pushed back to where your father placed me?' Lillian flailed her hands around in the air theatrically. 'Your father ruined my life, Victoria. I won't have him ruin it for the *second* time!'

It's all about you, isn't it, Tori thought, a glimmer of defiance silently raising its head once again.

'Do you really think he would be proud of the way you're acting?' Lillian griped. 'You must *not* let the Stevens down anymore. You won't get an offer as good as what you're getting from Matt. You'll be lucky if you end up with anyone! At this rate the best you can hope for is someone whose job it is to sweep the floor and you really think I'd willingly stand here and allow th…'

'What *really* happened to my father?' Tori said, her eyes fixated on the dusky pink heavy velvet drapes surrounding the bay window.

Cut off mid-sentence, Lillian froze from the unexpected question. 'What on earth are you talking about?'

Tori could immediately see by her mother's stance that the question was unsettling her, even though she was trying to hide it. 'I know what you *told* me, but I don't believe it.'

'What do you mean, you don't believe it?' Lillian screeched having regained her mojo. 'Are you calling me a liar, you insolent, ungrateful, selfish little…'

'I'm not calling you anything,' Tori muttered. 'I just think you haven't told me the complete story.'

Lillian's over-plucked eyebrows rose almost comically half way up her forehead. 'Like what? What is it that you think I haven't told you? Like I've already said, your father was an underhand liar and a criminal, but you won't accept the truth. Fact facts, Victoria!'

Rage bubbled in the pit of Tori's stomach. 'He wasn't *any* of those things!'

'Exactly how do you know? Because he played games with you and took you out? You were a child when he was killed, Victoria. A *child*. Children aren't told everything for obvious reasons. Grow up, you silly girl!'

'But it doesn't make sense…'

'You just don't *want* to believe your father was a bad person. He was involved in things he shouldn't have been and paid the price. Rightfully so!'

Tori stood up in anger. 'Are you saying he deserved to be

murdered?'

Lillian smiled, her thin fuchsia lips twisting into a sneer. 'You have *no* idea what he was involved in, Victoria. Your father was a loser, just like *you*. He made me believe he had something to offer and then condemned me to hell. I'd already been cut off from everyone and everything that mattered and then he made things even worse!'

'What was he involved in that was so bad?' Tori asked.

'I've already told you and I won't discuss it any further,' Lillian snapped, fixing Tori with a stare. 'All I will say is that I had *no* idea of the double life he was leading and I don't want to think about it ever again, so please leave it.'

Tori resumed staring at the curtains. *Her mother had to be lying.* She had the right to know all the details, even if she didn't like what they were. She would find out one day, but it was clear her mother hadn't the decency to tell her. 'At least explain how this 'deal' came about for me to marry Matt?'

Lillian sighed dramatically. 'Like I've told you *countless* times, the Stevens helped us get back some credibility. I'd been ostracised thanks to your father, remember? And after he was killed, well…'

What a hideous travesty being ostracised from those all-so-important circles, Tori thought spikily. She'd have preferred to stay where they'd been without any of this. 'But why? What was in it for them? Why would they do that for you?'

'Because Richard fucking *owed* me, that's why!' Lillian screeched, her face puce red.

Tori stared at her mother in shock. In all her twenty years she'd only heard her mother utter *that* word once before - on the day her father had been killed. 'What do you mean 'owed you'?'

Quickly composing herself, Lillian straightened down her tailored lilac skirt. *Stupid, stupid. She shouldn't have allowed the girl to rile her this much.* 'I don't know why I said that.' She forced a smile. 'I'm being silly. I've always blamed Richard. He was the one who set me up on a date with your father in the first place and it all went wrong from there.' *You're saying too much. You promised Richard that would never be spoken of. Stop it NOW!*

Tori frowned. 'So, Richard and my dad were friends.'

Lillian laughed. 'Friends? No, I wouldn't say that. They just knew each other from where they studied, that's all.'

Tori looked at her mother thoughtfully. There was definitely more to this. There was so much she didn't know, but it was clear her mother's account would always be vague and she doubted if any of what she'd heard today was true either.

Lillian scowled. She knew she'd said things Victoria would think about. She could tell by her expression. *Damn. But she hadn't gone into anything in detail. It was ok.* 'Think what you like. Richard and Susan have always been lovely people. They tried to help.'

Tori raised her eyebrows. If they were lovely people then they wouldn't be putting conditions on that friendship by making her marry their son.

Lillian studied Tori's whirring mind. She had to ensure her daughter did not discover it had been *her* who had been paid off. Jack's life insurance had been predictably paltry and they wouldn't have had this house or any of the luxuries they'd enjoyed if she hadn't had the foresight to make Richard pay what was due.

Any why shouldn't she have insisted Victoria was properly looked after by promising their son as her husband? She'd never admit that she hadn't really cared about what happened to her daughter. It was just an easy way back into the correct circles if their families were tied.

She'd never wanted the blasted child anyhow. When she'd fallen pregnant she knew there was no way her family would ever accept her back - especially with a child fathered by the working class, but once Jack was out of the picture at least she no longer had to keep up the charade of playing 'mother' like she'd had to do in front of him.

It was Victoria's fault she'd been trapped further into the

mess and would always have that association because of her. Now, *yet again* her daughter was the crux with the ability to drag her life into the toilet for the *second* time. Lillian shook her head in irritation. Jack's blood was most definitely running through the veins of his child.

When all was said and done, even Richard had his limits. He'd made it clear the other night when she'd been summoned for a 'meeting' that she'd already received *more* than her dues and if Victoria didn't act the part he'd stop the marriage. She'd been *certain* Richard wouldn't have dared to do that. After all, she could still tell everyone about his association with Jack… And was Susan even aware of the whole story? *She doubted it.*

Lillian sniffed in contempt. This presumption had backfired in her face when Richard had pointed out that too much time had passed for her threats to make a blind bit of difference. He'd almost taken *pleasure* in saying that after he'd ensured *her* dirty laundry had been thoroughly aired, then whose words did she think people were more likely to believe?

As much as she hadn't wanted to accept it, Richard had been *right*. Everyone would believe him over her and she knew it.

Well, she wasn't having it. Victoria needed to understand what was at stake here, but in a way that was palatable and of course without discovering the truth. *She had to turn this around.*

'Victoria, it will be *you* who sullies your father's memory if you carry on like this. Whatever you think of me, it will be *his* name plastered around town by his misdeeds,' Lillian said, enjoying the hurt visible on her daughter's face. 'For years everybody has believed your father died in a car accident on the way to work. They believe he was a well-respected and upstanding man. If you want to ruin your liaison with Matthew and give his family no choice but to cancel the betrothal, then go ahead! It will be on your back when everyone finds out what sort of person your father was and what *really* happened to him.'

Tori had heard enough. Hastily getting up from the chair she left the room and rushed upstairs to her bedroom, knowing it was seconds before the tears came.

She had no choice. She'd have to marry Matt and acquiesce to his demands. If she didn't, her beloved father's name and reputation would be ruined beyond measure and she could not allow that to happen.

• • • •

'AND YOU'RE ALRIGHT about all of this?' Jeremy asked.

Matt glanced away from the girl he'd got his eye on at a table opposite. At least he had some decent eye candy in the wine bars, rather than the motley collection of skanky women frequenting the pubs they'd been forced to visit in the line of duty.

For once he was staying at his apartment tonight. Things were – to put it mildly, rather strained at his parents since the meeting with his father. He'd unwisely thought his mother would be more relaxed about the whole thing, but he'd been wrong.

It was best all round if there was a bit of breathing space between them until he could show beyond reasonable doubt that Tori had seen the light – which she undoubtedly would do if she had any sense and also until he'd turned this investment thing around – which now he reckoned was achievable. Matt grinned inwardly. He also hadn't wasted any time getting those duplicate pills into Tori's possession and the sooner they had the desired effect, the better.

His eyes returned to the girl opposite. There was nothing to stop him having some company in his own place in the interim either, was there?

'About Tori?' Jeremy pushed after Matt had failed to answer his question.

'What about her?' Matt snapped. *He was sick of hearing her bloody name.*

Jeremy leant closer, his voice lowered. 'About using her as

bait like you suggested. Are you sure you're ok about that?'

Matt sat back in amazement. 'Why wouldn't I be? It's not like I give a shit. Marrying her or not, I couldn't give a rat's arse. If Noel thinks Hunter has an interest in her, then I want to capitalise on it.'

'I agree, but will Tori go for it?' Jeremy was doubtful Tori would be happy about being used as a sexual decoy to turn Hunter's head for their benefit. She was hardly the most outgoing person and she most definitely wasn't what he'd describe as 'liberal'.

Matt sneered contemptuously. 'I would say that from now on she'll be doing *everything* I ask of her.'

Jeremy was not convinced, but he had little choice but to leave Matt to organise it. 'What if they get wind of this? Or what if it doesn't work?'

Matt's eyes wandered back to the girl sitting on the opposite table and finally catching her eye, smiled. 'Noel's in on it, so he's hardly likely to say anything. The only other people are me and you and *we're* not going to drop ourselves in it are we?' *Christ, Jeremy did ask some stupid questions!*

'What if Tori blows the whistle?'

Matt shook his head. 'She won't! She knows what would happen if she did.' He frowned. 'This not working isn't an option, Jeremy. The investment project is too important and if we don't get this back on track quick smart, then I'm fucked and by proxy – so are you!'

NINETEEN

SARAH SAT AT her desk while Tori hung her coat on the stand. She'd been fearing her friend wouldn't be returning to work because since that phone call to the office at the start of the week she hadn't heard a thing. A full week later, she was glad to see that she'd returned. *She must have been really ill!*

Hastily getting up from her typing chair, Sarah rushed over. 'Tori! I'm so glad to see you! I was beginni…' She stopped, clocking the faded bruises and remnants of a bust lip. 'Jesus! What the hell's happened?'

Tori faltered, unsure of how to respond. Combined with the make-up she'd slapped on, she'd thought the mess Matt had made of her face had healed enough to be concealed, but obviously not. She shouldn't have been that surprised. Sarah was astute and not much got past her.

'Tori?'

'I-It's nothing, I…' Tori wanted to run away. She didn't want to have to explain what her husband-to-be had done or that her mother had found it both acceptable and deserved.

'Nothing, my arse!' Sarah exclaimed, grabbing Tori's arm. 'You're coming with me and you're going to damn well tell me what's been going on!'

Realising resistance was futile, Tori allowed Sarah to drag her into the coffee break room. 'I'm supposed to be working! I've been off all week and I'll get sacked for hiding in here. I've only just arrived.'

Sarah shrugged off Tori's concerns. 'Don't worry about the boss. He's at a meeting.'

Sarah pulled out a plastic chair from around the table and shoved Tori down onto it. Sitting opposite, she checked no one else was in the room. 'This was *him*, wasn't it?'

Tori studied her hands. She couldn't look at Sarah. What could she possibly say? She didn't want to lie.

'Tori, *talk* to me. Was this him? That bastard you're stupid enough to want to marry?'

Tori realised she had no choice but to level with her friend – at least on some respect. Sarah wasn't the type to let it go. She nodded slightly, her gaze still fixated on her hands.

'The utter wanker!' Sarah spat angrily. 'Christ, I only saw him on Monday and asked him if you were ok. The fucking liar said you had a stomach bug!'

'I could hardly come to work until I looked better...' Tori mumbled.

Sarah was fuming. *Absolutely fuming.* She knew that smug bastard had been hiding something, but she hadn't expected him to pull a stunt like this. 'I presume you've now finally left him?'

Tori looked up. 'I-I can't...'

Sarah was flabbergasted. 'And why the hell not? For God's sake, it's bad enough that he speaks to you like a piece of shit, but *this*? You've *got* to ditch him. It's not acceptable!'

Tori knew none of it was acceptable, but what was she supposed to do? Sarah didn't know what was involved, but even if she did, she wouldn't think it a plausible reason. 'It's complicated.'

Sarah scowled. 'No, it's fucking not! You say, *'I'm leaving you Matt, you're a fucking jerk'*, and then you walk out of the door. And just in case you're confused, that means you *don't* go ahead and marry the guy!'

'Y-You don't understand, Sarah. I ca…'

'You're damned right I don't understand! Jesus, I want to kill him myself!'

Tori felt warmed by Sarah's words. It showed she really cared which was a nice feeling, but unfortunately that wouldn't change the outcome.

Sarah pursed her lips. 'You think this will get better if you marry him?'

Tori wasn't stupid. She knew nothing would change the way Matt was. She wasn't one of those people who thought that she could change someone if she stuck with them. Oh no, she knew why she was in this position, but again couldn't explain that – not without everything coming out in the wash.

Sarah stared at Tori. She looked even more of a hollow shell than usual. She *had* to get through to her. 'It's only going to get worse! I mean, when I saw Matt on Monday, he was scheming something with Noel. Now what does *that* say to you?'

'I thought you liked that lot?' Tori said, trying not to question as to exactly *why* Matt had been in the White Hart with Noel.

'I *do* like them, well, most of them. Grin is ok and Hunter's a decent man, but *Noel*… he's a nutter. I'd go so far as to say he borders on psychopathic. I only put up with him because I've got the utmost respect for Hunter.'

Tori's stomach flipped again from the mention of Hunter's name, but still couldn't work out how Sarah could think *any* of that lot were decent knowing what they did.

Sarah studied Tori's face. 'I know your take on 'their sort', but believe you me, love, whether you agree or not, Hunter and Grin are good men. I have known them for years and if they knew that Matt ha…'

'You mustn't say anything!' Tori cried. If Sarah let it be known Matt had used his fists on her it would cause no end of problems. '*Promise* me?'

Sarah nodded sadly and sighed. 'If that's what you want, but Matt deserves the kicking of a lifetime. You need to leave him, you really do.'

'I just can't,' Tori replied quietly. 'Believe me when I say I don't want to be with him and I *certainly* don't want to marry him. I never have – even before this.'

'Then why are you?' Sarah cried. *This was exasperating!*

'It's too difficult to explain. I probably couldn't even if I wanted to.'

'What the fuck has he got on you?' Sarah spat. *There had to be more to it.*

'Nothing!' Tori said rather too hastily.

Sarah pursed her lips and frowned, her mind running overtime. 'I have to ask - did something happen between you and Hunter that night at the White Hart?'

'W-What?' Tori felt heat flood her system. 'Of course not!' *But she'd wanted it to, hadn't she? Oh yes, she'd wanted it to.*

Sarah shook her head. 'There was an atmosphere. The way you were looking at each other.'

Tori resumed looking down at her hands. 'Nothing happened, like I said.'

'Ok. I just thought it might have and Matt had somehow found out, hence this...' She waved her hand towards Tori's bruised face.

Shaking her head, Tori smiled sadly. 'It was to do with work actually. Apparently I screwed up a big deal for him by not acting the right way. He's been under a lot of pressure lately.' She knew it sounded like she was attempting to justify why Matt had hit her, but she wasn't. It was the closest she could get to giving Sarah the truth without explaining everything else.

'As much as I have utmost respect for Hunter and would trust him with my life, you don't want to get involved with him however tempting it may be.' Sarah's eyes twinkled. 'Don't get me wrong, I fully understand the attraction. After all, he's extremely easy on the eye and I wouldn't mind a bit with him myself if I didn't have my Colin.'

'Sarah!' Tori exclaimed, managing a smile.

Sarah's face turned serious. 'I mean it. You're not the sort who could be happy with what he would offer you. He's one of those tortured souls. He's damaged and would hurt you in ways that no one else could – even Matt.'

'I can assure you there's *nothing* going on between me and that man and there never will be,' Tori stated, whilst silently wondering what Sarah had meant by her description of Hunter.

Sarah nodded. *It looked unlikely that she'd get more out of this woman.* 'Let's get back to work, but we're discussing what you're going to do about that tosspot of a fiancé of yours later on.'

• • • •

HUNTER DISMOUNTED HIS bike and removing his crash helmet, shook his shaggy hair so that it fell around his shoulders. Sparking up a cigarette he looked up at the White Hart rising before him.

Pulling open the heavy door, he walked confidently into the tap room, nodding in response to the myriad greetings from the regulars. There was a steady number already in there, despite the pub having only opened its door for the morning ten minutes ago.

He walked up to the bar and smiled. 'Morning, Colin.'

Colin gave Hunter an easy smile. 'Morning, Hunter. How are you today?'

'Same old, same old. Pint please.' Hunter hadn't planned on stopping for a drink, but he always found the atmosphere comfortable and relaxing, so decided he might as well have a quick one whilst he was here.

Colin placed a freshly poured pint on the beer towel next to Hunter's crash helmet, then reached below the bar and retrieved an envelope. 'This month's cash is in there, mate.'

Taking the envelope, Hunter put it into an inside pocket of his leather jacket and smiled. 'Thanks. Feels a bit rude after we let you down last week.'

Colin waved his hand dismissively and winked. 'Just one

of those things. It's the first time you haven't been on hand, so don't worry about it. I will say though that Sarah's still cheesed off with you.'

Hunter smiled. That didn't surprise him. Sarah could hold a grudge for England. 'I can assure you it won't happen again.' And it wouldn't. That was the first and last time that any of his crew would antagonise him so much to make him fuck up and let someone down. He prided himself in delivering his promises and would not let that change.

Hunter quietly supped at his pint whilst Colin opened the days' post. He noticed the concentration as he studied a letter. 'Problems?'

'I don't know. It's a letter from the brewery. Our lease is up in two months. I knew it was due sometime around now.'

Hunter raised his eyebrows. 'You're not thinking of moving on, are you? It wouldn't be the same around here without you and Sarah.' On top of that, he doubted whether he'd be able to find another pub to use as a base that he enjoyed as much as he did in here.

Colin stared at the letter again. 'No, of course not. We love it here, you know that. As far as we're concerned, we were planning to renew our lease.'

Hunter frowned. 'So, what's the issue?'

'It seems the brewery have been approached by a company interested in buying the pub.'

'What sort of company?'

Colin shrugged and handed Hunter the letter. 'Some sort of investment firm is all it says.'

Hunter scanned the contents, his eyebrows knitting together. 'It doesn't mention a company name, but it does say someone will be arranging a meeting with you to view the premises.' *Could this possibly be the same place interested in buying the Factory?*

Colin took the letter Hunter handed back to him. 'Does this mean the brewery will sell?' he said, his voice holding a tinge of panic.

Hunter ran his hand across his beard. 'It sounds like they might be thinking about it, yes.'

'Oh shit! What will we do? Sarah will hit the roof!' Colin cried.

'I've recently had some twat digging around the Factory too. I told them I wasn't interested, but he kept turning up with a gimp from the bank.'

'It's different for you though because you *own* the place.' Colin grabbed a glass and poured himself a shot of whisky from the optic. 'I need a fucking drink. I'll have to put them off when they turn up. Get your lads to stage a bar fight or something!' He attempted a smile, but he was worried. *Very worried.*

Hunter could see Colin was concerned and although loathe to worry the man even more, he had to be honest. 'I'm not sure it would make much difference. If it's the same lot who want my place, they won't keep it as a pub.' His eyes narrowed. 'It would either be knocked down or turned into executive apartments.'

'Executive *whats*?'

'Apartments – flats.' Hunter scowled. 'Yeah, from what I've gathered their plan is to regenerate the area and buy up all the properties and turn it into a 'desirable' place - you know, like they've been doing in London docks?'

'You mean rip the soul out of the area and fill it with yuppies?' Colin said miserably.

'That's about the truth of it,' Hunter snapped irritated. If these people were now sniffing around other properties in the area as well as his then it looked like it might be as he'd feared. 'Listen, put the word out. Get in touch with as many other businesses and people around here as you can and see if they've been approached. I'll do the same. I thought it was just me, but it clearly isn't.'

He tipped the remains of his pint into his mouth and wiped the froth from his beard with the back of his hand. 'I'll come back in later and see what you've managed to find out.'

'I don't know how I'm going to break this to Sarah,' Colin

murmured as Hunter rose from the stool.

'One step at a time. I'll do everything in my power to ensure this area stays as we like it,' Hunter said. He would not be giving up his premises and his business without a damn fight. *This was his patch.* 'Make sure you let me know the minute you hear from the prick wanting a meeting or whatever it is he's contacting you about.'

Grabbing his crash helmet, Hunter stalked from the White Hart.

TWENTY

MATT GRIPPED TORI'S face and turned it towards him. His voice was soft, but the fierceness of his grip underlined his intentions to be anything but. 'Are you clear on what you need to do?'

Tori's immediate reaction, after flinching, was to rip Matt's hand away. His mere touch made her skin crawl, but she couldn't. She had to ensure she behaved *exactly* as she needed to: submissive and obedient. *Everything that he so desired.*

The fact that she wanted to yank his hand away from her face, followed by severing his entire arm and shoving it down his throat was irrelevant. A bit like she hadn't wanted to allow him take down her knickers when she'd walked in from work and let him take her roughly on her bed. She hadn't wanted any part of him *near* her, let alone *in* her. Again – something else she was used to having to get on with, whether she wanted it, liked it, enjoyed it, or not. And she could safely say it was *none* of them, but what was forefront was what Matt had said she needed to do.

When he'd said she was the key to ensure the investment plan gained back its momentum, she'd been shocked. Actually, that was an understatement. She'd thought he'd been joking until she'd realised that unfortunately, he wasn't.

'Being as you ballsed everything up in the first place, this is the *least* you could do, is it not?' Matt had said, talking as if what he was saying had been *normal*.

Well, it *wasn't* normal. *He wanted her to change Hunter's mind about selling his property.*

'How am I supposed to do that?' she'd asked, somewhat naively, realising her mouth was hanging open in utter amazement. She might have known it would involve something unsavoury.

'Close your mouth, Tori!' Matt had snapped. 'You look like you just stepped off the Sunshine Bus! I know it's a putrid thought – the prospect of having to be nice to one of *them*, but if it means we get what we need and you can redeem yourself in my parents' eyes, then I'll get my promotion and everyone's happy.'

Even though she knew what he'd said, she'd still struggled to take on board that she was hearing correctly. 'So, you want me to throw myself at someone to get you a work deal?' She'd refused to allow the hurt to show on her face.

Matt had sighed loudly. 'Oh, stop being so over-dramatic! It's hardly like I'm suggesting you become a hooker and walk up and down the road touting your wares in a mini-skirt and boob tube!'

Tori had known Matt was trying to act reasonable and pretend that how she felt mattered, but it was all an act and he'd been itching to punch her again for having the audacity to question his demands.

'But I wouldn't know how to go about it,' she'd blathered. *And Hunter? How could she throw herself at him?*

Matt had sniggered. 'I can vouch from my experience with you you're certainly not clued up on *that* subject, or anything really, but you're going to have to work it out.'

Tori had reddened. *Yes, she was inexperienced.* She hated sex and she hated Matt. Thanks to him, the tiny amount of confidence she'd once had was now non-existent. 'Hunter doesn't like me. He's made that clear!' *Surely Matt would realise this could never work.*

'I don't want you to fucking *marry* him! I don't even want you to sleep with him. All I w…'

'*Sleep* with him?' Tori had squeaked, the prospect had ignited that burning throbbing again, but it still remained a fact that the only man she'd slept with or had even *touched* was standing in front of her.

Matt had taken another measured deep breath, desperately trying to control his temper. 'Like I was trying to explain… I'm not saying you have to sleep with him. I just want you to get under his skin. Get into his *head*.'

'But…'

'You need to make him like you. To *trust* you or make him feel sorry enough for you to *want* to fuck you! Whatever! I don't care which way you do it, but time is of the essence and this needs to be done quickly. Like *yesterday*.' Matt had stroked Tori's hair in one of his ultra-false gestures. 'You need to make him to *listen* to your opinion.'

'Since when do I have an opinion?' she'd snapped, realising by the instant change in Matt's demeanour that she should have held her tongue.

Lurching towards her, he'd grabbed her around the throat and she'd begun trembling, angry with herself at her weak reaction.

'Stop pissing about! I *need* his property. Convince him it's a good idea to fucking sell it,' Matt had hissed. 'Achieve this in whichever way you want, but *no* shagging. You belong to me and I'm not having that sexually transmitted disease putting his cock in the woman who's marrying me!'

Realising he'd got his point across, Matt had dropped his grip. 'If it means it'll get the job tied up, signed and sealed, I'll allow you to kiss him and at a *maximum* stretch, give him a blow job, but that's the cut-off point. Do you understand?'

Tori had nodded dully, still not quite able to believe what was being asked of her. 'When you do want me to start this?'

she'd asked, her voice monotonous. *Dead.*

'Tonight!' Matt had barked. 'Get yourself ready and try for once to look attractive.'

Returning to the reality that she was sitting in Matt's car outside the White Hart, Tori knew she had not responded to anything he'd said.

'Are you on this fucking planet? I said, are you clear on what you need to do?' Matt's anger and impatience was growing.

Tori nodded. 'Yes,' she squeaked. She knew what she needed to do but had no clue as to how to achieve it. She was the *last* person who should have been picked for a stunt like this.

'What if he's not there?' she whispered, hardly daring to voice the question.

Matt sighed. 'Go and fucking find him, you thick cow! Do I have to explain the bleeding obvious?'

'Won't it be suspicious that I'm looking for him, or suddenly being over-friendly?'

'I doubt whether he's intelligent enough to notice, but if he does, then think of a suitable story to back up your actions. What you say is up to you. I really couldn't give a shit as long as I get what I want. I haven't worked all this time to get passed over for the job that's mine,' Matt raged.

It's only your job because Daddy is the boss. You haven't worked hard at all – you've let everyone else do that whilst taking the credit, Tori thought.

Leaning over, Matt coldly kissed her cheek and opened the passenger door. 'Off you go. I don't need to tell you to make your own way home, do I? I can hardly come and pick you up.'

Tori got out of the car even though her legs felt like they were glued to the footwell. 'What happens if something goes wrong?'

Matt narrowed his eyes. 'It better not, Tori. It had better fucking not.'

• • • •

SARAH WAS PLACING freshly washed glasses back in their rightful place below the bar when she sensed the atmosphere shift. Thanks to the area she was brought up in she was observant of anything which could signify problems or notable changes and it held her in good stead for running a boozer.

Quickly glancing up, straight away Sarah saw Tori standing just inside the doorway, nervously looking around. She pursed her lips. That twat of a fiancé hadn't been in. She'd not have missed the opportunity to give the slimy bastard a piece of her mind if he had. She'd promised Tori she wouldn't say anything to any of the Reaper crew, but she hadn't promised she wouldn't rip a piece off that wanker, Matt, the next time he had the bloody nerve to show his sneering face in her pub. She would very much enjoy telling the cowardly toenail what she thought of him.

Tori clearly hadn't noticed her. In fact, she hadn't even glanced over because she was too busy searching the room. Sarah sighed inwardly. Had she now been reduced to scouring bars looking for that good for nothing waste of space of hers?

Taking a deep breath, Sarah slipped from behind the bar. Placing her hand on Tori's shoulder, she was dismayed to see her friend jump out of her skin at her touch. 'Tori? What are you doing here?'

Tori's wide blue eyes blinked rapidly as she turned towards Sarah. 'I, er… I…'

Sarah gently steered Tori towards the bar, nodding to Colin to pour a drink. 'Who are you looking for? Matt, I presume?' She was unable to keep her venom from her voice. 'I'll save you the trouble, he hasn't been in.'

Tori smiled tightly. 'No, I wasn't looking for him. I wasn't looking for anyone. I'm allowed to come in here, aren't I? It's a public house, isn't it?'

Sarah squeezed her shoulder, completely unconvinced by Tori's fake bravado, knowing full well it was an act. 'Of course!' She plonked the drink Colin had poured in front of Tori and motioned towards a stool.

'Oh, erm, I'd better not. I'm supp…'

'Supposed to be *what*?' Sarah cocked her eyebrow. 'Like you said – this is a pub. I assume you came in for a drink being as you're not looking for anyone…' She eyed the still visible bruising around Tori's eye and cheekbone that another layer of foundation had not managed to completely cover. 'So, I'll ask again. Who are you looking for?'

Tori blanched. If her motives were so obvious, she didn't much fancy her chances in pulling the wool over Hunter's eyes. 'What do you mean?'

Sarah gritted her teeth. She wanted to help Tori, but if she wasn't prepared to level with her, then how could she? Against her will the first flickers of irritation formed. 'Unlike you, I've had no choice but to watch for signs of suspicious behaviour. It's a necessary trait around these parts, but being as you're not prepared to be honest, I'm not sure what you expect me to do?'

Reddening, Tori turned towards Sarah. 'Unlike me? What the hell do you know?' she snapped. 'Not a lot, that's what!'

Sarah raised her eyebrows. Tori hadn't risen to anything in the past, so that must have hit a nerve. Her irritation escalated further despite her wish to remain calm. 'And who's fault is that?' she cried. 'I'm trying to help you, yet you're not making it easy!'

Tori stood up. 'I've never asked to you have my back, Sarah. I also didn't say I was looking for anyone, but you presumed that because I'm on my own.' She had to cover her tracks. None of the Reapers were here so she would have to look elsewhere. A fission of dread formed in her stomach.

Sarah chuckled despite herself. 'Oh, have it your own way. You're such a bad liar, you really are!'

Tori grabbed her bag from the bar. 'I thought you were my friend!'

Sarah reached out to grab Tori's arm as she rose from the stool. 'I *am*, but…'

'But nothing!' Tori snapped. 'I should go.'

Sarah sadly watched Tori make her way across the tap room and out through the double doors. Her first instinct was to follow but realised it wouldn't help and just hoped that whatever the problem was, it wouldn't cause the girl any further issues.

TWENTY ONE

'ANYTHING I CAN get you, baby?' Georgie purred into Hunter's ear, wrapping her arms around his waist from behind.

'No thanks,' Hunter said in a friendly, but dismissive tone.

Georgie ignored the slight stiffening she felt through Hunter's body denoting the unease of her proximity and she dropped her hold. Her theory that he may have developed deeper feelings for her was incorrect if this display was anything to go by.

After his attentive and frequent recent summoning, she'd really begun to think she was finally getting somewhere with the man of her dreams, but now he'd resumed acting like she didn't exist. He blew hot and cold like a bust hairdryer. It was driving her crazy and she didn't know what she should do about it.

Taking another bottle from the bar, Georgie sashayed back to the group of easy chairs where some of the other bikers' women were sitting. Smiling widely, she plonked herself down and reached for a cigarette. It was important she didn't look miserable. The men didn't like that. They wanted their women to be sexy, happy and eager to please. She knew the score, but then she wasn't officially Hunter's woman. Even though it was an assumed role she'd happily slotted into as far as everyone else was concerned, she knew deep down whatever her and Hunter's relationship was, how she felt was *very* different from how he did.

Her eyes ran back to where Hunter stood with Noel, Grin and some of the others at the bar. They were deep in conversation. Something was going down, but she of course, like the rest of the women, had no idea what and wouldn't dream of asking. *Information was given, not requested.*

Georgie didn't know what else she could do to capture Hunter's heart. She picked at the leg of her skin-tight leather-look hot pants and took a swig from the beer. She looked good – everyone said that and was eternally grateful her long association with the white powder she loved so much had not had any detrimental effect on her looks – at least not yet.

Georgie frowned. Maybe that was it? Maybe Hunter didn't like the amount of gear she took? No, it couldn't be that. He'd always been more than generous with what he gave her and he wasn't averse to the stuff either. She was always on call when he needed her and always seemed to satisfy him between the sheets. Furthermore, he knew he'd got her heart, despite her promising herself that was the *one* thing which would never be up for grabs.

Finishing her beer, she pushed herself from of her seat and reached the bar just as the buzzer rang signalling someone was at the entrance to the Factory.

'See who that is, Georgie,' Noel barked. 'You know who not to open the door to.'

. . . .

TORI STOOD NERVOUSLY at the large doorway. Her heart was thundering and she felt self-conscious in the figure-hugging red dress that Matt had insisted she wore. She'd already almost broken her ankle walking up to the door and the rows of large motorbikes lined up to the left of her was doing nothing to quash the ever-mounting nausea.

The *last* place she wanted to be was here and the way her brief visit to the White Hart had ended was running through her mind and impeding her concentration about what she was supposed to be doing when she finally located Hunter. *That's if she did.*

The thought that perhaps she should hide somewhere and return to Matt at the end of the evening, telling him that she'd looked everywhere, but the Reapers were out of town, had crossed her mind more than once. She also knew that if she did that, Matt would undoubtedly check, discovering she hadn't been to any of the places she'd said, so she had little choice but to go through with it.

Tori stared at the imposing large metal door looming in front of her. It had been a good minute since she'd pressed the buzzer. *Maybe there wasn't anyone here?* But then why would their bikes be lined up outside if that was the case? How long should she give it before walking back to the waiting taxi?

Before she could answer her own question, she heard bolts sliding from the other side of the door and her heart lurched. The whole way over she'd been preparing herself for two things: one - what she would say as to the reason for her appearance and two - how she would deal with Hunter. She'd just about managed to think of something which explained her presence, but as for the second issue she still had no idea.

The large door opened to reveal the small girl from the party. 'Hi, I… erm… I wondered if…' *Sort it out, Tori. Sort it out, for God's sake.*

'Hey, aren't you that girl that came to my party the other week? Do you remember me? You rushed off to the bathroom,' Georgie said, recognising Tori straight away. 'I thought it was you when I looked through the spyhole.'

'Spyhole?'

'Just so we can check who's here.' Sensing Tori's confusion, Georgie flapped her hand dismissively. 'Don't worry about it. What do you need?'

'Erm… I…' Feeling a cold dread wash over her, Tori

realised she was still standing on the doorstep. This was the bit she was unprepared for. She needed to think and quickly. 'I, erm... It's a bit awkward actually...' she faltered. *Think, THINK.* 'I don't suppose my fiancé is here, is he?'

Georgie frowned. 'Fiancé?'

Tori smiled weakly. *Why should this woman remember anything about her? She needed to do better than this. It was all sounding really lame.* 'I thought he might have come here – you know, to pick up some, erm...' *There. She'd alluded to drugs. That was something that shouldn't be altogether surprising.*

Georgie gave Tori a knowing smile. 'Ah, I know who you mean - the posh guy. No offence, like!'

'None taken,' Tori smiled. 'Is he here?'

Georgie opened the door wider and beckoned Tori in. 'You'd better come inside, but he's not here. Not unless he's hiding!' She laughed loudly.

Tori stepped over the threshold noticing Georgie's eyes. *Nice enough girl, but high as a kite again.*

'I guess he may turn up. He'll have to hurry though if he wants some gear. We're off to a party shortly.'

Tori fidgeted awkwardly in the large square entrance area. 'I don't want to disturb you. I'd better go.' She could now tell Matt she'd tried, but they were on their way out and couldn't hang around. *Would he buy that?*

'Nonsense. Being as you're here, you may as well have a quick drink. Besides, Noel may know more about it if he'd arranged to meet your man.'

He's not my man. At least, I wish he wasn't, Tori thought sourly, becoming nervous when Georgie shot the bolts back home. Now she was trapped. The prospect of being locked in somewhere with that dreadful Noel wasn't doing anything to help her nerves. 'Is Hunter here?' she muttered.

Georgie swung around suspiciously. 'Why do you want to know that?'

'Oh, no reason. He's the only other one whose name I

know, apart from Noel.' *Stupid, stupid thing to say.*

Not looking entirely convinced, Georgie studied Tori. 'Yes, *everyone* knows Hunter,' she said. 'Which makes it difficult to get much time with him as I've discovered more and more lately.' She liked to make sure everyone knew Hunter was *hers.* Even if it wasn't official, she didn't see why she shouldn't publicly stake her claim on him. He never seemed to mind – well, if he did, he certainly hadn't said so.

Tori made her smile appear genuine. *So, this was Hunter's girlfriend?* She'd had no idea. How on earth was she supposed to get close to the man, or whatever Matt expected of her if this woman was on the scene? *This was getting complicated.* 'I just thought he might know if Matt's been or was expected,' Tori continued, hoping this somehow justified her question.

Georgie relaxed. *This girl wasn't a threat. She knew how Hunter felt about the yuppies.* 'Well you can ask. Both him and Noel are here, so one of them should know. Follow me.'

Georgie made to walk towards the large room, turning back to make sure Tori was following, but stopped as she walked into the light. She frowned. 'What have you done to your face?'

'My face?' Tori asked, unconsciously raising her fingers to touch the area around her eye. *Shit. Her makeup job obviously hadn't been as good as she'd thought.*

'Yeah, your face,' Georgie pointed. 'You've got a black eye.'

Tori dismissed Georgie's comment as breezily as she could. 'Oh, that's nothing. Stupidly I slipped at work last week, clumsy thing that I am!' *That sounded almost convincing. At this rate she'd be as deceitful and underhand as everyone else and that prospect did not warm her.*

'Sorry, I should have realised!' Georgie laughed. 'I don't expect you posh lot do domestic violence!'

Tori smiled, but inside she felt like curling up. If only this woman knew what this 'posh lot' were like. Taking a deep breath, she followed Georgie into the large room leading off from the entrance area.

• • • •

HUNTER GRITTED HIS teeth as Georgie wrapped her arms around his waist yet again. He'd already told her once that he was busy. He needed to hear all the info the others had gathered about who had been asking questions over properties in the area and put this together with the small bits he himself had eked out this afternoon. How could he do that if she kept draping herself around him like a limpet?

Ok, so they'd pretty much discussed all they needed to, but that wasn't the point. He'd told her once and didn't expect to have to repeat himself. 'Georgie!' he snapped, removing her hands non too gently from his belt. 'I've already said th...'

Pouting, Georgie released her grip and moved around to face him, nodding in Tori's direction. 'I know that, but there's someone here to see you or Noel.'

'If it isn't Miss Aristocrat!' Noel drawled, following Georgie's eyes. 'Come over here darlin' and get yourself a drink.'

Hunter's mouth went dry as he slowly turned around, knowing full well who Noel was referring to. His cock twitched as his eyes rested on Tori. The tight red dress she wore outlined her stunning figure perfectly. Luckily for him he'd mastered the art of the 'poker face' otherwise the powerful rush of lust would be visible for all to see plastered across his face.

'She's looking for her boyfriend, sorry, *fiancé*,' Georgie continued.

'And why exactly would he be here?' Hunter growled, his voice low and throaty.

Tori faltered before walking towards the group. She tried to look anywhere else but at the man whose presence had already caused a distinct dampness in her knickers and hoped she wasn't walking as self-consciously as she felt.

'H-He mentioned he needed to pick, erm, something up. We were supposed to be going to a party and, erm, well, we had a bit of an argument. I-I thought to see if he was here.' *That sounded plausible didn't it?*

'So Little Miss Aristocrat lost her fiancé?' Noel snided in a false upper-class voice. 'How dreadfully remiss of you!'

Tori ignored the sniggers from the group of women sitting in the armchairs behind and refused to let Noel know his words had achieved any effect.

'Did he give you that shiner too?' Noel laughed. 'I probably would have as well if I had to listen to you all fucking night.'

Tori sensed Hunter's stance stiffen and the hairs on the back of her neck tingled.

Fury ignited at the very core of Hunter's being with the thought of that jumped up pretentious prick raising his fist to this woman. He raised his hand and gently touched the bruised flesh around Tori's eye. 'Is that true? Did he do this to you?'

Tori blushed furiously as shockwaves ricocheted through her body. She really should have checked more to make sure the bruising was properly concealed in bright light. It had been stupid of her to be so careless. She could also sense Georgie bristling, clearly unhappy her boyfriend had concern over another woman. This was horribly awkward and she needed to rectify it. She shook her head. 'Like I told Georgie, I was clumsy at work. No more interesting than that, I'm afraid.'

Hunter turned back to the bar and picked up his pint. He needed something for his hand to do before he ran it over Tori's delectably bare shoulders and pulled down the zip which held her dress together. 'Noel, have you arranged for that man to pick up more gear?' He was unable to hide his irritation. Had Noel continued with what he'd asked him not to do? To bring those yuppy fuckers here so that he could peddle the shit coke?

'Not me. I haven't seen the prick. He certainly hasn't been here' Noel grinned. It was clear Matt had moved on the idea they'd discussed and he'd been right in saying Tori would go along with it. In all fairness whether he liked to admit it or not, the stuck-up cow was doing a fairly convincing job.

Tori looked at the floor, well aware that the 'prick' Noel was referring to was Matt. That's what they thought of them all around here was it? This was stupid and pointless. Matt had to see this plan of his was *never* going to work. 'I-I must have been mistaken,' she said quietly. 'I'm sorry for disturbing you. I'll leave you to get on with things.'

'You may as well stay for the drink Noel was getting for you,' Hunter brusquely signalled to the Reaper behind the bar. 'Pour the woman a gin.'

Georgie stared at Hunter, aware the whole room was silently questioning why he should want this girl to stay. No one liked her sort – especially not inside the Factory. 'Hunter, we need to leave. We've got to get to that party. We're late as it is!'

'I didn't want to cause problems. I shouldn't have come. It was only on the off-chance Matt might be here,' Tori said loudly. 'I have a taxi waiting outside.'

Noel glanced at Hunter. 'That's settled then. Let's go! We don't want to be late to wet Dev's baby's head.' He liked it when one of the Reaper's old ladies popped out a kid. It was a good excuse to get slaughtered.

Hunter nodded in agreement and at this, everyone immediately grabbed their crash helmets and leathers and Tori's half-poured drink became dumped to one side of the bar.

• • • •

'YOU REALLY DIDN'T need to stay on my account,' Tori followed Hunter back into the large room, aware her eyes were watching the way his muscles moved under the denim of his jeans. 'I didn't want to spoil your evening. If I can just use your phone, I'll call the taxi firm. They were supposed to wait. I didn't expect them to drive off and le…'

'It's not a problem,' Hunter muttered, flicking the lights to the bar area back on, but leaving the rest of the room in darkness. Stepping behind the bar, he continued pouring Tori's abandoned drink and cracked open another bottle of beer for himself.

'Where's your phone? Can I u…'

'No need,' Hunter barked. 'I'll give you a ride home. I just want another drink first.'

'A ride home?' Tori repeated, realising she sounded ridiculously like a parrot. Did that mean he expected her to get on one of those motorbikes? She'd heard the rest roar off only minutes ago when the others had left and the sound had frozen her blood in her veins. 'N-No, it's fine thank you. I'll just call the taxi.'

'What's your problem?' Hunter yelled, his loud voice making Tori jump out of her skin. *This was one too many times she'd treated him like a piece of shit, the conceited bitch.* 'I know you don't like me, or any of us, but I'm not a rapist! I won't molest or murder you. I'm merely offering you a fucking lift.'

The ferocity of his voice knocked Tori off kilter emotionally like a brick to the temple and she wobbled unsteadily on her high stilettoes. She would *not* give this man the satisfaction of seeing her cry. She would not allow him to have further proof of her weakness.

Hunter ignored the immediate urge to rush to Tori's side. It was most likely another one of those ploys her type pulled to deviate from an uncomfortable situation. He was still smarting from her blatant contempt.

His anger surged again as he glared at Tori's pale face. Did he detect the slight wobble of her bottom lip there? *Oh, for God's sake! Seriously?* 'Don't you ever get bored keeping up this pathetic act of how wronged you are? Look at the face on you!' he roared. 'Gets you attention from your boyfriend, mummy or daddy does it? It won't work with me, lady!'

Tori stared at Hunter's grey eyes flashing with anger. *How dare he mention her father! What did he know?* She bit down on her lip to try and stop her angry tears from escaping. 'What the hell do you know about my life?' she screamed. 'You know *nothing* about me!'

Hunter suddenly launched his bottle of beer against the wall where it smashed into pieces and ignored the terrified squeal that came from Tori's direction. 'What do *I* know about your life? I don't, apart from that it was and *is* a hell of lot better than mine!' he spat. 'You haven't got the first clue about what it's like to suffer and you think you can turn up at my place like Lady-Fucking-Muck, looking for that poncey joke of a man that you're stupid enough, or more likely, *greedy* enough to marry! Then when I'm kind enough to offer you a lift home, you all but accuse me of having dodgy motives.'

Hunter moved away from the bar and closer to Tori, watching as she flinched. 'I don't *need* to rape or intimidate women. Not that I ever would. Your attitude sickens me,' he barked. 'I'm supposed to be at a mate's party and instead, I'm listening to you insult me. *Again*. And it will be the last time, I can assure you.'

Tori mutely stared at Hunter facing her with pent-up, barely controlled aggression. She hadn't meant her refusal of a lift to insinuate anything. 'Like I said, you know nothing about me,' she said. 'Why assume I was thinking that? It shows what a chip on your shoulder you have.'

Without averting his hard gaze, Hunter smiled sarcastically. 'I can see your fear. In your *eyes*.'

Tori swallowed uncomfortably. He was right: she *was* scared, but not because of what he might do to her. In fact, it *did* scare her, but it was the prospect of him putting his hands and mouth on her, which elicited the reaction. *What he would feel like…*

She dismissed the notion and forced a thin smile. 'If you must know, I don't like motorbikes.'

'Bit too rough and ready for you?' Hunter scoffed. She could brush her reaction under the carpet as much as she liked, but he wouldn't be fooled by back-peddling. 'Or is being spotted with a Reaper enough to lose you your place in society?'

Unable to help herself, Tori laughed and Hunter eyed her suspiciously. Despite his irritation, he was still inexplicably drawn to her mouth and the way the eyes lit up. This was the first time he'd seen any spark of life behind her dead eyes and he liked it. 'Something funny?'

Tori leant on the bar. 'If you knew anything about me you would understand how funny what you just said was – in a bizarre, ironic way at least.'

Hunter shook his head in exasperation. *She was a strange one.* He waited for her to expand on what she'd said, but she said nothing more and he fought down the urge to ask. Annoyed with himself that this woman intrigued him so much, he walked back behind the bar and helped himself to another beer.

He nodded towards Tori's untouched glass. 'Are you drinking that, or do you have a conspiracy theory that I'm drugging or poisoning you as well?'

Tori rolled her eyes, almost enjoying that she was winding this man up. 'Well, I wouldn't be surprised. It's what *your* 'type' do, isn't it?' She smiled in a way which showed she was being sardonic. 'I'll tell you what. I'll call your bluff. If you've drugged me then you'll have to live with the fact that I was right.' With that statement, she tipped the contents of her drink into her mouth and swallowed it down in one.

Hunter continued looking at Tori, neither unfazed or impressed with her bad attempt at humour. He didn't want to give her the satisfaction of reacting. Silently, he poured her another drink and placed it in front of her. Walking around the bar, he sat on a stool opposite. Raising the bottle to his mouth, he cracked off the top with his teeth and spat the metal cap on to the floor.

Tori watched in silent fascination. He was too close. His proximity caused her blood to thrum. Suddenly remembering she was supposed to be doing what Matt wanted, she attempted to concentrate her mind. She needed to get to know him, to find out things, but that was going to be a lot harder than it sounded.

The truth was, Ash Hunter interested her. With a jolt she realised she *was* interested as to what lay behind his iron exterior and sensed there was a lot more going on behind the scenes than was immediately visible. 'What has made your life so hard?'

Hunter scrutinised Tori, ensuring his poker face remained

in place. He skimmed his eyes once again over her body encased in the skin-tight red dress and willed his cock to stop swelling. 'Nothing you would understand,' he muttered, almost to himself.

'Try me,' Tori said, secretly shocked that she'd uttered something that could be taken in so many different ways. She could feel the blush spreading from her chest up over her face.

Hunter grinned lopsidedly. She had no idea how much he'd *love* to try her. *Perhaps far too much…* There was something that set her apart from her sort. But was there? Was her beauty and his lust merely causing him to see her with a distorted perception?

He trusted no one. No one apart from his crew. Certainly no women – especially ones like her. He couldn't allow her to get under his skin any more than she already had. He watched her silently trying to peer into his soul. *She'd have a job*, he thought bitterly. *He didn't have much of one left.*

Hunter studied the discoloured and still slightly swollen flesh around her eye and cheekbone. And was that the remnants of a split lip? Despite his reticence he found himself still possessing the urge to find out whether she was telling him the truth about what had caused the damage to her face.

'What are you staring at me like that for?' Tori asked, breaking the long silence. His eyes were drilling into her head and probing around in an attempt to steal her thoughts. This sensation was so strong she wondered whether he *was* reading her mind and that thought horrified her because then he'd know the way he was looking at her made the need for his hands to be on her unbearably intense.

'What *really* happened?' Hunter asked.

'What do you mean?'

Hunter frowned. 'I mean, your *face*?'

Momentarily knocked off guard, Tori felt flummoxed. 'I-I… My face?'

'Yeah.' Hunter leant closer. 'The *bruises*?'

'I-I told you…' Tori shivered as Hunter ran his thick finger over her bottom lip. 'I…' Involuntarily she closed her eyes, anticipation shooting through her body.

Hunter studied Tori's perfect face as she closed her eyes. It would be so easy to pull her towards him and kiss her, then take her roughly up against the wall. His gnawing erection was extremely uncomfortable and he shifted in the seat. 'You're lying,' he muttered, moving his fingers away from her full lips before he lost control. 'Why are you allowing that prick to do this to you?' He felt his temper spike. 'Are you that desperate for the status which comes with his ring to put up with it?'

Tori's eyes shot open. 'W-What?'

'Why are you protecting him?' *What was so special about that obnoxious twat? Tori was so beautiful she could have any man she wanted. She oozed class and seemed intelligent too. It didn't make sense.*

'Y-You don't know what you're talking about.' Tori felt like she was drowning. 'You think I care about status? You think I'm that shallow?'

Hunter raised his eyebrow. 'Well, aren't you?' he said, then smiled smugly. 'So it *was* him. I knew it!'

Tori felt light-headed. *Shit, she was crap at this. He'd caught her off guard.* 'You're reading too much into things. I told you it was from work, but instead, you've basically called me a gold-digger!'

Feeling her heart racing and panic surging, Tori grabbed her bag. She had to keep a handle on her angst. She couldn't afford to have a meltdown.

Hunter frowned. 'Have it your own way,' he shrugged, standing up.

'Where are you going?' Tori asked, watching Hunter make purposeful strides across the room.

'To do what you originally asked,' Hunter said without turning back. 'I'm calling you a taxi. I've got things to do and haven't got time for this bullshit.'

TWENTY TWO

NOEL SLUGGED DOWN his fourth pint in quick succession and hoped his raging hangover would soon lift. He wiped the back of his sleeve across his mouth to mop up at least some of the beer he hadn't quite managed to tip in the correct place and then ran his fingers through his hair feeling the knotted remnants of last night's hair gel.

He really should have had a shower. If not only to make his hair feel less like it had taken up residence in someone's frying pan, but to also wash off any unsavoury residue left over from the bird he'd sunk himself into at Dev's.

He screwed up his face, wishing he hadn't made the drunken decision to ride that slapper bare back. *She'd been a classic contender for the clap.*

Noel watched Hunter make his way to the bar, glad it wasn't his round. He felt so rough he doubted whether he'd have managed to get up again and really needed the alcohol to hurry up and kick in to take the edge of this awful bloody hangover away before he dropped dead.

Half of this was Hunter's fault anyhow. He'd only ended

up putting so many away in the first place because he'd had to put up with Georgie bending his ear for what seemed like *centuries* before Hunter finally showed up. God, the girl had been going on and on and *on*.

'Was he still with that girl? What are they doing? Can you go back to the Factory and make sure everything's ok?'

No, he bloody well couldn't! He couldn't give a flying fuck as to what Hunter was doing, although given the chance of dipping his own wick into that posh bitch, Tori, wouldn't be something he would turn down. The difference was *he* wouldn't let a woman make him late for one of the crew's celebrations. *That* showed Hunter's priorities for what they were – *utter shite.*

Noel scowled. He'd been questioning Hunter's motives for far too long and it was getting more and more frustrating. Rafe would be turning in his grave if he could see what had happened to his beloved club since Hunter had taken the reins.

The Reapers were nowhere near the same as they used to be and sometimes it felt more a working men's social club than a motorcycle club. The only thing that resembled the old way was they rode bikes, wore the patch and of course still had the name. Where had all the chaos and devastation gone that he used to thrive on? Hunter was steering the whole club into being above-board and legit, whilst using the name and reputation to get what he wanted and pull rank in the city.

Noel absentmindedly picked at his fingers whilst keeping his bloodshot eyes trained on Hunter. He was talking to the landlady again. *Probably got a thing for her too.* Either way, he wished he'd hurry the fuck up because his mouth was like the bottom of a bird cage. Still, at least the rich ponce, Matt, had set in motion what he needed to do to help swing Hunter's mind into selling the Factory.

Noel swallowed down a smirk. If Hunter had indeed got a thing for that Tori bird as he suspected, then he'd be more than pissed off when he eventually realised she was also in on the set up. *The stupid cow. The rich never had any fucking morals.*

It was no skin off his nose. He'd been treated as a gopher

for far too long with Hunter speaking to him like he had the IQ of something in a pond. Well, he wasn't stupid and wouldn't be the one coming out of this with shit on *his* face. Hunter shouldn't be running the Reapers, that was quite clear. *He* should and before long he'd be claiming his rightful place.

It was, of course, an additional bonus that the posh prick had something to gain from it too and Noel wouldn't let the chance of that huge chunk of money Matt had promised elude him. There was no way in a million years he was missing out on that!

Furthermore, if Matt wanted his help in pushing Hunter towards Miss Aristocrat, then so be it. Fuck Georgie – she was a nobody junkie anyhow. She wasn't attached to Hunter and had no official claim to him, so bollocks to her.

Nah, it was a definite he could turn this around and believed the others were as fed up as he was with the rather pleasant way the club was run these days. There was a distinct lack of danger and it was fast becoming boring as shit. Surely he wasn't the only one who felt like this?

Noel tapped his foot on the floor impatiently. He needed more than what was available. A *lot* more and he was going to get it.

A smile spread across his unshaven face. If push came to shove, he'd use his trump card. He'd already sworn he wouldn't, but by God, he would if he had to. Enough was enough and if finally using the one piece of info he had against Hunter meant he could reinstate the Reapers to their full glory whilst making a mint from that posh cunt in the process, then so be it.

· · · ·

'I'M TELLING YOU straight up that wanker gave Tori a slap,' Sarah spat. She knew she'd promised she wouldn't breathe a word to any of the boys, but she hadn't been able to help it.

She'd got enough on her mind as it was since Colin had filled her in with what Hunter had discovered about this so-called property investment company. It really did look like there was a big risk of the area being redeveloped, because from what the boys had gathered, a large percentage of the other businesses, as well as the White Hart and Hunter had been approached. Even some residents on terraced streets not far from the Factory had been contacted too and it was worrying her sick. She loved this pub but had no control as to whether the brewery decided to sell. And now, to make things even worse it had been confirmed the potential buyer would be visiting tomorrow and to make sure the pub was presented favourably.

This property bunch clearly wanted their area and Sarah knew enough that most people would do anything for the right price. But aside from her own reasons for wanting things to remain as they were, this community was a good one. It was criminal to disperse people to live in a soulless and anonymous housing estate *somewhere* just so the yuppies could have yet another 'slums-to-palaces' regeneration project to choose from.

The thought of the heart, character and soul being ripped from the area made Sarah's skin tingle with dread. She'd been planning on asking Hunter what plans he had to try and stop this company, or how he would convince the people who had been approached not to sell, but her plan to get information out of him had been put to one side when he'd started going on about Tori's attitude.

Even though Sarah's nose was still slightly out of joint since Tori's outburst last night and she hadn't heard from her since, she wouldn't stand here listening to Hunter slate her friend. She grabbed Hunter's leather jacketed sleeve. 'I mean it though. You need to swear down that you won't do anything about it. I promised Tori.'

Hunter was less than impressed. 'I knew she was lying! You can't expect me to ignore this, Sarah. Not now I know for sure.'

Sarah eyed the man in front of her. The anger and resolve in his eyes were clear for all to see. She really shouldn't have said anything, so it was up to her to turn this around. She cocked one eyebrow questioningly. 'The one thing you're not taking on board here is that it's not *your* job to deal with it.'

'Of course it's my job! This happ…'

Sarah held her hand up knowing she was one of the few who could get away with straight-talking this man. 'No, it's not. Tori Morgan is not *your* woman. It didn't happen to any of the Reapers' women and it didn't happen on your patch either, so it's *not* your job to deal with it, see?'

Momentarily lost for words, Hunter scowled and swigged at his pint.

Sarah's attitude softened a little. 'It's nice how you want to look after her, but you need to step away from this one. You'll destroy the girl.'

'Look after her?' Hunter spat. 'What the fuck makes you think I want *that*? I'm just trying to do the right thing!'

Sarah smiled knowingly. 'I've known you a long time and I can tell, you know!' she winked.

Hunter tried to keep tabs on his building irritation, but it was becoming increasingly difficult. 'I think you're forgetting yourself, Sarah,' he growled.

'Yeah, yeah… Whatever you say. But do me a favour - as well as everyone – leave her alone!'

Hunter stood up rapidly. 'For fuck's sake, Sarah! You're out of line!' Downing his drink, he signalled to the others that they were unexpectedly leaving, ignoring the annoyance plastered over Noel's face.

Hunter strode out of the White Hart and jumped on his bike, quickly firing the engine. Roaring off along the road he didn't wait to see if any of the others were following. He needed to get away because Sarah had been right. *It wasn't his job to protect Tori, but he wanted to and that made him uneasy.*

• • • •

MATT POUNDED INTO Tori as she lay underneath him. It was difficult enough getting off without her being as unresponsive as a dead fish.

After she'd finished with that bonehead last night he'd been counting on her not appearing because he'd been involved in a thoroughly enjoyable session with a girl he'd picked up in a wine bar whilst out with Jeremy, but he *had* expected her to at least call, if not last night, then first thing this morning. However, she hadn't bothered. He'd heard *nothing* and much to his annoyance, he'd been forced to call *her* so that she could bring him up to date with what she'd achieved.

Predictably Tori had been vague about everything, so he'd instructed her to get her scrawny backside around here immediately to discuss what had gone on.

Pulling Tori's hips higher, Matt ignored the vacant look on her face and closed his eyes as he drove into her harder, sweat beading on his brow. *The fucking useless cow!* Only she could wear a two grand cocktail dress and turn up in a place full of rabid, horny bikers and when she'd got herself alone with the target, successfully manage to be told to leave.

Ok, so she hadn't been thrown out as such, but as good as. *Dismissed* was the word. The pointless bitch must have really pissed the bloke off for him to ring her a taxi. Now she didn't even have the decency to put her back into *this* and he needed to get her knocked up for his own sake. Even though he'd fucked that girl several times last night, he still felt unspent. *That was the downside of taking loads of coke.*

Grabbing a breast, Matt twisted it hard, smiling when he saw the pain on Tori's face. It was this that gave him the push he needed. Twisting it harder, she let out a yelp of pain and Matt pushed her knees up to her chest so he could get deeper. Feeling his orgasm mounting he gritted his teeth and thrust harder, pushing Tori down into the bed by his hands on her shoulders.

The sudden and much needed rush washed over him and with a long groan, he pulled out and rolled off. 'So, what are you going to do about it?' Matt said as he flopped back on the pillow.

Tori turned on to her side so that she didn't have to look at Matt. It was bad enough hearing the contempt and disgust in his voice without seeing it in his eyes too. *What did he expect her to do?* She didn't know. She'd tried what he'd asked, but it wasn't as simple as he thought.

Everything was always cut and dried with Matt. Black and white. For him, things followed set processes and rules and he had no concept of life not working from a flow-chart or textbook.

'Are you even listening?' Matt barked. 'You got all dolled up and looked good – even for *you*, but still couldn't manage to twist the fuckhead around your little finger when you had the chance! I bet you didn't even try.'

Tori sighed. She'd have to at least *attempt* to explain to him. 'Walking in and batting my eyelashes didn't mean he was suddenly going to start listening to everything I said. I don't even know the man. You can't expect him to discuss his property with me or take my advice!' she said incredulously.

'Why the hell not?' Matt propped himself up on his elbows. 'That's how most men work! They're quite simple to please and easy to get on side when they think with their dick.'

Tori burrowed further into the pillow. She didn't want to be having this conversation. Her nipples had already started to pucker with the thought of what was in Hunter's jeans, but the sad truth was she had no idea how to use her feminine guiles in that way and furthermore, she didn't think it was quite that easy. At least not where *he* was concerned.

'I get the impression there's a lot more to him than meets the eye. He's not a stupid man.'

Matt snorted. 'Maybe you're right. After all, he can't be *that* stupid if he had no urge to want to spend the night with you! What sane man would?'

Tori inwardly sighed. *Here we go.* Someone like Noel was more the sort that ploy would work on, but there was no way she'd voice that in case Matt decided she should turn her attentions to him instead. But Hunter – no – he was deep. *Intense.*

'He's definitely not gay,' Matt muttered.

'No, he's not,' Tori said a little too quickly. 'He's got a girlfriend.'

Matt laughed thinly. 'That lot don't have girlfriends. They have women they *fuck* and they have as many of those as they want.'

'He seems too respectful for that,' Tori said quietly.

'Are you winding me up?' Matt yelled. 'They don't know what 'respectful' means! Are you telling me that you actually *like* the jerk?'

Tori was grateful she still had her back to Matt so he couldn't see the reddening blush creeping up her face. 'Of course not! I just mean he's not as much like the others as you seem to think.' *He's nothing like the others. Nothing like them at all.*

'Oh, fuck off!' Matt jibed. 'They're all the same.'

'You're wrong. The problem is that he despises our 'sort' as much as we despise his.' It was true. It was clear Hunter held her in contempt, his general dislike was plain to see.

'You,' Matt said, turning Tori over to face him, 'are useless. *Regardless* of whether a man dislikes a woman, they won't turn down the chance of putting their cock into one. They don't have to *like* someone to do that!'

'Like *you*, you mean?' Tori spat before she could stop herself.

'What do you expect me to do? You're a frigid bitch. You don't like sex and when you do lower yourself to it, you're boring as fuck. I've got to find my pleasure somewhere.'

Tori remained silent. She didn't care. *He could do what he wanted if it meant spending less time with him.*

'Once we're married, you'll be pregnant by the end of the year. All we've got to do is produce a few kids and everyone will be happy. I don't have to like it and neither do you, but that's the arrangement and you're going to deliver that.' *And hopefully sooner than you think!*

Tori felt sick. The thought of her belly swelling year after year with Matt's offspring making her even more trapped made her panic levels suffocating. There was no way in a million years she'd be rushing to start that once they'd married and would drag it out for as long as possible.

'But first,' Matt continued. 'I need you to swing Hunter around. You know how much I've got riding on this and I haven't got time for you to worm your way in gradually.'

'I don't know what else I can do?' Tori whined.

'Despite what I previously said about how far I'm prepared to let you go with him, you'll just have to put yourself on a plate, that's what. Just make sure he double bags it. I don't want to catch anything.'

TWENTY THREE

IT WAS AWKWARD in the office. When Tori arrived, she'd wanted to speak to Sarah before anyone else came in, or before the day got properly started, but before Sarah had turned up the boss had appeared, along with the other workers who shared their office.

Tori glanced at her, but Sarah didn't look up, nor even seem to notice she was there. Her heart sank. She'd overreacted the other day in the White Hart and had behaved badly. Now it looked like she may have burnt her bridges with the only decent and genuine friend she had.

Tori faltered. She wanted to apologise and for things to go back to the way they were before. She'd been so on edge about what she was supposed to be doing that night she'd completely gone over the top with her reaction. Not that it in any way excused the way she'd kicked off, but it was the reason.

She should tell Sarah everything. That would explain it all. Tori frowned. Then again, that would mean more abject public humiliation, but if it meant putting things right, then maybe she should just bite the bullet and get on with it.

She studied Sarah as covertly as possible without making it obvious and spotted the dark circles under her eyes. The woman looked both withdrawn and preoccupied and a flutter of worry stirred. Sarah was always upbeat and positive, so it was unnerving to see her look so down. Tori set her chin resolutely. Sarah had been there for her when she needed it and after the other night, the least she could do was make the first move and see what was bothering her.

Glancing around to ensure the boss's beady eyes were not on her, Tori rose from her chair and moved the short distance to Sarah's desk. She placed her hand lightly on her shoulder. 'I just wanted to say I'm sorry about the other night. I overreacted and I...'

'Don't worry about it,' Sarah muttered without turning around.

Receiving no further response, Tori was unsure what to do or say next. It was obvious Sarah didn't have an interest in talking – either because she didn't want to make up, or something else was bothering her.

'A-Are you ok?' Tori pushed, gingerly touching Sarah on the shoulder again.

'Victoria? Have you run out of work?' The voice of her boss boomed over the quiet office.

Blushing like a reprimanded child, Tori hovered uncomfortably by Sarah's side. 'No, Sir. I've got plenty to do. I-I, er... I was just asking for some Tippex.'

Hearing Tori's excuse prompted Sarah to pass the bottle of Tippex over. 'Here you go,' she said quietly.

'Thanks,' Tori smiled, taking the bottle and scuttling back to her desk before she gave her miserable boss any further reasons to question her.

Knowing his beady eyes were still fixed upon her she steadfastly resumed her typing, making sure to make a big deal of applying Tippex to her work even though there were no mistakes to correct.

When Sarah had briefly glanced up, Tori has seen her eyes. They showed tell-tale signs of crying. *What on earth had got to Sarah to upset her so?* She wasn't the type to cry over something and nothing, so there was definitely a problem.

Screwing the lid back on to the Tippex, Tori repeated the journey and replaced the bottle on Sarah's desk. She casually lowered her head. 'Tell me what's wrong.'

'Come to the pub tonight and I'll fill you in,' she whispered.

Nodding, Tori returned to her desk. Matt wouldn't like that she wouldn't be going to the Factory to have a second attempt on Hunter, but he'd just have to put up with it. She'd already pointed out if she kept turning up it would look obvious, but he'd been insistent.

She wouldn't be doing as he asked. Not this time. She would find out what had upset Sarah first.

• • • •

GEORGIE PULLED STEADILY on the large spliff and blew the blue smoke out slowly towards the ceiling. She was enjoying the dream-like state her head was at rather than her usual hyper coked-up mentality.

She watched through heavy-lidded eyes as Hunter paced around his large private room distractedly. As he moved the muscles flexed fluidly in his legs and she ran her tongue over her lips in anticipation.

He was still acting distant and although she'd tempted him several times over the last few days, he'd been unusually reluctant to have much closeness with her. He'd only fucked her twice, which was most unlike him and her body was screaming with pent-up sexual frustration.

She also hadn't received any answers from anyone as to why he'd been late getting to Dev's bash the other night – short of waiting for Tori's taxi to turn up. Of course, she'd been unable to ask him outright because if she acted like a jealous harridan that would seal the death warrant of any chance of things developing further between them.

She'd grilled Noel, but he'd been off his tits and she hadn't been able to get much sense out from him. Not that she usually could and besides, she wouldn't trust anything he'd got to say even if he'd been sober.

Taking another long drag of the joint, Georgie inhaled deeply and held the smoke in her lungs for as long as possible to get the maximum effect. She stared transfixed at the small suncatcher hanging in the huge window casting sparkling reflections.

'You want some of this?' She offered the joint to Hunter who was staring mindlessly out of the big window over the industrial vista.

'No thanks,' Hunter muttered, wishing Georgie would bugger off. He needed to think and every time he'd got everything lined up in his head, she'd interrupt with a stupid question, or by pawing him and trying to get him into bed. He needed to be on his own for a while to find a solution to this property issue and he didn't need anyone infringing on that.

He'd spent this morning and most of the afternoon digging further into the company who had been approaching half the businesses this side of the city, but he'd learnt no more than what he already knew, which was frustrating to say the least.

He hadn't even been sure what he'd expected to find, if anything, but there wasn't anything that had flagged up as being untoward. The company was doing nothing wrong in offering people money to sell. People didn't *have* to and the company couldn't make them. But *could* they? At least two of the people he'd spoken to at the weekend had felt pushed into selling. The owner of a small grocers had told how the company had painted a bleak picture of how 'difficult' a shop like this would find competing with an upmarket delicatessen once the regeneration was complete.

Hunter knew this property bunch wouldn't get far if they *all* refused to sell, but half of the people approached didn't quite grasp that or see it in the same way. Another person had told how the company had honed in on how useful the huge chunk of money being offered would help in caring for his father who had been horrifically injured in a road accident a year prior. *How could he reasonably expect people to turn these offers down?*

On top of that, this company was offering almost *double* the market value. It was that bit which didn't make sense. Not a lot could compete with that. There was something else going on here and he was determined to find out what it was.

'Hunter?' Georgie wheedled, sashaying over to the window. As he slowly turned around, she provocatively removed her top freeing her large breasts. 'Are you coming to keep me company? I'm getting lonely…'

Hunter was past irritation. *She'd done it again.* Although she had the most magnificent breasts and he knew she was trying to please him, he wasn't in the mood. 'If you're lonely, go downstairs or to the pub. Everyone will be in one or the other. You also have your *own* house, so you don't need to hang around here. I need some space.'

Seeing Georgie's face drop, Hunter felt a stab of guilt, but not enough to retract what he'd said, or do anything to encourage her.

'Have I done something wrong?' Georgie asked in a small voice.

'It's nothing to do with you,' Hunter said impatiently. 'Why do people think it's always something to do with *them*?'

Wrapping her arms around herself in a sudden, rather pathetic attempt to cover her nakedness, Georgie sullenly retrieved her clothes from the floor. 'I'll get out of your way then, shall I?'

Running his hands through his hair in irritation, Hunter nodded bluntly, then turned his back and resumed staring out of the window. He knew she was expecting him to do or say something, but she'd be waiting a long time. He needed some space and he was going to get it.

Hearing the door close as Georgie left the room, Hunter quietly exhaled with relief. Now he could concentrate on the matter in hand. Much as he didn't want to, his next port of call would be setting up a meeting with those posh twats, Matt and Jeremy. They knew this property investor so they should be able to shed some light on the issue so that he could find out what the desperate need to buy the local area was all about, along with the over-generous offers.

Hunter frowned. But how would he know if they were levelling with him? He grinned slowly. *Because he'd make them talk if not, that's how.*

TWENTY FOUR

TORI SIPPED AT the third drink Sarah had poured since she'd arrived and leaned back against the sofa cushion. She looked around Sarah and Colin's lounge.

Two-bedroom living accommodation above the White Hart came with the brewery tenancy and Tori smiled at the homely feel of the place. The main room was an open-plan area, consisting of the lounge, a kitchen and a dining area. Although quite large, the area was still undoubtedly cosy and the different parts of the room were separated by alcoves formed when the previous separate rooms had been knocked through into one.

A large open fire roared at the end of the lounge area and a sofa and two matching armchairs were arranged in a semi-circle in front of it. The seats were covered with brightly coloured crochet throws and contrasting cushions and surprisingly this, plus the combination of the old-fashioned patterned wallpaper and garish pub-type carpet did not look ghastly, but gave the whole place a 'bohemian' look which she very much liked.

There were pictures on the wall including a large colour photograph of Sarah and Colin on their wedding day hanging next to the large bay window which was framed with old and worn maroon velvet curtains, identical to the ones around the bays in the tap room downstairs.

Tori placed her drink on the wooden coffee table in front of her and looked at Sarah. She understood completely why she'd preferred to sit up here to talk, rather than in the bar. The puffiness and redness of her eyes was visible and would have prompted questions from the regulars.

From Tori's side, being out of the bar was just fine by her because at least there was no way she would bump into Hunter up here. She was still cringing with how he'd dismissed her the other night and had no idea how she would react if she was face to face with him right now.

Matt, on the other hand had behaved *exactly* as she'd expected after she'd announced she wasn't going to go to the Factory tonight. He'd been irate – that was until she'd hit upon the brainwave of turning Sarah's upset into an idea for his cause. She'd cleverly explained her 'plan' so he'd ended up thinking the change in direction was *his* idea.

Knowing him well enough to use his over-inflated ego against him had worked and Tori had left to go to the White Hart, leaving Matt thinking *his* new idea was great. She of course, had no intention of doing anything Matt wanted her to do tonight, but she'd happily let him think differently. Sarah was her primary and only concern at the moment and that was all she cared about.

However, after Sarah had explained what was troubling her, Tori fully understood her friend's dread about losing the pub she loved so much. From what Colin had repeated about the meeting with the property investors this afternoon it had only made things worse and it did look like there would be a sale. Unfortunately before very long the conversation had inevitably turned to Hunter, but thankfully this time it had nothing to do with her.

'I don't understand what Hunter's got to do with it? He doesn't own the pub, so how can he be involved?' Tori asked.

Sarah swigged greedily at her fresh pint of lager. 'No, you're right he doesn't, but they're digging around his place too.'

Tori was thoroughly confused. 'The brewery is? Whatever for? Why would the brewery want his place? It's an old factory isn't it? Surely they don't want to turn that into a pub or bar?'

Sarah grimaced. 'There's no such thing as pubs where the yuppies are concerned. It's all bars, bars and fucking *bars*.'

Tori nodded. *She should know*. She'd been dragged around virtually every wine bar in a thirty-mile radius thanks to Matt and she hated them. She liked places like the White Hart – unpretentious and real. *Places with soul.*

'Besides,' Sarah continued. 'It's not the brewery who want to buy it. The brewery's buying nothing, it's been offered an amazing price to sell by the same investor who wants Hunter's place, along with half of the town. They're after a lot of the businesses as well as some residential streets for regeneration purposes.'

'A property investment company?' Tori frowned as the glaringly obvious truth sank into her brain like a stone. *How had she been so thick?* Her eyes narrowed. Matt had banged on about Hunter's place so much it hadn't even crossed her mind that it could be connected with the purchase of the pub. He'd omitted to mention the company who was going to save his neck and that of his career was also planning on buying up the whole area.

He'd only ever referred to the industrial site where Hunter's factory building was, but he and this company clearly had a much bigger idea to rip this neighbourhood apart and *she* was helping to orchestrate it.

There was no way she could tell Sarah what *her* troubles were now. Not after this. 'You said this company were offering good money?' Tori asked.

'Not *everything's* about money!' Sarah snapped.

Tori smiled gently. 'I didn't mean that. I meant if they're offering a good price, then maybe for most people it *would* be worth considering? I know it's different for you, being as you don't own this place, but for some of the others…'

'I don't know what the brewery have been offered, but according to Hunter, most people have been offered almost *double* the market value,' Sarah griped.

Tori frowned. Whatever was going on here she didn't feel Sarah was looking at this rationally. She had to think of the best way to put this across but suspected it wouldn't go down too well. 'I hate to say this, but you can't really blame them for wanting to take it if that's the case. Are you sure you're not thinking about this solely from your point of view?'

Sarah nodded sadly. 'Perhaps. It's just that it will rip out the heart of the community.'

Tori realised that, however this sort of thing was happening more and more frequently in so many places. It was the way the cities were moving forward. 'Even if everyone decides to turn this offer down, it's only a matter of time before another company comes along and tries the same thing.' She raised her eyebrows. 'Except the next time it may not be such a good offer…'

Regardless of Matt being involved in these deals and despite him hiding the extent of how many properties were involved, it didn't change the facts.

'Maybe you're right,' Sarah said miserably. She stared at the garish carpet, trying not to get herself lost in the gigantic psychedelic flowers.

'From what you've said, it does seem a very generous offer?' Tori reasoned.

Sarah frowned. 'Yeah, that's the problem. It *seems* like a good offer. *Too* good... I mean, aside from me and Colin not benefitting and only losing if the brewery sells this place and aside from not wanting to lose the community, perhaps for my own selfish reasons, I still think something's not right.'

Tori laughed. This gin was going down far too well and after finishing the third ample double, she'd begun to feel distinctly light-headed. 'Ever the cynic!'

'Maybe. Maybe not, but Hunter agrees and that's despite him making a *very* tidy return if he sold,' Sarah said thoughtfully.

'Why does everything revolve around what Hunter thinks or does around here?' Tori snapped, helping herself to another large top up of gin direct from the bottle.

'Because people *respect* him, that's why!' Sarah countered. 'Whatever you may think, he's turned a lot of things about around here – for the *better*, I might add.'

Tori snorted derisively. *She should slow down on the gin before she spoke out of turn again.*

'Look down your nose all you like, but it's true. There's a lot less trouble around here since he took lead of the Reapers!' Sarah snapped. 'Besides, he doesn't want this area full of those rich bastards either. Pushing us out again – like everywhere else.'

'And you say *I* have an attitude towards class?' Tori contested.

'So would you if you'd had happen to you what happened to him.'

'And what's that?'

Sarah paused. 'Not my place to say, but let's just say he's got his reasons.' She'd said enough. She knew what had happened to Hunter's family. It was common knowledge to anyone who had lived around here all their lives. As much as she liked Tori, she would not allow snotty comments about Hunter - the same as she wouldn't stand for him making comments about her. She liked both of them a great deal and wanted it to remain that way.

Realising yet again she may have overstepped the mark, Tori smiled. 'I think Matt may have information about this company. It could be a client of his from the bank, so I'll see if I can get anything from him that may be useful.'

Sarah frowned. 'I might have known he was something to do with this, however I doubt whether he'd tell *you* anything! Not with his attitude.'

'Well, I can but try. I won't mention anything to do with you. I'll act like I'm interested,' Tori smiled. Now she felt even more deceitful. If Sarah knew she'd been tasked with buttering Hunter up to sell, their friendship would be well and truly over. But she did have *every* intention of getting it out of Matt exactly as to what the score was.

On the face of it, as far as she was concerned, Sarah didn't want to lose the pub, but also needed to accept she had to move with the times. A good offer was a good offer – if that was what it was?

As for Hunter, well he didn't want anyone he classed as 'rich' moving into the area because of whatever chip was on his shoulder. That didn't mean it was the right decision.

· · · ·

MATT KNEW HE was attracting a thousand disapproving stares from the rest of the customers in the wine bar. He'd already had to smooth it over with the manager when Noel had arrived. He'd known Shawn would have immediately called security and asked him to leave otherwise, but luckily for Matt, he'd spent *far* too much money in this place over the last few years and had enough sway with the man to remind him of such.

With the reassurance that the rancid-looking biker was here under *Matt's* invitation and there would be no trouble, Shawn had accepted the fifty pound note shoved into his hand and reluctantly taken his word for it on the proviso that on the first sign of any trouble or provocation to any of his other guests, he'd be asking them *both* to leave. Matt would also be personally receiving the bill for any damage, as well as the bill for loss of trade.

Matt had to grudgingly accept this and scathingly eyed Noel lounging on the plush velvet bench of the cubicle they had been rapidly ushered to. The cubicle that was as much out of ear-shot and general visibility to the rest of the customers as possible.

When Noel had called insisting on an urgent meeting, Matt had had no choice but to bring him to one of his usual haunts. He could hardly invite the man to his parents' house. As well as not wanting him to know where he lived, he knew his mother would have had a coronary if Noel had turned up. She'd have called the police and then he would definitely be in the shit. He could have possibly taken Noel to his apartment, but again – he didn't want him or any of those fuckheads knowing any addresses he was attached to.

Matt's first and obvious suggestion had been to go to one of the flea-infested dumps the skanky pigs frequented, but that had been ruled out as a no-go because their meeting could not be conducted *anywhere* where any of the Reapers were liable to appear, or anywhere where word could get back that they'd met.

This had piqued Matt's interest. It must be important for Noel to be calling out to *him*, rather than the other way around.

He watched the man theatrically scratching at his groin whilst grinning manically at the couple eyeing him with distaste from the closest table. He was obviously doing it for effect, but it was not helping the overall situation. 'Do you *have* to do that?' Matt hissed.

'Think I caught crabs from the slag I fucked the other night,' Noel said. He hadn't. At least he didn't *think* he had, but maybe he shouldn't joke about it. He could well have got more than he'd bargained for judging by the state of the tart, but only time would tell.

'Well, keep them to yourself!' Matt grimaced. *God, this guy was so manky and the sooner all of this was sorted, the better.* 'Ok, so you wanted to see me? What's the problem?'

Noel leaned forward on the table, his leather jacket squeaking loudly against the heavily polished wood. 'Giving you the heads up on something, that's all.'

Matt tried not to act impatient. 'Are you going to divulge this information then or not?' he said, reluctantly pouring Noel a glass from the expensive bottle of wine he'd bought.

Noel stared at the rich red liquid in the wine glass like it was cyanide. 'What the fuck is this?' he yelled.

'Keep your voice down!' Matt hissed. 'I'm trying to ensure we get left alone and it will be impossible if you carry on like this!'

Noel raised both his hands in sarcastic submission. 'Oooh, listen to him! Bringing the tone of the establishment down, am I?'

'Yes, you are actually, so just drink it!'

Pleased he'd garnered a reaction, Noel grinned. Picking up the wine glass with one meaty hand clamped around the delicate bowl, he downed it in one, coupled with a loud, slurping noise. 'Aaargh!' he cried. 'It's like bastard floor cleaner!'

Embarrassedly glancing around, Matt noticed several people looking in their direction. 'Seriously, pack it in! Just tell me what's going on.'

Bored with his game, Noel leant forward again. 'Hunter will be looking for you.'

Matt's eyebrows raised. 'For me?' He was genuinely surprised. He hadn't expected that. 'What for?' *Shit. Had he discovered Tori was setting him up? If so, he'd be well in the shit and it would completely blow his plan.*

This morning his father had been on his back yet again and he knew he didn't have much time to get moving. Whether he liked it or not, he was relying on Tori to sort this and she'd better not have screwed it up.

Oh God. She'd gone over the White Hart to see Sarah and said she'd have another crack at Hunter if she could. Had she blown her cover or dropped him in it? *Christ, he'd kill her if she had.*

'He wants to talk to you,' Noel continued, enjoying Matt's distinctly pale complexion. 'Is that a problem?'

'No! Not at all! Do you know what it's about?' Matt asked, regaining some composure. He didn't want to give Noel the satisfaction of knowing he was worried.

Noel grinned. 'Of course. He tells me everything! I am Vice President after all.' *And he'd very soon be President if this gimp helped him pull off what he needed to do to ensure that.*

'What's it about then and when did he mention this?' Matt glanced at his watch. He'd only got the call from Noel three-quarters of an hour ago and Tori had been gone nearly two and a half, which meant she'd had *more* than adequate time to fuck things up and drop him in it.

'Oh, he mentioned it this afternoon,' Noel said, beckoning the waiter over.

'What are you doing?' Matt cringed, panicking as the waiter made his way towards their table.

'I need a drink,' Noel said, smiling at the slim man who had approached.

'Yes, *Sir*?' the waiter said, attempting not to stare whilst Noel used the menu to pick some old food out of his teeth.

'Get us a beer, will you?'

'Beer?' the waiter questioned.

Noel slowly looked up and fixed the man with a manic stare. 'Yeah, beer. I take it you know what that is?'

'Yes, Sir. What sort would you like?'

Matt wrung his hands under the table. Surely the waiter knew that was not a suitable question to ask someone like this?

'What do you mean, 'what *sort*'? Any sort! I just want a beer. Anything's better than *that*!' Noel spat, nodding towards the expensive wine bottle.

'Yes, Sir.' The waiter then eyed Matt inquisitively. 'And *you*, Sir?'

'I'm fine, thank you. I'll be drinking *that*.' Matt also nodded towards the wine.

As the waiter rushed off, Noel grinned. 'You're actually quite funny sometimes, aren't you?'

'Not really,' Matt muttered. 'Now can we just get on with it?'

Sighing, Noel leaned back onto the table. 'Hunter's convinced there's something weird about the property company. He thinks the deals being offered are too good to be true. He knows you know the guy and your bank is involved, so he wants you to tell him the score.'

'Oh, for God's sake! You know as well as I do that when they've all accepted the 'double-your-money' deal, we wait until things start moving and then at last knockings when they're too far in to pull out, the offer will be changed to well *below* the market value. A sudden 'change in the economy' type of thing… Where do you think the massive cut we'll be taking will be coming from?' Matt griped.

He'd already explained this before. That's why Tori needed to convince Hunter to sell the Factory. Her job after that would be to make him talk to as many other reticent people as possible as it was such a 'good deal'. Had Noel not listened to a word he'd said?

'I *know* that, you fuckturd,' Noel spat. 'I just wanted to warn you so you were prepared and also to let you know I've suggested an idea to him, which, if he takes on board, will work well in our favour.'

Matt's eyebrows knitted together. *What could this knucklehead have possibly thought of that was better than his plan?* 'Oh, right and what's that?'

Noel grinned. *This ponce thought he was thick.* Well he wasn't half as dense as everyone presumed. *He* was fucking good and he would prove it. *This* would get him what he needed and he was going to damn well have it. 'I've suggested that Hunter plays *Tori.* That he uses her. Gets her to want him – which to be honest, I think she already does. That way he can get her to spill the beans.'

Sensing Matt's irritation, Noel held his hand up before he could interrupt. 'But of course, *you* will inform your darling fiancée of this change of plans and then – hey presto – you can tell her *exactly* what you want her to feed to him,' he smiled. 'If Hunter thinks he's playing *her*, then he'll believe what she's telling him is kosher.'

Matt swallowed his irrational anger about Noel's reference to Tori wanting Hunter. It wasn't like he *cared*. It was the principle. Christ! Her wanting someone like *him*! It didn't get much more insulting, but Noel had a point. A very good one actually, however much it pained him to admit it. Maybe the bozo wasn't quite as retarded as he looked.

Despite himself, a smile spread across his face. 'Do you know, I think you may well have something there,' Matt smiled.

Noel grinned. 'You must warn her before she plies him with anything or asks too many questions. We don't want him getting suspicious.'

Matt suddenly went cold. Bollocks. He'd been the one who had insisted Tori push as hard as she could to make headway with Hunter if she saw him tonight. 'Where is he now?'

Noel shrugged. 'No idea, but if he's out, he'll either be looking for you or in the White Hart.'

Matt sat up. 'Then you need to get over there. That's where Tori's gone!'

TWENTY FIVE

HUNTER LEANT HIS head against the cool tiles of the wall in the gent's toilets. He could do with a lot more pints than he'd restricted himself to tonight, but he'd had to ensure a clear head on the off-chance Tori showed up.

He walked back in to the tap room of the White Hart and took his seat at the table where he'd left his pint. He hadn't expected her to be here but *had* expected Sarah to be around and she wasn't either. Even Colin was absent and instead a woman who did occasional shifts for quite a few of the pubs was single-handedly manning the bar. When he'd first arrived he'd asked where Sarah and Colin were and had been told Colin was 'out' and Sarah was upstairs, unwell.

He could guess where Colin was. He'd mentioned the other day he was due to meet up with a mate who knew his stuff on legal things and was planning to pick his brains to find out if he and Sarah had any legal standing in the event that the brewery did decide to sell.

He knew they were worried about the prospects, but for him, things were different. He was astute enough to know most people were very tempted to sell, but if he was going to enforce that this did not happen, he had to be completely sure he was doing it for the right reasons. Just because *he* didn't want them to sell and break up the community and spoil his dealings wasn't, in his mind, solely a good enough reason to force their hand. Another example of how different he was compared to how Rafe would have handled this. Rafe would have gone for everyone with both barrels and manhandled them into doing whatever benefitted him and the club, *regardless* of whether it was detrimental to anyone else. He, however, didn't work like that.

Noel may not appreciate his way of thinking - always preferring the muck and bullets approach, but Hunter had had more than his fill of that. He enjoyed running the club and this town in a fair way – and it was *this* which garnered him the genuine respect he received, rather than false respect because people were scared, like they had been of Rafe. Admittedly, Hunter knew people were also scared of him – after all, they knew what he was capable of, but the difference was he would only dish that sort of stuff out if it was necessary, not just because he could.

He had to find out what was *really* behind these offers before he brought the strong arm down and he'd made the decision to do that any way he could.

Hunter frowned. He still felt uncomfortable with the plan that was now in place for a multitude of reasons. When Noel had approached him with the idea, his initial reaction was a resounding 'No'. He'd wanted to whack him in the face for even suggesting it, but the more Noel talked and the more he thought about it, whether he liked it or not, the idea was probably the only real way he'd know for sure that he was making the correct decision for the area.

It all seemed horribly unsavoury – working Tori for the sole intent of extracting information, but then again, he was unsure as to *why* this prospect irritated and disgusted him so much. The well-to-do wouldn't bat an eyelid doing something similar – in his opinion they *thrived* on such things, so why shouldn't he? Compared to things he'd done in the past, this didn't even figure.

It was hardly like it would be a chore to make Tori scream with pleasure and make her trust him enough to betray her fiancée. Considering he'd thought of doing nothing but that since he'd first seen her it didn't make sense. If he was brutally honest, he *wanted* to bed her. Plus, he genuinely wanted to know what was inside her head and save her from that jerk - not because it was fake and gained something he needed, but because he *wanted* to. Now, whether he wanted it was irrelevant because it was what he needed to do.

Hunter glanced at the barmaid eyeing him appreciatively like she had been all night and suddenly realised the rest of the bar was empty. He glanced at the clock on the wall – coming up to midnight.

He could really have done with seeing Sarah. He hadn't got time to wait for Tori to show her face over the next few weeks and he could hardly approach the posh pair of blokes. The whole point of the plan was to do this without them knowing the ulterior motive. He'd have a word with them anyway to see what lies he'd get fed, but Noel was right – Tori was the key to the truth.

Hunter knew they had a mutual connection. She felt it too and he needed to play to that. He scowled. If only he'd known this was on the cards before he'd virtually thrown her out the other night it could have been very different. It had been the perfect opportunity and if he'd fed her a few more drinks he reckoned he could have easily got somewhere with her, but that hadn't been an option. *Until now.*

Sarah, out of anyone might know where Tori lived and if he had her address, he could either turn up, or lurk around until she left the house. The barmaid was adamant Sarah had said under *no circumstances* was she to be disturbed by any visitors upstairs tonight and he'd been able to do nothing but respect that, despite the pressing need for information.

Hang on, maybe there was another way…

Getting off his chair, Hunter sauntered over to the bar

wearing his best smile. 'I'm sorry, sweetheart. I didn't realise it was so late. I've had a lot on my mind and didn't notice the time. I'll get out of your way now.'

The barmaid smiled. 'It's not a problem, Hunter. You're never in the way.'

Hunter inwardly grinned. *She'd be quite easy if the info was on hand.*

'Did you want another drink?' she purred.

'I'd better not. I really should get going. Another time maybe?' He leaned across the bar closer to the woman avidly drinking in every inch of him. 'Don't suppose you could do me a favour?'

'Me?' The girl twiddled her hair coquettishly. 'If I can, then I will.'

'Well, it's not so much for me, it's for Sarah. I need the address of a girl she works with. She asked me to deliver some kit for this woman who needs it for work, but I've lost the address she gave me,' he smiled. 'I really need to get it over to her otherwise she'll get in the shit, that's why I was asking if Sarah was about.' *Ok - total lies, but Sarah would understand eventually. Hopefully...*

The barmaid frowned. 'Oh, you should have said. I'm sure Sarah would have dealt with that. I tell you what, I'll go and see if she's still awake.'

Hunter grabbed the girl's arm as she made to go upstairs. 'Don't disturb her. Let her rest if she's ill. I think she keeps a diary behind the bar with addresses and stuff in. Could you have a look?'

The girl smiled widely, enjoying the feel of Hunter's fingers on her skin. 'Well, I suppose that would be ok being as she's asked you.'

'Thank you,' Hunter winked and leant casually against one of the bar stools as the barmaid fished the small book out from the side of the till.

'What's the girl's name?' she asked.

'Tori,' Hunter replied, the name almost sticking in his

throat as he impatiently watched the girl flick through the diary. 'Tori Morgan?'

'I can't see anything here, oh hang on – is this it? Funny spelling! T-O-R-I!,' she giggled.

Hunter forced a smile. 'Write it down for me, would you?'

The girl scribbled the address on a chewed-up scrap of paper and handed it to Hunter, her hand lingering longer than it needed as her fingers touched his.

'Thanks,' Hunter muttered, jumping to his feet. 'I'll be off then. Cheers for your help.'

'About that drink?'

'Yeah, another time,' Hunter said dismissively and quickly left the White Hart before the girl could say any more. He'd got one more thing he needed to do first.

• • • •

GEORGIE'S HEART LEAPT with gladness when she opened the door to find Hunter standing there. Ok, so it was just gone midnight and she was blitzed. She'd been snorting coke like no one's business the last few days and was so hyped she could barely control herself.

She clenched her teeth in an attempt to stop the incessant grinding. She knew she'd overdone it lately, but the more she'd taken, the harder the comedown and despite the promise to lay off it, the downers had been so severe she'd been left with no option but to shove more powder up her nose rather than spend the day curled up in bed sobbing from crushing desolation.

To help her keep her head above water shc'd had a few people over who were now laid haphazardly over the carpet in her sitting room, but it was hardly surprising. She'd needed to get her mind off Hunter's dismissal of her the other day. She hadn't seen him since that and had been beginning to think he was going to blank her for ever. She'd been wrong though because here he was.

Smiling widely, Georgie threw herself against Hunter's chest. 'Baby!' she cried. 'I've missed you so much!' She lifted her face up to his, her hands running through his hair. 'I *knew* you'd come back when you'd sorted your head out from whatever's been getting you down.'

Hunter gently extracted George from around him and held her at arms' length. 'Georgie, can we g…'

'Don't just stand on the doorstep, babe. Come in and shut the door,' Georgie interrupted, full of excitement. Grabbing Hunter by the hand she pulled him into the lounge. 'You'll have to excuse this lot. I've a few friends over.'

Hunter glanced in irritation at the various people spark out on the floor. He picked his way over them feeling the urge to crush their ribs into the carpet. He could tell Georgie was off her head and would struggle getting a word in edgeways with her like this, but he had to. He had no choice.

Knowing how the woman felt about him it was unfair not to nip this in the bud. He couldn't keep her hanging. *It had never been an issue before, but now…*

An image of Tori's face flashed into Hunter's mind. Regardless of what he wanted to happen or whether it ever did, this wasn't fair. Not that he'd ever made Georgie any promises. He'd always been honest - his heart was closed, but now… Now something had happened. He didn't know what, but he *did* know he respected Georgie too much to think of another woman as he bedded her and that's what had happened the last few times.

'Let me get you a beer,' Georgie chirped, making her way into the kitchen. 'Actually, let's get hammered. I haven't got much powder left, but I've enough for a few more lines each. That and a bottle of vodka and we'll be well away!' She smiled widely. 'It's great to see you.'

'Georgie…' Hunter said, sterner this time. 'I don't want a drink, I…'

Georgie swung around, one hand on his chest, the other pulling at his belt buckle. 'Ah, I see. I knew it! You've missed me and want to make up for it first! Let's go upstairs and th…'

'*Georgie!*' Hunter grabbed Georgie's hand. 'Listen to me!

I won't be staying.'

The sternness in Hunter's voice stopped Georgie in her tracks. 'W-What's going on?' she stammered.

A heavy sense of dread had hung around her from his recent lack of attention and although he'd always resumed his random relationship with her in the past, she didn't think he'd ever given her such a long period of inattention. Sure, Grin had attempted to allay her fears when she'd spoken to him about it. He, like everyone else, had said Hunter had a lot going on, but why had that suddenly changed? She'd been terrified he'd had enough of her but finding him at her door tonight had made her think everything was alright.

Closing the kitchen door to shut out the people on the carpet, Hunter sat Georgie down at the small table and held her hands. 'We need to stop whatever we've had together.'

Georgie stared at Hunter blankly. 'Whatever we've had? What's that supposed to mean? I *love* you, Hunter. You know that. What are you talking about?'

Swallowing her internal pain, she raised her eyes to the ceiling to stop the tears from falling. The thumping of the stereo from the living room was crashing through her head making her already over-wired brain even more on edge. She felt like ripping the plug out of the wall and screaming at all the people on her floor to go home, but she wouldn't. *She could still make this right.*

Looking back at Hunter, Georgie stared into his eyes. 'You must have had a bad day, honey. Let's just go to bed and you'll feel better in the morning.' *She had to turn this around, she just had to. She couldn't lose him. Not now. Not ever.*

'I'm sorry. That's not going to happen,' Hunter said, his voice low and clear.

Georgie's eyes narrowed. He couldn't bin her off like this. He *wouldn't* bin her off if she told him her news, but she couldn't – not like this. She needed him to genuinely want her, not because it was the right thing to do. 'Is there someone else?'

Hunter shook his head. 'No. There's no one else.' *Not yet, but he wanted there to be.* He wasn't going to say that though. He knew he was hurting Georgie and he in no way wanted to hurt her any more than he had to. 'My head's a mess and I can't see you anymore. I just want you to know that it's not you, it's me.'

He tilted Georgie's chin up with his fingertip. 'I'll always be here for you though. As a *friend*.'

Fat tears rolled down Georgie's face. *He meant it.* She'd been right all along. What would she do now? Her life was over without him. She pulled the remainder of the last wrap of coke from her pocket.

Hunter eyed the powder and stood up. 'I really am sorry, Georgie.'

'Can I at least have some more coke before you go? I'm going to need it,' she muttered in a small voice.

Hunter's jaw set in a hard line. 'You don't need it at all. You should knock that shit on the head. You're taking too much of it. *Far* too much.'

And I'm probably going to take a lot more now, Georgie thought. 'Is that the reason you don't want to be with me anymore? Because of the drugs?'

'No, it's not. As I said, it's me.' Shaking his head with despair, Hunter quietly walked from the kitchen and out of Georgie's house.

· · · ·

TORI REGRETTED THE amount of gin she'd drank at Sarah's. Her head was still spinning even though she'd walked home rather than take a taxi in the hope the cold night air would clear her drunkenness. She may as well have taken the cab and saved her feet for all the good it had done.

The only upside of all of this was that her mother wasn't in. She'd lost track of the days and it must be one of her mother's regular Bridge nights so she wouldn't be back until the small hours, if at all. She'd be far too busy quaffing champagne and gossiping for as long as possible.

Tori sat at her bureau and stared vacantly at the neatly stacked paper and matching envelopes contained in one side of it. At least she'd smoothed things over with Sarah and now understood what was eating her. Not that it made any difference, but she *would* be asking Matt why he hadn't told her just how many places were involved in his plans.

Tori opened the bottom drawer of her bureau and stared at the shoebox. She'd been meaning to look through that for *weeks*, but she'd been so distracted with everything else. It wasn't just that though - there was still a big part of her which was nervous about memories of her father resurfacing and what the box might contain. Even though it was such a long time ago, his loss stung as sharply now as it always had and she didn't want anything to ruin her good memories.

Due to the confidence boost of the gin, Tori reached down to pull the shoebox from where she'd placed it, but the sound of the front doorbell made her stop in her tracks. *Had her mother forgotten her key? Now wouldn't that be hilarious!*

Getting up from the desk and walking rather unsteadily along the long landing to the stairs, Tori smiled. She could just imagine the pained, slapped look of horror on her mother's over-painted face having to ring her own doorbell to get access to her own house.

Halfway down the stairs the doorbell rang again. 'Ok, ok!' Tori muttered impatiently. Approaching the large front door, she frowned seeing a silhouette through the stained and frosted glass. *That wasn't her mother...*

A bubble of fear simmered. It was well past midnight and if it wasn't her mother, then who the hell was it? It didn't look like Matt.

Unwilling to open the door, Tori stood close. 'Who is it?'
'Tori?'

Tori froze. *She recognised that voice. The voice that made every hair on her neck stand up.* 'Hunter? Is that you?'

'Yes, it's me. Let me in.' His deep gravelly voice resonated through the glass.

Tori trembled. Not out of fear, but from confusion and anticipation. *What the hell should she do? How could she let him in? What did he want?*

'Tori?' Hunter said once more. 'Let me in, will you?'

Gingerly, Tori unlocked the door and opened it slightly. Through the crack she looked up into Hunter's face, the sight of this man literally taking her breath away. Standing like a man-mountain, his blond hair was loose instead of tied in his customary ponytail and the moon silhouetted his large frame perfectly, only part of his rugged face was illuminated.

'W-What are you doing here?' Tori stuttered, wanting to kick herself for sounding like a moron.

'Just let me in,' Hunter hissed, placing his steel toecap in the gap of the door. He hadn't got time for game-playing. He'd had enough drama for one night and needed to get off this doorstep.

This was more than an affluent neighbourhood. Even though it was dark, there was no mistaking the large houses on this leafy avenue nicely set back from the road behind long drives gated by wrought iron gold-tipped railings. He'd left his motorbike further down the road so as not to draw attention by parking directly outside the house itself, but he still didn't want to be seen hanging around.

His gaze locked on Tori's. The blue of her eyes was clear even in the dim light. His heart sped up with her utter beauty. *Maybe she wasn't on her own? Maybe Matt was here? That was it. That was now his reason for being here.*

'Is Matt here?' Hunter asked, levering his boot so it opened the door a little further. He needed to get in the house. *He wouldn't get anywhere at this rate.*

'Matt?' Tori failed to hide the disappointment in her voice. 'I'd kind of guessed you weren't here for me.' She silently reprimanded herself for sounding like a pedantic child.

'I need to speak to him. It's important!'

Tori could see the resolve in Hunter's steely eyes and felt another immediate rush to her core. The man definitely had something about him that did strange things to her. She could sense he would not give up and go away however much she stood her ground. Realising she may as well let him in caused her to tremble even more with the thought of being alone with him.

'Hurry up then,' Tori muttered, opening the door fully.

Hunter stepped over the threshold and stood in the large square hallway lit only by a small lamp sitting on an occasional table. His eyes ran over Tori, seeing she wore only a satin negligee which skimmed gracefully and oh, so tantalisingly over her body.

Feeling his eyes undressing her, Tori blushed and wished she'd pulled on her robe. She felt even more exposed in his presence than usual. 'I-I was just about to go to bed,' she said in a futile attempt to explain her lack of clothes.

Hunter smiled softly, forcing himself not to brush the curl of hair away which had fallen across her face. 'I don't mind if you don't!'

Feeling even more flustered, Tori had no idea what to do. *Should she offer the man a drink?* She reminded herself he was looking for Matt, so whatever he had to say wouldn't take long. 'I'm not sure what you want me to say being as Matt's not here. He doesn't live here.'

'I gathered that. I didn't have his address, so I came here and thought you may be able to help.' *I want to kiss you*, Hunter thought, his eyes drawn to Tori's full lips.

'Who gave you my address?'

Hunter brushed his long hair away from his eyes. 'Does it matter? It's not difficult to find someone if you want to.'

'Is that so,' Tori breathed, feeling reckless as she took a small step further toward him, pulled by an invisible magnet.

'Tori,' Hunter said softly, his hand moving towards her face. *I'm going to have to kiss her. I need to kiss her. I'll ask questions later.*

Drunk on both gin and lust, Tori knew there was no point fighting it anymore. Her lips parted slightly, her face raising towards his.

The beep of a car horn and slamming door stopped her in her tracks. *Shit. Shit. SHIT. Was that her mother?*

Hunter looked confused when Tori suddenly dashed to the left and peered out of a small window in an adjoining room.

Tori spotted her mother slowly tottering up the driveway in her ridiculously high heels. By the look of her she'd had her fill of champagne but wasn't drunk enough not to notice a six foot four, long-haired biker standing in her hallway. She rushed back out to the hallway. 'Quick! It's my mother!'

Tori grabbed Hunter's hand and belted up the staircase. Besides being confused, he was on the verge of laughing. *Was he really running away from somebody's mother?*

TWENTY SIX

TORI PULLED HUNTER into her bedroom and shut the door behind her. She leant up against it, breathing heavily from the exertion and found a large smile breaking across her face with the absurdity of the situation.

She looked up at Hunter standing in front of her, perplexed. His leather jacket was slightly askew from where she'd dragged him and a giggle escaped from her lips. Whatever she had just done was ridiculous, but also amusing. For the first time in a very long time she felt alive.

Adrenalin pounded through her body. Her mother wouldn't come up here now - she never did. She'd go straight to bed, full of champagne. The problem was that left her alone in her bedroom with the most beautiful specimen of a man she'd ever seen. One which set both her body and mind on fire. This longing she'd experienced since the first time she'd set eyes on him, heightened.

A frown flickered across Tori's face. This was dangerous. Thanks to the gin she was being unusually brave, but if she didn't get this man out of her house right *now*, something would happen. Her body shook. She couldn't do this, but so wanted to. *Really wanted to.*

Unable to resist the pull, Tori raised her eyes to meet Hunter's, knowing when she locked eyes with him she'd be unable to stop the force he exerted over her.

'What's going on?' Hunter said, his voice low. 'Did that just happen?' Despite himself, he couldn't help but smile. 'I'm thirty years old, yet I've just been dragged upstairs to a strange woman's bedroom to avoid her mother!'

Tori suddenly felt horribly embarrassed and her confidence deflated. He was right. It was ridiculous and extremely immature. She lived and acted like a teenager. Grown women didn't behave like this. They were in *control* of their lives – unlike her, who had no choice and little say in anything.

Her smile fell. There was no longer anything amusing about this farcical situation. 'You don't know my mother,' was all she could manage to mutter.

Hunter had enjoyed the amusement on Tori's face. It was like a refreshing slap to his brain. It had been a long time since he had experienced any form of joy and he'd liked it. He liked *her*. No, he *more* than liked her. It was something... something he couldn't explain...

His eyes roamed over Tori's body, her satin negligee hanging from one shoulder. The outline of her nipples through the thin silky material made the throbbing in his groin increase. *Fuck it*. Regardless of what his plan had been when he'd made the trip to her house, all he could now think of was to be with this woman.

'No, I don't know your mother and I don't know *you*,' he said, his eyes drowning in the blue pools of Tori's gaze. He moved towards her. 'But I'm *going* to know you...'

Tori drew in a sharp intake of breath when Hunter placed his hand softly on her face and tilted it up to his. When his mouth came down on hers, she nearly passed out with the overwhelming rush that shot from her mouth through her entire body. Almost frozen with both fear and need, she remained stock still, her arms stuck down by her side.

Hunter placed his other hand at the small of Tori's back and gently pulled her towards him. *Her lips tasted of peaches*. When he felt her stance relax, her soft lips parting and her arms wrap around his neck, he knew that despite his frantic need he would have to take this slow. He would have to be gentle and for once in his life, he was good with that.

Tori clung on to Hunter's thick neck and with his tongue flicking against her lips, she succumbed, allowing him to explore her mouth. She could feel the hard outline of his manhood against her stomach and the unfamiliar achy beating in her core increased.

An involuntary moan escaped from her mouth and she moved one of her hands into the back of Hunter's long tousled hair. Even through the haze of gin, Tori felt horribly self-conscious – well aware she had little experience and thanks to Matt, what she did have had been thoroughly unenjoyable. This man, this *gorgeous* man would find her a laughing stock, like everyone else, and she couldn't face the humiliation. She would only disappoint him and she didn't want to.

Quickly making the decision that she should immediately stop, she was about to pull away when his mouth left her lips and traced down her neck, leaving tiny butterfly kisses along her throat. How could a man such as this, who did the sort of things she knew he must do, be so gentle? How could his touch be so soft? This gentleness took her breath away and despite her reticence and embarrassment, she was powerless to stop her intense urge. *She needed him.*

Hunter could feel Tori's resistance. 'Tori?' he murmured against the sweet skin of her neck. 'Do you not want this?' He hoped to God he hadn't misread the situation and put his lust before reality. He'd never wanted anyone like this before and the thought of not being able to experience this beautiful creature in his arms horrified him in ways he could not comprehend. The intensity of his need was not normal. He'd always been very much in control and now he was losing it. He could drown in this woman. 'Tori?'

Tori threw her head back as Hunter's tongue traced along

her collarbone and fissions of electric surged from places she didn't know existed. She couldn't stop now even if she wanted to. *And she didn't want to.* 'Don't stop,' she gasped.

Aware she'd never instigated anything before, Tori pushed Hunter's leather jacket from his shoulders, her fingers running over the rock-hard muscles underneath.

Releasing her momentarily, Hunter allowed his jacket to drop to the floor, then swept Tori up in his arms and carried her over to her bed, laying her down gently.

Tori quivered in anticipation as she looked up at the man who had just deposited her as if she was a feather. Her eyes drank in his fine physique outlined through the tight black T-shirt and she couldn't stop her eyes from trailing lower to the tell-tale bulge in his jeans.

Hunter rested on the bed with one knee, the other leg stabilising him on the floor. His eyes not leaving Tori's, he slowly pulled the thin straps of her negligee down exposing her pert breasts. His breath hitched as his thick finger lightly circled one of her nipples. 'You're so beautiful,' he murmured.

Tori moaned with pleasure as the soft bristles of Hunter's beard traced across her soft skin and his mouth covered her nipple, licking and sucking it in a way that made her quiver. Her mind was spinning. Matt had never made her feel like this. Never made her feel – well, she didn't quite know how to describe it.

Resting to one side, Hunter raised himself up onto his elbow and looked down at Tori. His finger traced across her bottom lip as she lay with her eyes closed, her nipples erect with need. He had to free his painful erection from the confines of his jeans before he exploded. Deciding now was the time to take this further – a *lot* further, he began slowly pulling her negligee over her hips.

'I-I...' Tori gasped, her eyes shooting open whilst nervously raising her hips to allow the flimsy material to be slipped down her legs.

Hunter groaned as the rest of Tori's body was revealed. Her

white lace knickers tantalisingly covered the part he needed to lose himself in. 'God, Tori…' He pushed himself off the bed, hastily pulled his T-shirt over his head.

Tori stared at Hunter shaking his tousled hair out, his wide muscular chest covered with tattoos. She watched with desire as he unbuckled the thick black belt around his hips and her already drenched knickers became even more soaked. She could hardly breathe when his jeans slipped to the floor and realising he went commando as his huge heavily veined cock sprung up to slap against his muscled abdomen, her eyes widened.

Hunter moved back to the bed. As a first for him he was trembling with the need to possess this woman. He knew she was watching him and could see her nervousness, so he'd take it gentle. Besides, he wanted to explore every single inch of her body.

Kneeling, he slowly pulled Tori's knickers over the ends of her feet and tossed them to the floor. Watching her press her thighs together in an attempt to conceal herself, Hunter smiled. 'Don't hide, I want to see you.'

Hunter placed his hand on Tori's flat stomach and brought his lips down, tracing a line of light kisses over her belly.

Feeling Hunter's tongue draw lower, Tori stiffened. *Oh my God, he's going down there. He can't do that.* No one had ever done that. Matt certainly hadn't. In fact, he'd never tried – not that she'd wanted him to, but despite her misgivings, she found herself parting her legs when Hunter's mouth reached the top of her thighs.

Feeling an overwhelming urge to grab Hunter's head and pull him towards her centre, Tori cringed. She wasn't like this. She didn't do things like *this*, but she was unable to control the unfamiliar lust raging through her.

Hunter pushed Tori's thighs further apart with his arm. He'd show her why she shouldn't be nervous. Plunging his mouth down, he closed it around her clitoris.

'Ohhh my God!' Tori squealed with both shock and

pleasure as Hunter's mouth sucked and licked, his swirling tongue causing strong sensations to pulse.

With one hand gently gripping Tori's hip, Hunter raised his head and slipped one finger into her, pushing gently against her inner wall, his thumb circling her hard nub. Hearing her moans and aware she was pushing upwards against his fingers, Hunter smiled. *She was ready.*

Tori realised she had little choice but to allow her body to do what it needed to do. She could hear herself moaning and she arched her back, uncaring of what she looked like as a strange heightened pleasure slowly built. She had no idea what was happening, but it felt good. So, *so* good and she wanted more.

Hunter watched Tori writhe, easily accepting his second finger and his cock jerked in response. *Christ, he'd have to take her soon. Real soon.*

When Hunter moved his hand away Tori opened her eyes and discovered he'd positioned himself between her shaking thighs. She ran her hand over his rugged face, her need raw. 'Don't stop…' she panted. 'I want… I…'

Before she could say another word, he brought his mouth down on hers, his tongue exploring, his kisses urgent. Feeling the huge head of his throbbing cock at her entrance, Tori lifted her hips.

Easing himself slowly into her, Hunter groaned into Tori's mouth. He had to keep a handle on his lust, he really did, otherwise he'd rip her in two and the *last* thing he wanted to do was to hurt this beautiful woman.

Grasping his muscular buttocks with one hand, Tori ran the other over the ridges of Hunter's back. *She wanted all of him.* 'Hunter…' she gasped.

Taking the hint, Hunter slowly pushed deeper and deeper. 'You ok?'

'Mmm,' Tori gasped as he stretched her, filling her.

Getting the green light, fully seated and feeling her wrapped around him like a perfectly fitting glove, Hunter began to move.

Thrusting slowly, he stared at Tori. Her eyes opened, connecting with his and he felt a jolt so strong it almost derailed him. He didn't say a word – he couldn't. It was the most intense experience he'd ever had. *It was odd, but oh so fucking good.*

Pumping harder, Hunter growled to himself in an effort to keep a lid on the fast-rising sensations. He didn't want this to be over for a very long time. He wanted to see this woman break apart when he made her come.

Tori was hypnotised by the metal grey depths of Hunter's hard eyes. She felt shocked by her seeming inability to control her body. Her legs were shaking, her breasts tingling, her nipples rigid aching points and the building strangeness rising from deep inside was all consuming.

Hunter's pelvis was grinding deliciously against her and with each thrust, his cock rubbed against somewhere inside that made her want to spread her legs further, to pull him deeper, deeper, *deeper*. The strong, throbbing, beating was becoming more intense and it was making her feel high, like she was rising up and up. *What was happening?*

Tori panted in erratic gasps, aware she was making rhythmic moaning sounds which were getting louder, but she couldn't stop. Her hand dropped from Hunter's back and began grasping at the cotton sheets. Closing her eyes, she arched her back.

Seeing the signs, Hunter thrust faster. 'Let yourself go. Come for me,' he groaned.

Unable to respond or do anything other than thrash her head from side to side, Tori felt the intensity getting higher and higher, higher and *higher*. 'Ohhhhh!' she screamed.

Hunter crashed his mouth down onto hers, partly to muffle her screams and partly because he needed to taste her and feel her velvet lips on his again.

The intensity within Tori rose to an almost unbearable point of unknown and Hunter's tongue working inside her mouth only heightened the feeling. Colours flashing in her minds' eye, she could no longer breathe as her body stiffened and her climax peaked, breaking with an indescribable rush of pleasure of which she had had no idea existed.

Panting and groaning into Hunter's mouth, the feeling ran for what seemed like hours before it began diminishing.

The clenching of Tori's walls around him made Hunter satisfied she had well and truly reached her peak, possibly for the first time and he decided to take her up again before he was finished. *If he had time.*

Tori gasped as Hunter slowly resumed his thrusting. 'Ohhh, I need...'

'Tori, you need this. You need me...' Pulling her arms above her head, Hunter resumed his grinding, driving pace. Keeping his eyes locked on hers, seeing her combined shock and pleasure as he ramped up his speed, he braced himself for release.

Just when she'd truly believed she was fit to drop, Tori felt her insides kick back to life and the waves immediately began to roll – this time a lot quicker.

Pushing back on to his haunches, Hunter pulled Tori with him. Grabbing her hips with his strong arms, he held her close and lifted her body with his thrusts.

Tori's legs wrapped tight around Hunter's hips of their own accord and her arms moved around the back of his neck. With each incessant thrust she felt herself draw closer and closer to that same feeling of abandonment.

'Kiss me, Tori. Kiss me...' Hunter growled, his mouth searching for hers. He was going to come any second. Running his hand down her slender back he pulled her hard against him.

'Ohhh!' Tori cried, feeling herself building fast.

'Come, baby. I'm almost there,' Hunter panted, pushing her backwards again. He needed it faster. *Harder.*

He clenched his jaw, pounding relentlessly into her soft flesh. Her legs jerked as she grasped at his hair and with a muffled scream, she came hard for the second time, followed by Hunter unloading into her with a guttural roar.

Beads of sweat dripped from Hunter's brow onto Tori's

face as his rush diminished. He moved his weight to lean on one elbow and brushed her damp hair from her face, stroking her cheek as she lay limply beneath him.

Tori tried to regulate her breathing and attempt to make sense of what had just happened. She didn't dare open her eyes. That had been categorically the most amazing experience she'd ever had and she felt like crying, both with confusion and pleasure.

'Are you ok?' Hunter whispered, his full lips brushing hers. He didn't know what to do now. What he'd just experienced, he'd never experienced before. Oh sure, he'd had some cracking sessions in the past, but he'd never had anything which had made him feel... *Made him feel what? What did he feel?* He frowned. *He didn't know. Christ, this was weird. Too bloody weird.*

Tori wanted to bury her face in his chest. Beg him to make her feel like that again. *She was ok. More than ok but confused.* The reality of the situation hit home. *She'd just slept with one of her arch-nemeses and she was engaged to be married.*

Hunter could see Tori's conflicting emotions and tried not to let his hurt show. He'd promised himself a long time ago that he wouldn't let *anything* hurt him again. Had she not experienced what he had? That connection? He knew it made no sense, but it was there. 'You want me to leave?'

Receiving no answer, he decided rather than wait, he'd make the choice for her. He jumped from the bed and pulled on his jeans, failing to hide the bitterness in his voice. 'I'll leave you to it. Wouldn't want anyone to find out, would we?'

Refraining from reaching out and grabbing him and begging him not leave, Tori swallowed the lump in her throat and silently watched as Hunter stepped out of the room and closed the bedroom door behind him.

TWENTY SEVEN

NOEL THOUGHT HE'D done well keeping his temper for so long. It had only been after half an hour of listening to Dave Griffin 'um' and 'ah' about everything that he'd lost his rag.

Actually, it had been more to do with being sick to the back teeth of Griffin telling him he wanted to hear what Hunter's advice was before making a final decision. *Why did everything have to be about Hunter?*

Hunter was screwing things up left, right and centre. If it wasn't for his stupid moral high ground, then the entire club would benefit, but oh no, he wanted to do things his way.

Noel gnashed his teeth. He hadn't meant to lose his temper with Griffin. It wasn't like he'd walked into the shop *planning* on staving the man's head in was it? No it wasn't, so it was hardly his fault.

'The man's in hospital,' Hunter spat, his anger raw. 'Do you really think attacking one of the community will help this club?' He had hardly been able to believe it when word had reached him this morning and the talk surrounding the situation was that the Reapers were taking revenge on anyone dallying over selling.

'If everyone thinks we want them to sell before we know

what's going on, then what chance will we have to keep this community together *regardless* of what I discover?' Hunter raged. Not that he was any closer to finding anything out. *He was even less likely to find anything out now, thanks to what occurred between him and Tori.*

Just the thought of that woman caused his cock to twitch. He angrily dismissed it. What had happened had been utterly stupid. How could he have been so remiss to let his lust impede business dealings or what he needed to do to ensure a good outcome? *Because he hadn't been able to help it, that's why.*

Now Noel had single-handedly made things even *more* difficult. Irritated beyond all comprehension, he fixed his glare on his second in command. 'Are you even taking this on board?' he roared. The man seemed more interested with sifting through bags of a new shipment of gear. 'Griffin's saying you threatened him into selling? What the fuck's that all about?'

Noel looked up from the large carrier bag of coke, ensuring he wore a hard-done-by expression. 'Well that shows you how fucking tapped the bloke is, doesn't it? I said nothing of the sort! I only went into his shop for a packet of fags. I didn't go there to discuss anything about any of this property bollocks. What the fuck do I know about any of that?'

He raised his hands theatrically. *That sounded convincing.* It was true. Well, *partly.* He *had* gone into the newsagents to buy some fags, but thought whilst he was there he may as well take the opportunity to see what Griffin's thoughts were and see if he could 'convince' him, friendly-like, to see reason.

'Besides,' Noel continued. 'I'd hardly threaten the guy into selling, not when you don't know whether the deal's kosher!' *Yes, he had. He wanted the bloody cash Matt had promised him and needed to get this shit moving.*

Hunter studied Noel. 'But why batter him?'

Noel rolled his eyes. 'Do you really think that was purposeful? The prick gave me no choice. He got it into his head that I was pushing him for a decision and was getting arsy. It was only when he whipped the baseball bat from under the counter did I realise I had to do something.'

Hunter frowned. That was fair enough. Noel would have had little choice in that sort of situation, but it was strange. Dave Griffin was probably one of the least likely people he would have expected to kick off. Especially at a Reaper.

Noel had already pre-emptied the conclusion Hunter was most likely to come to, so he'd previously formulated an answer. 'I think he's losing it. Only the other week the guy from the chippy moaned Griffin tried to charge him twice for the slate he'd racked up. He'd already paid if off the week before, then his wife mentioned something about early-onset dementia. It's all a bit sad really.'

'Either way I'll have to go and see Griffin to sort this out and smooth things over.'

Noel didn't want that. He *really* didn't want that. 'I don't think you should. *I'll* go and see him. After all, it's me who did the damage, so it should be me who puts it right,' he smiled. 'I'll also put the record straight around town regarding the sell-don't sell confusion.' *Like hell he would...*

Sensing Hunter's reticence, Noel knew he needed to keep a handle on it while he could. 'I am your second, Hunter. Don't waste time doing something I can do, especially when you need to get answers on this deal.'

Hunter knew that was true. He did need to sort it out. He knew everyone was waiting for him to find out the honesty of the transaction and now Noel had managed, whether it was his fault or not, to cast doubt as to his reasoning, it was even more urgent he got the information.

Sensing Hunter was veering towards letting him sort it out, Noel thought it wise to change the subject to the other relevant subject. Last night Matt had said Tori was at the White Hart, so after he'd left the wine bar he'd sped over there. He'd made sure he hadn't been seen. Hunter had been in the bar, but there was no sign of that woman, so at least she couldn't have ballsed it up before Matt had got chance to fill her in on the latest changes to the plan. Being as he hadn't heard anything different, he presumed that was still the case.

'Have you caught up with that ponce, Matt yet?' Noel asked.

Hunter shook his head. 'He wasn't in the White Hart and there was no one there who had any inkling as to where he lives. I mean, why would they? I did manage to get Tori's address though.' He kept his voice level. The last thing he wanted was Noel discovering he'd humiliated himself and let the side down by fucking the Ice Queen.

'Oh yeah? Have you been round there?' Noel hoped the slight squeak of panic wasn't detectable.

Hunter nodded. 'Yes, but she wasn't in. No one was,' he lied. He couldn't admit to anyone what had happened. Tori had made her feelings clear and thankfully doubted whether she'd be making their indiscretion publicly known either. She couldn't have been more embarrassed, that much had been obvious.

Noel breathed an inward sigh of relief and acted nonchalant. 'Probably a good job. Miss Aristocrat would have called the fucking cops if she'd been in.'

Or she could have laid underneath me, making me feel something I thought I wasn't capable of, whilst I'd made her come so hard she'd almost passed out, Hunter thought, his cock swelling once more with the image of Tori writhing underneath him ingrained in his mind.

Noel studied Hunter curiously. 'Are you alright?' *What was eating him?* Because that bird hadn't been in, he'd got his knickers in a twist? Surely the big man couldn't *really* be hung up on that snotty woman?

Hunter was snapped from his inopportune thoughts. 'What? Yeah, I'm fine.'

'I've arranged to see Matt later on as it happens,' Noel nodded towards the carrier bag. 'Another order of coke. Come along to that?' He grinned. He was doing well on coke where that yuppie was concerned. Any orders for Matt, he cut the normal stuff with everything available to triple its volume so it would be useless for normal resale, but *perfect* for passing on to them.

Hunter nodded. 'Ok I'll come with you and catch him on the hop. Me turning up is the *last* thing he'll expect.'

Noel smiled. *Unlikely. He's more than expecting you.* 'Meeting's at six.'

· · · ·

'ARE YOU FEELING any better about everything today?' Tori asked Sarah as they ate their lunch in the small break room.

They'd both been snowed under all morning so there had been no opportunity to talk until now, which had luckily given Tori a good few hours to think of answers to anything Sarah might ask that wouldn't give anything away. Not that any amount of additional hours would help. As it was, she'd been up half the night staring silently at the ceiling trying to make sense of what had happened.

How she would love to tell Sarah what had gone on with Hunter. She'd know what to do, or if not, at least give her an idea as to how the hell she should handle it. She'd already got Matt on her back. He'd called informing her he'd be picking her up straight from work. Something important which involved meeting Noel.

There had been little point expressing how much she didn't want to be anywhere *near* that man. Matt already knew how she felt, so it wouldn't have made a blind bit of difference if she'd repeated it. What Matt wanted, Matt got.

At first she'd worried he'd discovered what had occurred, but then reminded herself that he'd previously made it clear that if she had to take things further with Hunter to make his plan work, then that was what she'd have to do, so he could hardly complain. Except what had happened had been absolutely *nothing* to do with any plan. What had happened with Hunter had been what she'd *wanted*.

Tori felt a flush creeping up her chest. It was true. Regardless of the confusion between her deep-seated feelings for his type she'd always wanted to know what it would be like to feel his hands on her. *Now she did.*

It had been nothing like she'd imagined. In fact, she hadn't known *what* to imagine. What exactly did she have to base it on? Her experience of sex with Matt had always made her feel ugly, dirty and useless. Having only ever had this view that sex was boring and unenjoyable, she was intrigued that Hunter, by his proximity alone could ignite a strange desire in her. Desire was alien, but she hadn't in her wildest dreams comprehended what it would have been like in reality.

Despite her intention not to let her mind linger on what Hunter's hands and body had done, she felt the now familiar dampness seep into her knickers. Her nipples hardened, the lace of her bra moving against the heightened flesh making her even more uncomfortable. She squirmed in her chair and squeezed her thighs together in an attempt to quell the throbbing between her legs. *Dear God, what was the matter with her?*

Tori sighed. The matter was that Hunter had taken her to a place she hadn't wanted to return from. She'd been on fire with need for the man and this had not abated, which frightened her. It wasn't just the physical effect which frightened her, although that had been mind-blowing enough. It was the deep connection. Her soul had opened to let him in and now she couldn't get him out. She'd never felt like this about anyone and it was disabling her ability to function. How could she have allowed herself to sleep with someone like that? *Someone that…*

He'd been so gentle. So attentive. So *experienced…*

A pang of jealously flowed over her as she wondered how many women the man had been with to know so much about their bodies? How many women had he screwed senseless and then walked away from? *Like he had done to her.*

Her cheeks burned with humiliation. He hadn't been able to wait to get away from her. He couldn't have put his clothes on and gone out the door much quicker! *God, she'd been a fool. A complete fool.*

Now Matt was expecting her to still play to Hunter to get him on side. How could she do that now? How could she humiliate herself again? He'd had what he wanted and judging by his quick departure, it wasn't something he wanted to repeat. Matt's ploy of playing to Hunter's cock wouldn't work and he'd been stupid in thinking someone as inexperienced as her could possibly hold the interest of a man like that.

At least he'd got out of the house without any problems, so that was one less thing she had to deal with. She couldn't imagine what her mother would have said if she hadn't been flat out in bed and heard her daughter screaming like a banshee whilst a big, dirty biker brought her to a mind-numbing orgasm, not once, but *twice* in quick succession.

Tori reddened deeper. *Oh dear God, how embarrassing was she? Howling and panting like a dog. No wonder he couldn't wait to leave.*

'Did you hear what I said?' Sarah jolted Tori from her thoughts. 'I answered your question ages ago and you just sat there with a funny look on your face. It looks like *I'm* the one who should be asking *you* if everything's alright, rather than the other way around.'

Tori forced a smile. 'Perhaps I won't have such large measures of gin at yours next time!' If she hadn't been feeling the effects of that spirit she was sure she'd never have opened the door to the man. *Almost sure…*

Sarah grinned. 'To repeat what I said, being as you were clearly on another planet, yes I do feel a bit better. Well, not *better*, but perhaps a little more rational.'

Tori smiled. 'Good. I'm glad about that.'

'Although…' Sarah continued. 'I heard one of the Reapers put Dave Griffin in hospital. A threat to make him sell his property apparently.'

Tori shuddered. *See? This is what they did. Threaten and bash people who didn't do what they wanted. That, or just kill them… And now she'd slept with one of them…*

'I know, it's horrible isn't it? Dave's a lovely man. He's run that newsagents for years, but now he's got a fractured skull and is in a pretty bad way. It's strange though… Hunter wasn't for selling.'

Suddenly irritated by Hunter's name cropping up into the conversation like it invariably seemed to do *regardless* of who was talking, Tori placed her mug of tea down angrily on the table. 'Who knows what that lot want?' she snapped. 'Whatever suits them, I suppose.'

Sarah frowned. 'I don't know whether it's true. It sounds out of character to me. Griffin pays them, so why would they turn on him?'

Tori knew if she didn't stop this conversation she was likely to snap and bite Sarah's head off again, which she didn't want. They'd only just put things right between them.

Gathering her lunch box, she stood up. 'I'd best get back to work. Matt's picking me up tonight, so I need to make sure I've finished everything.'

Nodding, Sarah watched Tori hurriedly leave the break room. Something had needled her, but she had no idea what.

Twenty Eight

'I'M GLAD I CAUGHT you before you bumped into that bonehead,' Matt said, squeezing Tori's hand as she got into the passenger seat of his Porsche.

Tori eyed Matt suspiciously. He was being unusually nice and that never came without a very good reason – usually one she would not like. It was bad enough she was being dragged along to see Noel, but Matt being pleasant on top of that disturbed her even more.

'And why's that? I thought it was imperative I hurried your plan along?' Tori said acidly.

'That's the point,' Matt said, taking his eyes off the road momentarily to glance at her. 'That's why I said it was important. There's been a change of plan and I need to let you know before you see Hunter again.'

I won't be seeing him again if I've got anything to do with it, Tori thought dejectedly. With any luck, from what Matt had just said, it sounded like the whole thing may be off. She dearly hoped so. 'Oh, so what's happened?'

Matt grinned viciously. 'Last night I saw Noel. I met him at that wine bar we like.'

The one you like, you mean, Tori thought. She didn't like

the wine bars they'd been to. Correction – she didn't like *any* wine bars *or* going anywhere with Matt – end of story. 'You took Noel to a *wine bar*?'

'Long story and not a good one,' Matt grimaced. 'But the outcome is that he's convinced Hunter to do half the work for us. Now his aim is to try and get you on side.'

Tori nearly choked. '*Me*? What do I know?'

Matt shook his head. 'Thankfully, that point is irrelevant. Hunter's convinced the property deals aren't the real thing, so Noel suggested he work you so that *you* dish the dirt on *me*!' He grinned. 'Don't you see? It's brilliant! If he thinks you trust him and believes you feel something for him, he'll take the crap you feed him – which of course will be all the stuff we *want* you to say.'

Tori felt winded. Suddenly it all made sense. *That* was why Hunter had turned up last night with the bullshit that he was looking for Matt. *Oh for God's sake! How could she have been so stupid?* He'd even used the same excuse as she had to explain her presence at the Factory, yet she'd been so blind she hadn't noticed. *And she'd played right into his hands.*

Matt frowned at Tori's expression. 'What's the matter? It's a great idea and will back up what we're doing. We'll play the overgrown piece of shit back at his own game and he won't even realise until it's too late. The fucking idiot will think he's clever by believing he's getting one over on me, when really one of his own crew is setting him up.'

Tori looked up. 'What do you mean 'setting him up'? And why would Noel help you? It's quite clear they all hate us.'

Matt laughed and squeezed Tori's thigh. 'Oh, you really are a sad little innocent, aren't you? Noel and his lot might hate us and what we represent, but they don't hate us enough not to take our money when it's offered.'

'M-Money?'

'Yes, *money*. Hunter's time is numbered. Noel wants what he believes is his rightful place, which is that *he* should be running the Reapers. Do you know Hunter actually wants to find out if the deal everyone is being offered is the business? Apparently, every fucker in this town hangs off that idiot's word as to what to do for the best.'

Tori frowned. 'It *is* the right thing to do though, isn't it? I heard people are getting really good deals from these offers.'

Matt's eyes narrowed. 'Where did you hear that?'

'Something Sarah said.' As the words left her mouth Tori realised her mistake.

'You haven't told her anything, have you?' Matt asked sharply.

'All I said was that it sounded like a great offer. I might add you could have told me you were involved with trying to buy the pub and all those other places.'

Matt smiled. 'Why is that relevant? Good girl, though. You're learning. *Finally!*'

Tori studied Matt's conniving expression. *How she hated him.* 'Well, *isn't* it a good deal?'

Matt ran his fingers though his floppy fringe as he pulled up in the car park of the same wine bar he'd met Noel last night.

'What do you take me for, Tori? Do you really thing I'd get kudos with the bank if I brokered a deal to pay these skanks *double*? Don't be ridiculous!' This woman really was stupid. He'd thought for a moment that she'd finally got the gist, but clearly not.

Matt sighed. He'd have to spell it out as usual. 'Once they've all signed and the deal proceeds enough for them to be legally unable to pull out without incurring a hefty fine, then the offer will 'mysteriously' be reduced to less than half the original value.'

Tori's mouth dropped open. 'So, you *are* ripping them off?' *Everyone would be turned over – including Sarah's brewery. She'd lose the pub for nothing.*

Matt grinned. 'It'll make us a packet! It's worth paying Noel a huge chunk because without him on side we'd be sunk.'

Tori felt like screaming. 'And Hunter knows this?'

Matt frowned. 'No. Just Noel. Hunter's all for doing the

right thing, hence our need to convince him this *is* the right thing. He must believe everything's above board – which is where *you* come in. After that, everyone will take his word for it and things will go ahead. Then of course, BANG! it will fall though – for them at least. Hunter will be outed for betraying everyone's trust and Noel will get what he wants. As well as the money, he'll be Number One Reaper.'

Tori sat frozen in shock. *She was part of this? And Hunter was using her too?*

'Come on. We need to get in there. I don't want Noel offending anyone without me being there to smooth things over.' Getting out of the car, Matt for once, chivalrously opened Tori's door. He glanced across the tarmac. 'Looks like Noel's not on his own.'

As she scrambled out of the car Tori's eyes followed Matt's over to the two large motorbikes parked by the back fence.

'I guess that's Hunter's,' Matt shrugged. 'Even better. It kills two birds with one stone and you, *sweetheart*,' he pinched Tori's buttock, 'will have a bonus chance of making him want to go home to wank over you.'

Tori felt sick. *How on earth was she going to get through this?*

TWENTY NINE

IT WAS TAKING all of Tori's power not to choke on her wine. She really could have done without drinking at all. She felt rough after last night's gin consumption, plus wine was not one of her favourites on a good day, let alone on a bad one. However, she could safely assume the rising nausea was more to do with her present situation rather than the remnants of a slight hangover combined with minimal sleep.

She hadn't been paying any attention to what had been said so far either and knew she should be. Her concentration had been focused on not screaming or running away, along with looking at *anything* other than the man sitting opposite.

She didn't even have to glance in Hunter's direction to know he was scrutinising her because she could feel his intense stare drilling into the very base of her brain. That and the powerful electrical charge radiating from him like a sub-station. All she could think about was that the whole of last night had been fake. Hunter hadn't wanted her at all - it had been *everything* to do with making her want *him* and he'd succeeded.

Even with what she knew and the hurt of his fake behaviour searing her like a blow torch, his magnetism was still pulling at her and she despised herself for her weakness. She'd never fallen prey to the trap of desire before and the first time she had, it had to be with *him*.

Why had she not seen this coming? As if someone like Hunter would *really* be interested in her. She must have been totally bloody deluded.

A very small part of her felt guilt over what Matt had told her. If Hunter's intentions really were for the best of the people, how sad was it that someone he should trust – Noel - was willingly setting up to destroy him and to be despised by everyone - apart from Matt, Jeremy and the bank of course…

She glanced at Noel and grimaced when he belched loudly following the lager he'd just downed.

'Oh dear. I think I've offended your beautiful fiancée, Matt,' Noel jibed seeing Tori's expression.

'Don't take any notice. She's always like this!' Matt laughed, attempting to ingratiate himself further with the tough bikers. 'But she's not too bad when you get to know her.'

Tori swallowed her scowl, further resenting they were talking about her like a parcel. She forced herself to smile, acting like the vapid cow they clearly thought she was.

'Actually, you said she was a nightmare if I remember rightly,' Hunter said, his voice low and even. His expression gave away nothing. He knew as far as Noel was concerned, he was supposed to be making this woman want him, but he failed to see how he could achieve this now she'd shown her true colours.

He should have guessed. Why he'd even thought for one millisecond that there was something about Tori that was different he could not fathom, but it still pained him that there was still something… *Something else…*

Whatever happened he'd have to force himself to get on with it, but once he'd found out the real deal regarding this bloody property thing then he'd quite happily wash his hands of this and have nothing more to do with the woman ever again. He'd been punching above both his weight and his station – which she'd reminded him of without any shadow of a doubt.

He'd seen it as clear as day etched over her beautiful face when the reality of what they'd done had sunk in.

Hunter tipped his bottle of beer in his mouth, angrily resenting his body betraying his mind and making sitting in the cramped seat uncomfortable.

'I was only joking about Tori being a nightmare!' Matt said. *The guy had to feel he was getting something that was worth it, even if, when push came to shove, he wasn't. Tori wasn't worth any fucker's effort.* 'Yep, I'm a lucky man that she's agreed to be my wife, aren't I darling?' Grabbing Tori around the neck, Matt made a big show of clumsily kissing her on the cheek.

Tori stiffened. She risked a glance at Hunter who stared at her with a cold, fathomless expression.

Matt nudged Tori under the table subtly reminding her that she should be making conversation. Taking a deep breath, she smiled. 'So, have you all had a productive day?' *Oh God. Was that all she could think of?* Her smile remained frozen on her face like an embalmed corpse.

'Depends of what you mean by 'productive'?' Hunter growled, his face still devoid of expression.

Tori swallowed. *This wasn't going well.* He was acting like she'd never existed. The total opposite from how he'd made her feel last night. She'd *believed* he'd wanted her. He'd made every nerve and fibre in her body sing. *Alive.*

Blushing as the image of Hunter positioned between her thighs, her moans echoing around the room, forced itself into her brain, Tori shook her head to rid herself of the memory. She had to do better than this. If Hunter wanted to play her, then she could also do that. Right back at him, the two-faced bastard. *Let him pick up his own bloody pieces. He deserved everything he got.*

With a resolve she was unaware she possessed, Tori leant forward to accentuate the cleavage visible in her dark blue tightly fitted dress. 'Matt's been telling me about this property deal. Now, I know we don't know each other, but wow! what an opportunity!' *Have that Hunter! Now let's see you play your part. You're supposed to be messing with the mind of the thick rich bimbo – that's me, remember? The one who will tell you all her fiancé's secrets when you make her pant for you.*

Hunter watched Tori's demeanour, attitude and behaviour morph in front of his very eyes. He knew Noel was expecting him to come out with something suitable, but all he wanted to do was walk away. However, he had too many people depending on hm to allow that to be an option.

Flicking his smile on like a light, Hunter stared intensely into Tori's eyes. 'It looks like that, yes. A few things I need to check out first.' He forced his eyes to scan her exposed cleavage for effect, ignoring that it was doing nothing to quell his raging erection that thankfully the table concealed. 'But I'm sure time will tell all…'

'I didn't think you wanted to sell?' Tori countered, knowing Matt's eyes were shooting death stares in her general direction, most likely wondering what on earth she was playing at by asking that. 'But,' she added. 'Considering it a possibility is a really good idea and one you shouldn't ignore.'

She suddenly felt a cold sweat break out over her. *She couldn't do this.* Regardless of her previous bravado of playing Hunter at his own game, she just *couldn't.* She'd been ridiculed all her life by everyone and anyone and then she ended up in some weird encounter with a man of the type she'd always despised, but he'd made her feel more wanted than anyone ever had… *Loved… Desirable…*

To find out it had all been a sham had been more than she could bear and putting herself back in this position so soon after finding out about the betrayal was just… *It was just too much.* She unsteadily got to her feet.

'Tori, what are you doing?' Matt hissed and grabbed her arm, his fingers digging painfully into her flesh.

Hunter watched, his eyes narrowing at Matt's hold on Tori.

'I-I don't feel well,' she mumbled, the room spinning as panic started to overwhelm her. 'Excuse me for one moment.'

Matt had little choice but to release his grip and irritably watch Tori stumble towards the Ladies' toilet. He'd seen the way Hunter was eyeing him and he didn't want the idiot to think anything was amiss. She'd been doing surprisingly well until just and she knew what she had to do, so what she was playing at was anyone's guess.

He caught Noel's questioning glare and realised he'd have to say something to excuse Tori's sudden strange behaviour. 'Sorry about her,' Matt shrugged, smiling a bit too widely. 'She gets like this. Time of the month again, I expect.'

'That's women!' Noel laughed, 'Histrionics and bleeding! Why do you think I never bother getting involved any further than dipping my wick?'

Hunter scowled. 'Are you not going to see if she's alright?'

Matt flapped his hand. 'Nah, she does it for attention. Now, let's continue discussing these deals? I can tell you a bit more about the investment company involved. I've worked with them several times now.'

Hunter ignored Noel and Matt eagerly waiting for him to join the conversation. This was insane. He couldn't sit here like this, not whilst Tori had run off. He would have to find out what was going on with her, even if it resulted in an answer he didn't want.

Try as he might to switch off his feelings and whatever her motives were for allowing him into her bed, he couldn't. This wasn't one of those many encounters that he could take or leave. Unfortunate timing and mismatch of class and attitude it may be, but the strength of his connection with the woman had all but slaughtered him and flattened him like a road-roller. Whatever he should or shouldn't be doing made no difference. How he'd felt last night had been too strong and either he was going insane, or she was an Oscar-winning actress, but his instinct told him that neither of those options were feasible.

Pushing his chair back, Hunter rose from the table. 'I'm going to get more drinks,' he barked,

'But it's waiter service,' Matt said, confused.

'Then I'm going to stretch my legs,' Hunter muttered,

already moving away.

'Let him go,' Noel hissed. 'He's a stroppy fucker at the best of times and has been on a right one all day. He'll be back.'

. . . .

TORI STARED INTO the gilt-framed mirror in the Ladies' toilet. She'd splashed cold water on her face from the elegantly-styled taps, but that had done nothing to calm her combined rising panic and desolation.

She leant against the chair positioned in front of another mirror and placed her handbag on the shelf below. At least there weren't any other women in here preening themselves whilst she hid her flushed and blotchy face. The thought of walking back out through the bar to where Matt and the others sat caused another wave of nausea to rise. She couldn't do what Matt wanted. She could and would not prostitute herself for his benefit to a man that she'd already freely given herself to.

Tori stared at her reflection and brushed her dark waves away from her face in an attempt to appear less dishevelled. She took long deep breaths to regulate her racing heart, but then jumped hearing the outer door to the Ladies' slam open. *Typical. She'd known it wouldn't be long before someone came in.*

Pretending to admire herself rather than turning around to look at the newcomer, Tori scrutinised her makeup in the mirror. It was only when she glanced past herself in the reflection did she see Hunter leaning against the wall behind her.

She swung around quickly. 'W-What the...'

'Are you ok?' Hunter asked, his grey eyes locked to hers.

Tori remained frozen, unable to form coherent words.

'What exactly are you doing?' Hunter said, refraining from stepping forward and pulling her into his arms.

'Y-You can't come in here!' Tori spluttered. 'This is the women's toilets!'

'Do you not think I don't know that? I came to see if you

were alright.'

Tori felt the overwhelming urge to cry. To sob and throw herself against Hunter's chest and pound it with her fists. Ask him why he'd left last night. Why he'd let her believe he'd wanted her when it was only part of a ruse. Instead she looked down at the floor. 'Y-Yes, I'm ok,' she lied.

'You don't seem as sure of yourself as you were ten minutes ago. I hardly recognised you out there.'

That wasn't me, that's why, Tori thought bitterly. She was angry for allowing herself to be put in this situation. She had to get away from this man. He'd laughed enough at her expense. Grabbing her bag, she made to walk past him.

Hunter grabbed Tori's wrist. 'You haven't answered my question.'

Spinning around, Tori stared at Hunter angrily. 'You're the one who upped and left!'

'You didn't give me much choice! Your face made it clear that you'd made a horrible mistake! Cut the crap, Tori. I saw your expression when it sank in what you'd done.'

Tori's mouth hung open. 'What *I'd* done? What about what *you'd* done?'

'What, you mean put my mouth on you? Fucked you like you wanted? Made you come hard whilst you screamed for more? Which?' Hunter countered, a smirk forming across his face. *Still playing Little Miss Innocent, was she?*

Tori blushed deeply. He was inches away and the need to touch him was strong, but it didn't change that he was laughing at her. 'How *dare* you!' she yelled, a tear from anger and hurt rolling down her cheek. 'You know very well what I mean. I know you did all of that purely to try and get information out of me!'

The smirk disappeared from Hunter's face. *How the hell did she know that? And that wasn't how it had been at all.*

'Am I wrong? No? Well, you've had your laugh.' Tori was sick of this. She was leaving.

'It's ok then for me to be your mistake? Think you can treat *me* like a piece of shit?' Hunter spat. *He didn't care now. Game over.* This was between him and her and he wanted her to know she'd caused him pain.

'I've got no idea what you're talking about,' Tori said. 'I'm just the stupid rich bitch you forced yourself to fuck!' *Would she have still done it if she'd have known it was a set up? Probably, yes.*

Hunter raked his fingers through his hair in exasperation. Grabbing her hand, he dragged it to his crotch. 'You *really* think I didn't want you?' he growled. '*Still* really want you.'

Tori gasped, both from the audacity of what he'd just done and hunger. Unable to help herself she palmed the hard bulky outline of his erection.

Groaning, Hunter crashed his mouth down onto Tori's, his tongue invading fiercely. *This time he wouldn't be gentle.*

Afire with need, all thoughts of Hunter's betrayal wiped from her mind, Tori did nothing to resist when he yanked her dress up around her waist. Tearing her knickers off with one hand he dropped the shredded material to the floor and picking Tori up, slammed her against the wall.

Wrapping her legs around Hunter's hips, Tori threw her head back, a loud moan escaping as he impaled her, his mouth on her neck.

Pounding furiously, Hunter's pace was savage and Tori was unable to catch her breath and could do nothing apart from claw at his leather-jacketed back as she felt *that* feeling quickly gaining pace deep inside her.

Holding Tori steady, Hunter relished the rhythmic moans coming from her beautiful mouth. His cock felt like steel. *He'd been hard for her all fucking day.*

'There was no pretence, Tori,' he growled, driving harder and harder. 'I wanted you. I still want you. I want you badly and more than you know.' *He was going to come any second. Any second he was going to blow. He couldn't control the power this woman had over him. It was too much.*

Tori felt herself spasm as the waves of her climax rose

higher. Feeling him expand and stretch her further she clenched her insides, almost delirious with the height she was building to.

When Tori cried out, her orgasm peaking wildly, Hunter followed immediately with a guttural roar and neither of them noticed Noel slip away from where he'd watched through the crack in the door.

THIRTY

TORI HADN'T KNOWN how to react when Matt
congratulated her on her good work as they'd driven back from
the wine bar. She'd still been shell-shocked from the encounter
with Hunter and had unanswered questions in her mind.

She felt more than confused. Was something *actually*
happening between them and if so, where on earth could it go?
She didn't know why she should be asking questions. Surely
she knew it couldn't go anywhere? But she wanted it to, even
though it was impossible.

She hadn't really been with it when she'd left the Ladies'
toilets, her mind still half-delirious and her body like a rag doll.
Matt and Noel had been standing by the front entrance waiting
to leave, so it seemed at least they'd realised she'd been 'ill' and
would need to leave. But it hadn't been as simple as that. As
she'd shakily got into the car she'd been fully expecting Matt
to lay into her for ruining everything, but he couldn't have
seemed more pleased.

'I knew you had it in you! Well done!' he'd said, putting
his hand on her knee. 'Did you manage to get anything out of
him apart from a pint of semen?'

Tori stared at Matt, confused until he made it clear.

'In a way I wish I'd been the one to check on you guys rather than Noel. The whole thing has made me quite horny,' he'd laughed.

With horror, Tori realised Noel must have seen her and Hunter and reported back to Matt. She'd felt sick. Sick that Noel had seen and sick that it had turned Matt on.

'I was only joking about the semen of course. Even *you* wouldn't have been stupid enough to let that AIDS-riddled hooker-shagger ride you bareback!' Matt chortled. 'Maybe you'll be in the mood for a bit more when we get back?'

Tori looked out of the window into the dark night. Hunter hadn't used protection and she hadn't wanted him to. She hadn't wanted even the *thinnest* piece of rubber separating her from that man. Besides, it wasn't *him* that worried her – Matt was the one who slept with prostitutes, yet he'd *always* refused to use protection. It wasn't like she was going to get pregnant, he'd said, but the Pill didn't protect her from whatever diseases Matt had did it?

She shuddered. The last thing she wanted to spoil the warm satiated feeling Hunter had left her with was by having to put up with Matt's hands on her. *Oh God, what was she going to do?* However much she dressed it down, she wanted Hunter. And more than just wanted him physically.

With a sudden dawning of realisation she knew she needed to know more about the man himself; what made him tick, what had made him become a Reaper and why he was the president of the club. Also, from what she could fathom, as he was all of that, how did he have the heart she knew he had?

The memory of Sarah saying he was trouble and damaged filtered into her mind. What had caused that and what about his girlfriend?

Why was she being so ridiculous? Anyone with half a brain knew this couldn't work on any level. And whilst she'd been busy being moralistic about Hunter using her, she'd conveniently ignored that the plan was to do exactly the same to him. *Except she wasn't. How she felt was real.*

Returning to real life Tori realised she'd have to keep up the pretence as far as Matt was concerned. If he for one moment thought Hunter made her *feel*, then he'd ruin her for sure. At least Noel hadn't overheard their conversation because if he had, Matt would be nowhere near as happy.

'You still haven't told me if you got anything useful out of the bonehead,' Matt said, bringing Tori back to reality.

'I didn't get a lot of chance, did I?' Tori snapped. 'I was too busy reeling him in like you asked.' This was what she needed to say if she ever wanted to see him again. And she *did* want to see him.

Matt scowled. 'Don't get high and mighty. Just think of the money this will bag us.'

Tori frowned. She'd got an idea but needed to play it carefully. 'You've no idea how difficult it is.' *It wasn't difficult. Wasn't difficult at all.*

'You need to get him to talk. Get in his head and find his weaknesses.'

'If he has any…' she muttered.

'*Everybody* has them and we need to discover his. He needs to believe in you.' Matt grinned, still quite unable to believe how well his plan was going.

'I guess the problem will be getting him on his own,' Tori said. 'I can't hang around the Factory because it will look suspicious.'

Matt laughed. 'I don't think your mother would be too enamoured to find that fucker in her house either!'

Tori almost choked. *He'd no idea how close that had come to happening.* But it was true. Where could she go where she could talk to him and get to know him? Where could they be alone?

Feeling a twinge between her legs, Tori shifted in the seat. 'What about the White Hart?' she suggested. 'That would be ok. I mean, I've been in there before an…'

'That's no good. The rest of them go in there,' Matt countered. 'Maybe he has a flat where he takes his other birds?'

Tori felt sick with jealousy at the thought that Hunter may have lots of women on the go. Even Georgie was bad enough. She didn't much appreciate that Hunter was the sort to cheat on a girlfriend either, but even that didn't dampen her need for him.

'Don't forget it's part of his plan to work *you*. Not that he knows you're aware of that.'

Oh, but he does, Tori thought, still wanting to ask Hunter about that, although maybe she should just concentrate on *being* with him for the time they had, regardless of the reasons?

Matt's eyes suddenly lit up. 'That's it! Why didn't I think of this before?' he exclaimed. 'My apartment! You said it's a waste of money being unused, so *use* it!' He grasped Tori's hand. 'Go there. Take him to the apartment and learn about him. No one will see you, so that's the best option. We've got to remember we can't afford for you to be seen with a biker. Especially *alone*. I'd never live it down!'

'No, I don't imagine you would,' Tori mumbled, hoping Matt didn't hone in on her bitterness.

. . . .

WHEN GRIN TOOK the phone call he knew Hunter wouldn't be happy. In fact, if he knew him at all, he'd be devastated.

He knew things hadn't been *official* with Georgie, like nothing ever had been where women and Hunter were concerned, but there had been a 'thing' between them for a good few years, which was why it had been a complete surprise when the other day he'd learnt there would be nothing more between them anymore, apart from friendship.

Grin had fully expected Georgie to be heartbroken. He personally liked the girl – liked her a lot and it was well known that she was in love with Hunter. Unfortunately it had never been a reciprocated love, but in her coke-fuelled mind she'd always believed she could change that. That would never happen now and Grin only hoped Hunter wouldn't be burdened with regrets he could not alter.

Hearing two bikes roar up the drive, with a heavy heart,

Grin necked the last of his pint and braced himself to deal with the situation. He ran his hand over his bristly chin and signalled to the others in the room to make themselves scarce. He wasn't looking forward to this. *Wasn't looking forward to it at all.*

Hunter walked into the Factory glad to be back in one respect. At least here he would be safe from Noel's badgering for information on Tori. He'd not been quite able to believe Noel had been having a sneaky peak through the door, but even that hadn't been enough to remove the inward smile he wore.

Outwardly his face was neutral but *inside* he was positively glowing. The feel of Tori around him had been just as delicious as it had been before and he wished he were in a position where he could be with her right now. He'd love nothing more than to spend the rest of the night sinking himself into her over and over.

He wanted to see her again as soon as possible and if everyone else thought the reason for that was purely business then he couldn't foresee it causing any issues. Even though he'd had no answer either way from Tori as to why she'd wanted him to leave the other night, his need to be with her was too strong to question anything. Right now it was enough to know that her desire for him was as intense as his was for her.

Slipping his leather jacket off, Hunter placed his crash helmet on the rack in the large entrance area before striding into the bar room. He glanced around and blinked slowly. *Where was everyone?* The place looked like the *'Marie Celeste'* – apart from Grin loitering at the bar.

'Alright Grin?' Noel boomed, following Hunter towards the bar. 'We had a productive evening. Well, Hunter did anyway…'

Glaring at Noel, Hunter studied Grin's face. *Something was wrong.* 'What's happened?'

Grin smiled, but it didn't reach his eyes. *He was dreading this.* 'I've got you a drink.'

Frowning, Hunter picked up the pint. 'Are you going to tell me what's going on?'

Grin took a deep breath. 'Georgie's dead.'

Hunter paled. *Not Georgie. No, not Georgie.* 'How? When?'

Grin rested his hand on Hunter's shoulder. 'I'm really sorry, mate. The call came in about an hour ago. She was found this morning.'

Hunter ran his fingers through his hair in shock. 'Where?'

'Her house. One of her friends went round because she hadn't turned up where they'd arranged. There was nothing anyone could do. She'd been dead several hours.'

Hunter swallowed the lump in his throat. 'What happened?'

'Drug-induced heart attack, they think. They suspect it might be something to do with dodgy gear, or a plain overdose.'

Hunter tipped his pint down in one go. He hadn't given her any drugs for a good while. *Shit.* She must have run out and got it from somewhere else. Some stuff that wasn't clean. He gritted his teeth. 'I want to know who she scored from,' he roared.

Noel bit his bottom lip. He couldn't be sure, but he'd thought there was a bag missing out of that gear he'd cut for the posh prick. He hadn't thought much of it at the time because it was hardly likely Matt would dare question him if he was a bag short. But it had been stored in the usual place at the Factory, so Georgie could have got hold of it. *Holy shit. Hunter would kill him if the gear he'd cut had killed the girl.* He paled further. If it had killed her it could also kill whoever Matt sold it to and then the shit really would hit the fan on so many levels.

'Noel,' Hunter barked. 'I want a list of anyone Georgie's been in contact with who could have passed her laced gear.'

'Hadn't we better find out for sure what killed her before we start digging?' Noel blathered. He needed to think about this and get word to Matt to hold the gear until he said otherwise.

'Oh, I fucking intend to,' Hunter growled. 'And that's just for starters, but I want you to immediately get on to finding her recent connections.'

Grin rested his hand on Hunter's arm once more. He wasn't quite sure how to say this, but there was no other way around it. 'There's something else...'

Hunter looked up and saw the sorrow in Grin's eyes. 'What?'

'Georgie was pregnant.' Grin squeezed Hunter's arm. 'A couple of months along. I'm really sorry, mate.'

Hunter put his head in his hands, before standing up and launching his bar stool against the mirror, exploding it into fragments.

THIRTY ONE

COLIN LOOKED AT his wife and smiled. 'I'm glad you've got Tori coming over tonight. Don't worry about helping behind the bar.' He glanced around the pub. It was hardly over-busy, just a handful of the regulars and Rog strumming away on his guitar in the corner. 'It'll do you good to have a natter.'

Sarah smiled. She was very lucky to have Colin, but she didn't think he was as bothered about all of this upheaval about possibly losing the pub as she was. She'd had it on good authority that three people approached by that investment company had already signed the preliminary sale contracts. In fact, one of them had told her himself. He'd been on his way back from the offy with a bottle of champagne in his hand when she'd bumped into him earlier.

'We'd never get as good an offer as that again,' he'd said, overjoyed at the agreed price. Lowering his voice, he'd leaned closer. 'Plus I didn't fancy getting my head staved in by the Reapers like Dave Griffin did. It's easier to do as they say. Besides, it's not like we're losing out,' he'd grinned. 'Me and the missus will be drinking to our good fortune tonight, that's for sure!'

Sarah frowned. It really had gone around town that the

safest option was to sell. No one had heard anything different from Hunter. Saying that, no one had heard *anything* from Hunter. She herself hadn't seen hide nor hair of him, or any of the Reapers for two days straight and she was not best impressed. Look what had happened in the pub the last time they'd gone AWOL.

Hunter had assured her that would never happen again, but they were sailing a bit close to the wind. If they weren't in here over the weekend then she'd not be giving them their money.

She huffed petulantly. Their lack of presence was certainly not helping getting any further with the genuineness of these deals.

Thankfully, the three who had decided to sign were, at the moment, in the minority. The majority were still holding out for Hunter's word before they made their minds up, but Sarah knew if he didn't deliver soon they'd most probably go ahead and accept.

· · · ·

TORI HAD MIXED feelings about going to the White Hart. On the premise of getting away from Matt it was of course a benefit. He'd been in a foul mood since receiving a phone call and had been scooting around here, there and everywhere since, yet he wouldn't tell her what it was about.

She'd also not heard from Hunter since the night at the wine bar and Matt had been so distracted by whatever was bothering him she didn't dare mention moving forward with plan without him suggesting it first. She couldn't act too eager.

And what if Hunter was there? How could she act normal in the same room as him when, regardless of what Matt wanted, all *she* wanted was to fold herself in Hunter's arms?

Then of course there was Sarah. As much as she dearly wanted to spend time with the woman, the weight of the knowledge over the falseness of the deals was gnawing away at her. She felt a total bitch for having this information and not sharing it. Realistically, what sort of friend did that make her?

A bad one, that's what.

Her initial instinct was to tell Sarah what she knew. She'd wanted to do that since the moment she'd found out, but if she did, then the first thing Sarah would do would be to tell Hunter and then not only would Matt's plan go up the wall and in turn ruin her mother, as well as her father's memory, but it would also rip apart anything she and Hunter might have.

Tori still didn't know exactly what, if anything that something was, but every fibre of her body and mind needed to explore it. She couldn't feel this intense about someone without following it.

Taking a deep breath, she pulled her jacket down over her smart jeans and after handing some money to the driver, slipped out of the taxi and into the White Hart.

• • • •

MATT WIPED A film of sweat from his brow as he yanked open the door handle of the Porsche. 'Get in Jeremy. We'll have to try somewhere else.'

Jeremy got into the car and fiddled nervously with the seat belt. 'I didn't realise it would be passed on,' he whined. *Well, he hadn't.* When he'd sold one of the bags of coke to that girl in the Mortgages section, he'd thought nothing of it. She'd bought some before and besides, he'd had no reason to question what she was going to do with it.

This morning after Matt told him what was going on he'd steamed into the office the first chance he'd had and eventually got it out of her than she'd sold it on to another girl ready for a party tonight.

'What the fuck did that skank cut it with?' Matt muttered, almost to himself.

'I don't know, do I?' Jeremy snapped. 'You're the one who did the deal. You seem to have been doing quite a lot of things without my knowledge of late.' It still grated that Matt had been meeting Noel as well as Hunter behind his back and he suspected this wouldn't have been mentioned had the bad gear not come to light.

'Is he *sure* it was that batch he sold to us which killed the girl?'

Matt slammed the Porsche into reverse and screeched out of the parking space. 'No, but he thinks it might be and it doesn't take rocket science to work out that if anyone in *our* circles drops dead from laced gear then we're fucking sunk!'

It had been going so well. His father had called him into his office to congratulate him on finally getting the project off the ground. The investor had dropped in three signed contracts only this morning and Matt had been extremely pleased until he'd walked out of the bank at lunch to find Noel lurking.

'What the hell are you doing here?' Matt had hissed, diverting Noel away from anywhere visible from the windows of the bank. The last thing he wanted was anyone to see him with someone like *that*.

Despite his questioning, Noel hadn't been forthcoming. He'd just barked that if he didn't get the coke back then they'd both be in the shit.

That was in pleasant terms.

In reality, Noel had said that Matt would be 'fucking dead' if he didn't sort it.

Well, if he didn't sort it, Noel wouldn't be the only one lining up to kill him. He'd lose *everything* and then some and he couldn't allow that to happen.

It had only occurred afterwards as to whether Noel was aware the gear he'd handed over was dodgy but had dismissed this thought quickly. He wouldn't be that stupid. Besides, they were working together now, weren't they?

Either way, he had to get every bit back in case Noel's worries were founded. He'd managed to collect ten bags out of the eleven that had been sold already. It had been embarrassing. People had understandably not been happy and he had the distinct impression that his coke dealing side-line would take a nose-dive after this debacle, but that didn't alter the need to get the one outstanding bag back from whoever that tart in

Mortgages had sold it to.

Speeding down the road, Matt gritted his teeth. He wasn't happy. This day had started out good and now it most definitely wasn't.

• • • •

TORI HAD INITIALLY been on edge as she'd half-waited for Hunter to turn up, but now – two hours later with no sign of him or any of the Reapers and with a handful of gins inside her, she felt more relaxed and happy to listen to the music the guy in the corner was strumming.

Although Sarah had made a couple of references to the pub sale and her annoyance at the lack of Reapers' presence, it hadn't been anything where Tori had needed to lie about the knowledge she possessed, but it had been enough for her to realise she would have to say something before too long.

Her quickly escalating feelings for Hunter made it almost feasible to perhaps seriously consider walking away from Matt, regardless of the nuclear explosion it would cause, but she also had to try and rationalise the situation. Her whole life she'd held the deep-seated resentment and bitterness for bikers and knew that was a huge part of what was causing her inner torment. Her body was reacting in a way which was the polar opposite of her mind and the constant argument in her head was making her feel ill. *And she could only foresee that worsening.*

It was physical infatuation, that was all and infatuations did not last. She would do well to remember that and see it for what it was, rather than analyse it into something it could never be.

'Fancy another one?' Sarah nodded towards Tori's almost empty glass.

'Why not,' she laughed. 'But I don't think we'll be much use at work tomorrow if we carry on at this rate.'

Sarah grinned. 'Sod 'em. We do far too much work for that miserable balding bastard at the best of times, so it won't hurt for us to be not so 'productive' for one day, will it?'

Tori stood up. 'I'll get these ones in.'

Sarah handed Tori her empty pint glass. 'Do you know something? You've been a lot happier since you let your hair down a bit. It suits you.'

'Let my hair down?'

'Yes, you've been a different person these last couple of weeks – like Matt removed his chain from around your neck.'

Tori smiled tightly. *If only...* Had she become different? The main difference was, what with everything else going on, she hadn't been forced to spend much time with Matt. There also hadn't been any talk of weddings, although she suspected that wouldn't last long. The other reason of course was that she'd hardly seen her mother, but again that would only be a matter of time.

From Matt's side, his lenience was down to that he needed her for this plan to work and that wouldn't last for ever and as for her mother, she'd successfully managed to avoid her. Her mother presumed she'd been spending more time with Matt, which she approved of. It wasn't as if Matt would inform his parents or her mother that he was 'prostituting' his fiancée to the head of the Reapers to secure his promotion would it?

Irritation flared and Tori castigated herself. *She wouldn't think about that tonight.*

Sarah folded her arms and yawned theatrically. 'Are you getting more drinks or expecting waiter service? In case you haven't noticed, this isn't the Ritz!'

Laughing, Tori moved towards the bar. 'Same again please, Colin.'

Colin bowed. 'Yes M'Lady!'

Tori giggled. She loved it here. She felt at home with Sarah, Colin and the pub.

'I take it you girls are on a roll tonight?' Colin smiled, pouring a fresh pint, whilst with the other hand, shot a double gin from the optic into Tori's glass. 'If either of you pass out, don't expect me to carry you upstairs!'

Tori laughed loudly. 'We haven't had *that* many, Col.'

'Well, you just wa...'

Colin stopped mid-sentence as an almighty crash came from outside. 'What the fuck?' he yelled, slamming the half-poured drinks down and rushed towards the window. 'Oh shit! It's Hunter! He's slammed his bike into the back of your car, Sarah!'

'What?' Sarah screamed, jumping up.

Tori followed Colin and Sarah outside with a group of regulars. Hunter was laying on the pavement with Noel standing over him trying to remove his crash helmet. His bike was on its side in the road and Sarah's car had a huge dent in the back.

'My fucking car!' Sarah wailed. 'Hunter, you bastard! What the hell were you doing?'

'Is he alright?' Tori rushed towards Hunter. 'You shouldn't be removing his helmet. What if he's hurt his neck?'

'He won't have hurt anything!' Noel snarled, glaring up at Tori. 'He's too fucking drunk!'

Tori stared at Noel in horror and then at Hunter as Colin and Noel dragged the big man to his feet.

'We tried to stop him,' Grin said, dismounting his bike, having finally caught up. 'He's been drinking solidly all night and most of the day. He's lost it big time.'

Hunter ran his hands through his hair, then wiped blood from his lip. 'I'm fine. I'm just *fine* and I'm not fucking drunk!' he roared, staggering slightly as he shrugged Colin and Noel's grip off him. 'Colin, get me a drink and Noel, pick my fucking bike up!'

Turning his back, Hunter stomped into the White Hart, his stride unsteady.

Tori's eyes searched Grin's face and watched with despair as he shrugged apologetically. Turning, she followed Hunter and ignored Sarah's continued angry shouts about her car. He'd definitely been drinking. Quite heavily by the looks of it. She'd never seen him anything other than fully in control of his faculties before, but now he looked manic. *Almost feral.*

Catching up with Tori, Noel grabbed her arm. 'Leave him!'

he hissed.

'Get your hands off me,' Tori spat, shrugging Noel's arm away and continued into the tap room. Hunter was behind the bar helping himself to a pint. His eyes were narrow slits as he scowled at a man in the corner.

'What the fuck's your problem?' Hunter roared at the man. 'You're looking at me! What the fuck are you looking at me for?'

Slamming the pint down, he moved quickly from behind the bar and was in front of the man in the corner before he knew what was happening.

Tori stared in horror as Hunter lifted the man from his chair by his throat.

'If you've got a problem with me, then fucking say so, you cunt!' Hunter pinned the man up against the wall.

Tori felt sick. *Where was the rational man who had been so gentle the other night? Where was the man who had made her feel so special?*

'I'm fucking waiting…' Hunter spat, flecks of spittle spraying from his mouth. 'Do you know what? I'm sick of you lot. Sick of all of you! You sit there waiting for me to tell you what to do, then slag me off when I don't have the answers quick enough!'

'Stop this, Hunter,' Colin said, moving toward the corner.

Hunger swung around, his eyes wild. 'Stay out of it, Colin. I've always had respect for you, but no one seems to have any for me. Including this wanker!'

'I-I didn't say anything!' the man stammered, struggling to get the words out due to the intense crushing of his neck.

'You were going to though, weren't you? You lot think you get away with anything!' he screamed to no one in particular. 'Have you any idea what I do? I do bad things. That's who I am. I fucking *kill* people I do and you think you can j…'

'Shut the fuck up, Hunter!' Noel warned.

'And you can fuck off too. You're a fucking liability. Everyone knows you've got a screw loose! Forgotten what I did for you, have you?'

Noel had just about had enough. 'You can shut up right now. You're not fit to be in charge of the fucking club. Pull yourself together! You're losing the plot just because some tart topped herself with your baby inside her? Big fucking deal!'

Tori went cold. *Hunter's girlfriend was pregnant? Had been pregnant? And now she was dead? Had Hunter killed her?* Her knees felt weak and she leaned against a table for support.

'What did you say?' Hunter dropped his grip on the man pinned against the wall who scrabbled away as fast as he could.

Noel was a fighter, but nothing could prepare him for the lightening quick and unexpected volley of pure rage from Hunter launching a volley of heavy punches down on him.

'Hunter! STOP!' Sarah screamed as Noel crashed to the floor with Hunter on top, continuing to lay into him mercilessly.

'I'll fucking kill you!' Hunter roared, pounding his fists into Noel's already bleeding and blackening flesh.

Grin ran towards Hunter. *He had to stop this*. Noel shouldn't have said that about Georgie or the baby. He knew Hunter was devasted and guessed he'd had no idea the girl he'd binned off a few nights ago had been pregnant with his child. He'd been with him all night and day – mainly to keep an eye on him as he'd insisted on drinking himself stupid – something he hadn't done for a *very* long time. From there, he'd alternated between crashing depression to raging anger. The man had drunk himself almost sober by midday and he'd tried to talk him into getting his head down and getting some sleep, but Hunter had just started on the spirits again.

Grin had thought things had calmed down a bit. That was until Hunter had muttered something and then staggered out of the Factory. When he'd heard the engine of Hunter's bike roar into life he'd not quite been able to believe it. The man could hardly walk, let alone ride.

Both him and Noel had desperately tried to catch up with him and somehow stop the suicidal journey, but Hunter had been riding like the wind and it had only been from pure fluke that he hadn't dropped the bike, or ploughed into oncoming traffic as he'd veered all over the road. The damage to Sarah's car was *nothing* in comparison to what could have happened. Regardless of this, what was important now was that he had to stop Hunter from battering Noel to death.

Grabbing the back of Hunter's leather jacket, Grin tried to pull him away, but Hunter effortlessly removed him by head-butting him square on the bridge of the nose.

Grin reeled, blood pouring down his front whilst Hunter resumed his attention to Noel. Sitting astride him he smashed the back of Noel's head into the floor.

Before Tori realised what she was doing, she'd run into the corner and thrown herself at Hunter. 'Stop this, Hunter. Stop this NOW!'

About to blindly launch into whoever had got in his way, on realising who it was, Hunter stopped still. His drunken eyes struggled to focus. 'Tori?'

Tori knelt down next to Hunter as he sat astride Noel's inert body and put her hand on his blood-splattered face. 'Yes, it's me. You need to stop this. Do you hear me?'

Hunter grasped Tori with both hands, pulling her against his beer-drenched leather jacket. 'Oh God, Tori, is it really you?' he slurred.

A pin drop could have been heard in the tap room as everyone stood in suspended animation.

'Tori,' Hunter slurred, drunkenly covering her cheeks and throat with kisses. 'You're here. You're really here?'

Tori ignored the entire room staring at them in a combination of shock and disbelief. She also tried to reconcile her utter disbelief from what she'd seen this man, whose mouth was pressed to her neck, unleash on these people with her need to comfort the man she loved.

Loved? Did she just say 'loved'?

'Hunter you need to get up. We need to help Noel,' Tori whispered, tenderly stroking his face.

'I need you,' Hunter groaned, his hands drunkenly pulling

at Tori's clothes. 'I wanna be in you again. I think I love you…'

Sitting on the floor pinching his nose to stem the blood, Grin watched the unfolding spectacle. *Was he seeing things?* He knew they'd all joked about Hunter having a thing for Tori, but it was true. And if what he'd just said was also true, then he'd also slept with her? *Christ, this would put the cat amongst the pigeons.*

Colin had seen enough. The prospect that he could soon also be on the receiving end of Hunter's out-of-character aggression didn't come into it. Striding over, he pulled Tori away. 'Get your hands off her *now* and get the fuck off my floor!'

He wasn't having this. Wasn't having this at all. He watched Hunter's eyes narrow. 'I'm not having it, Hunter. Have you seen what you've done?' he roared, nodding towards Noel and Grin. 'And now you're pawing Tori!'

Something must have filtered into Hunter's drunken mind because he pulled himself to his feet and focused on his surroundings. He ran his hand through his matted hair and swayed unsteadily. 'I'm sorry… I…' His eyes brimmed with tears.

Tori's heart felt like it would break. She moved forwards.

'For God's sake, Tori! Leave him!' Sarah yelled.

'I can't see him like this. *Please*, Sarah. Is there anywhere I can take him?' Tori begged.

Sarah studied Tori. *Oh fuck!* She'd been right. Something had gone on between those two, but it was worse than that. Tori had fallen for him. She could see it in her eyes and the way she looked at him, touched him. The scariest thing was, even though Hunter was very drunk, she suspected he'd somehow fallen too. *He'd said he loved her…*

She wiped the back of her hand over her forehead. 'Take him upstairs,' she muttered. 'Make him some strong fucking coffee.'

'Sarah?' Colin questioned unbelievably. His wife was seriously going to allow this man who had turned into the lunatic he'd managed to keep under wraps for so long into *their* flat with a woman he clearly wanted to stick his dick in?

'It's ok. He'll be ok with her, trust me,' Sarah said quietly, her eyes locking on Tori's. *She wanted some fucking answers, but that would have to wait.*

'Thank you,' Tori mouthed to Sarah as, with some difficulty, she steered Hunter to the stairs leading to Colin and Sarah's living quarters.

'Sarah, I'm sorry about your car, I'll pay for it.' Hunter tried to get his hand in his pocket but couldn't quite coordinate himself. 'Colin, I'm sorry ab...'

'Save it, Hunter,' Colin snarled. He was not impressed. He was *less* than impressed – he was disappointed.

'Sort it out tomorrow, Hunter,' Tori said. 'Let's just get you sobered up.' She left everyone staring after them in confusion, whilst Sarah busied herself at Noel's side, dabbing at his bleeding cuts.

THIRTY TWO

TORI WASN'T QUITE sure how to handle this. She stroked Hunter's hair as he slept. She'd watched his massive shoulders heave as he'd retched into the bucket placed next to the sofa, but now he was sleeping it off.

Her mind was spinning. Spinning like a roundabout. She didn't know what to think. He'd said he thought he loved her, but he was drunk, so surely he didn't know what he was saying? He couldn't mean it, could he?

And what about the other stuff he'd said before Noel had desperately tried to stop him? *That he'd killed people...*

This hadn't come as too much of a surprise, even though she dearly wanted it not to be true. After all it was only the stereotype of what she believed people like that did. Regardless of stereotyping, she'd heard it from his own mouth. He'd killed someone – or perhaps even more than one person? And what had that to do with Noel? What had he done?

Tori swallowed against the tight band invisibly constricting her throat. How could she quantify her feelings for a man such as this?

But what were her feelings? She looked at the man lying back with his head against the arm rest of the sofa, his eyes closed and had no choice but to accept it for what it was. Regardless of what her brain wanted her to feel, it wasn't just lust, she was utterly and unavoidably in love with Ash Hunter.

Tori brushed her hair away from her face in despair. *How could this happen? And what about his girlfriend?* She was dead and she'd been having his baby. She felt disgusted he'd known this and still slept with her. Her cheeks flushed with shame. What sort of man did that to a woman? A *pregnant* woman?

This man, it seemed.

Tori felt a wave of nausea rise. She was in love with a man who cheated on his pregnant girlfriend and was using her for information.

But was *she* any better? She was with Matt and had slept with another man for the very same reasons. Except *her* reasons weren't the same. For a start, Matt had wanted her to do it. He'd *encouraged* it. Furthermore, she hadn't done it for information, she'd done it because Hunter had made her body sing and she'd *wanted* him. The attraction was suffocating. *It still was…*

Despite her churning mind, Tori ran her finger gently down Hunter's face, brushing against the contours of his defined cheekbones and strong jaw.

'Tori?' Hunter mumbled, his eyes opening. 'I'm sorry. I'm so fucking sorry.'

'But Georgie?' she asked quietly as his hand caressed her cheek, burning her flesh with his touch. *Had he loved her?* 'Tell me about her.'

Hunter ran his hand through his hair, still matted with Noel's blood. 'We were in one of those… one of those sort of *strange* relationships. The sort that wasn't really a relationship… Not to me anyway…' he slurred.

'You *cheated* on her with me and she was pregnant? How could you?'

Hunter's bloodshot eyes shot open. 'I didn't know that. And I didn't cheat - It wasn't like that. I didn't know…' With difficulty he pushed himself up on his elbows and tried to focus on Tori.

'Don't use the term 'strange relationship' as an excuse. How could you not know?' Tears pricked Tori's eyes.

Putting his head in his hands, Hunter shook it slightly. 'I didn't. I just didn't... I never promised her anything. We got on well. I liked her, but I couldn't get involved...' he said, concentration evident as he attempted to form his words coherently.

'I'd stopped anything we had several days ago.' He looked desperate. 'I didn't know she was pregnant though - she never said. She never told me. I-I'd have stood by her for the baby. I'd have been there for her, I...'

Tori studied Hunter. He was still nowhere near sober despite the coffee and the short sleep, but at least seemed slightly more coherent. Despite the burning questions she decided to remain silent and let him talk.

'Tori,' Hunter clumsily touched her hand. 'I had to leave things with her. Before... before we...'

'Before we *what*?' Tori snapped. *Before you fucked me for information?*

'I couldn't keep sleeping with her when all I could think about was you. It wasn't fair. Georgie loved me and I had too much respect for her to do that. I didn't even know whether you wanted me as much as I wanted you...' He dropped his hand. 'Even if you hadn't wanted me, I had to leave things with her because it was only you...'

Tori remained motionless. *She didn't know what to think.*

A tear rolled down Hunter's face. 'The baby... I should have been there. I-I didn't know. I'd never...'

Tori was unable to stop herself from pulling Hunter's head against her and wrapping her arms around him. 'I'm so sorry about Georgie and the baby, I really am.'

'I always wanted children,' Hunter mumbled. 'I thought it might somehow make the past better.'

'T-The past? How?' Tori dared herself to ask. 'What happened in the past?'

Hunter shook his head. 'It's irrelevant now, really. My heart's been dead for so long.' His voice reverberated against her chest. 'It's been dead all of these years and you... you've done something... You've made me feel, I don't know... Made me feel...'

'Hunter... I...'

'I saw your face that night. I know you don't want me. You know I'm a bad man and don't deserve anything. I...'

'You're not a bad man,' Tori whispered. 'I...'

Hunter pulled away, his eyes now angry. 'That's the point. You don't know shit. I've done shit things.'

'What shit things?' Tori asked, not wanting to hear the answer but was unable to refrain from asking. 'You said you'd killed someone. Isn't that what you lot do?' She couldn't contain her bitterness.

Hunter sighed. 'I've killed many people, Tori and hurt a lot more, but there was one...'

'One *what*?' Tori pushed. What made this man so complex? Killing people seemed to be second nature for people such as him, so why would one particular killing bother him? Worryingly, she realised she hadn't felt particularly affected by his admission. What was the matter with her? She didn't understand herself sometimes.

Hunter thought for a moment. *What the hell was he doing?* 'It doesn't matter...'

Tori saw Hunter's shutters come down. 'It matters to me. One that was *what*?' she repeated.

'There's some things I can't explain, or perhaps don't know how to,' Hunter said slowly, his eyes hard. 'Let's not say any more. All I want to know is could you want me? I mean, like *really*? I know what your fiancé's plan is. Was it all just about that?'

Tori paled. *He knew? How did he know?* 'W-What?'

'I know, Tori, but right now I don't care. I just care as to whether what I feel for you is real. That connection. That...'

Hunter's fingers seared Tori's skin as he traced them down

her arms. *But hadn't he been only doing it for the same reasons?*
'But, you… you…'

'Forget what you think,' Hunter said, his mind now
surprisingly lucid. 'I want to know if you're a sham. What I
think you feel is a sham…?'

Tori dared to look into his eyes. 'I-It's not a sham. I… I…
You make me… I…'

Hunter pulled Tori towards him. 'I don't know how we're
going to do this. How the fuck we can do *any* of this, but we
need to try. We need to find a way… All I know is that I need
you…'

Tori focused on Hunter's mouth. *He was right.* She had no
idea how to deal with her conflicting emotions or the
unanswered questions still burning, but she had no choice. She
needed to be with this man. *Somehow she had to be with him.*

Seeing Tori's almost indistinguishable nod, Hunter gently
pressed his mouth to hers, relief, guilt, abject terror and love
coursing through him all at once.

• • • •

AFTER FINALLY GETTING everyone out of the bar under
the strict instructions that not a *word* about what had been
witnessed here tonight would be repeated, Sarah and Colin had
spent a long time cleaning up the broken glass and righting the
upended furniture.

The regulars had been easy to convince, but Noel and Grin
had been another story. Grin was still gobsmacked about
everything and not very impressed about his newly broken
nose. Noel, when he'd finally come round and Sarah had
patched him up as much as possible, was less forgiving. His
initial reaction was to find Hunter and pick up where they'd left
off.

Sarah had lied. She'd said Hunter had gone and thankfully
Grin had had the common sense not to point out her untruths
and tell Noel that he was upstairs. After some convincing from
Grin, Noel had conceded to leave and she'd felt it a good job

because judging by the state of his face it would probably only take one more punch of that magnitude to do damage which she would not have been able to fix without the aid of an operating theatre.

Sitting at the bar with a well-earned drink, she was struggling to get her head around what had actually happened tonight and why.

Colin finished his pint and glanced irritably around his tap room. 'I'm not sitting here any longer,' he griped. 'This is our pub and upstairs is our fucking flat, so I'm going up now.'

Sarah nodded. 'I'll come with you.' They'd given Tori and Hunter space for several hours and although she fully expected Hunter to have passed out, Tori hadn't reappeared and she hoped she'd been correct in standing her ground against Colin. That it was safe for the woman to be on her own with the man who had so disappointed her tonight with his behaviour.

She knew Colin was not pleased and knew there would be an argument at some point soon about it, but she'd thought she'd been doing the right thing.

'You do realise I'm not happy about any of this, Sarah?' Colin muttered as they slowly walked up the stairs to their lounge. 'Hunter wasn't in any fucking state to be alone with anyone, let alone your friend. His hands were all over her, or they would have been had I not stepped in.'

'It certainly was out of character,' Sarah agreed.

'I know you have a lot of time for the bloke, as do I. And I know that I don't know him as well as you, but I think that sometimes you forget what a savage he is deep down.'

Sarah said nothing. She acknowledged Colin was probably right. A lot of people knew what the Reapers had done and were capable of – or at least they knew *some* of those things, especially when Rafe had been in charge, but regardless of what Hunter had done in the past and was capable of, he was different. But perhaps she'd been naïve and he wasn't quite as different as she'd wanted to believe. It had been quite an eyeopener for her to see first-hand what he was like unleashed.

Colin pushed open the lounge door, half expecting to see the place trashed, Hunter passed out on the floor and Tori trembling in the corner, bleeding with torn clothes. *He'd never forgive himself if that was the case...* 'I tell you Sarah, if he's done anyth...'

Both Sarah and Colin stared mutely at the scene in front of them – the opposite of what they'd expected. Hunter lay on the sofa with Tori curled up on top of him. Both were asleep, fully clothed and his arms were wrapped protectively around her. One of her hands was in his hair, the other was placed flat against his chest.

'What the fu...' Colin exclaimed before Sarah nudged him into silence.

'Shh! Don't disturb them,' she hissed, seeing Hunter stir and gently stroke Tori's back.

Sarah had previously had her suspicions that something was going on between those two. After the earlier incident it was possible, *just*, that it was the drink talking and that Tori was too 'nice' – even though she admitted that theory was clutching at straws, but it was no use. However absurd and impossible it was from what she could see in front of her she may well have been right.

Colin stared at Sarah as she dragged him into their bedroom and quietly closed the door. His face felt like it had been slapped with a wet fish. 'He's... he's...' *He couldn't grasp any of this.* 'He's got a thing with *Tori*? For fuck's sake Sarah, did you know about this?'

Sarah's lips pursed. 'I had a theory but I didn't know for certain – she's said nothing to me. It certainly looks that way though, doesn't it?' *It could never work. It was a bloody disaster.*

She kicked off her shoes and sat on the edge of the bed. 'Let's get some sleep. It's late, but whatever happens I want some fucking answers. From *both* of them.'

THIRTY THREE

RICHARD HAD NO choice but to discuss this with Matthew during work hours. He couldn't bring up the subject at home because Susan would invariably ask why he was so interested and that was something he certainly didn't want to have to explain to her, or *anyone*.

This was all so frustrating. It was finished, or it *had* been until this morning. He needed to know exactly why he'd seen his son conversing with one of *them*. His blood ran cold whenever he saw any of those damn Reapers, but it had frozen solid in his veins when he'd driven around the corner on his way to the bank and spotted Matthew talking to one of them in broad daylight.

How he'd avoided steering into something he had no idea, but somehow he'd parked up and made it into the bank. He'd even got through the first three meetings of the day without showing the creeping dread he was experiencing, but there was only so much he could stand before the incessant need to discover what was going on threatened to overwhelm him.

When a knock sounded loudly from the other side of the glass door to his office, Richard glanced up. 'Come in,' he barked.

'What's up, Dad?' Matt said, walking into his father's office and shutting the door behind him. *He'd got a meeting in half an hour.*

He smiled. Thankfully things were back on track now he'd located the girl who had possession of the last missing bag of suspect coke. He'd handed the lot back to Noel on his way in this morning and ok, it hadn't been the brightest idea to pass a carrier bag full of drugs over in public, but what choice did he have? Noel had been *insistent* he got it all back as soon as.

Matt frowned. Noel hadn't looked too good. His face was a complete mess, like he'd been battered by a bunch of prize fighters, but he hadn't liked to ask what had happened and no explanation had been offered. It had been clear the man wasn't in the frame of mind to divulge any information. In fact, he'd hardly got more than two words out of him.

Personally, Matt thought he'd deserved a 'well done' at the very least for retrieving the suspect gear considering he'd been searching around half the night, but no – he hadn't even got a 'thanks'. It was *him* who had the right to be pissed off. *He* was the one who had been messed about because Noel's stuff had been rogue.

'Sit down,' Richard barked. He stared at Matt intently. 'What were you doing with that man?'

Matt blinked. 'What man?'

Richard slammed his hand down on the sheaf of paperwork on his desk. 'Don't act stupid. You know full well what man I'm talking about! The biker I saw you with this morning?'

Matt stared at his father in shock. *How typical for him to be driving past just at that point. He'd been with Noel for less than a minute!* Sweat formed at the back of his neck. *Quick, think of something...* 'Oh, that? He was asking for directions, that's all. Why?'

Richard's eyes narrowed. 'Why would one of the Reapers be asking for directions? Those bastards know every single back road, rat run and bloody sewer around this town.'

Matt raised his eyebrows. He was surprised his father even

knew who the Reapers were, but then again, *everybody* knew them. *Best play it cool.* If his father knew he'd got underhand deals going with Noel, even if it was in the interest of the bank, he'd go berserk. Besides, it was imperative it was believed he'd pulled everything off regarding the investments himself.

'I don't know. He was asking for a particular office.' *Think, think!* 'I guess that lot don't have much call to come to the financial district very often,' Matt laughed.

Richard scrutinised his son. 'I don't want you having anything to do with those people,' he spat.

Matt withheld the urge to ask why this should rattle him so much. 'I don't think you need to worry about that.'

Richard turned his gold pen around in his fingers. He couldn't make too much of a big deal or it would seem strange. He had to control his escalating worry. 'Make sure you have nothing to do with them. Even directions!'

He placed his pen back on the desk and folded his hands together. 'Surely you realise it isn't a good advertisement for a member of this bank to be seen fraternising with *them*.' He paused. 'Especially one who will be the Manager.'

So, that was still on the table? Matt smiled. *It had better fucking be.* 'I have to occasionally see certain members of the Reapers because one of the properties in the regeneration portfolio belongs to them.'

Richard frowned. 'I appreciate that, Matthew, but do *not* speak to them in public, do you understand? Perhaps Jeremy should deal with that specific property? He was overseeing it originally anyway wasn't he, so hand it back to him.'

Matt wasn't handing *anything* back to Jeremy. *He* was running this project, not Jeremy and wouldn't have him getting any kudos from this because his father had developed a complex. 'There's no need for that. I'll make sure there are no public dealings. I rarely need to see them anyway,' he lied.

He'd been more than correct with not informing his father of how they were making this deal work. Christ, based on this reaction he'd have a heart attack if he knew that he'd been to parties with them, got Tori to bed the Reapers' president for information and bought coke from the resident psycho to deal amongst the bank staff… *Yeah, keep that to himself for definite, no matter how astoundingly brilliant his plan was.*

'You need to ensure that,' Richard muttered. 'And Victoria?'

Matt went cold. *Fuck! Was this what this was all about?* Had he discovered what he was doing and was waiting for him to say? That's the sort of thing his father did. He was like a Gestapo interrogator who tricked people into admitting things. 'T-Tori?'

'Yes, you know – your *fiancée*. Is she toeing the line since the last little 'chat' we had about her - shall we say - *attitude*?'

Matt breathed a sigh of relief. 'Yes, yes, she's doing everything she should be. She's been really good like I said she would.' It was true. Surprisingly, Tori had done all that he'd asked and was making great inroads. It wouldn't be long before the project would take off now she'd bedded that fuckhead. She'd astounded him with her resilience to that dreadful situation. Clearly the prospect of losing everything had given her brain that much-needed slap.

Richard knitted his fingers together and rested his chin on them thoughtfully. 'And did you decide to try what I suggested may help?' He raised his eyebrows. 'With the special tablets?'

Matt smiled. 'Yes, but I haven't any news as to whether they've had the desired effect yet. Well, she hasn't said anything, but regardless of that, everything's going well and this deal's running nicely on track.'

'Good, good,' Richard said, glad for confirmation that nothing untoward was occurring. He hadn't realised until today how much fear and dread those Reapers still commanded from him. Plus, if Victoria was subdued that would be even more of a comfortable situation.

. . . .

'WE SHOULD BE at work, Sarah. *Both* of us,' Tori said, her

anxiety levels rising.

'They'll just have to put up with that, won't they?' Sarah snapped.

Tori hadn't meant to oversleep and was surprised it had been possible judging by the uncomfortable position she'd woken in. Although uncomfortable, it had also caused warmth to flood through her when she'd realised she was lying in Hunter's arms. That was until the recollection of the previous night had seeped into her mind.

Raising her head, she'd studied Hunter's gorgeous face inches from hers and brushed a strand of his dark blond hair away from his face. Even though it had still been caked and matted with Noel's dried blood he was still the most amazing looking man. *Perfect.*

But he'd said a lot last night. A lot of which had worried her greatly and some which had made her glow, but none of it mattered if it had purely been the drink talking. Even if it hadn't been, it still didn't change the overall desperate situation they were both in, or at least, *she* was in.

Part of her fears had been allayed when, with a hungover groan, Hunter had awoken, his usually crystal-clear grey eyes bloodshot and heavy.

'Christ, I feel fucking awful!' he'd moaned.

Feeling shy and nervously waiting for excuses and apologies to flow, Tori had self-consciously pushed herself off and made to get up.

'Where do you think you're going?' Hunter had asked, pulling her back towards him with a strong arm. 'I may be hungover, but I haven't lost my memory.' His smile dropped momentarily. 'I never do…' he muttered. 'I meant what I said last night.'

Tori had felt herself flood when Hunter's hands had trailed sensuously down her thighs and pulled her further up his body towards her, his rock-hard erection pressing against her stomach.

Hunter had gently pulled Tori towards him, his lips meeting

hers. She'd desperately wanted him, but unfortunately they'd forgotten they were lying on a sofa in the middle of Colin and Sarah's lounge and when Sarah had appeared in the doorway it had been clear neither of them would be walking away from this as if nothing had happened.

Not prepared to wait a second longer for an explanation, Sarah had sternly instructed both of them to *'get their arses off my fucking sofa and talk!'* And so they were sitting around the dining room table with Colin and Sarah opposite.

What made it even worse was that Tori hadn't had time to think how she would handle this situation, or what on earth she would say. What she *did* know was she would have to put her cards on the table, even if that meant Hunter walked away in disgust. She couldn't do this on any level if she wasn't honest with everyone. There had been too many lies in her life already.

The information she'd withheld from Sarah alone had been playing on her mind for long enough and she needed to tell her what was going on. Her heart was controlling her right now and she'd never felt more certain about anything. She glanced at Hunter and hoped somehow she could balance this constant arguing in her head and override the gulf between their two worlds.

Hunter swigged at his steaming tea like it was water. He liked a good throat-burner in the mornings to blow the cobwebs away. Under the table his hand lingered on Tori's thigh and was doing nothing to diminish the raging erection still straining incessantly against his jeans. He looked at Sarah who was cutting daggers whilst remaining silent, clearly waiting for him to speak.

Colin wasn't looking at anyone. Hunter could see the man was struggling to control his temper and he understood that. If it had been the other way around he'd have been livid too and for that he was extremely sorry to have been the cause.

'I'll talk, shall I?' Hunter said, lighting a cigarette. He glanced at Tori sitting stiffly in the chair next to him, her eyes wide with fear.

'I will start firstly by apologising. And I mean *really* apologising. I let you down, Sarah. Actually, I let *both* of you down and I'm very sorry.' He locked eyes with Sarah. 'You and Colin are the *last* people I would disrespect or upset purposefully and I know I have done both. I was out of control.'

'That's not an excuse,' Sarah spat. 'You came in here, kicked off an...'

Colin raised his hand. 'Let him speak, Sarah.'

Hunter nodded at Colin. 'I'm not justifying what I did. I lost control. That's all I can say. Apart from I didn't know Georgie was pregnant.' He felt Tori stiffen. 'Had I known, I would have done the right thing by her, I think you know that.'

Blowing out a plume of smoke slowly, Hunter stared at a point on the wall. He found it difficult to talk about stuff like this, but he owed it to this couple and perhaps Tori too. 'I loved Georgie in my own way, but I could never give her what she wanted. As you know we've had an on-off thing for years. She asked for nothing - apart from my heart, which was the one thing I couldn't give her.'

His face hardened. 'I called anything we had off a few nights ago, because I... because...' He shook his head, unable to formulate his words. 'I had no idea she was carrying my child. If I had, I would still have ended the one-sided relationship, but I would have been there for her.'

Hunter paused, aware the room was so silent it was almost ghost-like. 'When she died I felt guilty, so I went on a bender.'

'I've never seen you like that before,' Sarah said. 'And I didn't like it.'

Hunter nodded. 'I've been like that a *lot* of times in the past and I know it's not good enough, but...'

'I know what happened when you were young and that it fucked you up, but it's st...'

'What happened?' Tori cut in.

Hunter shot Sarah a glare and turned to Tori. 'Nothing for you to worry about.' He switched his attention back to Sarah. 'I've controlled myself for a *very* long time.'

'But wh…'

'Look, I just tipped over the edge - it's as simple as that.' Hunter pulled a wad of money from his pocket. 'This is for the damage to your car.'

Tori watched him push the pile of folded notes over the table towards Sarah.

'My car isn't worth that much,' Sarah said, scowling.

'Irrelevant. Take the fucking money, Sarah. And Colin, I'll replace anything that got damaged in the bar. Just give me the bill,' Hunter said, watching Colin nod stiffly.

'And what about this joke regarding you two?' Sarah glared at Tori. It stung that her friend had not told her about any of this. 'How long has this ridiculous shit between you been going on?'

Tori felt like crying. She knew she'd hurt Sarah by keeping things from her and had suspected her reaction would have been like this if she'd breathed a word about how she felt about Ash Hunter.

'I think I can speak for both of us in saying that it's been brewing for some time.' Hunter looked at Tori and gently touched her hot cheeks. 'But nothing happened until I stopped things with Georgie.'

He ran his hand through his hair. 'I'll be honest. I've been struggling with how I feel,' he continued, still looking at Tori intensely.

Sarah snorted. 'You're deluded. You *can't* be together. It's fucking ridiculous and your club will never allow it. Besides, you're too… too different.'

'I don't give a fuck about any of that!' Hunter roared. 'I want her.'

Sarah pursed her lips. 'You've wanted a *lot* of people and fucking had plenty since I've known you.'

Tori cringed. *What Sarah was saying she was just one of many and nothing special. Nothing different…*

Hunter's eyes narrowed. 'Like I said, Sarah, I have a lot of respect for you, but that doesn't give you the right to talk to me like that.' He clenched his jaw. 'You have no idea how I feel.'

Sarah glared at Hunter. She probably was speaking out of turn but she didn't want Tori getting ripped to pieces. 'So, how exactly *do* you feel, Hunter?' she raged. 'Tori has a lot to lose here. A hell of a lot.'

Standing up, Hunter smashed his fist down on the table. 'What? That wanker, you mean? The fucking prick wh...'

'Hunter, that's enough!' Tori said, pulling at Hunter's T-shirt. *This was getting stupid and she had to say something.*

'I think you've said all there is to say, Sarah.' Colin shot his wife a look. 'The man has been big enough to apologise and to give his reasons. That should be good enough. I can't imagine someone like Noel doing that, can you? You've got no right to expect him to explain his feelings.'

'Oh, shut up!' Sarah griped. 'I can do what I want. And that's another thing... What are you going to do about Noel? He's supposed to be your Vice Pre...'

'I tell you what, Sarah. If you really want to fucking know how I feel, then I'll tell you.' Hunter was still standing up, a vein in his neck twitching wildly. 'I'm in love with this woman.' He grabbed Tori's wrist and pulled her to her feet. 'Do you hear me? I fucking *love* her and I'm not prepared to walk away from this. For the record, I don't give a shit about Noel or what he thinks.'

Tori swayed unsteadily at Hunter's words, feeling like her legs would give out any minute. She still had to tell Hunter and the others what she knew and it would shatter everything. Her head was spinning. The other option was to say nothing and let it run. At least whilst she sorted out what to do about Matt and his threats. No. It was no use. She couldn't do that.

Sarah was gobsmacked by Hunter's admission. She'd had her suspicions, which had only been backed up by what he'd drunkenly said last night, but she hadn't thought it could *really* be possible. Not from Hunter. Lust, yes... but *love*? She shook her head sadly.

She turned her gaze to Tori. Now, she didn't look too happy

about Hunter's declaration. Could it be she'd been mistaken and the feeling wasn't mutual? Sarah's heart slightly ached for Hunter. If what he'd just said was genuine, then for him to admit that must have taken a hell of a lot and must be the 'real deal' for him. It was not something she'd foreseen in a million years and for it to happen with someone like Tori made it even more difficult.

'You don't seem too happy, Tori?' Sarah said quietly. 'Was that not something you expected to hear?'

Hunter's head swung around to look at Tori and her stomach sunk further. 'No, I didn't. It's all been a b…'

'You don't feel the same?' Hunter interrupted, pain raw in his face, quickly masked with his usual neutral expression. *Fuck, fuck, FUCK!* Quickly dropping his hands from Tori's waist, he turned away.

Tori placed her hand on Hunter's arm. 'NO!' she cried. 'It's not like that. That's not what I meant. Oh God…' She felt tears spring from her eyes. 'You… you've made me feel… so different…'

Hunter turned to face her once more. '*Different*?' he spat. 'What's that supposed to fucking mean?'

Tori swallowed hard, sensing Sarah and Colin shuffle uncomfortably in their seats. 'You've made me feel strong for the first time in my life. You've made me feel… things… Things I never knew existed,' she blushed.

Hunter didn't move a muscle and refrained from wiping the tears from her face. *That statement didn't mean shit. She still hadn't said how she felt. Had he just blown his soul for fuck all?*

'I-I…' The words stuck in Tori's throat. 'I-I'm scared.'

'Is this about Matt again? Your status?' Hunter spat. He wasn't going to stand here and be publicly humiliated for much longer. 'Spit it out, Tori or at least let me leave with *some* fucking self-respect!'

'I'm scared because of how I feel about you,' Tori blurted. 'I'm so in love I feel drugged. It's physically painful.'

Hunter relaxed, his arms circling Tori's waist again and

pulling her towards her. 'Tori... I...'

Tori placed her hands against Hunter's chest to stop him from kissing her. If he kissed her then she'd never be able to do it. 'But there's something I need to tell you first.' She turned to Colin and Sarah. '*All* of you.'

THIRTY FOUR

SARAH GLANCED AT Hunter stubbing out yet another cigarette in her ashtray. His initial anger had turned to shock, then back to anger and had stabilised at logic.

Tori's admission of what was going on behind the scenes where that rat of a fiancé of hers was concerned had shocked them all to the core. She, for one, had been on the verge of throwing the girl out of her pub by her hair. The look of fury on Hunter's face could have sunk a thousand ships. That had been until Tori had filled them in with exactly *why* she'd been involved. Even so, Sarah could hardly get her head around it.

It did make a bit more sense as to why Tori had felt so strongly against bikers if her father had been murdered by one and also why she put up with the crap Matt had been dishing out if she was trying to protect her father's name and her mother, although from what she gathered about Lillian Morgan, she wasn't sure why Tori was so hell bent on doing anything for that woman whatsoever.

Hunter's mind was in overdrive. He stared at the table in front of him. He'd been aware Tori had been sent to get information which he couldn't be too put out about – after all, he'd been guilty of the same thing, but it didn't change what had happened between them. What was bothering him more was Noel. *Noel was setting him up?*

The one consolation he took was that at least the death of Tori's father had been nothing to do with the Reapers, he could assure her of that. He knew or had been party to *everything* the club had been involved in for a *very* long time - much longer than he'd been president and so could safely say there had been *no* hit carried out on someone around here who had been undercutting their dealing. That situation had only ever occurred once and it had been with a rival group of bikers from London.

But Noel? *The two-faced sneaky piece of shit.* He felt the adrenalin pounding in his veins. If that fucker was here right now he'd kill him with his bare hands without a second thought. His initial reaction had been to go straight back to the Factory and rip him to fucking pieces, but instead Sarah had insisted they make a plan. *A plan to sort this out once and for all.*

Hunter scowled. How was he supposed to think about anything apart from how he would make Noel suffer?

Tori, meanwhile, sat limply in the corner of the room. She'd distanced herself from the other three to give them time to calm down. Her eyes were red and swollen from crying and she hadn't known where to look, what to do or say once, like verbal diarrhoea, she'd blurted her secrets from her mouth.

She couldn't work out whether they despised her or not. Hunter's face had been a seething mass of rage and the combination of shock and hurt on Sarah's face had stabbed deep at her heart. Every last ounce of Tori's strength had been sapped and she quietly waited for the firing squad to decide her fate.

'Right. Here's what I suggest,' Sarah said, breaking the silence. She had no idea if this would be acceptable to anyone or even feasible, but she had to suggest *something*. Without saying the words it was obvious Hunter was leaning towards wreaking havoc on Noel and she couldn't say she blamed him. Tori, on the other hand, looked as though her life was over. Personally, although her initial reaction had been to slap Tori's pretty little face for her betrayal, she knew something had to be decided before everything went even more tits up in every conceivable direction.

Checking she had everyone's attention, Sarah cleared her throat. 'I suggest we carry on as normal.'

'You *what*?' Hunter yelled in disbelief. 'You expect me to carry on with that treacherous cunt, Noel, as if nothing has happened? Are you insane?' It had seared his flesh that Noel felt he'd be better running the Reapers than him, he was letting the side down and would do whatever he needed to gain control of the club.

'I think you'll have to, Hunter. It's the only way we can stop them in their tracks without people getting killed.' Sarah eyed him accusingly. 'I know what you must want to do.'

'And you wouldn't be wrong!' Hunter spat. 'Being as you think you have all the answers, how do you propose we do this?'

'Well…' Sarah bit her bottom lip. 'Tori, firstly you must behave normally with Matt. As far as you're concerned everything *is* normal.'

'How can I when he finds out I've told you?' Tori squeaked, her eyes wide. *Matt would kill her if her mother didn't get to her first.* 'I can't even go home after this.'

'Yes you can. Matt won't be aware anything's changed unless one of us screws this up,' Sarah said, eyeing Hunter. 'We need to play them at their own game. If they don't know *we* know they'll play straight into our hands and cause their own destruction.'

'At least you now know the property deals were fake and your gut instinct was right,' Colin added. 'But how do we stop people signing without Matt and Noel realising we're on to them?'

Sarah pursed her lips. 'One step at a time. I haven't thought about that yet. The most important thing is to how to act initially, but we'll sort something out.'

'How long will all of this take?' Tori mumbled. Her head was scrambled. 'Matt's on a tight deadline to close this deal so they'll be planning on ramping it up sooner rather than later. It won't take him long to work out something's gone adrift and when he realises I've shafted him by telling you, he'll kill me for sure.'

'He'll have to get through me first!' Hunter snarled. 'This won't work, Sarah. I don't want Tori anywhere *near* that fucker. She can come to stay with me at the Factory.' His arm locked protectively around Tori's trembling shoulders.

'You see! You're doing it already!' Sarah snapped. 'Stop right now. Tori *has* to go back to Matt. She'll have to put up with his shit. She needs to listen to him, go along with *everything* he says and continue to sleep with him, do you understand? It has *got* to be business as usual.'

Hunter's teeth clenched, making a horrible grinding noise as he fought to control his rage.

'If Tori moves into the Factory, then you're fucked. The club won't run with you if they think you've swapped sides.'

'Why does it have be about sides?' Tori cried furiously.

'Because that's how it works around here,' Sarah said sharply. 'Tori, I haven't got time to babysit your emotions, I really haven't. Get yourself in check or throw yourself to the wolves from both fucking sides and accept that wanker of a boyfriend of yours has won, because I'm telling you that will be the outcome if either of you start doing the shit coming out of your mouths.'

'Sarah,' Colin said sternly. *She was getting on her high horse again.* 'You really need to t…'

'No, Colin. It needs to be said,' Sarah yelled. '*Someone* has to spell things out. I'm not standing by and letting psycho Noel turn over the only decent Reaper this town has had in a long fucking time. Neither do I want some jumped up prick dictate and ruin the lives of countless decent people around here. That includes *you*, Tori. You've already put up with far too much from that greedy bastard and that selfish mother of yours to last you a lifetime and it stops *here*. What's a bit longer of putting up with them – however galling it may be, if it means we can expose them for what they are with minimum casualties?'

Hunter nodded slightly. *Sarah was right*. Once it all came out Noel would be lynched – himself being at the front of the queue and Matt would lose everything. He smirked. If he had anything to do with it Matt would lose his fucking life, however he wouldn't add that into the mix just yet by voicing it.

He looked at Tori longingly. *He needed to protect her and wanted to be with this woman.*

Watching Hunter's mind tick, Sarah frowned. She could almost taste his thoughts. 'You two can always come here if needs be to, well… spend some time together, however I appreciate this isn't the best and most usual way to begin the 'romance of the century'.' She smiled slightly at her inability to hide the sarcasm. *Why the hell should she? She hadn't asked to be involved in this bullshit.*

Colin frowned. 'That's not a good idea. It would only be a matter of time before someone noticed them disappearing together upstairs and I don't want to be part of any of this, if truth be known.' He didn't need any more trouble brought to his door.

'Maybe you're right,' Sarah mused. She had to remember whatever she suggested inadvertently involved Colin too. This wasn't even her battle to fight, but he knew what she was like and that she'd feel compelled to try and help sort the mess. *And she would!*

'Matt wants me to work further on Hunter in his unused apartment,' Tori said quietly. 'He'd already said spending too much time at the Factory will cause suspicion.'

'Well isn't he the clever one!' Hunter snarled. *How he'd love to wring the bloke's neck.*

'We discussed it the other day, but then he got side-tracked with a mad rush getting something for Noel,' Tori added.

'And what was that?' Hunter asked.

Tori shrugged. 'No idea. He was running around like a headless chicken, but I'll find out.'

Hunter's eyes narrowed. *And if you don't, I will…* 'Ok, let's do it. Sort out with Matt about this flat of his and we'll go there. You can continue getting info from him and acting suitably horrified about dealing with me and I'll do my part at the Factory. And yes, Sarah, I'll behave myself with Noel. For now…'

'But what should I do about contacting you. How will I know when I'm meeting you and how do I get this to tie up with what Matt wants me to do?' Tori asked.

Hunter smiled. 'Don't you worry about that. You'll know.'

Tori nodded. It was hardly the way she'd wanted or expected things to go, but at least everything was out in the open from her side. *There also might be light at the end of the tunnel.*

THIRTY FIVE

MATT CONTINUED THRUSTING, whilst twisting Ginny's hair tightly, enjoying that she liked it a little rough as much as he did. His head was rushing, courtesy of the fresh coke Noel had given him for personal use as a freebie to make up for the previous 'mistake' until he'd secured another batch to sell. *That's if he had any customers left.*

What with all the stress he'd been under lately he'd felt it only right he should have a bit of time out, so he'd jumped at the chance to go on a bit of a bender with Jeremy and Ginny.

Jeremy was good in that respect. Even if he wasn't the best at much else, he certainly wasn't tight with his sharing ability. For instance, he had no problem sharing Ginny. And Ginny, well, she was up for a lot more than Tori, so it worked out well.

Matt glanced over to where Jeremy was snorting another line of coke whilst watching Ginny get a seeing to. He seemed to be enjoying himself. He'd said it before but would say it again. If only Ginny was the one he'd been promised to then he wouldn't feel half as hard done by. Still, at least this way he got the best of both worlds.

Matt twisted Ginny's hair harder and he grinned hearing her yelps. 'You love this don't you?' he growled, his arousal intensifying.

'Yes, oh yes,' Ginny panted, digging her false nails into Matt's buttocks. 'Harder, babe. Harder!'

Matt duly obliged, pushing Ginny's legs up towards her chest and driving home hard.

Ginny smiled. She was giving it all with her moans and groans of pleasure. She had to find a way to get into Matt's life on a more permanent basis. She'd never quite understood what his obsession with Tori was, the dull frigid bitch. It was clear *she* did more for him than Tori ever could, so what exactly was her hold?

Her mind had been working overtime for many months on that question. She'd even grilled Jeremy over it, but all he knew – or rather, all he'd *said*, was that it was something which been agreed ages ago and that was just how it was.

Although Jeremy was ok and Ginny kind of liked him, he wasn't a *patch* on Matt what with what he could offer. Matt's status alone would afford her so much more, both in social standing and in clothes, holidays and whatever she wanted. Plus, that would only increase once he'd got his promotion. The house they could live in would be mint and she didn't doubt there would be many elite parties.

She couldn't see Tori enjoying or appreciating any of that. The woman didn't enjoy or appreciate *anything* and nothing pleased her. She hadn't even been around that much lately and was absent again tonight, but she hadn't much cared. The less time she had to spent in forced conversation with that vacant cow, the better.

Ginny knew something was going on behind the scenes with the boys as they were always discussing things out of earshot, but she was used to that. She had no particular wish to know anything about their boring jobs. Her only concern on that score was what it could afford *her*.

The date of Matt's marriage was looming closer and she'd quite happily accept being his bit on the side, as long as Jeremy was happy and Matt offered her an attractive enough package.

That was unless she could go one better. Being Matt's bit on the side wouldn't be *anywhere* remotely close to having the kudos that being his *wife* would bring.

The more she thought about it, the more she wondered whether it was achievable to get him to change his mind and pick her over Tori?

Pushing her escalating frustration over the unjust situation to one side, Ginny forced herself to concentrate back on the here and now. Matt needed to be reminded once again exactly what he *could* have full time, should he choose it.

· · · ·

WHEN THEY'D FIRST arrived at the apartment – separately of course, the minute the door had closed behind them, Hunter had lifted Tori on to the breakfast bar. Kissing her hungrily and in too much haste to remove any clothing, he'd pulled her skirt up, pushed her knickers to one side and thrust straight into her.

Standing up against the breakfast bar, Hunter had slammed into her with such force and speed she would have shot clean off the surface she'd been sitting on had he not had a firm hold of her. His mouth had invaded hers with such a state of frenzy and his frantic driving pace had pushed her extremely quickly to a terrifying height. Tori's climax had been so strong her mind had whited-out as her orgasm exploded around her. She'd screamed loudly but hadn't cared in the slightest.

The second time they'd made love had been in the large walk-in double shower. Stripping off his jeans and T-shirt, Hunter had let them fall to the marble floor of the bathroom and Tori had quivered at the sight of his large muscular body. Pressing her against the tiled wall, the cold against her back had contrasted sharply with the hot jets spraying from the multiple shower heads as the water had cascaded onto their entwined bodies.

Coming hard once again, Tori had been glad Hunter's strong arms had been supporting her. Her jerking, shaking legs would not have been capable of holding her upright when the rush of pleasure had coursed through her, rendering her incapable of anything else but surrendering to it.

For tonight at least, they had convinced themselves they were a 'normal' couple who just happened to live in this sumptuous apartment in one of the most sought after areas of town and that they didn't have the dilemma which they had found themselves in hanging precariously over their heads.

She'd been overjoyed when Matt had agreed she should take Hunter to the apartment tonight, but she'd done well in acting suitably horrified. She'd had no idea how she would let Hunter know of the plan, but thankfully, Sarah had sorted that out and contacted him.

Tori had wanted to ask Hunter what had happened at the Factory but had refrained. She'd wanted to enjoy this 'normality' for as long as possible, knowing they would have to discuss the subject that neither of them wanted to broach before long, but there would be time enough for that later.

Once their desperate initial urge had been sated, Hunter had carried her to the bedroom and laid her on the bed, where she'd drifted into a strange reality. Her body, soul and mind were acutely tuned into the overwhelming, crushing love she felt and when Hunter had started to gently caress her once more, his kisses so tender, she hadn't felt like she would be capable, physically or mentally of him taking her again, but his touch, now no longer frenzied, but slow and feather-like, quickly proved her wrong.

Tori's body burnt as Hunter traced a line down between her breasts with his tongue and his fingers worked her closer and closer to orgasm. She ran her fingers over her erect nipples, shuddering as her own touch caused further ripples of arousal. Groaning with need, she pulled at Hunter's hair.

Making his way back up her body, Hunter's teeth nipped at Tori's throat before his mouth found hers. Positioning himself between her legs, he eased himself into her and moved slowly and she moaned as waves of love and desire merged into one.

Her fingers wound in Hunter's hair as he thrust slowly,

causing a ball of pressure to grow and her hips lifted further in time with his thrusts. She gasped helplessly. She was going to come. *Again.* Arching her back, she pressed herself further against him, holding her breath as the crescendo rose.

Crying out as the gently to build, but strong orgasm coursed through her, Tori clutched at the sheets as the waves rolled. Feeling Hunter expand further inside, her core clenched and spasmed as the final waves of her climax washed over her, finishing with Hunter growling loudly, his body stiffening as he flooded into her.

Sighing with complete satisfaction, Tori turned and rested her head on his large, hard chest. She drank in his smell – the manly scent that only *he* possessed and which alone made her nerve-endings tingle.

Being alone in the apartment had caused a huge outpouring of relief in as much that at this moment in time, nothing else existed. Just her and this man who had just made love to her in such a delicate way she felt she may burst with happiness.

They lay quietly for a while, content in their silence and Tori relaxed into Hunter's body whilst his hand gently stroked her hair.

'Tori?' Hunter said, his voice soft.

Raising her head, Tori propped herself up on one elbow and looked into Hunter's dangerously handsome face. She traced a finger over his lips and smiled. 'Yes?'

'You're fucking amazing,' he murmured, his hands running gently over her back.

Feeling him start to harden once more, Tori felt the unmistakeable tinge of desire and she smiled at herself in disbelief. *This man – Ash Hunter – had transformed her into an insatiable woman.*

THIRTY SIX

TORI HAD SUSPECTED it would be difficult to be in the same room as Hunter whilst acting like they hadn't spent the entire night thoroughly exploring each other's bodies, but it was going to be more difficult than she'd bargained for. A *lot* more difficult and she hadn't even set eyes on him yet.

Hunter had already told her, once they'd finally discussed the elephant in the room last night, that his plan for the next day was for Noel to get Matt to meet him in the White Hart and she should expect to accompany him. He'd smoothed things over with Noel, in as much as he'd forced himself to apologise for the kicking – and Noel being Noel, high on the ego-boost of Hunter's apology, had accepted it.

Hunter had then suggested Noel meet Matt to hand over some gear, but to bring Jeremy, as well as her and Ginny so as not to make anything look suspicious. Noel had liked this idea, especially after Hunter had reminded him he could also work on Tori and try to get further information about what Matt was planning.

Both Tori and Hunter knew Noel would immediately relay the plans back to Matt and of course, they'd been right. Within five minutes of speaking to Noel, Matt had been on the phone telling Tori they were going to the White Hart and to prepare for Hunter to make his next move.

It had all fitted in nicely with what she'd said to Matt when he'd grilled her about how she'd got on in the apartment. Interestingly, he'd seemed a bit taken aback that she'd spent *all* night there, but Tori had responded with the correct reaction.

'I'm trying to convince him that I want to be with him, aren't I?' she'd said. 'I think he's falling for it, although he treats me like a piece of shit and is very stand-offish, but still, I think I'm getting somewhere.'

Matt had looked suitably pleased that Hunter wasn't being too nice, but something had bothered him. 'I hope he's not better than me in bed?' he'd asked.

He'd tried to make it sound like a half-joke, but Tori had known the thought of anyone being better than him at *anything* would infuriate him deeply. She'd managed to look suitably horrified. 'Oh God, Matt. It's *disgusting*! He's awful! He's rough and it hurts me. The man makes my skin crawl.'

Tori had felt terrible having to say something like that about Hunter. He was beautiful and how he made her feel was *amazing*, but she had to keep up the act. She had to make Matt believe he was in control.

Matt had looked pleased with Tori's response and had patted her on the thigh. 'It shouldn't be for much longer. What info did you get?'

Tori had tried hard to look thoughtful. 'I think I've planted an idea in his mind. He hadn't mentioned anything about you, so I instigated it. I said that you'd been looking at another area for regeneration and wondered was it was about.'

Apparently she'd done well because what she'd said was to be used as the base for tonight's plan. Matt had instructed her to play along with anything Hunter may do, but she was to pretend she was telling him something in confidence. This 'something' was to be that although Matt didn't want him to know, it looked like the investors were thinking of pulling out.

Tori's job was to make out that Matt had told her the

investors thought the deals were taking too long to complete, but he didn't want Hunter to know anything was amiss. She was to insinuate alternative areas had been found which were contenders for regeneration instead.

She was to insinuate that Matt was hoping Hunter and the rest of the people involved in the project *wouldn't* sign because he stood to make more cash from the newer deal. This would then give her the further opportunity to beg Hunter to close the deals quickly and get the others to do the same as she didn't want him to miss out on such a great offer…

Matt was certain reverse psychology was the way to go and believed she would be the catalyst to finally twist Hunter's arm. Tori smiled. He clearly had no clue they were onto him and Noel and that was good.

Just the *thought* of Matt's face when he fell flat on his face propelled her forwards. She'd purposefully not dwelt too much on what this meant for her mother, because all she could think of was that she would not be marrying Matt and it was such a relief. She didn't care how everything else panned out if she had Ash Hunter by her side.

'Remind me why we're in this dump again?' Ginny's nasally voice was as ever, over-loud.

Jeremy glared at her. 'Because we need to pick up something, that's why. Now keep your voice down. We don't want to get kicked out,' he hissed.

Ginny rolled her overly made-up eyes. *Boring. Couldn't they even have a game of 'Spot the Scrubber'? Jeremy was getting far too serious lately.* Pouting, she turned her attention to Matt. 'I hope it's good stuff?'

Matt winked. 'Isn't it always?' *It had better be this time as well*, he thought, a flash of irritation sparking. Still, the gear wasn't the main reason they were here. He glanced at Tori who looked uncomfortable. She'd better remember what he'd told her to say. Tonight could clinch the deal once and for all.

'You shouldn't be arranging that sort of stuff to be done here. You know I don't like it,' Tori sniffed. 'It isn't right and you're more than aware I work with Sarah. It could make things really awkward.' She ensured she wore the correct expression. Sarah knew what was planned, but it would seem out of character if she hadn't made some remark about her unhappiness over the drugs. *She needed to get this spot on.*

'I see your absences of late have done nothing to change your miserable demeanour?' Ginny bitched, inspecting her long fuchsia talons in a blatant display of boredom.

Tori turned away and was sipping at her drink just as Sarah approached.

'Hello Tori. You in here again?' Sarah said. 'Nice to see you with your friends.' She nodded cheerily at the others around the table.

'Erm, yes... They fancied a trip over here for a change,' Tori replied quickly. She knew Sarah would say something along those lines. It's what had been agreed in case any of the locals commented on her frequent presence.

'Did we say we fancied a trip here? Must have completely slipped my mind, that one,' Ginny said frostily. She hadn't planned on *ever* spending another evening in this flea-infested dive. 'I didn't realise you'd been spending so much time here, Tori,' she continued, wondering if Matt had any idea his fiancée has been frequenting this place. *And without him too.*

Sarah smiled warmly, successfully hiding the utter contempt she felt for the conceited bitch. 'Actually, Tori's been very kindly helping me with some personal things, but everything's ok now, so I won't be taking her away from you guys so often I don't expect.'

'Can't say I noticed she wasn't around,' Ginny laughed loudly. 'Never mind!'

Sarah's lips formed into a tight line and she bit back a suitable retort. She began collecting some of the glasses in the hope it would divert the need from smashing the cow's perfect teeth out of her face.

'Actually, I need to grab something from Noel too,' Matt said, flashing his best smile in Sarah's direction. 'Do you happen to know if he'll be in soon?'

Sarah glanced at Matt's smarmy face and then at the clock. 'It's collection night tonight,' she said, smiling widely and secretly enjoying the look of distaste on Ginny's face. 'So he shouldn't be long. The boys always like a drink or two afterwards.'

She smiled at Tori's nervousness. 'Don't worry Tori, I won't let them bite you.'

Blushing, Tori tried to smile. She could kill Sarah for saying something like that. She didn't want any more attention drawn to her. She was already struggling knowing Hunter would walk through that door any minute.

Matt laughed. 'Yes, sorry about her. She gets ridiculously nervous. She's got a pathetic paranoia about certain 'types'. An unfortunate throwback caused by a silly incident in her past, I'm afraid.'

Matt's voice was condescending, patronising and downright nasty and Sarah found it even harder to keep the grin she wore in place. *What a horrible bastard this man was.* Saying that when he knew full well what had happened to Tori's father… 'Well, she'll be safe here.'

Sarah returned to the bar with the empty glasses before she forgot herself and said something scathing to that revolting piece of shit.

· · · ·

NOEL SAUNTERED INTO the pub. How he'd enjoyed Hunter's apology yesterday. How he'd *loved* hearing him being contrite over his behaviour and how bad he'd felt for taking his rage out on his trusted second-in-command.

He smiled. *Little do you know, Hunter, you fucking loser. I won't be Vice President for much longer.*

Noel would admit he'd found it hard to pretend he'd accepted the apology. Although he hadn't accepted it *too* quickly, he'd still had to accept it sooner than he would have realistically chosen, but he'd had little choice if he wanted to move forward with the plan. *And that he did want. Very much.*

He glanced at Grin. Grin's feelings were hurt over Hunter head-butting him more than anything else, but he'd accepted his apology gracefully. Like the rest of the club that man respected Hunter's authority without question, but that wouldn't last for much longer either - not when Hunter's judgement, along with everything else was questioned.

In fact, Hunter couldn't have played it better than if Noel had orchestrated it himself, but how he wished he hadn't been out cold when the overgrown bastard had drunkenly declared his undying love for Miss Aristocrat in front of a full room. Still, he'd use that against the twat when the time was right.

Grin had pulled Noel to one side the very next day and voiced his worries about it and if it worried Grin, then it would certainly worry the rest of the club too.

Noel smiled again. *Everyone* knew of Hunter's raw hatred for Tori's sort and if it looked like he was going to jump ship to *be* with one of them – not just a fuck, but actually *be* with one of them, that would cause more than a few questions over his sincerity.

Grin hadn't said it in so many words, but Noel deduced purely from the bits he *had* said that he wasn't overly impressed about Hunter's declaration, drunk or not, especially so soon after Georgie's death. Everything was about respect from where the Reapers stood and it appeared Hunter had very little of that and so he was gradually losing the respect of the others. *And that would only get a lot worse.*

Still, for now all Noel could do was enjoy being part of manufacturing Hunter's gradual demise. It would be fun to see him work Miss Aristocrat in front of everyone. Again, it would get everyone asking questions, even if it were only in their own heads. The man would sow the seeds of doubt himself.

Noel was also looking forward to seeing what Matt had instructed the posh bitch to do. *This would be a good night.*

· · · ·

HUNTER TRIED TO concentrate on what was going on around him, but his eyes were consistently drawn back to Tori sitting at a table in the main part of the tap room.

His flesh still tingled from the memory of her hands on him and the feel of her wrapped around him and he knew he would have trouble containing himself until the next time they could be alone. His body ached for her and he'd never felt need like it. His whole being was finely attuned to every little thing, making his senses crisp and heightened.

He knew he had to pull himself back down into his usual controlled state because he was no use to *anyone* like this. He just wasn't sure how he would do it. He'd never had to deal with anything like this before. He'd never been in love and now he'd fallen so hard it was crucifying him. He tipped his pint into his mouth. *Whatever happened he had to get a handle on himself and fast.*

Pushing himself to his feet, Hunter walked across the tap room. Passing Tori, his eyes burnt into hers. 'Tori,' he smiled, his heart thundering. Nodding at the others he continued towards the bar.

'Same again?' Sarah asked, making Hunter jump.

'Please,' he nodded.

'I've been watching you,' Sarah hissed. 'And I've been watching Noel watching you. You need to sort yourself out.'

Hunter frowned. 'What do you mean?' *He already knew what Sarah was going to say and she'd be right.*

'You're staring at Tori *all* the time! Put your feelings away and get your poker face on. We need to sort this.'

'I know…' Hunter grinned bashfully. 'I'm just not used to it.'

Sarah couldn't help but smile. It was quite sweet. She looked at the big man in front of her. There was no doubt about it. Ash Hunter had genuinely fallen head over heels by the looks of it. She squeezed his arm. 'All of this will come good in the end somehow.'

Hunter's face set in a resolute expression. 'It better had.'

THIRTY SEVEN

TORI KNEW WHAT the nudge Matt had given her under the table meant. *It was time to do her part of tonight's plan.* She'd also seen Hunter glance at her as he'd strode through the bar and had been aware of his eyes on her since the moment he'd walked in. Her heart had been racing, but now he'd gone in the direction of the toilets it had accelerated to fever pitch with the prospect of a few snatched minutes with him.

Picking up her handbag, Tori rose to her feet. 'I'm just popping to the Ladies.'

Getting no response, short of a small nod from Matt, she hastily made her way out of the tap room and into the back hallway.

There was no sign of anyone. *Where was Hunter?* Should she wait for him to leave the Gents, or should she go into the Ladies? She didn't want to miss him, but equally she couldn't lurk in the corridor in case anyone else appeared.

Without warning, Tori was grabbed from the side and pulled into a recess she had not previously noticed in the dimly lit area. Before she could do anything, Hunter quickly brought his mouth down on hers.

Wrapping her arms around his neck, Tori melted into him,

relishing the feel of his strong arms around her and his lips on hers.

Hunter reluctantly pulled away. 'God, Tori. You've no idea how much I want to bin this rubbish off and just take you somewhere else,' he murmured.

Tori pressed her nose into Hunter's chest, inhaling the smell of his leather jacket, which although had once frightened her, was now figuring nightly in her dreams. 'Me too.'

'But we have to do this, so...' Hunter took a deep breath. 'What's the plan?'

Tori hastily recounted Matt's instructions and Hunter frowned before a slight smile broke across his face. 'Oh, I've got it...'

'What? What are you going to do?' Tori asked nervously. 'Hurry, I need to get back in there.'

Hunter cocked an eyebrow. 'I'm going to have a little bit of fun with your lovely Matthew.'

Tori's heart sank. 'Don't mess it up. It wi...'

'Don't worry,' Hunter pulled Tori back into his arms. 'You're telling me that he's thinking of concentrating on a different area instead, right?'

Tori nodded, her arms automatically sliding around Hunter's waist.

'Ok, so I'll be understandably annoyed, won't I?' Hunter winked.

'Oh no, Hunter, you *can't*!' Tori cried, unable to hide the smile forming on her face.

'I won't hurt him. Well, not as much as I want to, but I may do a *little* bit, you understand? Noel will step in quick enough. Unfortunately I'll have to wait until this is all finished before I *really* hurt him.'

Hunter pressed his lips gently back onto Tori's, then released her. 'Now get yourself back in there. Give Sarah a quick nod if you can. She's expecting me to kick off. Then act upset. Tell Matt you've told me and I'm not happy.'

Tori's eyes widened. 'Are you not following me back in?'

Hunter grinned. 'I just need a moment to get rid of this,' he nodded towards the tell-tale bulge in his crotch. 'Go on, before I change my mind and fuck you instead!'

. . . .

'WHAT DO YOU mean by 'furious', Tori?' Matt cried, trying to keep his voice down. Panic rose as he glanced at the door leading to the corridor, which at present was still thankfully shut. 'Where is he?'

'He stomped back in the Gents, so I came straight out to tell you,' Tori said, concealing her enjoyment at the dread on Matt's face. She'd also given Sarah a subtle signal too, so at least she knew what was coming. She, however still had very little idea what Hunter would do and her heart pounded with adrenalin.

'What's going on?' Jeremy asked. 'What have you done, Tori?'

'She's done what I told her to do,' Matt said, his eyes watching the door. 'Look, I think we need to leave.'

'Leave?' Ginny squealed. 'Why? I haven't finished my drink!'

Matt stood up, but didn't get much further when, with an alarming crash, Hunter burst through the door from the back corridor.

Tori marvelled at Hunter's ability to change his expression from how he'd looked at her not two minutes ago into the feral mad man crashing his way towards them.

She stood up just as Hunter reached their table and grabbed Matt around the throat. Picking him clean off the floor, a table overturned as he was flung against the nearest wall.

Sarah tentatively watched from her place behind the bar. She dearly hoped Hunter would remember what the overall plan was and not, although it would have been very tempting, lose his temper and wreck everything.

Tori watched in silent fascination as Matt scrabbled around attempting to back away from Hunter who loomed over him whilst Noel began to make his way over from the dart board

311

area.

Reaching down, Hunter grabbed Matt by the lapels and yanked him from the floor, slamming him back up against the wall for the second time. He brought his face close. 'I hear you've had a change of heart about doing a deal with me and the people around here?'

'W-What?' Matt squeaked, his eyes darting to Jeremy for back up, which was pointless because both he and Ginny were rooted to the spot, their mouths hanging open in a comical fashion.

'You heard me, you prick,' Hunter roared, shifting his grip from Matt's lapels to his throat and applying a worrying amount of pressure. 'I said why have you changed your mind about dealing with us? We not good enough now?'

Matt gasped for breath as huge fingers crushed his windpipe. He looked up into Hunter's face. *Christ, he looked mental. That stupid bitch must have laid it on pretty thick for him to be this angry.*

'Did Tori say that?' Matt spluttered. He needed to keep up the pretence, even if his plan had gone horribly wrong. 'I-I don't know why she said that,' he gibbered. 'She must have taken what I said the wrong way.'

'And why would she have done that?' Hunter hissed, moving closer to Matt's puce-coloured face.

'She shouldn't have said anything,' Matt began, reminding himself of the script. 'But you know what she's like.' He attempted a smile, but only received more pressure around his throat.

Noel pulled at Hunter's shoulder. 'Leave him! You can't do that in here!' *He had to stop this. What the fuck was going on? This wasn't what he'd been expecting to happen. Both him and Matt had been sure getting that information from Tori would have worried Hunter, not turned him crazy.*

Hunter swung around to face Noel. 'This wanker is planning on binning off the deal and looking elsewhere,' he spat. *He was enjoying this.* 'Isn't that right, Matthew?'

'No, no it's not like that,' Matt blustered.

Hunter dropped his grip. 'Ok then, what *did* you say then if it wasn't that?'

Matt leant against the wall, his stomach heaving and gulped in huge mouthfuls of air.

Hunter grabbed Matt's floppy fringe and pulled him back up. 'What's the score then, dickhead?'

Matt had to think. Had to think *really* fast. *Shit, shit, SHIT!* He glanced at Noel, but remembered he needed to play the game too. 'All I said was we needed to close the deal, or the bank wanted me to look at other possibilities. It wasn't my idea! I'd wait as long as you like, but it is…'

'And you weren't going to bother letting me know about this?' Hunter roared, lurching towards Matt again.

Noel stepped forward. 'Wait, let's hear what the cunt's got to say.' Facing Matt and just out of Hunter's line of vision, he gave Matt a look - one that clearly signified he'd better think of something fast.

Taking the hint, Matt straightened himself up, mortified to be in the middle of a pub grovelling out of pure terror to this baboon. 'If you can close all of the deals by the end of next week then I reckon I can still swing it your way. I can smooth everything over and still get you those prices, I swear!'

Hunter's face broke into a smile – one of those smiles that left his eyes ice-cold. 'I'm very glad to hear it. We wouldn't want to think you wouldn't be getting us and the rest of the people the best deal, would we?'

Matt shook his head furiously. 'No! Definitely not! I can *assure* you it's all above board and I'll make sure this mix-up is rectified.' It was a good job part of his plan meant Hunter would lose his status around here otherwise he'd have to move to Jupiter once these deals had closed and he'd got his money.

Hunter grasped Matt's lapels again, but this time straightened them down. 'Good. I'm pleased we had this chat. You've convinced me now that we should sign, so I'll make sure everyone knows this and then I'll be back in touch with the contracts.'

'That's *fantastic*! I-I'm sorry for the confusion,' Matt simpered. *Thank fuck for that! It had worked!* The plan had only gone and fucking worked. *YES!* Although it had been a bit close to the bone for his liking, it had still worked – like he knew it would, the thick fuck.

Trying not to beam like a Cheshire cat, Matt smiled. 'Can I buy you a drink?' The *last* thing he wanted to do was to buy this freak a drink, but he had to appear grateful and sincere.

'No thanks,' Hunter snarled. 'We've got people to see.' He jerked his head at Noel. 'Let's go.'

Hunter forced himself not to look in Tori's direction otherwise he would be compelled to stay – and if he did that, then he knew there was no way he could endure sitting with this utter wanker without doing what he *really* wanted to do. *Which was to kill him stone dead.*

Without further hesitation, Hunter strode from the White Hart without a backwards glance.

• • • •

'THANKS A BUNCH for helping out,' Matt spat, glaring at Jeremy. He was in desperate need of another drink but couldn't bring himself to pick up his bottle of lager because it would underline to all and sundry how much his hands were shaking.

'What could I have done?' Jeremy garbled. 'The guy's built like a brick shit-house!' *There had been no way he was risking a beating off him!*

'You could have said something,' Matt moaned sulkily. He turned to Tori. 'And as for *you*, what the fuck did you say to rile him that much?' He had to scrape back some self-respect from *somewhere* and having a go at this stupid cow was the best option.

'Exactly what you *told* me to say.' Tori casually sipped at her drink. She really should pretend to be *slightly* concerned over Matt's welfare, but she was enjoying his humiliation too much.

'Wait a minute,' Ginny piped up, her thin cosmetically darkened eyebrows arching inquisitively. 'Would someone like to tell me what on earth is going on? Why would you be asking *her* to say anything to that… that *thing*?'

Jeremy waved his hand in Ginny's direction. The last thing he wanted to do was to explain any of this to her, although he suspected that even if she dropped it for now, she'd be back on his case about it later. 'It's a long story. Work stuff.'

Realising she wasn't getting anywhere, Ginny snatched her bag from the table and huffily stalked in the direction of the toilets.

Matt looked at Jeremy. 'At least it had the desired outcome.' He smiled widely. 'In fact, it worked a treat! The thick fucker fell for it hook, line and sinker, so the deal's done!'

'Not yet. Not until we get those signed contracts,' Jeremy added.

'Oh, we'll get them. He won't want to think he anyone's missed out because of his paranoia, will he? Little does he know though… *Yet*…'

Tori forced a smile. She was unsure what Hunter was doing by agreeing to get the contracts signed. If that happened then surely all of those people, including *him* would be legally bound into selling their properties for a loss? He knew this, so why had he agreed? 'I'll go and get us more drinks,' she said, pushing her chair back.

Grateful Sarah was behind the bar, Tori leaned up against the scuffed wood, glad for the support for her slightly shaky legs.

'Well, that was a fairly pleasing spectacle wasn't it?' Sarah winked, her voice quiet. 'Same again?' Seeing Tori nod, she began pouring the drinks.

'Why would Hunter say he'd sort the contracts? That's the *opposite* of what he should be saying isn't it?' Tori whispered.

'I don't know what his plan is, but I shouldn't worry about it. Hunter knows what he's doing, so trust him to deliver,' Sarah smiled. 'I've never known him not to.'

Tori sighed. 'I thought he was going to really hurt Matt for a moment.'

Sarah laughed and placed the fresh drinks on a beer towel. 'I can guarantee he'd have *wanted* to, but I'm also glad to see he's got his control back.' She raised an eyebrow. 'Did you see Matt's face? I thought he was going to shit himself or cry!'

Tori hid her giggle with a false cough and picked up the drinks.

Sarah touched Tori's arm, her face now serious. 'But I'll tell you now, Hunter *will* hurt Matt at some point without a shadow of a doubt.'

THIRTY EIGHT

HUNTER WATCHED MAX TURNER scan the contract for the sale of the Factory. He couldn't decipher the man's thoughts as his eyes moved quickly over the words – the guy had a poker face as impressive as his own.

He'd pulled in a favour. First thing this morning he'd made a trip to Max's – a lawyer who he'd had dealings with in the past and knew would be able to see if there were any loopholes that could be utilised. Ok, so he'd taken a gamble – a *massive* gamble with what he'd agreed with that prick last night, but he'd also had a sixth sense it was the right thing to do.

Max looked up, his forehead deeply furrowed. 'I'm pretty sure you're on to something here, but I want to double check with a guy who deals solely with conveyancing.' He stood up from his leather chair. 'I won't be long.'

Hunter tried not to get impatient as he waited, his foot itching to tap the floor. His mind drifted back to Tori. He'd left the White Hart without giving her any indication of anything and would have felt a lot better if he'd had the opportunity to tell her he'd be in touch soon. Instead, he'd left her with that bunch of pricks who he didn't doubt would have given her a hard time over what had occurred. Whatever happened he'd be seeing her soon. *He had to.*

Hunter frowned. He couldn't tell the rest of the club what was *really* going on. If Noel knew he was on to them then he'd do everything to stop it and furthermore, he had no idea if there was anyone else backing his VP. If the rest knew the truth, they'd lynch Noel and *he* wanted to be the one to do that.

It was horrible. Hunter had begun to suspect every member of the club. The men he'd trusted with his life he was now doubting and he had the distinct impression they were equally beginning to doubt him. He knew it would be difficult when he announced he was going to be with Tori, but they'd all just have to live with it. They would also have to live with the knowledge that Noel was a traitor.

Yep, things were going to become *very* difficult for quite some time, but there was no way around it. Then of course, he'd have to work out how to deal with Noel and that was probably the most difficult part.

Hunter had to face facts. He was risking completely losing the club, but he stood by doing the right thing by them all – everybody. *And that included himself.* To top it all, he'd got Georgie's funeral later. *It would be a trying day.*

Max re-entered his office amidst a cloud of expensive, strong aftershave. He chucked the contract on the desk in front of Hunter. 'As you suspected there's a loophole you can use.' Smiling, he sat down. 'Whoever the dickhead was that drew this up clearly didn't have enough legal nous! They've left themselves wide open.'

Hunter sat forward, the beginnings of a smile forming on his lips. 'Right. Good, so....?'

'So... if you look at Paragraph Two, 'Clause Thirteen A', you'll see that's the part which has been clumsily added into a standard above-board contract.' Max waited until Hunter had flicked to the correct place in the paperwork. 'You see? But if you look at 'Clause Two B', *that's* the one they should have removed. Leaving that second clause in after adding the other renders the contract in no way legally binding.'

Hunter smiled. 'So even when these are signed, they're a bag of shit?'

'Yes, they're not worth the paper they're written on, so you're good to go ahead and run with your plan. At first glance the contracts look fine, but I guarantee they won't stand up in court and I doubt it would even get that far.' Max scratched his chin and smirked. 'When you're ready to pull the rug out from under their feet, all you have to do is casually point out the bit they forgot to remove, then stand back and enjoy watching the blood drain from their faces.'

Hunter grinned. 'Cheers, Max. I owe you one.'

Max stood up and shook the big man's hand. 'Anytime, Hunter. Anytime.'

. . . .

TORI HAD BEEN glad to retreat to her bedroom after dinner. She hadn't relished spending the evening at home, but she hadn't heard from Hunter and didn't dare contact him without Matt's say-so. He'd been adamant she needed to lay off him for a day or two to make sure he did what was needed to close the deals.

The thought of not being around Hunter for even a *minute* made Tori feel sick and panicky, but she had no option but to accept it. There had, however, been no way she would spend the evening with Matt. When he'd said he'd pick her up later, making a lewd remark about needing to empty his balls, she'd quickly pretended to be ill.

Matt had tried his standard bullying tactics, but she had a bit more confidence at the moment and stood her ground, consoling him slightly by promising to make it up to him tomorrow. The thought of letting him anywhere near her now positively sickened her, but – like Sarah said, she needed to do what she had to do until this was over.

She'd even used the same ploy on her mother. Tori smiled to herself with her newly found deviousness against the people who had controlled her for so long. Her mother had started her usual interrogation over dinner about where she'd been lately, but Tori had placated the situation by saying in a happy tone of voice that she'd been almost *living* at Matt's because things were going so well between them. It was only when her mother progressed to talking about wedding rehearsal dates had she drawn the line and made an excuse of going to bed with a sudden migraine. The words *'It's only four months away now, Victoria'*, were still ringing in her head.

Despite her yearning to be with Hunter, Tori also knew it was good to have a bit of time to herself. Things had been so chaotic lately with so many different and worrying things her head was mashed. Leaning back against her chair, she exhaled deeply. She stared at the door at the bottom of the bureau before opening it, her hands shaking slightly as she retrieved the shoebox.

Was this the right time to look? Would her already scrambled brain cope with the emotional slap seeing anything to do with her father?

Taking a deep breath, Tori removed the lid from the shoebox, staring at the mishmash of contents and pulled out a Christmas card. She opened it, her eyes brimming with tears as she read the words written many years ago:

> *Daddy,*
> *Happy Christmas 1978.*
> *I love you MORE!!!!*
> *Love love love*
> *Tori*
> *xx*

Tori smiled through the tears. They'd always played that game. Every night when her father tucked her into bed and placed a kiss on the top of her head, she'd say: *'I love you, Daddy'*, and without fail, he'd reply: *'I love you MORE!'*

The only time she ever got to say that to him was in cards or notes, because if she ever said it out loud, he'd counter with

'Yes, but I love you more, more and MORE than that!'

Closing the card, Tori continued picking through the shoebox. There were a few more cards - again from her and what looked like a few old pay slips. Her eyes were then drawn to some photographs. Pulling them out, her fingers trembled as she stared at her father's face, captured forever on film.

The first photo was the one she'd looked at when she'd first located the shoebox, so she skipped straight to the next one. This one must have been taken just before she was born as her mother was heavily pregnant. Sitting next to her husband on a worn-looking sofa, she wore a light-coloured dress stretched over her huge belly.

Tori studied the picture. Her father's hand was gently resting on her mother's bump and her mother – although a very beautiful woman when younger, looked sour as usual. Her face showed no sign of happiness whatsoever.

Tori irritably flicked to the next photograph. More sour-faced pictures of her mother and one of her as a baby. One of... *Who was that?*

Tori picked up the creased picture and studied it. Her father stood behind a large fallen tree trunk along with three other men, none of whom she recognised. His hands rested on the shoulders of a woman sitting on the trunk.

Tori peered closer. The group in the picture has been taken from some distance. It wasn't her mother. Even though the photo was black and white, the woman's hair was far too dark. In fact, it looked jet black. The woman wore a white blouse and short skirt, her shapely legs were crossed and her hand was on the hand of the man stood behind her. *Her father's...*

She turned the picture over and read the scrawled handwriting:

'Me, Jack, Bill, John and Ed'

From what Tori could see the woman was breathtakingly beautiful and looked blissfully happy, but who was it?

She moved to the next photograph. This one was of her father and the same woman. Closer this time. They were facing each other – staring into each other's eyes with what she could only describe as pure love.

Tori swallowed. *She must have been a girlfriend.* She looked away from the picture, tears brimming. She wasn't upset. Why would she be? It would be absurd to think her father had only even been in a relationship with her mother.

Her eyes moved back to the photograph as she wondered what had happened between them. They were clearly deeply in love. Intrigued, she grabbed the next photograph. Another photo of her as a baby. *Were there any more of this woman?*

She flicked through the remainder of the photographs, stopping at another one which showed the group again. Judging by the presence of the fallen tree in the centre it had been taken in the same place as before. One of the men present in the other group was missing, with another man standing in his place. Clearly they had been taking turns with the camera. She was just about the place the photos to one side and continue rummaging when something made her stop and look back at the photo.

She frowned, half-recognising the man on the end. She wracked her brains trying to place his features when it became suddenly clear. *It was Richard. Richard Stevens – Matt's father.*

Tori paused. That wasn't such a big deal. She knew they'd studied together, so the photos must have been taken around that time. What a shame she didn't get on better with Richard, or she could ask him who this woman was. She must have been someone special for her father to have been looking at her in that way and to have kept the photographs and she was intrigued to know why it hadn't worked out between them.

Tori continued looking through the shoebox and pulled out a badly crumpled and yellowed newspaper cutting. She gingerly unfolded it, smoothing out enough of the deep creases to enable the aged thin paper to be legible. It was so badly creased it looked like it had been screwed up into a ball at some point before being unfolded again.

She peered at the tiny print. It was an obituary:

'Leila Cooper, beloved sister, daughter and mother.
Missed by all. Your death will be avenged.'

Tori frowned. Was this the woman on the photograph? And what a strange thing to write on an obituary: '*Your death will be avenged.*' It also said she was a mother, but there was no mention of a husband.

Scolding herself for trying to analyse something she had no clue about, Tori folded the cutting up as best as she could without further damaging it.

Why would her father have kept this unless Leila Cooper was indeed the woman in the picture? Should she ask her mother? Maybe she would know?

Almost slapping herself for her stupidity, Tori hastily dismissed the idea. Even it her mother did know who this woman was, she was hardly likely to admit her husband had looked at anyone else. She'd never hear the end of it. This shoebox had to be a collection of her father's personal things which her mother had not known about, otherwise it would have been disposed of along with everything else when all traces of him had been removed.

Tori, however, was inquisitive. She loved family history and felt excited to have had a glimpse into her father's past. Placing the shoebox back in the bottom of the bureau for the time being, she sat back to think of how she could find out more.

THIRTY NINE

IT HAD BEEN a productive day but a difficult one. Hunter walked out of Georgie's wake and sat on the wall outside. He needed a bit of space. Lighting a cigarette, he looked up at the dark night sky and exhaled slowly. It was strange being back at Georgie's house. The last time he'd been here it was to dump her and look what had happened.

Taking a deep breath, he realised he needed to rationalise things. He'd always been honest with Georgie and prided himself on that and despite her manic behaviour, if she'd known he'd fallen in love she would have been happy for him. Even though it hadn't been with her, she'd cared enough about him to be pleased and would have known it was a near miracle for his heart to have finally opened.

However, he was unhappy to have drawn blanks on where any dodgy gear could have come from. He was sure that was what, if not had caused, had at least contributed to Georgie's death and for his own peace of mind he needed closure on it. The word had been put out, but he'd had no info as to whether she'd scored from anyone they didn't trust. The only place she'd ever got her drugs from was the Factory and their gear had always been top notch, apart from that one pathetic load they'd dumped on Matt.

Noel had sworn down Georgie hadn't had anything from him recently and Hunter believed him. *Even Noel wasn't low enough to pass known shite to one of their own.*

The knowledge of Georgie's pregnancy still cut Hunter to the bone. It had been hard watching the coffin containing the girl whose heart he'd broken, together with the child he'd never meet, be lowered into the ground.

Grinding his cigarette out on the pavement, Hunter sparked up another. The music was still thumping from inside the house, the wake going strong. He smiled sadly. Georgie would have approved. That girl loved a good party.

The only good thing to have come out of today was getting the confirmation he'd needed regarding the contracts. After leaving Max's he'd managed to see ten people involved in the deal and informed them it was good to go, so they should go ahead and sign. He still had plenty more people to get around, but word of mouth that he'd okayed the deals was sure to spread like wildfire.

The news that he was signing the deal hadn't gone down well in the Factory. Admittedly it wasn't the best day to drop that bombshell what with Georgie's funeral, but he'd had to say something before word got out. Understandably everyone had been shocked, short of Noel, who had tried his best to act surprised, but he hadn't fooled Hunter.

Hunter knew full well the Reapers would talk about his decision but wouldn't dare question him. Especially not today of all days.

All he'd added to the news was that he'd find somewhere else for the Reaper's base once the Factory had sold. In reality, that wouldn't be needed because there would be no sale. There wouldn't be a sale of anything, but it was vital everyone believed there would be otherwise everything would be blown.

• • • •

GRIN WATCHED HUNTER from the window of Georgie's

front room. Things were not going well in the slightest. After the shock had worn off, the entire crew had been livid over Hunter's decision. He couldn't blame them and wondered what had happened to Hunter to make him sell out.

There he'd said it, even though it was only to himself. It was what everyone else was thinking and he could only foresee that worsening.

'So basically Hunter's decided, after all the shit he promised all these years, that he'll allow our patch and half the city to be overrun with fucking yuppies!' One of the crew had ranted after Hunter had left.

Watching the others nod in agreement, Grin had listened to plenty of mutterings of 'Rafe would turn in his grave...', 'Has Hunter gone soft?', or 'Since when has it all been about money?'

There had even been a few comments about 'putting in a transfer to a *proper* club'.

Grin didn't know what bothered him more: that Hunter should have had such a drastic change of heart - so against everything he stood for, or that his recent behaviour was so erratic.

'Aright, mate?' Noel said, clumsily hooking his arm around Grin's neck. 'What's up?' His eyes followed Grin's gaze to Hunter still sitting on the wall. 'Hmm, he's dug himself a hole, hasn't he?'

Grin didn't respond. *What was there to say? Even though Noel was wasted, he was right.*

'Silly fucker! You should have voted for me when you had the chance,' Noel slurred, nodding in Hunter's direction. 'This is what women talk you into if you let them. That sort of shit would never have happened with me, as you well know.'

Slapping Grin on the back for good measure, Noel staggered off in pursuit of another drink and a willing girl he could play with.

Without taking his eyes away off Hunter's back, Grin tipped the rest of his beer into his mouth. *Was Noel saying this was something to do with Georgie?* Suddenly a rush of cold ran over him. *This wasn't about Georgie, this was about Tori.*

No. It couldn't be - Hunter had already told him he was playing her for information regarding her boyfriend's deal, but he'd noticed the way he looked at her. He wasn't that good an actor to hide it. And what about what he'd said the other night when he'd been drunk? *He'd said he thought he loved her.*

It all made sense. That conniving bitch had somehow, against all the odds, hooked Hunter. She'd reeled him into her poisonous web and he'd fallen for it. He was genuinely in love with the stuck-up bitch and too stupid to realise it was all in aid of her fucking boyfriend.

Grin raked his fingers through his hair. *What the hell was he going to do?* On one respect he wanted to rip Hunter's throat out for doing this to them and being too blind to see, but on the other hand – it was *Hunter*. He loved him – he was like a brother and if he made this public, the man would be ripped apart.

He nervously lit a cigarette. He would speak to him. Either that or go and see the woman who had made Hunter somehow believe he was in love under false pretences and dispatch her. He'd never offloaded a woman before, but there was too much at stake here.

Feeling his blood pressure rise, Grin tried to calm down. He'd wound himself up into a frenzy. No matter how much he didn't want to believe it was possible that Hunter was selling them up the river, it very much looked that way.

There was nothing else for it. He'd have it out with him – even if it were to just get his side of the story.

· · · ·

HUNTER REALLY WASN'T in the mood for a conversation. He'd had enough today, what with everything, and although he'd expected questions, he didn't want them *tonight*. Grin was one of the more rational members of the club and it was of no surprise that he should be the chosen mouthpiece for everyone else's grievances, but it didn't change that this was not the right time.

'Can't this wait?' Hunter grumbled, staring aimlessly into the dark night.

'No, it can't,' Grin said, his voice uncharacteristically aggressive.

Turning to face him, Hunter crossed his arms over his broad chest. 'Go on then. I'm listening.'

Although Grin had calmed down, he didn't like Hunter's dismissive attitude. The man had changed. He never thought he'd see the day when Ash Hunter thought it acceptable to batter a club member. Neither did he think, he himself, would have received a head-butt for no reason other than the man being drunk. He also had never envisaged Hunter would get turned over by skirt – especially one from the class he despised so much. How could the man sell the Reapers out for a few quid because some rich slag had pulled the wool over his eyes?

'The Reapers have been going for over fifty years, Hunter,' Grin said, his bitterness clear.

Hunter sighed. 'When did I say anything about disbanding? I'm just selling the Factory.'

'*Just*?' Grin spat. 'That's the club's home! Do you not think you should have discussed it with all of us before making a decision?'

Hunter's eyes narrowed. 'It's *my* place, not the club's. The club just uses it. If I want to sell my own fucking place, then I don't see why I should have to discuss and ask permission from *you* or anyone else!' Although what he said was correct, if he'd *really* been thinking about selling the Factory, he *would* have discussed it out of courtesy. This whole situation would be so much easier if he could just tell everyone what was really going on. *Damn Noel and his fucking games.*

'Maybe,' Grin said. 'But I didn't think we worked like that. We're supposed to be a *family*.'

Hunter gritted his teeth. 'You don't think I know that?' Would he be doing all of this if he didn't see them as his family? No, he wouldn't. He was protecting the club and the area like he always had. Everything he did and everything he'd *ever* done was for the club or for the people in it, regardless of what he'd been left to personally carry as a burden on his back.

Grin snorted with derision. 'If you did then you wouldn't be selling us and everyone else out!' He couldn't stop what he wanted to say from coming out of his mouth. 'Rafe would have turned in his grave if he thought you'd pull a stunt like this!'

Hunter stared at Grin. 'And that's what you think, is it?'

Grin swept his arms in the direction of Georgie's house. 'It's what *everybody* thinks. Noel's right. We should have voted *him* in!'

Hunter couldn't help but smile despite his building anger and Grin stared at the sneer across the man's face. 'You find this amusing? Well, it's *not*! What's the matter with you? You're letting that posh tart use you as a puppet!'

Hunter sprang to his feet and grabbed Grin. 'Don't you fucking *dare* speak about Tori like that,' he spat, but the sound of Grin's laughter in response to his anger made Hunter drop his grip and stare at him.

'Oh my God,' Grin said. This situation was *far* from amusing, but he felt almost on the verge of hysteria. 'It's true!'

'*What's* true?' Hunter frowned.

Grin put his hands in his hair as if to tear it from his scalp and flopped down onto the wall in despair. 'You *are* in love with that woman. Oh my God, Hunter. What are you thinking? Can't you see she's playing you so her boyfriend can get what he wants? Noel was *right*!'

Hunter's mouth set into a line. *So, Noel had been feeding the fire?* 'It's not like that.'

Grin stared at Hunter, his eyes cold. 'So, you're not denying it? For fuck's sake! You stupid bastard!'

Sighing, Hunter sat down on the wall next to Grin. *He was going to have to tell him.* 'No, I'm not denying it. Believe me, I've shocked myself!' He lit a cigarette. 'Don't ask me how it happened, but it did.'

Sensing Grin was about to launch into another tirade,

Hunter held up his hand. 'But before you say anything else, you need to hear the rest.'

. . . .

NOEL LOUNGED IN the armchair, savouring the feel of his cock being worked by the skinny nameless girl kneeling between his thighs. As her tongue flicked around him he pushed her head down, ignoring the strange gagging sound she made.

Things were going nicely to plan. Aside from this pretty little tart giving him head, he'd done well. He'd seen the look on Grin's face and hadn't even had to say much to fuel the hostility. The tension amongst the Reapers when Hunter had dropped the bombshell about selling had been thick enough to slice clean through with a blunt plastic picnic knife and he'd already heard that word had got around town that go-ahead had been given for the regeneration deals.

The disconcerted murmuring amongst the rest of the crew – especially as the drinks had continued flowing once Georgie's wake was in full swing, had left him in no doubt as to the success of his plan. It wouldn't be long until Hunter's reign was well and truly over and *his* would begin.

'Put your back into it!' Noel growled, grasping the girl's hair and pressing down harder. 'I ain't got all fucking day!' He'd already got his eye on another girl who'd been giving him the look earlier and he wanted to make sure he had a go with her too before the night was out.

Yeah, everything was good. Several of the signed contracts would have by now already winged their way to Matt-The-Ponce's desk, which would have given the prick a hard-on for sure and judging by the word he'd had on the street there would be more contracts following suit on Monday. This was all on target to wrap up by the end of next week as planned and then he'd get his money.

And along with the money, he'd also be claiming the 'President' patch for his leather jacket.

FORTY

RICHARD HAD BEEN both surprised and pleased to hear a further ten contracts had been returned and signed, for the regeneration project. It appeared his son had been telling the truth when he'd said everything was on track, so maybe he'd been a bit hasty in presuming he was slacking.

He'd also been happy to receive confirmation Victoria was finally toeing the line and doing what he'd expected from a future daughter-in-law. Matthew hadn't been spending much time at home recently, but whatever he'd been doing was obviously working. Not only was he getting his leg over, but the girl was behaving herself and playing the game - which could mean one of two things. She'd either accepted that she must behave if she wanted to be part of his family, or that she was indeed already pregnant.

Matthew hadn't mentioned whether she was or not, but he had a hunch that she was. Things were working out well. *Very well indeed.*

There had only been one issue which had bothered him. Whilst they had been talking, Matthew had mentioned Victoria had asked about a picture. The stupid bitch reckoned she'd found a photograph from the old days with him on. Why on earth would there have been a photograph of him lying around Lillian's house, unless the sour old bat had developed some secret fantasy about him?

Smiling to himself, Richard found the thought quite amusing, but joking aside, it ceased to be funny when Jack Jacob's name had crept in the conversation.

Matthew had only mentioned it out of passing as a throwaway comment, but the hairs on the back of Richard's neck had stood up and prickled. Nevertheless, he tried to act uninterested. 'I don't remember any photos being taken of me and Victoria's father,' he scoffed. 'I barely knew him!'

'Oh, it wasn't just you and him. Apparently, there was a group,' Matt explained.

'A *group*?' Richard wracked his brains but couldn't think of a situation where there could have been a group photograph taken. 'It must have been a college picture. Class photo or something?'

Matt shook his head. 'I haven't seen it, but from what Tori said, I don't think so. She said there was a fallen tree, but she was more interested in the woman.'

Richard felt immediately sick. 'What woman?' he forced himself to ask, now knowing exactly who was on the photograph.

'I have no idea. Like I said, I haven't seen the picture so I can't describe it. Tori was really interested though. She said, judging by the other photos she'd seen, she thought it must have been her father's girlfriend – before Lillian of course.'

Richard felt sweat gather at the back of his neck and resisted the urge to push his fingers into his shirt collar.

'Was it his girlfriend?' Matt asked. 'Hey, imagine Lillian's face if she knew that?' He couldn't help but chuckle, easily able to imagine her magenta lips pursing, making the wrinkles around her mouth pucker, causing it to resemble a cat's arse more than it usually did.

Richard wrung his hands. No matter how he felt it was important he played this cool. 'How should I know if whoever this woman was had been his girlfriend? Like I keep telling you, I hardly knew the man. It probably wasn't even me on the photograph. I certainly can't remember it,' he lied. *He could remember it alright. Remembered it as clear as if it were yesterday.*

That day they'd gone into the woods Leila Cooper had looked even more stunning than usual. It had been a beautiful day and they'd eaten the sandwiches she'd brought with her. It had only been supposed to be her and Jack going out that day but bumping into Jack as he'd gone to meet Leila, Richard had invited himself, Bill, John and Ed along too and Jack had been too polite to refuse.

As the sunlight had filtered through the trees, Richard remembered it reflecting on Leila's raven hair making it appear almost blue. He'd been even more incensed at that particular moment as to how the hell Jack managed to bag such a looker. Gypsy or not, Leila had been by far the sexiest woman he'd *ever* set eyes on.

'Are you alright?' Matt asked, studying his father's face.

Shaken from his thoughts, Richard hastily pulled himself together. He needed to play this differently. 'Yes, I was just recalling what you described to see if I could remember anything.'

'I'll ask Tori to bring the photos next time she comes over. Then you can see if it's you and if so, it might bring back some memories.'

Richard didn't need a photograph to bring back the memories of *that* day. He shook his head. 'Don't do that. If you ask her for the photos she'll only get her hopes up that I'll be able to tell her something of interest. We don't want to disappoint her.' *But he needed to see that picture to make sure it was him and if it was him, then he needed to destroy the bloody thing.*

He felt quite sick. All this time he'd believed there was nothing in existence to link him with Jack-bloody-Jacobs, let alone linking him to the gypsy.

'See if you can get the photographs without her realising,' Richard suggested. 'I'd be interested to see if it's actually me on there. I don't think I've got any pictures of myself from back then and it would be nice to remind myself just how good-looking I was!'

Matt stared at his father, amazed to hear him say something containing a hint of humour. He didn't think he'd heard him say anything that could be classed as such since 1980, if at all.

'It would be nice for Victoria if I could confirm something too. Not that I'm promising that of course, hence why it's best if you get them without her knowing.'

Matt raised an eyebrow. 'Gosh, have you had a change of heart about Tori? You want to do something nice for her?' *It looked like all was well and truly home and dry for this wedding and wedding equalled money, plus promotion, so this was a good sign.*

Blustering, Richard realised he was running the risk of acting over-eager and needed to back-track a little. 'Not especially, but like you said, if she's been doing so well lately, then she's making an effort and has finally seen the error of her ways, so it won't hurt for me to make a little effort back, will it?'

Matt frowned. *Was his father ill?* Along with his non-existent sense of humour, he couldn't remember the last time the man had done anything *remotely* in anyone else's favour, unless there was something in it for him. It was a trait he'd always very much admired.

'Ok, the next chance I get I'll act interested and then she'll show me the pictures and I'll know where she puts them.'

'That's a good idea,' Richard smiled.

'Look who's here,' Susan cried, suddenly entering the living room. Holding the door open, Lillian followed her in.

'Hello Richard,' Lillian glided over amongst a cloud of floral perfume and air-kissed Richard on the cheek. 'Hello Matthew.'

Bustling over to the nearest chair, she made herself

comfortable. 'I hope you don't mind me turning up unexpectedly?'

'No, of course not,' Richard lied, glad neither Susan nor Lillian had entered the room a few minutes earlier to hear any of what they had been discussing. He glanced at Matthew, hopeful he'd have the good sense not to mention anything about photographs, Jack Jacobs or other women.

'Here you are,' Susan gushed, handing Lillian a glass of white wine.

'Thank you. I wanted to run some dates for wedding rehearsals past you. We really do need to get them in the diary sooner rather than later,' Lillian simpered. 'It's not long now and you know how quickly everyone's schedules fill up at this time of year. We don't want to run out of time to plan.'

'Absolutely not! Everything needs to be perfect,' Susan agreed. 'What dates did you have in mind?'

'Well…' Lillian fished a folded piece of paper out of her handbag. 'I've pencilled in four or five dates as a starting point, but they of course depend on everyone's availability.'

Unfolding the paper, she sipped at her wine. 'I would have brought Victoria, but unfortunately she went to bed with a migraine. I know she'll happily fit in with whatever works for you.' She smiled widely. 'She's getting very excited now I'm pleased to say.'

Leaning forward, Lillian patted Matt on the knee. 'I think you've been wearing her out with your charm, what with all the time you've been spending together lately.'

Richard couldn't help but add a comment that he knew would irk Lillian no end. 'Will we need to arrange adjustments to Victoria's wedding dress, Matthew?'

'*Richard!*' Susan exclaimed, embarrassed. 'What a thing to say!' She rolled her eyes at Lillian. 'He doesn't think sometimes, he really doesn't!'

Lillian gave a tight-lipped smile. If Victoria had got herself pregnant before there was a ring on her finger then she would never live it down. The humiliation would be bad enough, let alone her daughter's promiscuity visibly showing in a wedding gown. *She felt faint with the thought of it.* 'My daughter has been brought up better than to behave like that, so I hope she's been acting correctly during the time she's spent here recently?'

Matt felt a horrible sinking feeling plummet from his throat in the direction of his feet as his parent stared at him in confusion. He didn't think it would go down too well if he explained he'd spent very little time with Tori lately because she'd been too busy following his instructions to sleep with a Reaper whilst he'd been having a most enjoyable time with a couple of his favourite high class call girls and Ginny. Oh and the rest of the time had been spent catching up with Noel, which was never enjoyable, but unfortunately very much of a necessity.

'But Victoria's not be…'

'Not been any trouble at all,' Matt interrupted his mother from uttering the words he knew she'd been about to say. *His parents had not seen Tori for weeks.*

He glared at his father. Why had he made insinuations about a possible pregnancy? For fuck's sake, he knew what he was trying to do on that score – it has been *his* idea after all, but he didn't want any additional hassle. Especially from his mother, or worse, *Lillian.*

Tori hadn't mentioned any hint of pregnancy, but that was hardly surprising. The stupid bitch was that backwards when it came to sex and everything that went with it, she probably wouldn't even realise until her belly was huge and there were kicks coming from inside her.

'That's right,' Richard jumped in, quickly getting the hint and giving Susan a hooded stare. 'Victoria's been no trouble. In fact, she's been a *joy* to have around.' He knew Susan would be asking him what was going on. He expected Victoria and Matthew had been spending some quality time together at his apartment to ensure a baby was in situ.

What was important right now was that he did not want Lillian having any fuel to throw at him or say he didn't know what his own son was up to. Whatever happened though, he'd be finding out.

Richard then turned to Lillian, desperate to change the subject. 'Let's have a look at what rehearsal dates you've suggested then, shall we?'

• • • •

HUNTER KNEW THIS was a bad idea, but he couldn't help it. It was late, but he *had* to see Tori.

Grin had not taken the news about Noel well. At first he'd struggled to believe the man would do such a thing and that was a fully understandable reaction. He'd felt the same himself, but unfortunately it was true.

Not wanting to knock the door of Tori's house, he stood in the shadows and looked up at the imposing house. If he was caught hanging around he had no doubt that the police would be called.

There had been no other way to get in touch, apart from this. He couldn't wait for Sarah to get a message to her. All he could do was hope what little knowledge he possessed about her house and the location of her bedroom would be enough to make sure he picked the correct target.

He eyed the double bay window of the living room at the front of the house. The curtains were closed, but the light was on. He could however, sense no movement from within and could hear no noise.

Bending down, Hunter scraped a handful of gravel from the wide drive and stepped back further into the shadows to the left of a large, immaculately pruned topiary hedge. Taking aim, he threw some of the gravel as lightly as he could, but hard enough to make a noise against the glass of the window he believed was Tori's room. Hearing the stones hit the window, he remained motionless and waited with bated breath.

Nothing.

Taking aim once more, he repeated his shot, but again received no reaction, not even a flicker of curtains or any sign of movement from that bedroom, or anywhere else. *Maybe this was the wrong room, or perhaps Tori was out?* Stupidly, he had not considered that to be a possibility and his skin crawled with irritation at the thought that she may be with Matt.

Deciding he couldn't stand here throwing stones at windows like a teenager for ever, Hunter gave it one last shot and his heart lurched when the curtains twitched and Tori appeared at the window.

Checking no one else was in any of the downstairs windows, Hunter stepped from the shadows, quickly beckoning her to come down. Retreating back into the refuge of the tall shrubbery he waited for a very long minute before Tori appeared on the driveway, looking around frantically as to his whereabouts.

Hastily pulling her behind the foliage, Hunter greedily pressed his mouth against hers, relaxing as he felt her arms wrap around his neck. He knew he could little afford to get side-tracked, but it was with reluctance that he pulled his lips away and looked down into her face. 'I had to see you!'

'You're crazy!' Tori replied breathlessly. 'But I'm glad you did. I've missed you like ma...'

'Things have gone tits up,' Hunter interrupted. 'I've had to tell Grin the score.'

'W-What?' Tori cried. 'Why?'

Hunter frowned and ran his finger gently down Tori's cheek. 'I had little choice. Noel's stirring like mad. He's trying to incite problems within the club.'

'So Grin knows... knows about you and I? That it's real?' she said in a small voice.

'He already knew Noel's version – that I'm supposed to be playing you, but he guessed himself that I've fallen in love with you for real. I guess I'm not a great actor.'

Tori warmed at his words. How she wanted to just take him inside and let him wrap her in his arms.

'He thought you were playing me for Matt's gain and I'd fallen for you regardless like a dumb fuck.'

'God, he must hate me…' Tori whispered.

'He didn't think much of you, no – but now he knows the truth.'

'But now Grin knows about Noel what will he do?'

'He's ensured me he won't do anything or let on to the others what he knows.'

Hunter trusted Grin not to do or say anything if he said he wouldn't. Actually, he had little choice but to trust him, but he didn't know if Grin could control the growing resentment from within the club.

'This is all going to get nasty if we can't get this wrapped up soon,' he said, seeing the panic in Tori's face. 'Every minute this continues the more likely it will blow up in my face. I need to close this so Noel and Matt are exposed.'

Tori felt nauseous. There were so many implications if this didn't work the way they needed it to. Furthermore, how would she *ever* be accepted as being with Hunter by the other Reapers even after this had all finished? Suddenly everything seemed extremely unattainable.

Sensing Tori's rapidly burgeoning desolation as to how they could possibly have a future, Hunter gently cupped her face with both of his big hands. 'Listen, don't worry. I'll work this out. We just need these deals wrapped up. I'll speak to everyone needing to sign and once this has closed at the end of next week, Noel will receive his pay out from Matt. It's then that I'll go in with both barrels.'

Tori clung to Hunter, the prospect of what could go wrong speeding around her body. 'But what if you get lynched by the club before that?'

Hunter clenched his jaw. It was a very feasible possibility. The bad feeling had indeed escalated a lot quicker than he'd imagined, but he'd be damned if Noel and that posh prick would bring him down. *Whatever happened, he'd find a way.*

'We're going to be together, Tori.' He pulled her closely against him. 'Now I'd better get out of here before someone sees me and calls the cops. I just wanted to bring you up to date.'

He pressed his mouth to hers briefly. 'And I wanted to see you of course!' he winked.

'My mother's out,' Tori whispered feeling his hardness growing against her stomach.

'Nevertheless, I still have to leave.' Hunter hastily pulled away. 'I'll be in touch soon.'

'I love you...' Tori whispered, her voice barely audible as she watched Hunter disappear back into the shadows.

FORTY ONE

'VICTORIA?' LILLIAN SCREECHED as she slammed the front door noisily behind her. 'VICTORIA!' *Where was that girl?*

Richard and Susan had agreed to the preliminary rehearsal dates she'd suggested, as had Matt and she'd been glad to hear Victoria was finally impressing the Stevens with her improved behaviour, but she hadn't been impressed by the comment Richard had made about a possible pregnancy. She'd presumed he was joking until she'd sensed the atmosphere change. It felt like they were hiding something and she didn't like it. In fact, it had made her feel thoroughly queasy. *Surely she would know if her own daughter was pregnant?*

Lillian's eyes narrowed. Maybe that was why Victoria had been virtually absent these last couple of weeks? Maybe she hadn't wanted to spend much time around in case her secret was discovered?

'*VICTORIA!*' Lillian bellowed once again, her blood pressure rising. 'Are you even here?' Had that migraine been an excuse not to accompany her to the Stevens'?

Slamming her handbag on the hall table, Lillian moved up the stairs. She would get to the bottom of this. She wasn't having that deceitful little bitch of a daughter of hers hide things. *How dare she think that remotely acceptable!*

She might have known the girl would inherit that sort of stuff from her father. Was it not bad enough when she'd got out of the taxi not five minutes ago to spot one of those grotesque bikers clambering onto his bike like an oversized gorilla? The bike had been parked only a few houses down so what the hell was one of those despicable creatures doing around this neighbourhood? *This was a nice area, not a ghetto!*

Pursing her lips, Lillian made her way along the landing. Without fail she would get in touch with the Neighbourhood Watch Team first thing in the morning. She would *not* put up with that sort cruising around here and needed to ensure it was stopped immediately.

Lillian pushed open Tori's bedroom door seeing her daughter sitting on the bed with headphones on and rifling through a tatty shoebox. 'I've been calling you. Did you not hear me?'

Swinging around, Tori pulled her headphones from her ears and hastily pushed the shoebox to one side. 'Sorry. I was listening to music.'

'I thought you were ill?' Lillian said, her eyebrow arched suspiciously. 'Miraculously disappeared has it?'

'W-What? I took some tablets and it…'

'Is it not bad enough to return from the Stevens' and see one of those rancid 'Ropers' or whatever they call themselves, hanging around?' Lillian screeched. 'I mean, around *here* of all places?'

Tori nearly choked on her tongue. *Hunter?*

'You don't know anything about that, do you?'

Tori paled, the blood draining from her face like an emptying bath. 'M-Me? W-Why would y…'

'You might be hiding that along with everything else!' Lillian folded her arms. 'Is there anything you want to tell me?'

Tori blinked several times in quick succession. *What had she discovered? Had Matt said something?*

'Lost for words? I might have known. You have *one* chance to tell me the truth and I mean it, my girl!'

Tori faltered. *What was she supposed to say?* She repositioned herself to shield the shoebox containing her father's things from her mother's line of sight.

Lillian could bear it no longer. She wasn't stupid. She could see her sly two-faced daughter was hiding something. 'Well, *are* you?' she spat.

Tori stared at her mother, confusion evident in her expression. 'Am I what?'

'Don't act dumb! You are, aren't you?' *Oh God. This was her worst nightmare come true. Victoria was pregnant.* Lillian lunged forward and slapped Tori hard around the face.

Tori raised her hand to her face in shock and touched the burning red imprint her mother's hand had made.

'Don't you *dare* play the innocent with me, you silly girl! Is there *nothing* you won't do to cause humiliation? How could you be so stupid to get yourself pregnant?'

Tori could only sit and attempt to ingest what she'd been accused of. *Pregnant? What the hell had Matt said, for God's sake?*

Lillian paced up and down the room, her face red with rage. 'How far along are you?' If she had to get that dress taken out, she'd go crazy. Maybe an abortion would be better rather than face the shame? There would be plenty of time for this after they'd got married. *Christ, how could the girl have been so irresponsible?*

Tori finally found the resolve to speak. 'I'm not pregnant!' she cried.

Lillian froze. *She wasn't? Or was her deceitful daughter lying again? Lying just like her father had done the whole time.*

Tori saw the doubt on her mother's face. 'Seriously, I'm not.'

Lillian, in a combination of relief and confusion, perched on the end of the bed like a bird. 'You're not?'

'No, I'm *not*,' Tori spat, getting irritated.

'Richard said th…'

'*Richard*? Why would he say that and furthermore, how would he know even if I was?' *Had Matt told his father she was pregnant and if so, why?*

'He said something that made me think that was the case. They seemed to be hiding something and I th…'

'Well, whatever they were hiding, it wasn't *that* and nothing to do with me!'

'Don't start being insolent. I've a right to know if you've put me in a difficult position!' Lillian glanced past Tori. 'And what's *that*?'

Tori stiffened, realising her mother was looking at the shoebox. 'Nothing… Just some old stuff.'

'Like what?' Lillian snapped.

'Leave it alone!' Tori yelled, standing up.

Lillian froze once again – this time for two reasons: one – her daughter had dared to shout at her and two – that looked like… 'Is that your father's?' she gasped.

She elbowed Tori to one side. 'Oh my God! It *is* your father's! Where did you get that from? There should be none of his things left in this house!' she screamed. 'I want no trace of that man anywhere near me!'

'It's my father's and so therefore it's mine!' Tori yelled as her mother attempted to take the box.

For once Lillian was a loss as to what to do. She'd erased that man from her life as much as she'd been able to, yet there was still a box of his possessions lurking around.

Tori stared at her mother. 'I just want to know what happened.'

'Well, you won't find it in *there*, will you!' Lillian sighed. Feeling suddenly exhausted, she sat down on the edge of the bed once more and sighed. 'I've already told you what happened. Your father was leading a double life. He was dealing drugs with bikers.' Lillian flapped her hands theatrically. 'I mean, can you believe it? With *bikers*? Why would he do that? He never seemed the type.'

Even after all this time Lillian struggled to understand why Jack would do that. Regardless of everything, she *had* loved him once – even if he'd ruined her life by taking away her status. One thing was for certain and that was she'd *never* forgive him for dying a criminal's death.

Tori sat back. This was the most her mother had ever voluntarily divulged hinting that she may have feelings. 'It seems like you're unsure?' *Could it be that deep down her mother didn't entirely believe it either? She*, herself, still struggled to believe her father would have been involved with or risked anything like that. 'I mean, how do you *really* know that to be true?'

Lillian sighed. 'Well, no one ever will for certain, I suppose, but I got it on good authority that was the situation,' she said quietly. If Richard hadn't admitted Jack had been involved in dealing, she'd never have guessed. Jack had certainly been good at hiding his double life from her, but then he would be. He'd have known she'd have never accepted it.

Tori frowned. *She'd got it on good authority?* 'Who said this? The police?'

Lillian nodded her head. 'The police agreed it bore all the hallmarks of a gang-related attack. They hadn't anything to link Jack to anything but admitted gang runners are rarely on the radar in the first place, so that wasn't surprising.'

'So, who…'

Lillian had had enough of this conversation. *If Victoria really wanted the truth, then she could bloody well live with it.* 'Richard told me,' she spat. 'Richard – you know, your *fiancé's* father.'

'R-Richard?' Tori spluttered. 'Why would Ri…'

Lillian shook her head resignedly. 'Put it this way, Richard didn't want to tell me.'

Tori remained silent, almost hypnotised by her mother's words.

'Richard admitted your father had been involved with dealing drugs at college and he'd tried to stop him doing it even back then. After we all got married we drifted apart, so we had very little do with each other.' She flapped her hand. 'I mean, Richard would never have liked being involved with anything like that. He's far too well-bred, we all know that, but there's so much you don't know about your father. It seems there was a lot *none* of us knew about him.'

Lillian looked both wistful and angry at the same time. 'I was also aware that both your father and Richard knew of some rather unsavoury characters a very long time ago, namely a horrible gypsy-type woman, who thinking about it, must have been part of this drugs thing.' *She wasn't going to admit to her daughter that the awful woman had been Jack's girlfriend.*

Tori's senses heightened. *Had that been the woman in the picture?* 'Did Richard tell the police this?'

'God, no! He wouldn't have admitted he'd ever known anyone who dealt drugs, or *those* sort of people. His reputation would have ended up as sullied as mine,' Lillian said bitterly.

'But why did Richard help us out after my father...' Tori stopped as the penny dropped into place. 'Oh my God! You blackmailed him, didn't you? You bloody well blackmailed Richard.' She wiped the back of her hand over her forehead. 'After the killing you threatened to expose his connection with my father knowing his people would disown him. *That's* why you said he 'owed' you wasn't it?'

Lillian swung around, her eyes flashing. 'Tell me why I shouldn't have? If he hadn't introduced me to Jack, then I wouldn't have lost everything. We needed to start afresh Victoria and I didn't see why Richard shouldn't make that happen. Why should I have been the only one to suffer?'

Tori sat back, barely able to catch her breath. *So, her mother had been blackmailing Richard for all of this time?* 'Does Susan know about this?'

'Of course not!' Lillian scoffed. 'And she's not going to either!' she hissed.

'And Matt?'

Lilian shrugged. 'Only what *you* told him.'

Tori said nothing, realising the promise of marriage had been part of the blackmail deal too.

Lillian stood up agitatedly. *She'd already said far too much.* 'So now you know everything that I know and remember, if you want to keep your father's reputation clean as far as everyone around here is concerned, then you'll never breath a *word* of this. Now throw that stupid box away with whatever rubbish it contains and accept what I've told you. Your father was clearly not a nice person. That's the truth and you're going to have to live with that and just get on with your life.'

Lillian walked out of the bedroom, slamming the door behind her, leaving Tori to curl up into a ball and sob quietly into her bedspread.

FORTY TWO

SARAH PLACED HUNTER'S pint in front of him and eyed him curiously. She knew the brewery had made the decision to sell the White Hart, because Colin had received a letter this morning stating that their lease would not be renewed and they would be in contact when a suitable notice period for vacating the premises had been determined.

This would have occurred regardless of what Hunter's word had been to the rest of the area. His influence didn't stretch as far as a national brewery, but it stretched everywhere else because for days she'd been hearing that people had signed their contracts as advised.

The plan was on track, but prayed Hunter was correct in what he'd discovered about the paperwork not being legally binding. If that lawyer friend of his had fucked up, then far too many people had just been sold down the river.

Hunter had brought Sarah up to date about levelling with Grin and that he was doing his best to keep tempers and resentment contained, but it was evident from the general shift in attitude that all was far from well in the Reaper's camp. She could tell that a mile off just by the way the other bikers glared with disdain at Hunter each time his back was turned. It wouldn't take long before Grin, or anything Hunter could say would stop the lid on the angrily bubbling cauldron from flying off.

Watching him sip his beer, Sarah frowned in concern. Hunter looked drawn and tired and it showed clearly in his rugged, handsome face.

She knew he wasn't the only one who this was hitting hard. At work the last couple of days, Tori had been even more of a shell of herself – almost like a ghost. She would guess this was primarily from waiting for the combination of fallout from Matt and her family, along with the lack of contact from Hunter.

'When will you be able to see Tori?' Sarah hissed when Hunter leant forward to pick up his cigarettes. 'It's ok. For once no one's looking at you.'

'I've no idea. I haven't heard a word from her.'

Sarah nodded. 'Tori told me Matt didn't want her seeing you for a few days to add more pressure to the contract signing.'

'Well now they're all signed, so soon it will be time to expose both Matt *and* Noel,' Hunter spat. It was getting more and more difficult to put up with the accusatory glances and pretend to listen Noel's 'consolations' of *'they'll get over it soon enough',* when *he'd* been the one who had instigated this whole mess.

It was choking him not being able to pull his Vice President up over the whole thing and sort him out once and for all. And in truthfulness, he had no idea how long he would be able to keep himself from doing what he very much needed to do where that man was concerned.

'You're still keeping a lid on yourself though, aren't you?' Sarah asked, almost able to read Hunter's thoughts.

'Only just,' he muttered, ignoring Sarah's expression. 'Don't start. It's easy for you.'

'*Easy*?' she cried. 'You've got to be joking!'

Hunter gave Sarah a look that immediately made her realise she'd spoken too loudly. Helping herself to a gin, she tipped it into her mouth. 'Sorry. Everything's getting to me.'

Hunter gritted his teeth. 'I know the feeling. How's Tori?'

'Not too great. Very quiet. She doesn't say much.'

'That bastard best not be giving her a hard time,' Hunter spat. If he found out that to be the case, he'd pull the plug on all this shit right now, regardless of the flack it would generate.

'No more than usual, I don't expect. Just keep your emotions in check, Hunter,' Sarah said sternly. 'But I agree. The sooner all this is sorted, the better.'

· · · ·

'ARE YOU COMING in for dinner or not?' Susan called through the downstairs study door, her voice spiky with impatience.

'Yes, I won't be a minute,' Richard answered. 'Just a couple more minutes.' He pulled the photographs from his pocket, like he had done several times already and pushed them onto his desk with shaking fingers.

The light from his gilt desk lamp illuminated the group of people clustered around the fallen tree. *It was definitely Leila Cooper and that was definitely him.*

At least Matthew had retrieved the pictures and he'd said he'd got all photos from the box. As suspected, when he'd feigned interest, Tori had willingly shown him. It hadn't been difficult to see where she had then placed them, so the minute her back was turned, he'd swiped them, stuffed them in his pocket and replaced the box in her bureau without her being any the wiser.

Richard knew Matthew probably thought it a bit odd to ask three times whether he'd got every single one of the photographs, but he'd had no choice but to check. He couldn't risk these being left hanging around, not now he knew of their existence.

Matthew had confirmed he and Victoria had been busy 'baby-making' at his apartment, which explained the close shave the last time Lillian had been around. He'd had to say something to Susan though because he'd promised her he'd find out. Obviously he'd kept quiet about the baby plans, but equally she'd not been entirely happy that their son was sleeping with Victoria before their marriage. Susan was old-fashioned on a lot of subjects, but like he'd pointed out, he'd only made out to Lillian that Victoria had been staying with them because she would have approved even less otherwise.

Richard had known that by underlining Lillian's attitude to be archaic, embarrassing and unwarranted considering Matthew and Victoria were almost married, it would force Susan to grudgingly accept the situation. There was no way she'd have wanted to be put on a par with the woman.

Richard glanced back down at the image. Leila had been a looker that was for certain. *Shame she'd had no class.*

He knew Tori would eventually notice the photos were missing, but by then it wouldn't matter. With any luck it would be quite a while before she even bothered looking in the shoebox again.

'*Richard?*' Susan called again.

'Yes, I'm coming.' Richard flicked the switch of his shredder on and hearing the motor fire into life, hastily fed each of the four photographs between the metal gnashing blades.

· · · ·

'MATT INSISTED I remind you there's only a few days left before the end of the week, but to do it in a way where I tempt you with my wares...' Tori smiled, sliding her hands under Hunter's T-shirt, her fingers running over the hard ripples of his abdominal muscles.

'Yeah, I expect he's right,' Hunter murmured, his hands inching up Tori's thighs as she lay next to him on the bed in Matt's apartment. 'You wouldn't want me to lose interest now, would you?'

Hunter had been more than pleased to receive a message via Sarah to meet Tori at the apartment. It couldn't have come too soon. He'd been in desperate need of seeing her. He'd been mulling over something for a couple of days now and the time they'd been forced to be apart had only strengthened his resolve to make the decision to go ahead easier than he'd thought. It had been simple to concentrate on reasons why he shouldn't, but reality didn't come in to this one. It was how he felt and his mind was made up.

Tori lay wrapped in Hunter's arms and she pressed her nose into his chest, delighting in his hair tickling her nose. She was so happy she felt she may burst, but despite her happiness, she knew there was an awful lot she didn't know about this man, but did it matter? Not really, not whilst he made her feel the way he did.

'Hunter, I've realised I don't even know how old you are!' she exclaimed. *And who called their lover by a nickname? It was crazy, but she loved it.*

Hunter stroked Tori's hair. 'I did tell you once before, but you've obviously forgotten. Why is it so important? Have you decided I'm too old and decrepit for you?'

Tori laughed. 'Yes, that's it. You're positively *ancient*! No, come on, how old are you?'

Hunter propped himself up on his elbows. 'Guess.'

'Oh, I can't! I don't know!' she exclaimed. 'I'm hopeless with ages. Thirty-three? Thirty-one? Thirty-four?'

Hunter flipped Tori over on to her back and pinned her down in one move. 'You cheeky bitch!' he teased. 'You think I'm *that* old?'

Tori giggled as Hunter trailed kisses down her neck. 'What then?'

'I'm *thirty*, Tori,' he laughed, his voice muffled against her throat. 'A whole *ten* years older than you. How unacceptable!'

Tori laughed, but it didn't change that she wanted to know more. 'I know nothing about you. How about your parents? You never mention them?'

When Hunter froze, Tori knew she'd said something uncomfortable. She lifted his head up and looked into his eyes. 'What's the matter?'

Hunter flipped himself off Tori and propped himself up

against the pillow. 'My parents are dead.'

Tori gasped, raising her hand to her mouth. 'I'm so sorry. What… what hap…'

'They were killed in a car accident. That's all there is to say.'

'I understand. At least to a point. As you know my father was killed.'

Hunter nodded, recalling what Tori had told them all recently. 'What was your father like?'

Tori snuggled against Hunter's chest. 'He was great. The best! I loved him with all of my heart. He was the most wonderful and kindest person ever.'

'I wish I'd met him,' Hunter said, softly stroking the top of Tori's head.

'So do I. I think he'd have approved of you, even though my mother will throw herself from a bridge when she finds out we're together.'

Hunter frowned. 'How will you deal with her?'

Tori shrugged. 'I genuinely don't know and at this precise moment I don't care – I'm too happy! I'm also sure she wasn't truthful about my father. She's always made him out to be a bad person, but I don't believe it.'

She sat up and leant against the headboard. *Should she tell Hunter about what she'd discovered about Richard? She would, but not now. Other things were more important.* 'I know it's easy for a devoted daughter to have a biased view if they love their father to distraction and don't want to think he wasn't what they thought, but I genuinely believe he wasn't what she said. I'll piece together what happened someday.'

Hunter smiled. 'I'm sure you will and I'll help you. We'll do it together.'

Tori beamed. 'That means so much to me. Thank you. I've also found some photos of him that I'd never seen before. I must show you.'

Hunter smiled. 'I'd like that. I mean it Tori. I might have done some bad things in my life, but I'd do anything for you.'

Tori paused. That was a valid point. She'd guessed from what had been said before and from things Sarah had said that he'd been involved in stuff which she suspected she would not like, but he'd already admitted killing people, so how bad was bad? 'You said you'd done bad things. I want to know what those are.'

Hunter took a deep breath. If he was going to be with this woman – which he was – then he had to at least make sure she knew exactly what he was and just hope she loved him enough to see past it. *This would be a gamble.*

'Like I said before. As I said, I've killed several times. Most were necessary, a couple weren't and one was a mistake,' Hunter said clearly, his grey eyes boring into Tori's. 'Where I come from these things are part and parcel, but the mistake shouldn't have happened and it has always bothered me.'

Tori didn't respond. Her mouth moved, but nothing came out. She suspected this renewed confirmation was only the tip of the iceberg. She wanted to look away but was hypnotised by his gaze drilling into her soul. 'I... I...' Her voice was barely louder than a whisper.

Hunter traced his finger across Tori's bottom lip. 'If we're going to be together it's important you know what I am. I'll tell you more about it someday if you really want to know, but not now,' he said. 'The main thing is if you can't accept the shit I've done then you need to walk away because I can't change what has happened in the past. I also can't promise I won't do it again.'

Tori hesitated. *How could she walk away?* She'd never felt like this about anyone. 'I-I just need you to be honest.'

'That is one thing that I always am, so you don't need to worry about that.'

Tori smiled. Being with a man such as this went against everything she believed, but for the first time ever, she understood the old saying: *'you can't help who you fall in love with...'*

'I won't be walking away,' she whispered. 'Just don't hide

anything from me.'

'I can assure you I won't be doing that.'

'I should hope not!' Tori rose to her knees and slowly undid Hunter's belt buckle and palmed her hand over his crotch.

Hunter groaned as Tori unzipped his jeans, his cock springing out. His fisted his hand down his heavily veined shaft to relieve a little of the unbearable aching as it pulsed in readiness.

Moaning loudly as Tori's lips, followed by her tongue circled around the sensitive head, he could barely control himself when she took him fully into her mouth. 'Oh God, Tori, that's good.' His hips thrust in impatience. 'Too good.'

It had been far too long since they'd been alone and his desire was torturous, but he refused to allow this to be over too quickly, however tempting it was for release. However much it pained him to not feel her mouth around him, he gently pulled Tori up, and kissed her. His hand made its way into her knickers and his kisses got harder as he worked her. Stopping to pull his T-shirt over his head, he then removed Tori's top and unclipped her bra, his mouth closing around one of her nipples.

After letting his jeans fall to the floor, Hunter took no time in positioning himself between her thighs. *He wanted to look at her.*

Pushing himself into her willing flesh, Hunter growled as she closed around him. He thrust fast, his need intense and overbearing. Tori bucked underneath his pounding hips. He needed this woman. Needed everything about her and he would not be letting her go.

He slowed his pace almost to a halt. *Now was the time. He'd been planning to wait, but it had to be now. It had never felt so right.*

Tori looked up into the grey eyes she loved so much. 'Don't stop!' she panted, her hips pushing upwards with the need to feel him moving inside her. 'Hunter?'

Hunter brushed his lips against hers and moved a wisp of hair away from her face. 'Tori,' he growled. 'Marry me?'

Tori's eyes widened. 'W-What?'

Hunter smiled lopsidedly, almost shyly. 'I'm serious and I know it's quick, but will you marry me?'

'Yes! Oh yes, I will!' Tori squealed, a tear escaping from her eye.

Licking the lone tear from Tori's cheek, Hunter smiled and resumed, this time slow and gentle. *She said 'yes' and he was going to marry this woman.* He had no idea how they would make this work, but he was marrying her whatever it took.

FORTY THREE

'YOU'VE ASKED HER to *what*?' Grin said, unable to conceal his shock.

Hunter grinned. 'Marry me. I've asked Tori to marry me and she's said yes.'

Pushing the door open, Noel blustered into the small room at the back of the Factory. 'Am I hearing things correctly?' *Why was Hunter updating Grin before him? It had been his idea to play Tori, so surely he should be the first to know anything new?*

Turning, Hunter forced himself to smile. 'Yes, you're hearing correctly. Is that good enough for you?' *Shit. He hadn't realised Noel was about otherwise he wouldn't have said anything.* It had been a good job he didn't go into any more detail because Noel couldn't know his proposal was real.

Noel sneered. 'Jesus! You didn't have to go *that* far!'

Grin glanced between Hunter and Noel. This was awkward. If Noel found out what was really going on, things would be trashed. *He needed to say something.* 'That's what I thought.'

Hunter shrugged. 'Just trying to make her believe as you wanted.'

Noel frowned. 'Not sure why you've gone the extra mile. I mean, the deal's nearly all done and dusted, so there's not really much left to get from her.'

'Just thought I'd keep the act going well.' Hunter despised talking as if this was false. He felt as if he was sullying Tori and how he felt by pretending otherwise, but there wasn't a lot he could do. *Not yet, anyway.*

Noel laughed. 'You've done well. She must have fallen for your irresistible charms, hook, line and sinker to accept you, the stupid bitch! At least you don't have to do this for too much longer.' *Tori was doing well – he had to give her that.* She'd done a great job of making Hunter believe she really *did* want him. It was hilarious. Matt must be pleased and as long as Hunter continued to think he was playing Tori then things were all on track, apart from one thing.

Hunter stared at Noel, careful to keep his expression neutral and not reflect the incessant rage hearing this traitor speak about Tori disrespectfully. 'Good. It's getting quite grating.' He moved towards the door. 'Got to get moving as I need to sort a few things.'

Noel stood up. 'Wait a minute! There's something I need to ask you about. It's the...'

Hunter raised his hand. 'Haven't got time, mate. I'm pushed as it is.' *The word 'mate' in relation to Noel stuck in his throat like a fish bone.*

'But Jeff Da...'

'We'll catch up later.' Hunter shouted over his shoulder as he left the room, closely followed by Grin.

Noel screwed his face up with irritation. Hunter had told him that all the contracts had been signed, but according to Matt, there was still one outstanding. It was Jeff Daniels' off licence. Why the bloody hell was Daniels dragging his fucking feet? He'd have thought that man, of all people would have been the first off the mark to sign.

Countless times he'd been in there on his collection and the cantankerous old bastard was forever griping about being sick of all the winos and deadbeats continuously asking for stuff on tick, or the groups of kids hanging around trying to trick him into thinking they were old enough to purchase their four-packs of Tenants Super.

Daniels had said for *years* that the day couldn't come soon enough when he could retire and he was yearning to sell the business, as well as the poxy flat above that he lived in and finally have some form of life.

Oh, Noel had heard Daniels' miserable spiel on repeat for eons, but now he had the opportunity to do exactly what he'd been bleating on about, he was the *only* one holding it all up.

From the short conversation he'd had with the Reaper who had been tasked with finding out what the delay was, it seemed Daniels had had a change of heart and was unsure whether it was right for him – regardless of what he had previously said he wanted and what Hunter had advised.

'Don't forget there isn't *really* a deadline by the end of the week. I only said that to force Hunter's hand,' Matt had sneered when he'd informed Noel of the latest spanner in the works.

Well, it was alright for Matt, wasn't it? All that seemed to be getting on that prat's wick at the moment was moaning about photos of Miss Aristocrat's bloody father!

He personally hadn't given a shit about any of it until he'd heard a name. A name he hadn't heard for a very long time and one which he hadn't thought he'd ever hear again. He'd given nothing away, but this tiny snippet of information Matt had unknowingly handed him had turned his trump card into the *ultimate* one.

Noel clenched his teeth. None of this changed that Matt may not have had a fucking deadline, but *he* did. He needed this money and it was the right time to get it. The unrest within the club was close to breaking point and being as Grin was smoothing the situation over every chance he got, he might eventually even turn things around for Hunter and that would be more than detrimental. *He couldn't take that risk.*

Now Hunter wouldn't even make the time to discuss anything. Something else was more important. How was he supposed to get this sorted if Hunter was slacking and not noticing there was still a contract outstanding and not wanting to even hear about it?

Well, he'd just have to do something about it himself. If he paid Daniels a visit and 'helped' him come to the correct decision then it would be sorted in a few more days, but he didn't have a few more days. He needed to finish this *now*.

Noel snorted a fresh line of coke from the table. There had to be another way. Smiling slowly to himself, he wiped the powder residue from under his nose with the back of his sleeve.

There *was* another way and he knew *exactly* what it was.

• • • •

'IT WAS SO NICE of you both to make the effort to come and discuss the arrangements for Matt and Tori's nuptials,' Lillian wittered, smiling at Jeremy and Ginny. 'You've both been exceptionally good friends to both of them over the years and I hope that is reflected in their wish for you to be best man and maid of honour?'

Tori smiled dully at her mother's simpering, questioning why she was bothering attending this pointless wine and biscuits evening. It was the first she'd heard of Ginny being her maid of honour. Why would she want that nasty cow to have anything to do with it?

She smiled, reminding herself that there was absolutely no point in wasting time thinking about it. They could plan all they liked, but this wedding was not going to happen. *She was marrying Ash Hunter and soon she would be rid of Matt for ever.*

She stole a sideways look at Matt thinking that the usual smug expression of his would soon be gone. It was all quite amusing. It someone had told her six months ago she would accept a marriage proposal from a biker, she'd have presumed they were hallucinating. She grinned. It was madness, utter madness, but nothing had ever felt so right.

'Is something amusing you, dear?' Lillian said, her tone friendly, but her glare meaning the opposite as she eyed her daughter. *Did she really have to sit there with a stupid smile plastered across her face whilst everyone was busy organising the most important day of her life?*

'I'm just happy, that's all,' Tori replied, ignoring Matt's frown.

'What will I need to do as maid of honour?' Ginny asked, her voice shrill. 'Do I get a special dress? I don't want to wear something that will clash with my hair.' She flicked her extensions flamboyantly.

Tori scowled. Personally, Ginny could take her place as the bride if she liked. She'd do much better at being Matt's wife - except of course, *she* wasn't part of the deal.

'Of course you will, my dear. You can have any dress of your choosing, providing it fits with the colour scheme,' Lillian gushed. *If only Victoria could be more like this girl.* 'It's so exciting,' she chirped, clasping her hands together. 'I can't believe in just over three months it will be finally official between you two love birds.'

Tori choked back a laugh. *Love birds? More like vultures!*

'If I had it my way, we'd have already been married by now,' Matt said, his tone sharp.

Tori felt a shiver of apprehension as he grabbed her hand, purposefully digging his nails into her skin.

Lillian eyed Matthew. *She hoped he wasn't getting fed up, not at this stage.* 'I know what you're saying Matthew. It's been extremely frustrating and you're right – you would have been married by now if Victoria hadn't dragged her feet over the dates.'

'We're very eager to start a family, aren't we darling?' Turning to Tori, Matt's eyes cut into hers, almost daring her to disagree.

Tori nodded stiffly. *What was Matt doing this for? He'd start her mother off about pre-wedding pregnancies again at this rate.*

Ginny laughed. 'Oh, I'd hate to be all fat and covered with stretchmarks!'

'Pregnancy is all part and parcel once you're married, Virginia. It's what's expected,' Lillian scoffed. 'No one says you're going to enjoy it, but it's what is done.' *And it ruins your life.*

'For the record, I intend to keep Tori pregnant for several years,' Matt said sourly. He stood up, pulling Tori with him. He was hoping to get through the evening and deal with what he'd discovered later, but it was grating on his mind too much to leave it any longer. 'Now if you don't mind excusing us, I want to spend some time with my wife-to-be.'

Tori glanced around, confused. 'I thought we were discu…'

'We've discussed everything that needs to be discussed from our side. Let's leave everyone else to get on with their side of things,' Matt said, leaving no room for any misconceptions. They were leaving and leaving *now*.

Tori felt rather sick. Matt was in a terrible mood and had been since the minute he'd arrived. Her heart raced. *Had he found out what she'd really been doing?*

• • • •

MATT HADN'T SAID a word to Tori during the drive to his apartment and she hadn't dared ask why they'd come here either because it was clear he wasn't in the mood.

She glanced around the now familiar surroundings of where she'd been so blissfully happy only the night before, finding it in stark contrast to how she felt standing here with this man. Just by *being here* with Matt tainted the beauty of what she'd experienced here with Hunter.

Angrily yanking a bottle of wine from the huge American-style fridge, Matt poured himself a large glass. He stared at Tori as he leant against the kitchen island unit. 'Well?' he spat.

Tori was unsure what he wanted her to say or what he was asking, but something was clearly very wrong. 'I-I don't know what you're asking?'

Matt's face turned red as he slammed the wine glass down onto the surface and strode towards Tori. 'You don't think you perhaps might have told me that wanker asked you to marry him?' he screamed.

'W-What?' *How had he found that out? Shit! How should she play this?* 'I-I haven't had chance, I w…'

'You haven't had *chance*?' Matt roared, backhanding her around the face.

Tori reeled with both shock and pain and stared wide-eyed at Matt. 'I-I thought…'

'You thought *what*?' Matt spat. 'You thought it was a good idea?'

Tori struggled to pull her head together. *She had to remember the plan.* 'I-I didn't expect him to do that. I thought you'd be pleased?' she said quietly. *This was awful!*

'But you accepted! You know full well he believes he's playing *you*!' Matt was wild-eyed, the tendons in his neck taut.

'W-What else was I supposed to do?' Tori stammered. *He was frightening her now.*

Matt raked his fingers through his hair. 'How I've refrained from belting you in front of everyone I really don't know!' he spat. 'You stupid bitch! You should have said something like 'I can't', or 'No'. We don't need him anymore, you know that. The deals are all signed, but if this gets out…'

Tori stared blankly. 'But he…'

'But *nothing*! Jesus wept!' Matt shook Tori roughly by the shoulders. 'I thought you were *finally* growing a fucking brain! If this gets out, I'll be finished!'

'I-If *what* gets out? I-I don't understand.'

Matt stared at her in amazement. Did she not understand that if his circles learnt about this then he'd be a laughing stock and so would she. They'd be ostracised from everything worth anything.

He'd been horrified when Noel had called to congratulate him on Tori doing such a convincing job with fooling Hunter and he'd had to pretend that he'd known about it. How he'd managed to refrain from smashing the phone against the wall, he didn't know, but he still ended up having to cut Noel off.

He'd called literally just as he'd been about to leave to go to Tori's for this stupid wine and biscuits thing. Even if he hadn't been about to go out, he'd have had to make an excuse to get Noel off the phone because he'd been angry. *So fucking angry.*

'You don't understand?' Matt yelled. 'You don't fucking *understand*?' He grabbed Tori around the throat. 'I had to put up with that fuckhead Noel calling and telling me what *you* should have, you mean? You could have at least given me some warning! You must have known I wouldn't be happy?'

Tori clawed at Matt's hands closing around her throat as she struggled for breath. 'Matt… I…'

'Noel overheard Hunter telling that mong with the teeth, so who else has he fucking told?' Matt spat. 'Jesus Christ! You may have done such a blinding job on him that he's stupid enough to believe you'd marry him, but it this gets out – which it will the way he's playing his mouth, then we're sunk. Fucking *finished*! Can't you do *anything* properly?'

Matt released his grip and Tori slumped to the floor gasping for breath. 'Oh yes, that's right – act all hard done by and wronged. You stupid, *stupid*, pointless fucking bitch!'

Tori gathered her speeding thoughts. *Why would Hunter have told everyone? Had he done that on purpose?* 'I-I'll tell him I've changed my mind,' she blathered. *She couldn't let this mess up. Not now they were close.* 'I'm sorry.'

'You're *sorry*?' Matt screamed. 'You're fucking sorry? It makes no difference what you say if this gets out. The damage will be already done. But it's ok that you're sorry once I've lost my fucking job!'

'It won't get out. I'm sure of it.' Tori reasoned. 'Why would it?' She needed to calm this down. 'You're overreacting. No one knows them from our circles.'

'*Overreacting?*' Matt's voice was so high-pitched it sounded like he'd blown a gasket. 'I'm overreacting? Gossip such as this travels like fucking wildfire. It's not every day that one of our sort would agree to marry someone like *that*. Especially when they're engaged to someone like *me*.'

He almost laughed at the ridiculousness of being jilted at the alter for a scrubber thug like Hunter. Except it wasn't even slightly funny if people believed his fiancée would accept a man like that. What would that make him look like?

'Oh my God! If my parents hear about this then they'll know I was involved with a deal with the Reapers and I'll lose everything. They'll cut me out!'

'I-It won't come to th…'

'Shut the fuck up, Tori!' Matt roared. He'd had enough. Yanking her to her feet, he ripped at her clothes.

'What are you doing?' Tori screamed, her eyes darting wildly around the room as she tried to get away from Matt's hands.

'Taking what's *mine*,' Matt sneered, forcing Tori over the kitchen island.

'No, Matt. Don't be like th…'

'Shut up! You've done enough damage. You need to act properly like the wife you're going to be,' he spat. Unzipping his trousers, he roughly shoved himself into Tori. 'You need to tell that twat to keep his mouth closed. You need to make sure he puts this right. Do you understand?'

Overriding the pain in her rib cage as it was crushed against the side of the wooden surface, Tori nodded, refusing to let the tears fall. This whole situation *had* to be over soon because she couldn't take much more.

FORTY FOUR

HUNTER WAS GLAD to sit in the relatively calm atmosphere of the White Hart and get a couple of pints down his neck. He wasn't even up for conversing with Sarah. Thankfully, she could tell he wasn't in the mood for talking and had left him to his own devices, happy in his own company. Not that he was particularly happy with his own company. He wasn't happy about *anything* right now – apart from Tori and even *that* was difficult, thanks to everything else.

He'd had a close call with Noel before and it could have been a different story if the man hadn't made himself known. Hunter irritably pulled a cigarette from his packet and lit it. He was getting slack. He should have said nothing at all. At least not until he'd made sure no one else was about. It had been uncharacteristically remiss and there was no room for stupid mistakes like that from anyone – especially *himself.*

He wondered what else Noel had wanted to discuss. He probably should have waited to listen, but every second he spent in that man's company was another second that made it harder to act normal. *Things were not normal.*

Glancing at his watch, Hunter decided to have one more pint before hitting the road. He couldn't hide in here on his own all night however tempting that prospect was. Getting to his feet, he was making his way towards the bar when the main door slammed open with force. Swinging around, he knew there was trouble the minute he saw Grin's face.

'There's a problem in George Street,' Grin said under his breath.

Hunter hastily grabbed his leather and helmet. 'What problem?'

'I don't know, but we need to get over there,' Grin muttered. 'I have a horrible feeling it's something to do with Noel.'

• • • •

WHEN HUNTER ARRIVED at George Street to find the off licence being dowsed by water from the attending fire engines and groups of people huddled in the street, he'd been able to tell straight away the situation was far from good.

Luckily, people living in the flats above the adjoining shops in the terraced row had successfully escaped and their buildings were only smoke damaged, but the same couldn't be said for that of the off licence. He'd waited until a body bag was removed from the shop and put in the back of a vehicle before he'd fired his bike and roared off in the direction of the Factory.

Once inside, he'd pulled Noel into the back room and it hadn't taken him long to get to the bottom of it and prove Grin's suspicions correct.

'What the fuck were you thinking?' Hunter roared, facing the man casually swigging from a beer bottle.

Noel rolled his eyes. 'Chill out! I did you a favour! Daniels was dragging his feet. The cunt wanted to do his own thing and it was wasting time,' he said with a smile on his face. 'You hadn't even noticed there was a contract missing. I tried to tell you, but you were too busy.'

'What, so you thought you'd just go and burn him to a crisp rather than wait?' Hunter raged.

'Why not? For fuck's sake, it was for *your* benefit! The deal would have fallen through if I hadn't done something. This way it can still go ahead as planned, just with one less property available due to 'unavoidable natural causes' rather than opposition. Now, *that* would have delayed things.'

Hunter raked his fingers through his hair. He could feel the red mist descending at the rate of knots. Lurching forward, he grabbed Noel in a chokehold. 'You stupid bastard! You did this without consulting *me*?'

With some difficulty, Noel extracted himself from Hunter's grip. 'With *you*? Like I said, you didn't have time to listen and what fucking use are you anyway?' he spat. 'I'm having to sort this out being as you're so half-soaked and deluded. It's my job as second-in-comm...'

'This has *nothing* to do with me, but *everything* to do with you!' Hunter spat. *This was the last straw. He couldn't hold back any longer.* 'I know what you've been doing, you lying cunt! You've been working with that ponce to set me up.'

Noel's eyes sparkled with pent up rage. *So he knew, did he?* 'And why the fuck not? You're not fit to run the Reapers. It should be *me*!' he spat. 'You're fucking finished here, Hunter. *Finished*!'

Hunter ground his teeth. *It would be so easy to kill Noel.* He wanted to. Wanted to *badly*, but he was a Reaper and Reapers *never* killed other members, regardless of the circumstances. The worst punishment a fellow member could get was to be officially banished and that was worse than being dead.

He had to play this a different way. '*You're* the one who's finished. I'll be exposing you and your arsehole of a posh friend for what you are,' Hunter laughed tightly. 'You're out of this fucking club, Noel!'

Noel straightened down his leather jacket, ruffled from where Hunter had grabbed him. 'I don't think so.' *And when he was out of the club, he'd kill him.*

Hunter couldn't help himself. He needed to rub it in just how much Noel's snide plan had backfired. 'And you also might like to know that me and Tori are getting married – as in *really* getting married and you and Matt will lose everything.'

Noel stared at Hunter in amazement and then laughed. 'And you actually think she'll marry you? For fuck's sake, you're more stupid than I thought.'

Hunter raised his eyebrows. 'Am I? Why is it then I know she was sent to play me and that she knows I was supposed to be playing *her*?' He enjoyed watching the gravity of his words radiate into Noel's brain. 'Ah, you've worked it out, have you? Me and Tori have been playing you and Matt – not the other way around. What we have is *real* and you're both fucked!'

Noel shrugged. *So it hadn't quite worked out as planned, but he'd still be getting his money.* 'Doesn't change that half the area's been sold though, does it? And I should tell you that the price will be cut to less than half,' he grinned. 'I've done you up like a kipper, mate and I don't give a rat's arse about you and Tori. It's irrelevant and furthermore, because you've talked everyone into these deals it'll be *you* who'll be outed!'

Hunter smiled. He was an inch away from Noel's face in a stand-off.

'What are you going to do now?' Noel jibed. 'Smash my face up again? You lost half your respect around here the last time you did that, but then everyone's worked out you don't adhere to club rules.'

'I *always* honour club rules,' Hunter barked.

'Yeah, that's why you want to be with the enemy. Remember your family, do you? Remember what was done to them?' Noel laughed, his eyes flashing with malice.

Hunter gripped Noel around the throat. 'That's out of order.'

Noel ripped Hunter's grip away once more. 'But it's true.'

Hunter clenched his jaw in frustration. *He wasn't going to talk about his family.* 'You're wrong about the contracts - they're null and void. Do you *really* think I wouldn't have made sure of that?'

'Yeah, right!' Noel scoffed.

Hunter shrugged. 'Think what you like. Just wait and see…

And I'll be announcing to the club what you've done.'

A flash of panic ripped through Noel. He knew enough about Hunter to know when he was bluffing and he wasn't. If the club found out he'd tried to turn everyone over he'd be ripped apart and that he could not let that happen. *Hunter was not going to win this one. It was time to use his trump card.* He'd waited far too long as it was, plus with this new information he had it couldn't be better.

Squaring up to Hunter, Noel grinned. 'You do that and I'll tell the rest of the club how you fucked up your initiation.'

Hunter paused. *What did Noel know about that? Only him and Rafe knew what had really happened.*

Noel relished the look on Hunter's face. 'You didn't think I knew? You had no idea I've known all these years, did you?'

Hunter scowled. *This was bollocks. Noel was playing him and he wouldn't fall for it.* 'I don't know what you think you know, but I doubt it's anything that would concern me. I've got nothing to hide.'

As Hunter turned to leave the small room, Noel smiled. *That smug expression on his face wouldn't be there much longer.* 'I wouldn't be too hasty, Hunter.'

Hunter swung round, his eyes narrow slits. 'Get fucked, Noel. Your plan has failed.'

Noel folded his arms across his chest and grinned. 'Ok, have it your own way. You think it hasn't pained me having to act grateful to *you*? That I should be thankful for you taking revenge for my mother when I had no need to?'

Hunter froze, his hand on the door handle.

'Yeah, that's right... All these bloody years I've acted like you did me a fucking favour...'

Hunter turned, his eyes blazing. 'What the hell are you talking ab...'

'I *heard* you, Hunter!' Noel spat. 'I fucking heard when Rafe informed you that you'd taken out the wrong man!'

Hunter stared at Noel. *How could he have heard that? Rafe had made sure they'd been on their own.*

Relishing the tinge of worry and questioning of possibility on Hunter's face, Noel continued. 'I was in the flat bed. You know, when you and Rafe disappeared in his pick-up truck. I sneaked in under the tarpaulin. It was supposed to be a laugh… I was only… what? Fifteen years old? I was planning on jumping out on you, but then you started talking… Remember?'

Glad to see he'd got Hunter's full attention, Noel casually lit a cigarette. 'Oh yes, I heard it all. *You'd* been given the job of getting all the gen on my mother's bastard rapist and you spent, what? Months and *months* gathering all the shit together, didn't you?'

Hunter felt a nerve twitching frantically in his neck and he wished it would stop. He ran through the plausibility of staving Noel's head in and just walking away. 'You d…'

'Then after you'd been given the go ahead based on what *you'd* researched and carried out the hit, it was only then that it came to light that you had, in fact, ID'd the wrong fucking man!' Noel squared up to Hunter. 'I *heard* Rafe ball you out for getting it so fucking wrong. I heard it with my own ears!'

Noel threw his hands up in the air. 'Do you not realise that you were my *hero*? I loved you for avenging my ma, but then I had it all ripped away hearing that conversation.'

Hunter remained stock still, unable to fully process that all this time Noel had been aware of what had really happened, yet always acted the opposite. *Shit. This was not good.*

Noel's eyes narrowed further. 'Oh yes, I heard it quite distinctly when Rafe told you that *no one* was to ever know about it. It would stay between you and him. You were his son and you'd have been fucked within the club for screwing up so badly. But you weren't even his son either, were you? Not a *real* son. Yet he still protected you and covered your fuck up, but what about ME?'

Noel paced around the small room. 'He said I was *never* to know because it was important I believed justice had been done. And you – you spineless piece of shit –accepted that, yet I was left knowing the *real* pervert was still around whilst having to act grateful to *you*.'

'Rafe said it would be best that way,' Hunter muttered. *There was no point denying it. Noel had indeed heard every word of that night.*

'And that was definitely easier for you!' Noel roared.

'It's *never* been easier for me!' As much as he didn't want to, Hunter owed the man at least some form of explanation. 'I wanted to continue and find the correct person the second I knew I'd fucked up.'

Noel laughed hollowly. 'But you didn't bother…'

Hunter shook his head. 'I did. I started to, but I was instructed to stop. Rafe didn't want anything else done. As far as everyone else was concerned the job had been done.'

'Oh, *that's* alright then!' Noel spat. 'As long as it was better for everyone else! Fuck what I wanted, yeah?' He threw his cigarette butt on the ground in rage. 'Not that I give a fuck, but did you actually ever stop to think about the poor bastard you wrongly took out?'

Hunter folded his arms across his chest. He wasn't going to freely admit just how much it had gutted him that he'd screwed up. Not to Noel or *anyone*. 'There wasn't a lot I could do afterwards!' he spat.

A malicious grin spread across Noel's face. 'How convenient. Hunter the Hero! And you did some right hardcore shit to that geezer too. Oh, they hushed that up too didn't they, but we all knew.'

Hunter didn't want to think about that either. He had no problem meting out justice in the worst ways possible, but his first killing had scarred him because he'd got it so wrong.

'The club will hang you, Hunter. Reapers don't accept anyone who won't take responsibility for their own screw ups.'

'So, you're blackmailing me over this regarding your deal?' Hunter said. *He wouldn't be held to ransom for anyone.* 'I'll tell them then myself, shall I?'

Noel smiled widely. 'See it whichever way you like, but there's one more thing…' He scratched his chin in fake thoughtfulness. 'Do you even know the name of the man you killed?'

Receiving no response, Noel got right up in Hunter's face, his voice now quiet. 'I do. It was Jack Jacobs.'

'Well if you know, why are you telling me?' Hunter said, getting fed up. 'I'm fully aware of his name!'

'Then I'm surprised you haven't noticed by now that the man you wrongly murdered as none other than the father of your beloved Miss Aristocrat!'

Hunter almost laughed. *What on earth was he talking about?*

Noel's face broke into a cold, wide grin. 'Don't get confused by names. Ask Miss Victoria Morgan what her name *used* to be. She may be able to bend her own rules to a point where you're concerned, but not *that* much!'

FORTY FIVE

HUNTER HAD BEEN riding for two hours. He wasn't going anywhere in particular. He had no clue *why* he was going where he was going, exactly *where* he was going, or if he reached anywhere, *what* he would do.

His mind was reeling over what Noel had said. He genuinely had no clue what to do about what he'd discovered. He vaguely remembered walking out of the back room in the Factory leaving Noel standing where he'd left him. He had no memory whatsoever of what he said, if anything, in response to Noel's bombshell and he had even less idea if he'd said anything to anyone else. All he knew was that he'd had to get out of there.

The entire time he'd been on the road his brain had been in a continuous loop. Could what Noel have said been true, or had he somehow manufactured it to mess with his head?

That Noel knew the truth surrounding his initiation couldn't be disputed, but for that man to have been Tori's *father*? Surely that couldn't be possible?

Hunter wracked his brains to remember each exact word Tori had ever said about her parents and the small amount of information she'd divulged concerning the circumstances surrounding his death. She'd said it was bikers, but also a drug deal? It *couldn't* have been the same person. And what was this about her changing her name? Why would she have done that and furthermore, how would Noel know?

Glancing at the road signs, Hunter took a left back towards the city. He couldn't ride around randomly for ever. He needed to find out if there was any shred of truth in Noel's words and if there was…

Hunter shook his head angrily. Whatever happened now, he couldn't expose Matt and Noel at this precise moment, but things would hit the fan regardless. Noel was right - he was finished. Now it was known that the contracts weren't worth the paper they were written on, Noel would fast be ensuring *everyone* knew about it.

It was no good. He'd have to expose them regardless of what happened to him and take it on the chin. It was only what he should have done *years* ago, but there was one person he needed to see first.

If what Noel said was true and Tori learnt of this from someone else then it would be even more awful than it already was.

. . . .

MATT STOMPED INTO the hall of his parent's house and irritably tossed his blazer on the coat stand. He could have done without having that unexpected grief Tori had caused. He hadn't dreamt she'd do something so stupid. *Fancy accepting that idiot*!

He nodded to himself, satisfied he'd got his point across at the apartment. *He was still the boss, no mistake*.

She'd hardly said a word when he'd dropped her back at her mother's. Hopefully Lillian wouldn't ask questions as to their early departure from that stupid wine and biscuits thing. He wouldn't put it past Tori to bleat out some other crap to cause even more problems.

'Ah, Matthew – you're back!' Susan glided out from one of

the rooms off the large hallway.

Matt's heart sunk. He'd been hoping to avoid his parents. Turning, he smiled, hoping it didn't look forced.

'Have you had a nice evening?' she gushed. 'Have you come from Lillian's? Weren't you going over there to sort wedding things out? Is Victoria ok?'

She frowned at the strange expression plastered across her son's face. 'What's the matter? You seem a little, shall we say, agitated?' She threw her hands up in the air. 'Oh no! You haven't argued have you? Victoria's not playing up again is she? Please tell me sh...'

'Nothing like that,' Matt interrupted, perhaps a little too brusquely. Remembering himself, he bit back his irritation and smiled. 'Everything's fine. Tori's fine. We're *both* fine!'

Susan let out a melodramatic sigh of relief. 'Well, I'm very glad to hear it!'

Matt forced yet another smile. 'I think I'll go and have a bath. It's been a long day.' *Anything to get away from this questioning.* He had only managed four steps in the direction of the staircase before his mother stopped him.

'Oh, I almost forgot!' she cried. 'There was a phone call for you. It sounded important.'

Matt's hackles tingled. 'When was this? Who was it?'

'About ten minutes ago. The man said he was from a property company.' Susan frowned. 'He was very stand-offish if you must know - almost rude, in fact. He said it was urgent and wants to meet with you immediately. Tonight, he said. Why would someone be ringing at this time in the evening, Matthew?'

Matt knew full well it wasn't the property firm because for a start, they hadn't got his home number. *This was Noel and if he'd called for an immediate meeting then something must have gone horribly wrong.*

Not giving any indication that bile was rising steadily up his gullet, Matt played his rising panic down. 'Big investors do this sort of thing all the time,' he blathered. 'They class something like running out of stamps as 'urgent'!'

'He didn't sound like a big investor to me,' Susan sniffed, suspicion in her voice. 'He sounded rather common, truth be known.'

Matt laughed. 'You'd be surprised what some of that lot sound like, but they're the real deal, believe me! Money and credentials coming out of their ears!'

Susan pursed her lips. 'Shouldn't your father be made aware of this?' Richard had locked himself back in his study the moment dinner had finished and he'd hardly said a word to her throughout the entire meal. *Something she'd be picking him up on later.*

'No! *I'm* handling this account, so I'd be grateful if you could just let me get on with it. I *do* know what I'm doing, you know!' Matt scoffed.

'Of course you do, dear.' Susan smiled condescendingly, watching Matt yank his blazer back off the coat stand. 'Where are you going? I thought you were having a bath?'

'I've got to go and see what the investors want,' Matt barked.

'What? Now? You're actually going back out?' Susan said, amazed.

'Yes. It's urgent isn't it?'

'But I…'

Matt shut the front door behind him before his mother could get any further questions in.

· · · ·

TORI SAT IN HER bedroom doing nothing, short of staring at the wall. She was unsure how long she'd been sat there for – it could have been hours.

When she'd returned from Matt's apartment, she'd been relieved to find Ginny and Jeremy had gone and her mother had retired to bed. She didn't think she'd have been able to bear any snide remarks, comments or questions on top of Matt's behaviour.

Exposing him and that foul bastard Noel could not come soon enough. She hadn't enough strength left to deal with this situation any longer and it was running the risk of suffocating her.

She'd hurriedly had a scalding hot bath to scrub all traces of Matt from her body, but her skin still crawled with revulsion. The apartment was now ruined for her too. She would not be going there again. Not with Hunter. Not with anyone. Matt had shattered every beautiful memory she'd had of being with the man she loved within those same four walls.

She still couldn't work out what Hunter had been thinking of by telling everyone they were getting married. How had he been so careless to announce that at this stage? At least Matt had bought that it had been part of the plan, but she hoped it hadn't delayed everything being finished within the next couple of days.

Hearing the unmistakeable roar of a motorbike Tori's ears pricked up. Rushing to the window, she pulled back the curtains and stared out into the night. She squinted at the figure dismounting the huge bike in front of the house. *Oh God. It was Hunter.*

Heart beating rapidly with a mixture of elation and worry, Tori rushed down the stairs, giving her mother's bedroom door a quick glance over her shoulder as she went. *Soon she'd be free of all of this.*

Tori yanked open the front door just as Hunter reached the top step. She threw herself against his chest and pressed her face into him, inhaling his familiar smell. 'I'm so glad you're here,' she cried.

Hunter wrapped his arms tightly around Tori, comforted by the feel of her small body crushed up against his. His whole being relaxed for a split second before the reason as to why he was here flashed back into his brain.

Pushing onto tiptoes, Tori pressed her lips against his. 'Why did you tell everyone about us getting married? It got back to Matt and he went crazy. He…'

'Did he hurt you?' Hunter interrupted, anger surging at the very thought.

As the memory of Matt forcing himself on her filtered through her, Tori began trembling. 'He, he was angry… I-I couldn't stop him. I…'

'I'm going to fucking kill him,' Hunter spat. *What had they all done for everything to end up like this?*

'It doesn't matter,' Toni protested. 'Not now. Not now you're here.'

'It *does* matter, Tori,' Hunter raged. '*Everything* bloody matters!'

Tori frowned. *Something had happened. She hadn't even stopped to think about that in her relief on seeing him.* 'Come upstairs quickly. My mother's asleep. She won't see us.'

'I really don't care if your mother sees us or not,' Hunter muttered. *This had all gone too far.* He had no idea how, or even *if* he could broach the questions he so desperately needed to ask.

He studied Tori's face for any resemblance, however slight, to the man he'd so brutally butchered, but found none. A glimmer of hope radiated. *What Noel said might have been an elaborate and extremely clever wind up after all.*

Following Tori upstairs and shutting the door behind him, Hunter wanted to forget about the reasons for his visit. When she began unbuttoning his jeans even knowing that obnoxious bastard Matt had had his way with her earlier wasn't enough to dampen his urge to bury himself in this woman. But he needed to speak to her first. 'Tori, I…'

'Shh…' she whispered, wrapping her hand firmly around his cock which had hardened on cue.

Unable to help himself, Hunter lifted Tori off her feet, depositing her on the bed and followed her down, his mouth on hers.

Frantically pulling up her clothes, he wasted no time in ramping up a steady rhythm, enjoying the feel of her moans vibrate against his lips. *He belonged with this woman and she belonged to him. There could be no other way.*

• • • •

'WHAT DO YOU mean, he knows?' Matt hissed.

'Keep your voice down!' Noel barked. 'Isn't it suspicious enough that we're both in the toilets?'

Matt controlled his ragged breathing. The last place he wanted to be was in the White Hart toilets with this man and listened with mounting panic whilst Noel recounted what had happened between him and Hunter.

Cold sweat dripped freely down the back of his neck. 'Fuck! So, you're telling me the contracts won't stand when he contests them after the price is dropped?' *This was just about the worst-case scenario EVER and one he hadn't even contemplated as being an option.*

Noel nodded. 'Basically, yes.'

Matt leant his forehead against the cubicle wall, extremely uncomfortable that he was locked in a toilet stall with this freak of a psycho and also that he was stupid enough to press his skin against a filthy partition wall which someone had probably died against, or at the very least, wiped shit on. But even these two disgusting situations paled into insignificance compared to hearing that everything he'd worked so hard for was fast on its way down the sewer.

'Oh Christ! I'm fucked! What am I going to do?' Matt wailed. Tori had been correct. Hunter was cleverer than he'd given him credit for. And how the hell had the loopholes in the contracts been missed? Which idiot had got them legally checked and drawn up?

Matt's teeth grated together. *Jeremy, that's who.* He'd entrusted that part to bloody Jeremy, being as it was supposed to be his skill set. He might have known. He might have bloody well known he'd fuck it up. Jesus Christ, he was going to wring his neck!

Noel smiled. 'You need to chill out bec…'

'*Chill out*?' Matt screeched. 'What are you talking about? How in Christ's name am I supposed to do that? Are you insane? It's *me* who's lost everything not y…'

'I've told you once,' Noel growled, pressing Matt's face painfully into the wall. 'Keep your fucking voice down and if you can't, then I'll pull your bastard voice box out and shut you up myself!'

Swallowing nervously, Matt attempted to calm down. *Sometimes he forgot exactly who he was dealing with.*

Satisfied Matt had finished squawking, Noel released his hold. 'As I was saying, you need to chill out.'

Matt stared at Noel. It was easy for him to think that way. His life was a mishmash of beer, chirping birds and pointy sharp stabby objects. This man wouldn't have the first clue what any of this meant. 'But Hunter will expose us and what we've done, don't you see? On top of that, the contracts will all be revoked and we'll have nothing, whereas he'll *still* come out of this smelling of roses. Unlike us.'

Noel grinned manically. 'And that, Matthew, is where you're totally wrong.'

Matt sighed. *Wrong? He wasn't bloody wrong!* Noel must have taken weird shit tonight if he was that deluded. 'How on earth do y…'

'Hunter won't be exposing us and the contracts will go through as planned with the lower price. We'll get everything we expect. He'll be the one blamed and we'll be just fine,' Noel winked. 'Nothing's changed. At least, not for us.'

Matt felt like his tongue had fallen down the back of his throat as he almost choked with the futility of Noel's words. 'How can that happen?'

'Because,' Noel sneered. 'I decided to finally use my trump card.'

FORTY SIX

IN THE AFTERGLOW of sex, Hunter twirled strands of Tori's hair around his thick fingers as she lay her head against his chest. He should have just come out with what he needed to ask the minute he'd got here, rather than get side-tracked into bed.

A horrible sinking feeling resumed in the bottom of his stomach. He knew deep down that if he'd said what he'd needed to say when he'd arrived he would have lost the option of sinking himself into the woman he loved so fiercely. *And that thought made him sick with utter despair.* He stared at the wall to keep his rollercoaster of emotions in check.

'Are you going to tell me what's happened?' Tori murmured.

'Happened?'

'Obviously something has. I can't see you just turning up here otherwise?'

Hunter realised he had to concentrate. He needed an answer to his burning question before he told her that their plans had gone somewhat awry. Even if what Noel said was bullshit, which he hoped with every fibre in his body it was, he'd still have to explain that when he exposed Matt and Noel, it would also expose his mammoth fuck up all those years prior and he would be finished in this city. It didn't offer much of an incentive, nor a good grounding for marriage.

He sighed. 'Noel's causing trouble.'

Tori sat up abruptly. 'Oh no! What's he done now? Everything's still on track to finish, isn't it?' Tears brimmed in her eyes. '*Please* tell me it's still on? I can't bear this anymore. I've *got* to get away from these people!'

Pulling Tori back against his chest, Hunter scowled. *Whatever happened it looked like he would let this woman down either way.* 'Nothing major,' he lied. 'He's just being difficult.' Now was not the time to mention that alongside everything else, Noel had torched and murdered the only unsigned contract holder.

This wasn't going to work. He couldn't make her life any worse. Every minute she was involved with him it was destroying her. In fact, he was destroying *everyone* around him and it had to stop.

'Let's talk about something else for a minute,' Hunter continued, forcing his voice upbeat. *This was a good way of broaching the subject.* 'Have you found anything else out about your father?' The words almost stuck in his throat. *Please God, don't let it be the same man.*

Seemingly placated by Hunter's words, Tori frowned. 'No, I haven't had chance to think about anything. There's been too much going on. I can't concentrate and I…'

'Why don't you tell me his name?' Hunter asked, the words burning. 'I could do some digging? It's obviously Morgan, but what was his first name?' *He was glad Tori couldn't see his face. He could barely breathe.*

'Wait!' Tori cried, jumping out of bed and moving to the bureau. 'I'll show you a picture.' She bent down and retrieved a tattered shoe box. 'His name wasn't Morgan, by the way.' She glanced over her shoulder. 'That was my mother's idea. She changed our names back to her maiden name after he died so not to be 'associated' with the whole thing. I, of course, had no say, but his name was Jack – Jack Jacobs.'

Hunter's heart crashed and he felt frozen in time as Tori's father's name echoed around his head like a ping-pong ball. *JACK JACOBS... Was it possible for there to be more than one?*

Tori excitedly lifted the lid off the shoe box. 'Let me show you.'

Hunter felt a strange tremoring inching along his arms to his fingertips. He remained silent in the hope it may somehow change the outcome.

'Oh, that's weird…' Tori exclaimed, frowning.

'What is?' Hunter asked, amazed that he'd been able to utter anything out loud.

Tori emptied the shoe box onto the bed. 'I was sure I put the photos back in the top of this box. Oh, wait. Here's one.'

Tori pulled out the photograph of her mother and father. 'You can probably tell I'm in situ on this one,' she laughed, pointing to her heavily pregnant mother. Handing the photo to Hunter she smiled. 'And there's my dad.'

Hunter forced himself to look at the black and white photo, ringing sounding in his ears as he stared into the face of the very man he'd murdered. *Shit. SHIT. It was him. Noel wasn't bullshitting. By mistake he'd killed the father of the only woman he'd ever truly wanted and loved.*

Tori frowned Hunter's expression. 'Are you alright?'

'I-I don't feel too good actually,' Hunter muttered. He quickly handed the photograph back to Tori like it had burnt his fingers. *He couldn't look at it. Didn't want to look at it.* What the hell was he going to do? He either needed to tell her or end it. Which would be worse for her?

Tori continued rummaging through the contents of the box. 'Half of the photos have gone. I don't understand how that could have happened.'

Hunter watched Tori. It was clear how much all of this meant to her. He had little option but to walk. Discovering she'd slept with and wanted to marry the man who had murdered her father would be more than she would be able to cope with.

If the boot had been on the other foot and she had been the

one who had killed *his* family, he would hate himself more than he hated her. No, he couldn't do that to her. She must never find out - not for his sake, but for her own sanity. Walking away was the only decent thing he could do.

'Ah!' Tori exclaimed. 'Here's another one.' She passed a second photo to Hunter.

'I don't really think I n…' Before he could finish, she'd already placed the picture in his lap.

'I've been trying to discover who this woman is,' she said excitedly. 'Look at their faces for God's sake. It's as clear as day how in love they are! I'm intrigued!'

Despite not wanting to, Hunter glanced down. His eyes landed back on the man who he could barely look at and then moved to the woman. He squinted closer. *Was that… Could it be?*

'Don't they look crazy about each other?' Tori continued, smiling to herself, oblivious of the torment on Hunter's face. 'I found other things too which I think must be to do with the same girl in this photo. There were also photos with Richard wh…'

'Tori,' Hunter interrupted. 'I've got to go.'

Tori froze. *Had she done something wrong*? 'What do you mean? Where are you going?' She grasped Hunter's arm. *He was acting strange. He'd been strange since he'd got here and now he was acting even stranger.*

Hunter pulled out of Tori's grip as gently as he could and got out of bed, hastily putting his clothes on.

'You're scaring me,' Tori whimpered. 'Tell me what's wrong. What have I done?'

Hunter turned towards Tori and softly touched her cheek. 'You haven't done anything. Nothing at all…' *Oh Christ, how could he do this?* How could he walk away from this woman? He loved her. Loved her more than *anything*.

No. It was wrong. He couldn't continue knowing what he now knew and he wouldn't shatter her heart by telling her the truth. He'd rather she despised him and be sheltered from the poisonous knowledge. *It was only what he deserved.*

'Hunter?' Tori placed her hand over his still resting on her cheek.

Taking a deep breath, Hunter resumed his poker face, replacing all expressions of gentleness and love with a cold mask. 'I should've said this when I first got here,' he said, his voice icy.

'S-Said what?' Tori felt sick, knowing something impending.

'I came here to tell you that we need to end this.'

Tori breathed a sigh of relief. 'I know. It'll all be over in the next couple of days won't it? You said the plans were still on track and th…'

'Not the deals. Not Matt and Noel. Forget about that.' Hunter's voice was stern. *God, he hated himself, but it was the only way.* 'I'm referring to us.' He dropped his hand from Tori's face and grabbed his jacket. 'I can't do this anymore.'

Nausea rushed through Tori and she staggered slightly as the impact of his words hit home. *He couldn't be serious?* 'W-What?'

Hunter shrugged his leather onto his shoulders. 'I said, it's over. That's all I have to say.'

'I don't believe you! We love each other,' Tori said, barely able to comprehend what she was hearing. 'What's happened to make you say this?

Hunter raked his fingers through his hair. 'Look. We both knew it was never going to work.'

'But I want it to work. We can *make* it work. We *have* to!' Tori threw herself against Hunter. *He didn't mean it. She couldn't let him go.*

Peeling Tori away from him, Hunter scowled, despising himself even more than he thought possible. 'Give it a rest, love,' he said patronisingly. 'I can't believe you seriously fell for it!'

'F-Fell for what?' A horrible churning sickness picked up speed in Tori's belly.

'It was just the plan, baby. Just part of the plan,' Hunter

grinned. 'Thanks for the info though. Because of you I know who the usurpers are within the club, so take consolation from that.'

He felt like screaming. He could see Tori's pain from his words. This was the last thing he wanted and the last thing he meant. It was taking all his power not to scoop her into his arms, tell her he didn't mean a word of it and that he loved her to distraction, but he couldn't. He mustn't for *her* sake.

'Y-You mean you…' Tori's voice was tiny. *Broken.*

'We've had a bit of fun though!' Hunter winked. 'Christ, Tori – you take things *far* too seriously! What's the big deal? I just wanted to get one last shag in before I told you the score.' He shrugged his shoulders dismissively. 'Get yourself up the aisle with Matt and do your thing like you originally planned. You'll be fine. See you around, babe.'

Before he gave in to the intense urge to stop all of this once and for all and tell the woman he loved the truth, Hunter strode from Tori's bedroom without looking back.

FORTY SEVEN

NOEL DIDN'T CARE what it fucked up. *He was doing this.* He pulled the throttle on his bike aggressively. He owed Matt fuck all and now, being as Hunter had completely screwed up everything he'd believed would happen, he needed to see what he could salvage, if anything.

He hadn't even expected Hunter to return to the Factory tonight, He'd presumed he'd do one of his usual disappearing acts to lick his wounds and let the truth sink in, but despite everything, the bastard was getting the last laugh.

Noel had been quite happily propping up the bar and drinking with the others, unable to hide his happiness. Despite being asked several times why he was in such a good mood he'd held off the big announcement. He wanted the full crew to hear it and also wanted Hunter present so he could relish the outpouring of hatred which would occur, but that was not going to happen tonight.

Arriving back unexpectedly, Hunter had beckoned him into the back room and casually informed him that *he'd* be the one to announce his and Matt's set up to the rest of the crew. He was also calling a meeting of all the contract holders and informing them that the deals were well and truly null and void and *why*.

Hunter had spoken rationally and calmly, which had grated right on Noel's wick. He hated it when he couldn't elicit the reaction he wanted and he'd wanted Hunter to be roaring and spitting fire, but he wasn't. He was *calm*. And when Hunter was calm it was even more worrying because that meant everything was completely controlled.

Hunter had said that once he'd levelled with everyone about his initiation fuck up he'd voluntarily step down as president and move on. He was going solo – not attached to any particular chapter or even any club. He'd be going on the road full time.

Noel had tried to throw in a dig about Tori to rile him, but even that hadn't worked because he'd even called things off with her. He'd had it all planned.

No, he'd horribly underestimated Hunter's ability to deal with the situation, which only left the obvious. Hunter had accepted he'd lose his place but was determined to take him down with him. And Noel suspected it wouldn't be Hunter who would be coming off worse.

He scowled. *He wasn't having that*. This wasn't just *his* problem – it was also Matt's and Matt was about to get the opportunity to think of something to put this right. *Something fucking good*.

The posh twat had always been mega-cagey about divulging his address. Did the sad fuck think he couldn't find out where he lived if he wanted to? These people seriously didn't have a *clue* as to how things really worked, did they? That lot with their poncey Filofaxes and index cards. Did they think it was difficult to get things done? *Well, it wasn't*.

Noel's scowl deepened as he rode along the road towards Matt's address, noting how the scenery got greener with more trees along the roads and lawns, posh gates and driveways. The further he rode, the longer the drives became until most of the houses were not even visible from the road. The ones that were partly visible behind large rows of trees, ornate ironwork or walls topped with frozen lions on pedestals were so big they could solve half the housing crisis. *Christ, the whole thing made him bloody ill.*

Well, Matt wouldn't be impressed with what he'd got to say. He'd seemed happy with what he'd been told when he'd left earlier, but things change and now it was down to *him* to think of something before more than just Jeff Daniels went up in flames.

Noel slowed down and squinted through his visor at the brass house plaques for an inkling of the correct property location. Finally finding it, he parked up and sighed at the eight-foot-high black iron electronic gates and intercom system in front of him.

Great. It was time to be the property investors again, Noel thought, stabbing his calloused finger on the buttons.

· · · ·

TORI HAD BARELY been able to move since Hunter had left. She lay curled up on the bed, her face swollen and red and her pillow sodden from the tears. Even her ribs hurt from the wracking sobs that had quaked through her body, but for now she was cried out.

Now she just felt empty. Empty and numb. She placed her hands over her eyes in an attempt to cool her hot skin. She could hardly believe she'd been so stupid. How could she have been so ridiculously naïve to *really* believe that Hunter genuinely wanted her? Everyone had been cleverly concocting things, including her, so why had she been so dense to think that the same could have applied to her?

But it *hadn't* occurred to her. She'd believed him. She'd *felt* his love for her in her soul. How could she have dreamt that up and got it so wrong?

With considerable effort, Tori pulled herself up against her pillows. She hadn't dreamt it up. None of it. Hunter *did* love her. What he'd said tonight had been lies. She frowned. He was protecting her from something, but she didn't know what. He'd promised her he'd always be honest, but now he'd broken that.

His whole demeanour had changed from the deep love she'd seen in those grey eyes of his to callous and scheming contempt. Like he was *laughing* at her. *Like Noel. He'd been acting like Noel.*

Maybe this was who he really was? Maybe this was what Sarah had meant by 'damaged'.

The thought sickened her to the bone, but nowhere near as much as the prospect of being without him. How could he do this? How could he make her feel what she felt and then expect her to carry on with Matt as if nothing had happened?

Tori put her head in her hands. She'd told him all of those things about her, about Matt, her mother and what had happened to her father and it had all been fake?

She shook her head angrily. It wasn't fake. There was no way it was fake. Hunter was as much in love with her as she was with him, so why was he doing this? There had to be a reason. There *had* to be because she couldn't not be with him.

There was nothing – *nothing* on this earth that could make her not want Ash Hunter.

· · · ·

MATT HAD JUST been glad it had been him who had answered the intercom rather than anyone else. His mother had retired to bed long ago and his father was still locked away in his study.

What he hadn't been glad about was the second he'd heard the voice he'd known who it had belonged to. And now Noel was standing in his parents' kitchen telling him that everything had gone tits up again. How could everything change so drastically in the space of a couple of hours?

'You'd best sort this,' Noel hissed, helping himself to a bottle of lager from the large refrigerator.

Matt stared at Noel uncomprehendingly. 'Me? *You* were the one who said everything was fine. I presume you didn't expect that fuckhead to call your bluff, did you?'

Noel glared at Matt. *Thought he was some kind of cunt, did he?* 'Call my bluff, my arse!' he snapped. 'Hunter's got shag all left to lose now because he knows he's finished. Not just in this town, but in his head too.' He pulled the bottle top off with a sickening crunch of his teeth and spat it on to the floor. 'And that's how I know he'll go through with this unless you come up with something to convince him to do otherwise.'

Matt grimaced at the bottle top lying on the tiles. He was surprising himself with how calm he was being and presumed he'd have had a meltdown if Noel had come out with something like this, but clearly the thought of drawing his parents' attention to the biker in their kitchen was enough of an incentive to hold himself in check. Hearing a floorboard creak above him, he glanced around nervously.

'What's the matter?' Noel sneered. 'Worried Mummy and Daddy will catch you hanging around with the big, bad biker?'

Matt bit back the remark he wanted to scream at this obnoxious blockhead. *Did he not think he hadn't got enough to worry about without juvenile digs?*

'Pull faces all you like,' Noel said. 'I personally don't care what happens to you. I just want my fucking money!' He jabbed Matt hard in the chest. 'And you need to make sure I get it. You need to think of something so Hunter doesn't open his trap. We need to give him a reason to keep it closed.'

Matt frowned, unsure what he could do if Hunter was willing to sacrifice himself in favour of the truth. And what could he do without dropping himself in it? It really was beginning to look like they were well and truly fucked.

'At least you can go ahead with your poncey wedding,' Noel muttered.

Matt looked up startled. What the hell had that got to do with it? 'What makes you think that wouldn't be happening? Unless you've got even less faith than I have that we can dream something up to get us out of this?'

Noel laughed loudly and Matt cringed as his guffaw ricocheted around the large expanse of kitchen.

'Did I forget to mention the latest?' Noel said, unable to

conceal his sneer. *This would surely piss Mr Posh-Knob off.* 'Tori marrying Hunter of course!'

Matt snorted with derision. 'Oh, for God's sake! She only said that as part of the plan! She told me!'

'That's where you're wrong,' Noel said smugly. 'That's what I thought, but that's not the case. It was fucking *real*! Despite everything, they went and fell in love. Ridiculous isn't it?' He slapped his hand against the polished granite work surface and chuckled. 'I mean, it's fucking *hilarious*! I never thought in a million years Hunter would *ever* fall for someone – let alone something like *that*! Jesus, he'd have been a laughing stock!'

Matt stared at Noel, unsure whether he was winding him up or not. Gradually realising the man was being straight, he felt burning rage simmering.

'Yeah, he was going to drop us all in in and then fuck off with your missus!'

Matt's hands curled into fists and he dug his nails into the soft flesh of his palms in an attempt to quell his fury.

'But don't worry, you won't lose face. He's dumped her.'

'He dumped *her*?' Matt cried. So, Tori really *had* accepted that freak? Over him? *No. No way. No fucking way!*

Noel grinned. 'Like I said, I used my trump card. I admit I thought it would solve everything, but it only seems to have partly had the effect I expected.'

Matt angrily brushed his floppy fringe away from his eyes and focused. The *last* thing he wanted was to give any indication that any of this bothered him. But it did. How *dare* Tori pull a stunt like this. How dare she embarrass him this way. She'd have gone through with it too if she hadn't been dumped. He'd make her pay for this.

'Listen to this. Years back Hunter topped the wrong target by mistake. He didn't think I knew, but I did. It was covered up by the President at the time because Reapers don't do things like that. They also don't withhold information, no matter how bad, so Hunter will be outed for dishonesty when everyone finds out.'

'So, you blackmailed him with *that*?' Matt asked incredulously. 'It didn't work though did it because he's telling everyone himself.'

Noel smiled. He wasn't about to give Matt any further information as to why Hunter had been tasked with that specific job for his initiation. The prick didn't need to know his personal information, but he *did* need to know the rest.

'Ah, but there's more… It was *you* who helped to up my trump card,' Noel grinned.

'Me? How? I didn't know anything about any of this.' Matt didn't really care either. All he wanted was to stop Hunter from opening his mouth. *That and paying Tori back ten-fold.*

'Because you gave me a name and I put two and two together.' Noel swallowed the last of his beer.

'Name? I don't know what you're talking about,' Matt snapped. He was getting annoyed. He wasn't in the mood for stupid guessing games. He needed to think, think, *think* about what he was going to do.

'Yes, you told me Tori's father's name.' Noel smiled seeing Matt's confusion. 'Yep, Hunter was Jack Jacob's killer.'

• • • •

RICHARD HAD ONLY left his study to fetch another drink. He was putting off going upstairs because even if Susan was pretending to be asleep, she would miraculously regain consciousness the *second* his foot touched their thickly carpeted bedroom floor. He'd then be grilled over his lack of conversation during the evening meal. He'd been married to her for too long not to be able to pre-empty the situation and could sense it a *mile* off.

He walked down the hallway only to hear voices. Stiffening, he edged towards the large kitchen, but on the verge of bursting in, he stopped on catching a glimpse of Matthew and someone with a leather jacket. A leather jacket with a patch. *That patch.*

Icy cold, Richard stood in the shadows, watching as the freak biker from *that* club walked out of *his* house with a parting shot at Matt to 'fucking sort it'.

He waited a few more seconds before walking into the kitchen. 'What in the name of Christ was that person doing in my house, Matthew?' Richard watched his son jump in shock.

Matt stared at his father. *Shit. Could tonight possibly get any worse? How much had he heard?* In fact, did that even matter? Whichever way he looked at it he was sunk. It was all done and dusted. He would have to tell his father what had been going on. He sighed heavily. He'd find out within a day or so anyway.

'I'm waiting, Matthew,' Richard spat. 'Did I not tell you quite clearly that you were not to have anything to do with those people? Why the hell are they coming around here?' All sorts of unsavoury thoughts shot into his head as his mind flashed back to what he'd fed through the shredder.

'I didn't know he was coming around,' Matt said quietly.

'What did he want? You'd better start talking and talking *now*!' Richard barked. If Susan knew one of those types had been hanging around her kitchen, she'd divorce him.

Matt sighed. He pulled out a bottle of beer from the fridge and motioned to a chair at the breakfast bar. 'You'd better sit down.'

FORTY EIGHT

DRIVING AWAY FROM the bank Matt breathed a heavy sigh of relief. It wasn't over yet, because now he'd got to go and meet with *them*. He didn't want to talk to Noel and he *certainly* didn't want to talk to Hunter, but he had no choice. He just had to hope against all hope that Hunter agreed to his suggestions and that it wasn't already too late.

At least what he'd spent the *entire* night worrying about had now been dealt with, so that was one less thing on his mind.

He'd woken this morning with a crawling sense of dread in the pit of his stomach remembering the night before hadn't been a bad dream and was real. There had been no sign of his father at breakfast and so therefore it had been with great trepidation that he'd arrived at the bank with the very real prospect it would be his last day of working there.

Last night, after he'd hesitatingly told his father everything: his actual involvement with Noel, the Reapers and what he and Noel had planned out, he'd thought it would all be over. He'd fully expected to have no job, no home, no prospects and to have been *thoroughly* disowned when he'd been summoned to his father's office first thing on arriving at the bank, but none of it had happened. Quite the opposite, in fact.

His father's reaction to everything, well – to say it had dumbfounded him would have been a gross understatement. Matt couldn't begin to understand why his father was prepared to do what he'd promised to, but he certainly wouldn't argue.

Not only had his father not reacted badly considering, but he'd even appeared impressed by his resourcefulness. Admittedly he hadn't been happy about any of it, but he hadn't taken any action either and now Matt had been given a way out without losing anything. *It couldn't have been better.*

The only thing he'd left out of last night's conversation, apart from the drugs, was that Tori had been planning to ditch him for that overgrown thick skull. He hadn't felt it relevant. Actually, that wasn't entirely true. He hadn't said anything because he was embarrassed. *Toe-curlingly, witheringly embarrassed.*

Matt scowled. He hadn't even *started* on Tori yet. In fact, he hadn't even seen her, but he would be doing so. Furthermore, he would be marrying her - that much was clear. And from now on, he would be *very* careful as to when he let her out of his sight – if *ever*.

Pressing his foot down harder on the accelerator, Matt sped towards where he'd arranged to meet the Reapers.

· · · ·

RICHARD'S HAND SHOOK slightly as he picked up his tumbler of whisky. It had taken some fudging, but he'd managed it. He'd jigged around a few portfolios and now he'd got the cash needed to get this complete disaster shoved under the carpet. *And there it had to stay.*

'Is there something you're not telling me?' Susan eyed her husband suspiciously, watching him fumble with the bottle as he poured himself another whisky. 'Don't forget we've got a Bridge evening tonight.'

'I can't make that,' Richard mumbled. *There was no way he could even think about going.*

'What do you mean?' Susan cried. 'We're playing the

Mercers and it's an important round.' Her candyfloss hair quivered dramatically.

Richard smiled apologetically. 'Sorry. I really can't. I've got too much to do.'

'Like what?' Susan placed her wine glass on the table. 'What's going on, Richard?' She folded her arms over her chest. 'Are you having an affair?'

'W-What?' Richard very nearly spat whisky over Susan's extortionately expensive sofa throw. 'An affair? Of *course* not! What made you think that?'

Susan's brows folded. 'Well, you've been acting oddly for a while, so I'd like you to tell me what's going on.'

Richard stared at his crystal tumbler. He accepted he'd probably been acting a little strangely the past few days, but he could hardly tell Susan the *real* problem after all this time. Besides, it was done now – *hopefully*... He'd still have to think of something. Something that was both credible *and* partly true whilst making sure he omitted everything else in the back story.

'If you must know it's work.' He sighed deeply when Susan remained silent. He hated it when she did this. It meant she was waiting for him to embellish and he didn't want to.

'I really didn't want to say anything, but it looks like I'm going to have to.' Richard took another sip from his whisky to make it look like what he was about to say was difficult. 'Do you remember the big investment project Matthew has been working on?'

Susan nodded. 'Of course! Only the other night a very rude man called about it. It sounded like he'd come from the ghetto rather than a large firm. Urgh, he was quite common.'

Richard's ears burned. *So, the Reapers had been phoning as well as turning up had they?* He'd definitely done the right thing. He could not run the risk of having them anywhere near him. Being as Matthew had been so insane to make underhand deals with them, of all people, which he might add, had now gone horribly wrong, it posed the risk of them digging for dirt *very* real. And if they did that, then they could come across something else – something a *lot* worse. And that wasn't an option.

Richard looked up. 'Unfortunately, the whole regeneration portfolio has fallen through.'

'*What*?' Susan sat rigid. 'Oh my God, Richard! This was so important to Matthew. He must be devastated! Why did it happen?'

'It wasn't anything Matthew did,' Richard said. *It was everything Matthew had done actually. Everything. And because of his stupid bloody son he'd been the one who'd had no choice but to sort it. What else could he do? Nothing, that's what.*

'I told you he wasn't ready for something as big as this. Or was it something to do with Victoria? If that little cow has ruined our son's career, I swear to God th…'

'It wasn't anything to do with either of them,' Richard interrupted. *He had to knock that on the head.* He didn't trust Victoria not to drop Matthew in it. Fancy using her as a plant to get information from the Reapers! Brilliant move, but it could have easily gone wrong. For instance, what if someone had seen her? Matthew however, had assured him that hadn't happened and Victoria's part had all been above board. Thankfully, all she'd done was chat to them, but still, it had been a ludicrous thing to do.

'Matthew has done everything and more to make the project work and even Victoria has been supportive by all accounts. I can assure you it's not down to any incompetency on our son's part.'

Susan stared at the ceiling dramatically. 'But won't this look bad on him? Has this lost the bank money?' Wh…'

'Relax! The bank knows it wasn't anything he did and I'm not being blamed for giving him the project either. They were placated by the compensation the property company have offered.' *They might be if that were the case – which it wasn't. The bank knew absolutely nothing about any of it and it needed to stay that way too.*

Besides, he knew damn well all his wife was concerned about was whether this would affect his retirement package. He'd already gambled several things to pull together the extortionate sum required to pay that damn Reaper off and make sure he wasn't on Matthew's back. The next thing to do was to conceal the huge hole in the bank's overall investment portfolio this whole mess would leave.

If the bank ever got wind of this then it would be *his* head on the chopping block because it was *him* who was in charge of everything after all, not his son.

In reality, the project didn't have to be pulled at all. That was the worst thing about it. What Matthew had manufactured would have netted the bank *millions*, even after that disgusting Reaper's cut, but he'd had no choice but to abort it when Matthew had said another Reaper was about to expose him and his underhand deals to all of the contract holders and there would have been uproar.

Sweat formed as Richard imagined hordes of the great unwashed invading the bank headquarters, screaming about bad practice and being ripped off by the bank manager's son. There would undoubtedly have been an investigation and then he'd *definitely* lose his retirement package. And that wasn't all. From what Matthew had said, it would be a double-pronged attack. The rest of that flea-ridden motorcycle club would be baying for that Reaper dunce he'd been dealing with and the moron would be coming for Matthew as pay back. *Oh, he more than most knew how that type worked.*

Richard sighed. The portal Matthew had stupidly opened with the Reapers was like a septic wound which had to be sealed and sealed well.

It wasn't over yet either by any stretch of the imagination. Not until he had confirmation the proposal had been accepted. Only *then* would it be over and he wasn't going *anywhere* until Matthew got back tonight with news, so Susan and her Bridge evening would have to damn well wait.

Richard plastered a smile on his face. 'Don't worry about

Matthew. Go and enjoy yourself tonight and send apologies for my absence.'

Susan flapped her hand. 'Oh, but Matthew must be so disappointed. From what he said the project was almost complete.'

Richard nodded. 'These things happen, I'm afraid.' He could wring Matthew's neck for this, but outwardly he had to keep it all under wraps. Despite the damage that had been caused by this recklessness, his son would still get his promotion and everything would carry on as normal, because it *had* to.

He frowned. Thinking about it, maybe it would be best if Matthew took a position in another city for a while to ensure there were no reprisals and then return once everything had blown over. *That may be the most sensible option?*

'Look Susan, Matthew is upstanding and successful – everything we wanted him to be. He's getting married shortly and even *you* must admit Victoria has changed for the better. Don't forget there will be grandchildren soon, I don't doubt.'

Susan smiled, but inside she felt differently. She wasn't convinced Richard was being entirely truthful as to why the project had fallen through. Neither was she convinced that Victoria had in any way changed for the better.

· · · ·

'WHAT'S GOING ON?' Sarah asked, eyeing Hunter necking the pint she'd poured. She'd been surprised to get word that he'd called an impromptu meeting for all the property holders in the White Hart tonight.

She'd been trying to discover what was going on for *days* but hadn't heard a thing. Oh, she'd heard about Jeff Daniels being 'mysteriously' burnt to death along with his shop. He'd been the only one not prepared to sign the deal, so everyone had their suspicions as to who had been behind that, not that they'd say, but she knew without any shadow of a doubt.

She knew it had been down to the Reapers – it was the way

they worked, or rather it *had* been until Hunter had taken charge and then that sort of thing hadn't happened anymore. Not unless a certain one of them was involved. She glared at Noel.

Why was that man still being allowed to get away with things like that? Was Hunter losing his touch or did he just not care any longer? Come to think about it, why was Noel still even *here*?

Tori hadn't been at work for two days either and Sarah had no idea what had gone on. Being as they'd all devised this plan between them, she'd thought she'd have been one of the first to be updated, but she'd presumed wrong. She'd expected more from Hunter - a *lot* more.

Even Colin had been snapping at her, feeling the need to continuously point out that he'd told her not to get involved, but she'd chosen not to take his advice and now look what had happened.

Sarah scanned the room full to the brim with both town folk and Reapers. All the Reapers were jovial enough and Noel was very pally-pally with the others and undeniably happy, which was even more disconcerting.

Her eyes traced back to Hunter, his posture rigid and his expression cold as stone. He looked drawn. His rugged face was tired and his strikingly handsome looks faded.

Being as she hadn't received any response from her previous question she nudged him. 'Hunter?' Sarah hissed. 'You need to tell me what's going on. We were supposed to be in this together, yet you haven't said anything and now you've called this meeting?'

Hunter leant forward. 'Shut the fuck up, Sarah,' he growled. 'You don't know what you're talking about.'

Initially shocked at being spoken to in that tone of voice, Sarah quickly became irritated and grabbed his arm. 'Don't play the hard man with me, Hunter. It won't fucking work. *You* involved me in this and now you're shutting me out. Why have you called this meeting and more importantly, why the fuck has Noel not been outed yet?'

Hunter clenched his jaw. It was bad enough he'd conceded to the offer that prick, Matt, had put on the table. He couldn't decide whether he'd accepted it for the right reasons or purely to save his own back. And then there was Tori. He wanted to know how she was but couldn't ask. He hadn't slept since the night he'd left her and doubted he ever would again.

'Hunter! Just answer my damn questions, will you?' Sarah cried.

'I'm not beholden to you!' Hunter roared, causing the whole pub to fall silent.

Sarah stared at Hunter. *He was losing it. What had happened to make him like this? He'd morphed into an unfeeling jerk. This wasn't him.* 'Are you and Tori alright? Is that what's causing your attitude problem?' she whispered.

Aware he shouldn't have raised his voice and glad that the pub had now resumed its usual background chatter, Hunter shot Sarah an ice-cold grey glare. 'Me and Tori are done.'

'Done?' Sarah couldn't believe it. *That's why Tori had been absent from work.* 'I thought th…'

'You thought wrong,' Hunter snapped. 'It's over. I finished it. It wasn't working. I got caught up in the plan. It was never real.'

Sarah stared at Hunter. *Never real? She'd never seen two people more in love. What was he hiding?* 'I don't th…' Her words were diverted as the main door opened and Matt and Jeremy walked in. 'Oh my God. What the fuck are they doing here? Why haven't you sorted this?' she hissed.

'Because I fucking can't, that's why,' Hunter growled. Turning from the bar he walked towards the raised area over by the dartboard. *It was time to speak to this lot.*

· · · ·

SARAH HAD INITIALLY been overjoyed to hear the property investors were pulling out. She'd thought she may have even broken some of Colin's ribs she'd hugged him that hard.

Wasn't this good news? It sounded ok to her, so why hadn't

Hunter just said? It slowly dawned on her that something was not the ticket with this whole situation.

She'd listened carefully whilst he'd spoken to the crowd. To be fair, the majority had taken the news well. There had been a handful who had not been happy, but he'd done well smoothing things over.

There had been a few hecklers, especially when Matt had taken the stand to explain things from the bank's point of view, but the offer of compensation to anyone incurring a financial loss from signing early had soon put paid to that.

She'd watched Hunter whilst Matt had been speaking. His face remained neutral, but she could detect the burning resentment and anger radiating from him.

Sarah could tell his rage was directed towards Matt. God, she hated that man too. Hated him with a passion and couldn't work out why Hunter was still dealing with him. Noel still walking around was an even bigger mystery.

And what had happened between Hunter and Tori? Hunter had spoken like he hadn't given a shit about the woman, but she knew that was a lie. That man was deeply in love, so what was making him behave like this?

She had to go and see Tori. She *had* to. She wasn't going to get information from Hunter whilst he was like this. Throwing the beer towel she was holding onto the bar, Sarah slipped out of the back door before Colin noticed and tried to change her mind.

FORTY NINE

TORI HAD DARK circles underneath her eyes and her skin was blotchy. She hadn't slept, nor eaten and felt like death physically and mentally. *And now this.*

She stared yet again at the pregnancy test in her hand showing a thick blue stripe that left no room for doubt over its accuracy. She'd been hoping that somehow in the last two days since she'd done it, the test results had changed, but it hadn't. The blue line was still there bright and clear and she was still most definitely very much pregnant.

Maybe her mother had a sixth sense after all? She'd denied being pregnant, when she probably already had been.

How had this happened? She was on the Pill. She hadn't been ill or taken antibiotics, so how could it have failed? She didn't even have a clue how far along she was. Her mind had been so all over the place the last couple of months she had no recollection of her cycle.

In fact, the only reason she'd even done a test was the burning urge that she *needed* to do it for some unexplained reason. She didn't feel different. No different at all, so maybe it was wrong? These tests could be sometimes couldn't they?

'Victoria?' a voice shouted from the landing.

Quickly chucking the test into a carrier bag and stuffing it down the side of the bed, Tori tried to pull herself together.

Without knocking or waiting for an answer, Lillian burst into Tori's room and stood in the doorway. 'You have a vi… Dear God! Look at the state of you! You'll have to go to the doctor's if you're no better tomorrow,' she cried.

Tori stared at the floor. She wasn't ill but had to say something as to why she hadn't been to work and locked in her room for the past two days. The only thing she was suffering from was intense heartbreak. Oh and because she was pregnant with a choice of two men as the father. One of whom hated her guts, manipulated and beat her and the other who she desperately wanted and loved, but who had now decided he didn't want her.

Lillian pursed her lips in irritation. 'Did you hear me? You have a visitor.'

Tori sat bolt upright. *Was Hunter here? Had he come for her?* Her eyes lit up. 'Who is it?'

'Some drab woman who said she works with you. Sophie or something,' Lillian sniffed. 'I really wish you wouldn't tell people like that where you live. She looks decidedly cheap.'

Tori stood up, her legs shaky. 'I think it must be Sarah,' she muttered, trying not to show her excitement. 'And she's *not* cheap!' *Had she brought a message from Hunter?*

'Hmm, well. Each to their own opinion,' Lillian said under her breath. 'I've put her in the drawing room.'

· · · ·

'TORI!' SARAH CRIED as her friend entered the room. She pulled her in for a hug. 'Are you ok? You're not are you, that much is obvious. You look dreadful.' She smiled slightly. 'Don't think your mother's too impressed that I'm here!'

Tori managed a weak smile. 'She's never impressed with anything. Did Hunter send you? What did he say?' She hadn't meant to blurt that out, but she was too impatient. She needed to know what he'd said and where he wanted to meet her so that they could sort all of this rubbish out. She knew he hadn't meant what he'd said. That was now proved because he'd sent Sarah to fetch her.

Sarah frowned. *How should she handle this?* Hunter hadn't sent a message. He hadn't even *asked* about Tori.

Tori tried to read Sarah's face. She could see she was thinking about what to say, rather than saying it. Suddenly a worrying thought ran through her mind. 'Oh no! He's ok, isn't he? Has he been hurt? Where is he? I must go to him.'

Once she'd told him about the baby, he'd be even happier. She wouldn't tell Sarah yet – Hunter should know before anyone else. Her face fell slightly remembering there was a chance that this life inside her may be Matt's. But she'd hardly slept with Matt lately, so it stood more chance that it was Hunter's, didn't it?

Sarah watched Tori sadly. It was obvious she believed Hunter had sent her, but he hadn't. *She'd have to tell her.* 'Tori, you need to…'

'I *knew* it would be ok!' Tori babbled, happy tears rolling down her face. 'I couldn't believe he'd walk out on me like that. He's trying to protect me from something, I know it.' Her eyes widened. 'Has Noel done something to him?'

Sarah shook her head. *It was no good.* 'Hunter's not hurt. You need to stop and listen to me. He told me you've split up.'

'H-He told you th…'

'I hate to tell you this, but he didn't send me. He didn't even ask about you, sweetheart.'

Sarah watched Tori attempt to hide the wobble in her bottom lip. 'I don't know what's going on, but you're right that something is. He's in the White Hart right now with Matt and Noel.'

'With Matt and Noel? But he's supposed to be outing them!'

Sarah shook her head. 'It's not happening. The deals have been called off by the property company, *allegedly*... Hunter isn't saying anything else.' She didn't like to admit it, but the thought had crossed her mind that perhaps Hunter had fooled *all* of them. Maybe all of this had been an elaborate plan and he was on side with Noel after all?

'W-What did he say?' Tori whispered.

Sarah shrugged. 'He was strange. He was as cold and spoke to me like dirt. He's *never* done that before, *ever*. He said you and he were just part of the plan.' *God, she hated being the bearer of bad news.*

'T-That's what he said to me. He came here two nights ago,' Tori said softly, smiling at the memory. 'We made love. It was *wonderful*, as always.' She brushed the tears from her cheek. 'Afterwards we chatted and he offered to do some digging about my father. We looked at photos, but then... then he changed. I-It was like he'd morphed into a different person. He looked at me like I meant nothing.' Tori's face crumpled. 'He acted like *Noel*. It was awful.'

Sarah screwed her face up. 'Like *Noel*?'

Tori nodded. 'Cold. Unfeeling. Sarcastic. Like he didn't care about anything. He spoke to me like shit. It was so unlike him.'

Sarah pursed her lips. 'But you don't believe any of it?'

Tori shook her head. 'I keep flipping from one to the other, but no – I don't. It just doesn't make sense.' She sighed. 'We were so much in love. I could *feel* his soul within me. It's something I've never felt before and I swear it wasn't just from my side. The way he was with me... There isn't any way someone could have put that on.'

Sarah sighed. *She didn't think so either.* She grabbed Tori's hand. 'Come on.'

'W-What?' Tori asked, startled.

'I agree with you. I don't think this is right either. Something's wrong and we're going to find out what!'

'He's made his mind up Sarah,' Tori cried. 'He said we were done and then he walked.'

'And you're going to let him?' Sarah raised an eyebrow. 'You don't believe that and for what it's worth, neither do I.

I've known Hunter for years and his acting ability is shite. If what you've said is true and for the record, I believe you, Ash Hunter is as crazy about you as it gets! If he was putting that on then I'll eat my fucking hat! There's *no way*! He's in love with you, Tori – big time!'

'D-Do you think so?' Tori stammered. Could her instincts be right after all?

'I *know* I'm fucking right!' Sarah snapped. 'Now grab your coat. We're going to the White Hart. He'll still be there and he's going to damn well level with us!'

HUNTER HAD DONE what was needed. He'd smoothed everything over and everybody was ok. *Everybody apart from him.*

Sure, on the outside he was fine. He hadn't had to admit his fuck up and still retained his integrity – as far as everyone else was concerned at least, but inwardly he was dead.

He stared at Matt, wishing that looks alone could kill. That man was smug enough – as was Noel. Yeah, everyone was happy. Matt would walk away intact with no smear on his name because it was all the property firm's fault as far as anyone else knew.

Noel would be receiving a massive pay out for his 'inconvenience' and the townspeople were none the wiser about being a hairs' breadth away from being totally and utterly ripped off by the pair of them. On top of that, the Reapers, apart from Grin, were still blissfully unaware there was a snake in their midst.

Hunter ground his teeth. It was just *him*. Oh yes, on paper it looked like he'd got away with not having to expose his ill deeds, but he'd had to let those warped two-faced bastards get away scot free, whilst he'd been forced to walk away from the love of his life.

His heart skipped a beat as Tori's face flashed into his mind. How he wanted her, yet she must despise him. But whether she hated him or not, there was no way he would let her marry that ultimate wanker.

Hunter raked his hand through his hair, hoping he was doing the right thing. The next part of his plan was the only way he could possibly deal with this. The only way he, and he suspected Tori would be able to function without each other would be if one of them wasn't around. *And it was going to be him*. But he wasn't planning on letting her go and had every intention of getting her back, but there was something he had to do before that could happen.

Grin hadn't understood at all. He hadn't understood why Hunter would have told him what he'd said about Noel and Matt only to let them walk away and then put Noel in charge!

Hunter realised it sounded absurd. All he could say to Grin was to trust him. He would be back, but only when he'd sorted everything out.

He had a plan. This time he would find out once and for all who should have been the target for his initiation hit and that was what he should have done in the first place all those years ago. He would find out who had raped Noel's mother. The target was linked to Jack Jacobs and he was going to find the bastard. Then and only *then* would he return, tell Tori the truth about what he'd done and only hope that her love for him was strong enough to somehow be able to forgive him.

It was a long shot, but if he had the name of the *real* culprit to give her and he could explain how it had happened, then there was a slight chance they could make it work.

One thing was for definite and that was they couldn't make it work whilst he was withholding something from her as important as this, so he had no choice but to go and find the information. He had precisely three months before she walked down the aisle.

Hunter took a deep breath. Tori may well have to continue

hating him in the interim and believe the lies he'd said for her own sake, but it would make sense in the end. It *had* to.

Hunter glanced around. He'd wanted to catch Sarah and put things right with her before he left, but she was nowhere to be seen, so it would have to wait. Every minute he remained here was another minute he was without the woman he needed to enable him to breathe air.

Nodding sadly at Grin, Hunter rose from his chair. He trusted Grin to repeat what he'd told him to say if anyone asked further questions. He may not understand right now, but he knew the man had enough faith in him to realise there was a damn good reason behind all of this.

. . . .

'ARE YOU SURE about this?' Sarah asked, grimacing when the gears crunched as she manoeuvred her way around a roundabout.

'Never surer about anything in my life!' Tori said resolutely. She'd made her mind up. She was going to tell Hunter she wasn't accepting what he'd said and that she wasn't going *anywhere* without him.

She would announce this in front of everyone in the White Hart if she had to. *Including Matt.*

She wasn't going to marry Matt Stevens. She was marrying Ash Hunter and that was the end of it. She'd grabbed enough clothes to last her a few days and would stay at the Factory from now on. She'd quite happily never see her mother or Matt *ever* again and didn't care what happened to her, what they did, or what they thought. She *would* be with the man she loved and no one could stop her.

She placed her hand gently on her flat belly. This was *Hunter's* baby inside of her. It wasn't just wishful thinking – she could just *tell* that this baby had been made with *love.*

Sarah squeezed Tori's hand. 'You're doing the right thing. Something's caused this turnaround and only *you* can stop it!' She smiled. 'Go and get your man, sweet cheeks.'

Buoyed by Sarah's words of support, Tori smiled, no longer desolate. 'How much longer?' she asked impatiently, her heart clamouring in her chest.

'I'm going as fast as I can!' Sarah crunched yet another gear. 'A couple of minutes. They'll all be there. They were involved with the big 'discussion' when I left and you know what they're like. It'll drag on for hours.'

Sarah had to admit she was excited. Apart from wanting Tori and Hunter to be happy and discovering what was behind this debacle, she also couldn't wait to see the look on that disgusting bastard, Matt's face. Not to mention the expression of pure rage Noel would also be wearing. She swerved into the street of her pub. 'Here we are!'

Tori breathed a sigh of relief seeing the line of motorbikes neatly parked outside.

'Ready?' Sarah pulled up alongside the kerb and yanked the handbrake into position.

'Definitely!' Taking a deep breath, Tori stepped out the car.

· · · ·

SARAH KNEW SOMETHING big had happened the minute she stepped into the White Hart. Her heart plummeted like a rock. The packed room was virtually silent, apart from a few mumblings and everyone looked rather shell-shocked.

She didn't think anyone had even noticed their arrival. Certainly no one had looked around to see who had entered the tap room, which was unusual. It was like they were all on a different planet. *Apart from Noel.* His raucous voice rambled on excitedly in the background.

'Tori!' Matt shouted, suddenly noticing her in the doorway. 'What are you doing here?'

'I-I…' Tori looked around as Matt made his way over. *What was wrong with everyone and where was Hunter?* Her eyes darted rapidly around the room looking for his familiar silhouette.

Striding up to Tori, Matt placed his arm possessively

around her shoulder. 'I'm glad you're here, but I'm afraid you've missed all the excitement.'

'She knows the property deals are off because I've already told her.' Sarah barked. She glared at Matt, willing him to remove his poisonous arm from around her friend. *God, she would love it when Tori told him she was leaving him for Hunter and there would be nothing he could do about it.*

Matt waved his hand dismissively. 'It doesn't surprise me that you told her, but that's *old* news,' he sneered. 'The latest is *very* unexpected…'

'Spit it out then being as you think it's so important!' Sarah snapped, wishing Hunter would hurry up from wherever he was so Tori could say her piece and wipe the smarm from this piece of shit's face.

'Are you ok?' Sarah said quietly to Tori who stood stock still, clearly looking for Hunter.

'Why wouldn't she be?' Matt snarled. 'In fact, everything couldn't be better as far as *I'm* concerned. Come on, darling, let's go home, shall we?'

'I don't th…' Tori faltered.

'Oh, I forgot to tell you what's happened. Silly me!' Matt smiled nastily. 'Hunter's gone.'

'What do you mean, *gone*?' Sarah barked. *That was ok. She'd take Tori to the Factory instead if needs be.*

'He's gone. Left town.' Matt paused for effect, gloating in satisfaction at the pain on Tori's face. So, it *had* been true. She was in love with that jerk. *Well, not anymore.* And if she thought she would get away with that then she had rocks in her head, but for now he'd take her agony as his starting point.

'L-Left town?' Tori stuttered, feeling nauseous and faint.

'Yep! He's gone solo,' Matt continued. 'He announced it to everyone. He's stepped down as President.'

Tori glanced at Grin with panicked eyes. *This couldn't be true.* Seeing his slight nod, she felt like she might throw up.

'And guess who's President now?' Noel grinned, sauntering over. 'Me! Great isn't it! Finally get some *proper* order back in this town.'

Sarah's mouth dropped open. '*You*?'

'Yep and Grin's my VP,' Noel said proudly. 'Hunter's instructions.'

Tori's heart splintered into a thousand pieces. *Oh Jesus...* She glanced at Sarah who looked equally as shocked.

'I'll find out from Grin as to why,' Sarah hissed in Tori's ears. 'Don't worry, we'll sort it out.'

Matt pulled Tori to one side and spoke quietly in her ear. 'Don't think I don't know the truth, you little bitch. Hunter doesn't want you. You're playing things *my* way from now on, otherwise I will fuck you and your mother up for good big time. There's a *lot* you don't fucking know.' He grinned inwardly. *He'd save the best part in case he really needed it but looking at her face he didn't think he'd have any problems with Tori Morgan again after this.*

'Come on,' Matt said brightly. 'Let's get you home. We've got a wedding to plan!'

Tori didn't see much point in resisting. She'd been wrong. Hunter didn't love her and now she really *was* stuck with Matt. Things had come full circle. She was back to where she'd started. It wouldn't have been quite so painful if she wasn't now aware what *real* love was.

She didn't look at Sarah. It was fruitless. She was finished and had to accept it. Robotically she followed Matt from the White Hart.

NEXT IN THE SERIES

HUNTED #2
THE FAMILY LEGACY

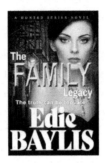

Unsure of whether Matt or Hunter has fathered the child growing inside her, Tori's unwanted wedding to Matt grows closer, but is there light at the end of the tunnel?

Unfortunately, Tori hasn't counted on another man present in her life. One who is more instrumental in her misery than she realises.

Sometimes the truth is too late in coming and makes bad things happen and sometimes a hidden legacy can cause the most horrific thing of all…

MORE FROM THIS AUTHOR

SCARRED SERIES:

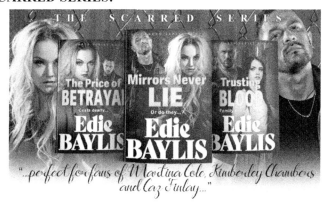

MIRRORS NEVER LIE | THE PRICE OF BETRAYAL | TRUSTING BLOOD

Disappointed to find out the promise of avenging his wrongful incarceration had already been carried out without him, Zane Morelli stepped out from prison. It didn't take long to realise that what he'd been told of the death of the man who had set him up was a lie.

A lie told by Zane's own firm. A firm who had already overstepped the mark during his absence by scarring his face in retribution for their wrongful belief that he had betrayed them.
But the truth was now loud and clear. The man who had succeeded in getting Zane banged up was alive and so therefore, would be paying for what he did.

This should be easy for someone like Zane, but there is another person with a grudge. Not only with Zane, but with his target.
And Zane hadn't thought Erin Langley would prove such a thorn in his side.

MORE FROM THIS AUTHOR

ALLEGIANCE SERIES:

TAKEOVER | FALLOUT | VENDETTA | PAYBACK |JUDGEMENT

Daddy's girl Samantha Reynold hadn't bargained on unexpectedly needing to step into her father's shoes and take over the family casino business.

Pampered and spoiled, Sam knows nothing about the rules of this glamorous but deadly new world. She has a lot to learn and even more to prove. But she won't let her family down, especially when it looks like they could lose everything to their biggest rivals – the Stoker family.

Eldest son Sebastian hasn't got time to pander to pretty girl Samantha as she plays at being boss. Rumours are swirling around the streets of Birmingham that have the power to rip the Stoker family apart and destroy everything they've built.

MORE FROM THIS AUTHOR

RETRIBUTION SERIES:

AN OLD SCORE | FINDERS KEEPERS | THE FINAL TAKE

Three families... One prize...

Teagan Fraser had no idea what she was getting herself into when she took on an assignment as a live-in carer for Dulcie Adams – a retired dancer from a Soho club. Dulcie has waited forty years for her lover, Michael Pointer, to return, but she's been living in hope for a time that never came and left looking after something important, which Jonah Powell and his firm want back.

In addition to the notorious Powell firm, there are others wanting to claim what they believe is rightfully theirs and they'll do anything to get it back. If only Dulcie wasn't around it would be a lot easier, but she's difficult to shift...

A lot can happen in a short space of time and Teagan might wish she'd never become involved.

More From this Author

DOWNFALL SERIES:

UNTIL THE END OF TIME | ESCAPING THE PAST | VENGEFUL PAYBACK

Dive into Seth and Jane's train wreck of a life, where drugs, alcohol and obsessional love means this downright dangerous pair will do *anything* to ensure nothing gets in their way.

They do bad things. *Very* bad things and their promise to love each until the end of time turns into a war against each other.

A war neither of them can win.

** This series contains written depictions of graphic violence, sex and strong language. It also contains some themes that may be uncomfortable for certain readers. **

ABOUT THE AUTHOR

Over the years Edie has worked all over the UK as well as in several other countries and has met a lot of interesting people - several of whom have supplied ideas for some of the characters in her books! She has now settled back in central England with her partner and children, where she is pursuing her writing.

Edie writes gritty gangland and urban fiction for Boldwood Books and Athame Press.

Edie's series so far include her latest – the *Scarred* series; the *Allegiance* series; the *Retribution* series, *Hunted* series and *Downfall* series.

When she isn't writing, Edie enjoys reading and is a self-confessed book hoarder. She also enjoys crochet and music as well as loving anything quirky or unusual.

Visit www.ediebaylis.co.uk for the latest news, information about new releases, giveaways and to subscribe to her mailing list.

Edie Baylis

gangland | crime | urban

THRILLER AUTHOR

Connect with Edie

https://fb.me/downfallseries

https://www.goodreads.com/author/show/17153586.Edie_Baylis

https://twitter.com/ediebaylis

https://www.amazon.co.uk/Edie-Baylis/e/B075FQHWCZ/

https://www.bookbub.com/authors/edie-baylis

https://ediebaylis.co.uk/

info@ediebaylis.co.uk

https://www.fantasticfiction.com/b/edie-baylis/

https://www.instagram.com/ediebaylis/

https://www.tiktok.com/@ediebaylis

https://www.pinterest.co.uk/ediebaylis/

Join Edie's Mailing List

Subscribe to Edie's mailing list for the latest news on her books, special offers, new releases and competitions.

https://ediebaylis.co.uk/signup.html

CWA MEMBER

ACKNOWLEDGEMENTS

Thanks to the people that kindly read my drafts of *The Status Debt* – you know who you are and I appreciate your time and feedback.

Thank you for reading *The Status Debt*. I hope you enjoyed reading it as much as I did writing it!

If so, would you please consider leaving a review on Amazon and/or Goodreads.

Reviews from readers are SOOOO helpful and especially important to us authors and without you we would have nobody to write for!

Thank you once again and hope you enjoy the rest of my books.

Edie xx

Printed in Great Britain
by Amazon

46576241R00239